LITHIUM-6

LITHIUM-6

RISTO ISOMÄKI

TRANSLATED BY OWEN F. WITESMAN

This is a work of fiction. Names, characters, organizations, places, events, and incidents are either products of the author's imagination or are used fictitiously.

Text copyright © 2007 Risto Isomäki

Translation © 2015 Owen F. Witesman

All rights reserved.

No part of this book may be reproduced, or stored in a retrieval system, or transmitted in any form or by any means, electronic, mechanical, photocopying, recording, or otherwise, without express written permission of the publisher.

Previously published as *Litium 6* by Tammi in Finland in 2007. Translated from Finnish by Owen F. Witesman. First published in English by AmazonCrossing in 2015.

Published by AmazonCrossing, Seattle

www.apub.com

Amazon, the Amazon logo, and AmazonCrossing are trademarks of Amazon.com, Inc., or its affiliates.

ISBN-13: 9781503947733

ISBN-10: 1503947734

Cover design by Scott Barrie

Printed in the United States of America

PROLOGUE

Aboard the *Lucky Dragon No. 5*, March 1, 1954

Does it snow in paradise?

As a day began that would irrevocably change the world, Rongelap Atoll rested silently in the embrace of a calm Pacific morning. The slow, gentle ocean swell turned to breakers on the barrier reef protecting the island ring. Only harmless foam rolled onto the white sands of the beaches, quietly washing back and forth fine particles of coral. Palm trees swayed in the mild breeze. The slow, rhythmic lapping of the waves soothed the sleep of the locals in their huts. The humid air was warm and silken. If there was anywhere on earth that resembled paradise, it was here.

Out on the open ocean, two hundred miles to the west, a lonely fishing vessel rocked in the sluggish swell. This was *Daigo Fukuryū Maru*, the *Lucky Dragon*. Or, more precisely, *Lucky Dragon No. 5*, since four of *Daigo Fukuryū Maru*'s sister vessels had been lowered from the shipyard into the sea previously. A few days earlier, *Lucky Dragon No. 5* had sailed out of Yaizu Port with a crew of twenty-three, aiming to fill her hold with the succulent tuna sought after by Japanese consumers.

At 6:45 a.m., there were only traces of dawn. The crew was gradually gathering on the deck. *Lucky Dragon* had lowered its long line the night before. Soon they would see what had struck the hooks, and how good their fortune had been this time.

Then, suddenly, the western sky began to brighten.

"The sun is rising from the wrong direction," gasped one of the fishermen.

In an instant the horizon turned dazzlingly bright, and the ocean shimmered as though it were broad daylight. Overcome with a mixture of fear and wonder, the crew stood mute as they watched the western sky.

Seven minutes later a deafening roar filled their world; it was as if a thousand lightning strikes had struck at once, or as if an immense, invisible landslide had crashed down on them on every side. Somewhere far away a glowing fireball of mottled orange, yellow, and red rose above the horizon. Much later they would hear that the fireball had been nearly five miles across.

"Bikini is that way," said one of the fishermen. "The Americans are doing their tests again. It is *pikadon*!"

His companions flinched. Pikadon! A bomb like the ones that destroyed Hiroshima and Nagasaki, killing hundreds of thousands of people.

"They didn't announce anything," one of the fishermen said in disbelief.

"They don't always make an announcement."

The captain of the vessel appeared behind them. With a deeply furrowed brow, he looked at the western sky blazing with flame.

"Is that dangerous?" one of the men asked the captain.

The captain shook his head.

"No," he said firmly. "We are far outside the danger zone. At least twenty miles from its edge. Bikini is one hundred miles away. Let's get back to work."

The fisherman still seemed concerned.

"They've done their tests many times before," said the captain. "The danger zone has never extended this far. Not even close. If we'd been near Bikini, then there might be reason for concern. But one hundred miles away—no. Believe me. We're in no danger, even if the wind were blowing this way."

The fisherman calmed down some, because of course he believed the captain, but he was still concerned.

"It's just that they have bigger pikadon now than before," the fisherman said. "A thousand times bigger, I hear. They call them hydrogen bombs. The one they blew up two years ago was like that."

"Hydrogen bombs are bigger, yes, but their fallout isn't nearly as dangerous," the captain assured the fisherman. "They burn cleaner than atom bombs."

***

A few hours later, ash began falling on the ship. At first only a few large gray flakes floated in the air, but then the rain of ash thickened as if a large volcanic eruption had occurred nearby. To the eyes of the crew of the *Lucky Dragon*, the feathery particles looked like gigantic snowflakes, except that snowflakes were usually bright white.

Ash fell over the *Lucky Dragon* for nearly three hours, creating a thick layer of sediment. When the crew walked on deck, the soles of their shoes left tracks. Then the ash fall subsided, and soon only a few large flakes floated here and there in the sky. Then even they were gone. The captain ordered the crew to swab the deck clean, but many first collected large piles of ash as mementos and gifts. They stored the ash in large sacks and small jars.

Suddenly the captain noticed something strange.

"Ichiro," he said, addressing one of the crew members. "Your skin is red. You look like you were burned."

Ichiro turned to look at the captain.

"Ichiro . . . maybe you should go and rest," said the captain.

At that moment the captain realized, somewhat begrudgingly, that he wasn't feeling very well. There was a small, sharp pain at the corners of his mouth. He had been feeling discomfort there for several minutes, but it was becoming more pronounced, and he was annoyingly conscious of its existence. And deep inside his belly, an indeterminate malaise was churning. Like a big, solid lump growing heavier by the minute. Had he eaten something that had gone bad? His stomach was never upset.

Then he heard a sickly gurgling sound, and when he turned he saw one of his men vomiting violently over the railing and into the sea. A moment later, another man was throwing up, and then a third. The nauseating sensation clenching the captain's own stomach only grew worse. His head was spinning and his joints and muscles were beginning to ache—all at once, across his entire body.

The captain didn't know what the Americans had come up with this time, but it seemed that the enormous conflagration they had detonated over Bikini Atoll was something new. Something that made the fallout dangerous even hundreds of miles away.

"We have to leave," the captain said to his first mate. "We're going home. Immediately."

"But."

"Let's go. Now."

The fishing vessel turned toward the east, its engine at full throttle. But within moments the whole crew of the *Lucky Dragon* was sick and vomiting.

The wind did not relent. A few hours later the ashen snow reached Rongelap Atoll fifty miles away and Utrik Atoll two hundred miles away. The foliage of the palms and the sand beaches were covered in a blanket of gray particles, and ash from incinerated coral fell on the roofs of the houses and in people's hair. Children and adults plucked the flakes floating down from heaven and looked at them with smiles of wonder. This was something completely new to them, because in paradise it never snowed.

The next day all the residents of Utrik and Rongelap were seriously ill.

Almost sixty years would pass before the world would understand how much more dangerous it had suddenly become on that fateful day.

ONE
RAPID-L

"It can even be thought that radium could become very dangerous in criminal hands, and here the question can be raised whether mankind benefits from knowing the secrets of Nature, whether it is ready to profit from it or whether this knowledge will not be harmful for it. . . . I am one of those who believe with Nobel that mankind will derive more good than harm from the new discoveries."

—Pierre Curie
June 6, 1905
Stockholm
Nobel Prize Award Ceremony

1

When Chief Inspector Kenzaburo Niori saw the building, he immediately sensed that something was terribly wrong.

"Call for backup," he said to Akiko Nobura. "Something bad has happened here. Something very bad."

How could he know? Nobura wondered, but she wouldn't question her superior's order. A younger subordinate didn't do that. Especially if that subordinate was a woman with only a few years of experience on the force.

"And call a locksmith," Niori added. "Just in case."

Chief Inspector Niori looked at the twenty-story office building rising above him, the headquarters of the Yoshikawa Corporation. Its glass walls were dull green in the dim light of the night. In the lower lobby a yellow light glowed, but no one was to be seen, even though Mitsuru Kemba had said on the phone that there would be guards who would come out to meet them.

Niori tried the handle of the glass door again, but it still didn't open. He also pressed the buzzer for the umpteenth time. The security guards should have heard the noise, but no one came. The whole building was quiet.

Like a sealed crypt. He didn't like that thought.

Behind them, downtown Osaka's shining sea of lights hummed. Neon signs and LED video screens morphed on the walls of the taller skyscrapers. Here and there a window was illuminated, but most were still black. It was 4:10 a.m.

Akiko Nobura ended her call. "Two more patrols will be here in half an hour. The locksmith should be here sooner."

"Kemba is going to come too," Niori grumbled. After a pause, he added, "I have a bad feeling about this."

"Is something specific worrying you?" Nobura asked. "Everything looks perfectly normal."

"Kemba said the building should have eight security guards. Why aren't any of them hearing the door buzzer?"

Half an hour earlier, the CEO of the Yoshikawa Corporation, Mitsuru Kemba, had woken the chief inspector. The phone ringing had also awoken Niori's wife, Hatsuro, and their six-month-old daughter. Despite the fact that Mitsuru Kemba was a distant relative of Niori's wife and a revered family acquaintance, Niori had been hard-pressed to be friendly and polite.

But Kemba had practically begged him to pay a visit to the company headquarters. In the middle of the night, Kemba had remembered some minor thing he should have handled the previous day. He called one of the night watchmen, but the guard didn't answer. Kemba called the cell phones of two more guards, also with no response. Then he called the police, who promised to send a patrol. But when Kemba called back, he was told that the patrol had already been by and found everything in order.

Chief Inspector Niori had no desire to be up and about hours before his normal shift, but he knew he owed Mitsuru Kemba this service. So he had arranged to meet Kemba at the Yoshikawa headquarters. To accompany him, he roused Sergeant Akiko Nobura, who lived nearby.

Niori had thought he was wasting his time and simply acting out of courtesy to Mitsuru Kemba, but as soon as he arrived on the scene, he changed his mind.

This was going to be a very long day.

Moments later the two police officers saw the lights of an approaching car. When it pulled up in front of the building, a gray-haired man in his sixties climbed out.

"Thank you for coming so quickly," Kemba said, somewhat breathlessly, and squeezed Niori's arm with both hands.

Nobura greeted Kemba with a bow.

"The guards aren't responding to the buzzer," Niori said.

Kemba's expression changed.

"I knew something was wrong. Wait just a moment while I open the door."

Pulling out his keycard, Kemba pushed it into the reader. The lock mechanism did not respond.

"That's strange," he muttered.

"Eight guards is quite a lot," Niori said. "Is there something valuable in the building?"

"We do have an extremely valuable prototype on the premises right now," Kemba confirmed. "It's the first working unit of its kind to be connected to the power grid."

"What sort of device are we talking about?" Niori asked.

Kemba hesitated.

"The project is still mostly secret," he said evasively.

"Knowing exactly what we're dealing with may be important," Niori insisted, although he knew he was being impolite.

"You may be right," Kemba said, still more than a little reluctantly. "I suppose you have to know. In one of the lower levels we have a new Rapid-L series reactor."

"Reactor?" Niori asked in surprise. "What do you mean *reactor*?"

"Well, a nuclear reactor, of course."

"A nuclear reactor?" Niori said. "This close to the center of Osaka?"

Kemba's brow furrowed. "I know what you're thinking. People have a hysterical fear of nuclear power. I've gotten used to that response, but there's no good reason for it. What other form of energy has actually killed as few people as nuclear power? And besides, Rapid-L is a very special kind of reactor."

The lights of a quickly approaching passenger car appeared.

"That must be the locksmith," Akiko Nobura said. "It couldn't be either of the patrol cars yet."

"Rapid-L is a next-generation reactor," Kemba continued in a voice still full of concern and uncertainty despite his obvious pride. "Ultracompact, ultrasecure. The reactor itself is only six meters tall and a couple of meters wide, and only weighs seven point six tons."

"Ah," Niori said. "Is that so?"

The locksmith parked next to Niori's and Kemba's cars and approached the trio. He had a large toolbox in one hand. The locksmith gave them all an appraising look and then greeted Kemba first, immediately followed by Niori. Then he nodded in Nobura's direction.

"Is this where I was needed?"

"You're in the right place," Niori said. "Can you get that door open?"

The locksmith looked at Niori in surprise, more than a little dubious.

"May I assume you have authority for this?"

Niori showed the locksmith his police identification.

"Kemba-san is the CEO of Yoshikawa Corporation," Niori said, indicating the older man.

"I suppose I can open the door for you then," the locksmith said with a grunt. "I mean, I guess you know what you want."

Digging a small battery-powered saw out of his toolbox, the locksmith pressed the blade against the latch. The saw began to whine, first quietly and then with an increasingly shrill pitch as it picked up speed.

"A Rapid-L doesn't produce electricity using a steam or gas turbine like old-fashioned reactors do," Kemba continued. "It converts heat differentials directly into electricity using state-of-the-art thermoelectric cells."

"Sounds sophisticated," Niori admitted.

Niori didn't try to interrupt Kemba's spiel. He understood that Kemba was worried and that talking was how he was dealing with his anxiety. By giving his standard presentation, Kemba was trying to calm himself down and save face, convincing himself that everything was still fine.

"This will only take a few minutes," the locksmith announced. "Even though this metal is pretty hard."

The locksmith changed saw blades and continued to work.

"Before, using thermoelectric cells didn't make sense because the performance coefficients were only a few percent," Mitsuru Kemba continued. "But our new cells are two to three times more efficient. One Rapid-L produces two hundred kilowatts of electricity, which is the perfect amount for a power source for one residential or office building."

Niori looked at Kemba in confusion.

"But you're talking about nuclear reactors. Do you mean that small nuclear reactors could end up in apartment building basements?"

Kemba nodded.

"Exactly. Housing cooperatives could save millions of yen if they were able to produce their own power."

"There you go," the locksmith said and opened the door. He looked at the door in surprise and then turned to Niori. "Shouldn't an alarm start going off right about now?"

Niori thought this was all quite strange.

"You can send the bill to this address," said Akiko Nobura, handing the locksmith her business card.

Then she and Niori entered the building lobby with Kemba following behind.

"Reactors like this are also perfect for developing countries where it can be difficult to connect outlying areas to national electric grids," Kemba continued.

"Believe me, someday we will be manufacturing tens of thousands of them," Kemba said. "They're so reliable and safe to operate that they don't even need anyone to monitor them. In the future one operator could track the status of thousands of reactors over the Internet."

In the lobby, there was an abandoned reception desk with two wheeled chairs behind it. Niori walked over to the U-shaped desk and peered around, finding microphones, security monitors, and a couple of computers. Some of the monitors were on, and in one of them Niori saw a bird's-eye view of himself. In another monitor he saw the locksmith turning his car around. But most of the monitors were dark.

"Should these monitors be off?" Niori asked.

Kemba shook his head.

They walked into the middle of the lobby. Still it seemed no one else was there. Niori felt increasingly uncomfortable. Where were all the guards?

"You said you couldn't make contact with the guards," Nobura said. "What if something happened to the reactor?"

"That's impossible. The reactor computer is constantly communicating with the building servers. Everything was fine when I left home. The temperature was exactly what it should be, five hundred and thirty degrees Celsius. The reactor continuously feeds electricity into the building's power network. It's functioning perfectly. And besides, if anything were to go wrong, the reactor has a highly effective emergency cooling system. Much more effective than it actually needs to be, in fact. That's why it's so safe. The moment the temperature exceeds seven hundred and eighty degrees Celsius, the lithium release modules melt and—"

As he reached the back of the lobby, Niori stopped short, and his whole body tensed. He gestured toward Kemba, who immediately shut his mouth.

Kemba didn't know exactly what Niori had seen, but it made the policeman plunge his hand into his overcoat. When he pulled his hand out, he held a large evil-looking pistol. Niori gripped the pistol with both hands and gradually crept forward. Nobura drew her own pistol and followed him.

Kenzaburo Niori knew that over a million people died in the world every year as victims of violence. All because one person pulled a trigger, jabbed a knife, threw a punch, kicked, choked, or did something else that interrupted someone's vital functions. A million people. Every year. More or less every fiftieth person who died that year would be a victim of violence. That was a shocking number, even if the problem was much smaller in Japan than in most other countries. But it was simply a fact of life that humankind occasionally put aside the cultural and social norms that restrained aggression and violence. Whenever that happened, man instantly became his own primary cause of death. In times like those, grotesque ideologies multiplied like airborne plagues, and most of the people who died did so at the hands of their own species. Half, two-thirds. Sometimes even more. Not just one in fifty anymore.

Niori knew all of this, but none of the statistics he had memorized so carefully ever prepared him for situations like this.

In the hallway that led to the stairs, a security guard in a Yoshikawa Corporation uniform lay sprawled on his back. Under the man was a large partially congealed pool of blood. On his forehead were two round red holes only an inch apart. The skin was slightly raised around the holes, as if they were tiny craters.

They wouldn't be needing an ambulance. Niori heard Mitsuru Kemba's sharp intake of breath, and he turned to Nobura.

"We have to go see what's going on."

"Shouldn't we wait for backup?" Nobura asked.

Niori shook his head.

"This could be an act of terrorism. We don't have time to wait."

"But the Rapid-L is perfectly safe," Kemba protested. "Nothing can happen to it."

Niori could hear the shock in Kemba's trembling voice. He clearly didn't want to go into the basement.

"Nothing manmade can be designed to withstand every terrorist attack," Niori said calmly. "Not even a nuclear reactor."

Kemba swallowed.

Niori started down the stairs with Nobura close behind. The lights were still on, which was a relief.

For a moment Kemba fought with his competing senses of duty and caution but finally decided to follow.

At the bottom of the stairs, half on the steps and half on the floor, lay another security guard. Niori immediately noticed something strange.

Again the body lay in a large pool of blood. Beyond it, on the floor, were spatters of blood in a large arc several yards across. Next to the spatters was a trail of blood extending farther down the hall. It seemed like a trail left by something . . . as if something had slid across the floor.

At the far end of the trail lay that something.

Now Niori understood why the body had looked so strange from the top of the stairs. It was missing its head. He also saw that the dead guard was clutching a powerful submachine gun in one hand. Death had not loosened his grip on his weapon.

While he was studying in North America, Niori had once seen a bobcat kill a white-tailed deer. The deer had been large, probably weighing ten times what the bobcat did. But the bobcat had latched on to the deer's throat. The white-tailed deer was a magnificent, gentle animal. As Niori watched, it became obvious that the deer couldn't believe what was happening was possible, that another animal could be so brazen and ruthless. During the critical second, the deer didn't do anything. It was too shocked to act. Once the bobcat had the deer by the throat, the deer had no options. It couldn't shake the bobcat off because of the pain, or perhaps it didn't dare because it feared having its throat ripped out. Then, the deer's oxygen began running out. Its hind legs gave way, and, a moment later, the deer fell on its side with a forlorn, accusatory expression in its gentle eyes. The bobcat kept its grip on its prey's neck until the deer stopped moving. Then, it released its jaws and turned to look straight at Niori. He would never forget the expression on the bobcat's face.

"How . . . how could someone do something like this?" Kemba whispered behind him.

The guard had been armed. But he hadn't used his weapon as the attacker rushed at him and decapitated him, presumably with a razor-sharp samurai sword.

This was medieval. Why hadn't the guard fired his gun? Niori wondered. Again he saw in his mind's eye the image of the bobcat sinking its teeth into the neck of the deer.

"Keep moving," Niori said, noting the shock in Kemba's and Nobura's eyes.

The next body was a little way down the corridor. The guard's pistol hand had been cut off. Then the sword had been thrust through his heart. Blood was everywhere. This was a nightmare. Niori had sensed something bad, but he never could have imagined anything like this.

"Where is the reactor room?" Niori asked in a whisper.

"At the end of the hall," Kemba responded quietly. "On the right."

The fourth guard lay dead at the door of the reactor room. He had also been killed with a sword.

Things like this didn't happen, Niori thought.

The reactor room door was open. Niori peeked inside.

The room was less than fifty feet across—smaller than he had expected—with a slightly elevated ceiling. In the middle of the room was a cylinder about eighteen feet tall and six feet across, with various cables and pipes of varying thicknesses protruding from it. The lights were still on, and the reactor emitted a steady, almost soothing humming sound.

Three more dead guards lay on the floor. Under each was a large pool of blood. An acrid burning smell hung in the air. But otherwise... there weren't any terrorists, and Niori didn't see anything that looked like a bomb. Still, he was on high alert.

The nuclear reactor was right in front of him now. It really was astonishingly small, only three times taller than a man. It was hard to believe that it was pumping two hundred kilowatts of electricity into the building's internal power grid every second.

Motioning for Nobura to circle the other way, Niori walked around the reactor, looking for signs of a possible bomb. But he didn't see anything of the sort. Instead he noticed two wheeled welding carts loaded with bottles and hoses. Dark protective goggles also lay on the floor. The welding rigs obviously had been used recently, and the smell of burned metal was coming from somewhere close to them.

Niori caught sight of the digital thermometer display next to the reactor. It read 528 degrees Celsius, which was almost exactly the number Kemba had mentioned. The temperature had a long way to go before the red zone. Apparently the reactor was working normally, just as Kemba had claimed.

Niori quickly checked the bodies of the guards lying around the room. They had also been killed with a samurai sword or similar bladed weapon.

"What's the point of all this?" Niori asked, mostly to himself. "Why would someone do this?"

Chief Inspector Niori had served on the Osaka police force for twenty-two years, but he couldn't remember seeing anything remotely this violent. This was Japan, not America. Things like this didn't happen here, said an incredulous voice in Niori's head. Japan only saw 0.9 homicides per hundred thousand people every year.

Then he remembered that Kemba had mentioned eight guards. They had found seven dead. Where was the eighth?

A new thought popped into Niori's mind: This was staged. This was a display. Theatrics. Someone wanted to tell them something, and they were saying it in a way that would be heard.

But what was it all about? Was it meant to make them notice something or prevent them from noticing something else?

Was this terrorism? Or an antinuclear attack? Was the purpose to show them how easy it would be to blow up the reactor? To tell them that they could have done it if they wanted to?

A groan came from behind Niori.

"The LR modules," Kemba said.

Niori turned. Kemba looked even paler than before. He pointed at the side of the reactor.

"The LR modules," he repeated. "They took the LR modules."

2

Considering the time of year, the night was exceptionally warm. Even though it was two in the morning, a gentle heat still lingered in the air. A woman sat on the concrete floor of her balcony drinking her fourth glass of whisky. The floor was hard, but she didn't care and didn't bother getting a pillow to sit on.

She always told herself that things could be worse. Much worse. That was a useful idea and frequently brought her comfort. But when she had a really bad day—and there had been quite a lot of those lately—her depression wasn't mitigated by thinking that things could actually be much bleaker. On those days she curled up as small and tight as she could on her bed, wrapped her arms tightly around herself, and cried. Just a little, and usually not for very long. Always quietly enough that the neighbors wouldn't hear. Sometimes it helped, sometimes it didn't. Tonight crying didn't help.

The woman stood up, went inside, and took out the whisky bottle again. In her mind she relived those seconds that had changed her life. She had gone over it all thousands of times, unable to break the endless cycle of thoughts and questions. She knew well enough that the retracing wasn't going to help, that it would only drive her crazy. She shouldn't waste her time and strength grieving over the past. What happened happened, and there was no way to change it anymore. There was no point tormenting herself thinking about how things could have been. It was last winter's snow, spilled milk, water under the bridge, dust in the wind.

Normally she attacked these thoughts and questions the instant they arose; she forced them out of her mind, or at least pushed them far back toward the edges of her consciousness, into places where they were less bothersome. Even so, she knew they were still lurking somewhere in the great black seas surrounding her consciousness.

But sometimes the questions assaulted her so suddenly and with such violence that she didn't have time to ward them off.

When nothing else helped, she drank herself into a stupor. She tried not to do it very often, and so far she had been relatively successful. Sometimes she felt tempted to resort to stronger drugs than alcohol, but she hadn't succumbed yet to that. Because she had at least one reason she needed to stay alive and keep herself together. A person she would be responsible to for her actions for the rest of her life. Someone who might need her again someday.

The woman drank two more whiskies to calm her thoughts and put them in their proper place, locked into the compartments where every now and then they acquiesced to stay.

But right now an extra, anomalous weight pressed down on her. She would have preferred to forget it since the memories surrounding it were so unpleasant and fresh.

But . . .

And it was a big *but*.

What if it was important? And what if something terrible happened because she didn't tell anyone? Could she endure that? On top of her other struggles?

She sipped more whisky and tasted the words she had heard a few days earlier.

She shuddered. The words were mysterious and frightening. Hearing them had sent instant shivers up her spine. And what about what happened moments later? There had been something ominous about it all. Dangerous.

Unless she had only imagined it.

But later, when she looked up information about it online, her concern returned. And it was deeper than before. She had spent a long time considering whether she should share her worries with Michael. Finally she decided not to. She would have been forced to explain too much, to invent too many explanations and lies. Instead she asked one of her clients who worked for the government whom she could tell about it if that was what she decided to do. She had lied, saying she was asking for a friend and that she didn't know exactly what the matter was about.

The man had hesitated but finally gave her a business card from his wallet. Apparently he had collected it at a State Department cocktail party a couple of weeks earlier.

"Maybe he can help your friend," the man said. "But don't tell anyone where you got that."

"Of course not," she replied.

The card was on her table now. She picked it up as she sipped her whisky.

"Lauri Nurmi," she read in a whisper.

Strange name. An address in New York, telephone number, and e-mail appeared under the name. The acronym *NTU* was also printed on the card. NTU? She didn't have a clue what that stood for. She had looked in the phone book and online, but she hadn't found any NTU. The street view of the online map showed a nondescript office building.

She placed the card back on the table.

Should she go to the address? Or call? Or send an e-mail?

No. If she shared what she knew in an e-mail or over the phone, she could be tracked down. Maybe it would be best to simply go to the building and feel it out before deciding how much to tell—if she told anything.

"You're afraid you're going to get into trouble if you go," she said to herself. Not going would be much more sensible.

But could she do that?

Once again her thoughts forced her into a corner.

3

This is one hell of a mess, thought Julia Noruz. She wanted to light a cigarette. She was never going to make any sense of this.

"Not unless I can get a smoke," she said aloud.

Julia perched her eyeglasses on her forehead and stretched her arms. Her eyes felt tired, and a headache lurked somewhere around her temples.

Research reports on the consequences of the Chernobyl nuclear power plant disaster were piled on her desk. Some were in English or German, but most were written in Russian, Ukrainian, or Belorussian and printed in Cyrillic characters. Julia knew those languages, but in this case that didn't seem to be much help. With a few exceptions, she couldn't find any major mistakes in the methodology of the papers when she evaluated each of them individually. But the overall picture they formed didn't make any sense.

Julia sighed, her whole body screaming for nicotine.

Year after year the research on the aftereffects of Chernobyl had become increasingly contradictory. Pieces to a scientific puzzle collected within a viable theoretical framework should have led to an increasingly coherent constellation of interconnected facts. A smooth, even surface.

Like any other two-dimensional puzzle. It shouldn't be a jagged three-dimensional mass with sharp edges pointing out every which way. Ugly protrusions that were entirely the wrong shape to fit with any of the other pieces and which left gaping holes and giant voids.

"I give up. Someone is lying. Someone has to be lying. Why don't these results match up? And why can't I think about anything but cigarettes? Quitting can't be this hard—Mark Twain quit smoking thousands of times," she muttered to herself.

Julia tried desperately to focus on the problem.

"I can't see any pattern here. There isn't any rational shape."

And where was her phone? She would need to find that at some point too.

"OK, woman, calm down," she continued to herself. "You'll find it. It has to be here . . . You just have to take a breath and go through everything again. There has to be something here that you're just not understanding yet. There's always a pattern hiding under the surface. Even when it looks chaotic."

Julia stood up and tapped her forehead with her index finger.

"So, what do we have?" she muttered. "First we have a few dozen studies that found increased child mortality and birth defects in the three years after Chernobyl in England, Germany, Turkey, India, and other countries. OK, those are one category. Then we have seven hundred Russian, Belorussian, and Ukrainian studies reporting completely new diseases, increased mortality, and birth defects. That's another category."

Julia collapsed at her desk again. In addition to the first two categories, she had a miscellaneous collection of studies done in the West that applied more advanced research methods. These mapped child mortality and congenital defects in various locations in each country. The statistics were then compared with the amount of radioactivity each area received. All of the studies done this way produced similar results. Increased child mortality and congenital defects simply did not correlate with how much radioactive material each area received. In many cases there was actually a strong negative correlation, at least statistically, between radioactive contamination and child mortality: the more becquerels measured in the milk and forest mushrooms in the area, the more healthy the children. This seemed impossible.

"How do these pieces fit together?" Julia asked, continuing her monologue. "Or do they? Maybe they don't actually fit together at all. At some point I'll probably have to accept the fact that this puzzle is impossible to solve because the pieces are from a bunch of different puzzles. But if they don't fit together, someone has to be lying. Who could that be?"

Julia had a policy of rejecting conspiracy theories, but what else could explain the contradictions contained in the material sitting in front of her?

"So now I have to decide what kind of conspiracy I want to believe in," Julia said, still aloud. "Option one: thousands of Russian, Ukrainian, and Belorussian scientists and doctors have formed a giant antinuclear plot. Option two: thousands of Western scientists and doctors have formed a giant pronuclear plot."

Great. That cleared everything up. Julia liked straightforward problems. The only issue was the insignificant fact that neither option, while logically conceivable, made any sense.

"So you've started talking to yourself again, have you?" Lauri Nurmi said behind her.

Julia jumped.

"Who, me?" she said. "Never."

"How's it going with the smoking?"

"Excellent," Julia said, thankful for the interruption.

"That's good. We can avoid having ash all over the place," Lauri said. "At least from you smoking, that is."

"Do you want to be useful or just stand there criticizing me?"

"At your service, madam! What would you like me to do?"

"Bring me the shredder. I give up. I was thinking I'd put myself out of my misery before lunch so I don't change my mind in a moment of weakness."

"Ah," Lauri said, rubbing his stubble. "Sounds sensible. Clearly you've already chewed your nails to the bone. And how long have you gone without a cigarette this time?"

"A long time," Julia assured him.

"How long?"

"Well, pretty long."

"Precisely how long is 'pretty long'?" Lauri insisted. "Stop evading the question."

Julia looked at the clock.

"Well, if we're going to be precise, I've gone . . . exactly . . . sixteen minutes and twenty-three seconds."

"Not impressed," Lauri said, a bit too coldly in Julia's opinion.

He could be a little more supportive. What made him think putdowns were going to work better than encouragement?

On the other hand, Julia's instincts told her that although Lauri's comment was intended to be playful, the extra dose of harshness wasn't entirely accidental. Hmm . . . So Lauri wasn't in a very good mood. Usually there was only one explanation for that.

"You've been fighting again," Julia said.

"I don't understand why you always stick your nose where it doesn't belong."

"Oh, so that's how it is? And who was it who was just criticizing me about my smoking?"

"You're the one who asked us to cheer you on," Lauri pointed out acerbically.

"So it was a worse fight than usual," Julia said. "Should you really be together if it's always like this?"

"I think we'll make that decision ourselves."

Julia stood up. Walking over to the coffeemaker, she poured a full cup of black coffee and handed it to Lauri.

"Thanks," Lauri said. "If things with Alice and me go south, I might come knocking at your door soon."

Julia shook her head. "Right. That'll be the day."

"What's that supposed to mean?"

Julia sighed.

"Lauri, I'm older than you, I'm at least forty pounds overweight, and no one has ever called me beautiful. Alice, on the other hand . . . How could I ever compete with that? And you always fall for women like her."

"It isn't that simple," Lauri protested.

"In your case it is. Sorry."

"You've got a brain in your head though. That counts for something."

Julia turned around, crossing her arms and looking at Lauri in amusement.

"Well, that's nice to hear. A woman's brains count for something!" Then she turned serious. "But what I don't understand is why you can't grow up a little and apologize to Alice. Even if she is just a little too good-looking, that doesn't make her a bad person."

Julia was irritated that she had said anything, because now she was forced to continue.

"Alice is actually, as painful as it is for me to admit, a pretty damn nice person, and you're a fucking idiot if you drive her away. I'm sorry, but that's just the way it is."

Why was she defending Alice to Lauri again? Because Alice had always been friendly and decent to her, that was why. Even if there was something slightly irritating about the unflappable self-confidence that came from Alice's wealthy upbringing and timeless good looks. At least there was if you didn't come from a background like that and didn't have as good a self-image. If you weren't as thin and athletic and didn't compete in ultratriathlons. If you suffered from weight problems, if you had never had a relationship last more than a month, and if you couldn't even stop choking your own lungs with soot.

"You can't know what she's like at home," Lauri said and turned to leave. "Thanks for the coffee."

"No problem," Julia said. "But I think you guys should keep trying. I know I'm on the outside looking in, but I think you'd both have a hard time finding anyone else that fit you so well."

"That's easy for you to say."

"Yes, it is," Julia said. Opening her desk drawer, she pulled out a pack of cigarettes and slipped it into the pocket of her jacket on the back of the chair. Then she picked up the jacket and draped it over her arm.

"Where are you planning to go?" Lauri asked. "Out on the balcony?"

"I'm a Muslim, so I pray toward Mecca five times a day," Julia said in amusement.

"Ah, yes," Lauri said, his face in a crooked grin. "Do you really think anyone would believe an explanation like that? In your case?"

"Well, you aren't exactly a devout Christian either," Julia protested.

"But I'm not addicted to dangerous substances."

Lauri carried his coffee mug to his office and started sorting through his e-mail. There was a lot of it. He had only gotten through the first three messages when the telephone rang. The caller was his boss, Colonel Kenneth Andrews.

"I never would have believed I might find you at your actual place of employment," Andrews said with feigned surprise. "What on earth are you doing here?" he asked.

"Don't try to be funny, Kenneth," Lauri said. "It doesn't suit you."

"There's a visitor for you," Andrews said.

"I don't have any appointments."

"Be that as it may, there's a woman here who came to see you. She's been waiting half an hour already. Apparently she has something important to talk with you about."

Lauri glanced at his watch.

"OK, maybe I can give up a few minutes. You never know what kind of woman might cross your path!"

"I'll bring her to you."

A moment later Andrews was standing at Lauri's office door. He was a little older than Lauri, tall with blond hair. He had bewilderingly blue eyes, and Lauri had sometimes thought that in Hitler's Germany he probably would have been classified as some sort of honorary Aryan.

With Andrews was a woman dressed in understated but expensive-looking clothing. Lauri invited her in. She had thick chestnut brown hair and a prominent nose. The olive tone of her skin lent her a hint of the exotic.

Lauri thought she was attractive in a unique sort of way, but there was a hard and slightly bitter undertone to her expression that Lauri didn't like.

The woman extended her hand.

"Katharine Henshaw," she said.

"Lauri Nurmi," Lauri replied and indicated the chair on the other side of his desk. "Please, sit."

The woman sat down across from Lauri. Andrews remained standing near the door.

"How can I help you?" Lauri asked.

The woman looked at Lauri appraisingly.

Lauri didn't press or say anything at all, giving the woman time to come to her own conclusions.

Gradually she relaxed. Lauri thought she was finally going to tell him what she came to say.

"What does lithium-6 mean?" asked Katharine Henshaw.

4

Kenzaburo Niori spotted the abandoned truck with its driver's-side door and both rear doors hanging open. Two police cars were parked alongside the truck.

A small ocean of steel cargo containers—blue, red, gray, and black—were stacked around the harbor area. Here and there were heavy-duty Cargotec cranes on tracks. Farther away they could see taller cranes and the superstructures of enormous cargo ships anchored in Osaka Harbor.

"That has to be it," said Akiko Nobura, pointing to the truck.

Niori and Nobura pulled up next to the police cars.

They greeted the officers who walked up to meet them. Mitsuru Kemba got out of the backseat of one of the police cars and followed the officers. His steps seemed strangely apathetic and tired, and his hair was much grayer than it had been a week before. Niori thought Kemba looked as if he had aged ten or fifteen years in just a few days.

"So there's a body in the truck," Niori said.

The nearest officer nodded in response.

"Have you succeeded in identifying him?"

"Yes. His name is Saburo Morita."

"We guessed as much," Niori said.

Saburo Morita was the missing Yoshikawa guard, the eighth.

"At least he wasn't a traitor," Nobura pointed out. "If that's any comfort to anyone now."

Niori looked thoughtfully at the rear doors of the truck, which were hanging open.

"Were the doors like that when you found the truck?" he asked. "Or did you open them?"

"The doors were already open," replied another officer. "We haven't touched anything."

Once again the unpleasant feeling that things weren't exactly as they seemed crept into Niori's mind. Someone was toying with them. Someone was playing a game, and they didn't know the rules.

"This is act two of the play," Niori said aloud. "They wanted us to see this."

"I know what you mean," Nobura said. "I don't like this. I don't enjoy acting blind."

Kemba frowned. "I don't understand what you're talking about."

"We don't know what's really going on," said Niori. "Of course we understand what this looks like. But is it really about that or something else entirely? These are exhibitions . . . acts in a play. The guards in the basement killed with the samurai sword and this body here, in a truck with the doors wide open. For some reason whoever did this wants us to know that the LR modules were taken out through the port. Otherwise they would have disposed of the body some other way. Or left it at the scene of the crime."

Kemba looked at the stacks of cargo containers around them.

"How can we know that the modules aren't still here, in one of those containers?" he asked.

Niori looked at Kemba bitterly. Over the past few days he had learned that a Rapid-L series nuclear reactor's normal cooling system functioned on liquid sodium. But if something happened that made the reactor temperature rise above 780 degrees, the emergency cooling system modules would start to melt.

Inside the modules was a light isotope of lithium, the lightest known metal solid at room temperature. Lithium-6. Naturally occurring lithium was a mixture of lithium-6 and lithium-7. A Rapid-L used almost pure lithium-6.

When the lithium-6 first melted and then continued heating up, it would expand and force its way into the reactor. As it did, it would squeeze the incombustible gases normally in the reactor out of its way and into an increasingly small space, taking their place and stopping the reactor from melting down.

Now the Yoshikawa Corporation had been forced to stop and disconnect the Rapid-L installed in the basement of their headquarters because the lithium release modules from the emergency cooling system had been cut off and hauled away.

The operation must have required several men, but the police had no details to work from since the building security camera tapes were also missing. Niori had ordered his detectives to comb the nearby buildings for any surveillance tapes that might show pictures of the vehicles used by the robbers. Now it was very probable they had found one of them, presumably the one used to transport the LR modules away from the Yoshikawa headquarters.

"When you say you know what this looks like, what do you mean exactly?" Kemba asked Niori.

Niori didn't respond immediately. He looked out to sea. The open water was obscured, hidden behind the stacks of containers, cranes, and ship hulls. Niori wished he were surrounded by ocean and shoreline. He felt hemmed in.

"My grandmother's middle brother was working on a fishing boat named the *Lucky Dragon* in the 1950s," he said. "He became very sick after the Americans conducted a nuclear test in the Bikini Atoll. The *Lucky Dragon* was caught in the fallout."

"The Americans have never been terribly good at taking responsibility," Kemba said with a shake of his head. "How did your great-uncle fare, or did he die?"

"He survived."

"Were they in the test area by accident?"

"No. It was a completely new kind of bomb. Its fallout was deadly even far outside the test area."

"Oh, I see," said Kemba. "Very irresponsible. But I don't understand. What does that have to do with these thefts?"

Maybe it was better that way. Turning to Nobura, Niori left Kemba's question unanswered. Nobura looked at him in amazement, since her superior was rarely guilty of such rude behavior.

"What do you think, Akiko? Would it be possible to find out which ship the modules were loaded on?" Niori asked.

Nobura shrugged, surprised by the familiarity of her superior's use of her first name.

"We can try," she said. "Let's interview any possible witnesses and go through the port security footage. And see what the satellite pictures show. I can't see what more we can do. The radiation trail has been covered quite effectively."

"You may be right," Niori said. "Except that there is still one thing we have to do. In addition to everything you mentioned."

"And what is that?" Nobura asked.

"We have to tell the Americans."

5

Katharine Henshaw looked at Lauri Nurmi and waited. The weight of her question was palpable.

"What does lithium-6 mean?" she asked again.

Not the most common conversation starter, Lauri thought.

Lauri had always had a passionate interest in history, and his area of specialty was nuclear technology. He was particularly fascinated by the story of how American nuclear physicist Ted Taylor had once lit a cigarette with an atom bomb.

In 1952 at the Atomic Energy Commission's Nevada Proving Grounds, Taylor had set up a small concave mirror on top of an instrument case. Then he held his cigarette at the focal point and waited. When the atomic fireball flashed ten miles behind Taylor and his colleagues, the mirror focused the radiation from it to the end of the cigarette, which began to glow. Taylor took a few drags and then put it out. He had saved what was left of it, because he knew it might be the only cigarette ever lit by an atom bomb that hadn't burned up instantly.

Lauri wasn't sure whether the story was true, but several people had assured him it was. Taylor himself had said he kept the half-burned cigarette for a long time but then smoked the rest of it once by accident.

Lauri looked at Henshaw and wondered, a bit perplexed, what he should say to her.

"Lithium-6?" he said.

Andrews looked at him strangely from across the room, and Lauri suddenly realized he must have sounded absentminded and distant.

How innocent we were then, Lauri thought. So young and innocent—humanity in general.

Lauri was born twenty years after Ted Taylor lit his Pall Mall with a nuclear bomb. Taylor had been one of the most gifted and inventive nuclear weapons designers of all time. Five years later he was heading up a top-secret joint project between the US government and General Atomic called Orion.

Lauri could see Katharine Henshaw's expression growing impatient.

"Lithium-6 is the second most common isotope of the element lithium," Lauri began.

During Orion, the climate had been one of excess: the first nuclear power plants; intercontinental jet planes, satellites, and moon shots; submarines studying the deepest abysses of the ocean—all to create the illusion of technological omnipotence.

People believed that in the long run, nothing was impossible. Why would it be? Soon there would be bases and then cities on the Moon and Mars. People would fly to the stars. Ships and airplanes and maybe even cars would move under nuclear power.

Using small nuclear bombs would make digging canals and building foundations and mineshafts inexpensive and straightforward. Subterranean coal seams could be vaporized into natural gas using atom bombs, and small explosions could be used to produce precious elements that were otherwise vanishingly rare on Earth.

"Most lithium is lithium-7," Lauri continued. "The rest is primarily lithium-6."

He could picture Ted Taylor and that Pall Mall in his mind's eye. Starry-eyed naïveté? Lauri asked himself. Of course. Youthful daydreaming? Undoubtedly. Nowadays no one would think anything else—for example, about Operation Plowshare, the government's attempt to find peaceful uses for nuclear bombs. But . . . the real question was whether we'd really woken up or whether we were still living the same daydream. What if we were still asleep and only dreaming that we were awake? And if we were still sleeping, when would we actually wake up and get real? And what would it take to snap Sleeping Beauty out of her dream?

"Yes, so?" said Henshaw once the pause became awkward.

"Of course we need dreams, but . . ."

Henshaw raised an eyebrow at Lauri, but she quickly realized his thoughts were wandering far afield.

"So?" Henshaw repeated. "I understand all that already."

"Oh yes, the lithium . . ."

"I studied physics in college," Henshaw continued. "And I also know that lithium-6 or liquid sodium is used as a coolant in fast breeder reactors."

"Well, then you basically know as much as we do," Andrews said mildly.

He was still standing by the door.

Henshaw shook her head. She looked dissatisfied. "Isn't there anything more? Something unpleasant?"

"I don't know if I understand what you're getting at," said Andrews.

"What else can be done with lithium-6?" Henshaw asked. "Or, what I mean is, can anything bad be done with it? Anything really bad?"

Lauri and Andrews exchanged a quick glance. What should they say? Who was this person interrogating them?

Henshaw looked at Andrews, and her expression turned even more impatient.

"Isn't there anything else?"

Edward Teller, Lauri replied in his mind. The Hungarian nuclear physicist who, along with the Ukrainian-Pole Stanislaw Ulam, discovered the central principles of thermonuclear explosions and invented the hydrogen bomb. Actually, Ulam was probably the one who conceived the critical idea as he contemplated the secrets of stellar supernovae. Ulam realized how a small fission detonator, based on splitting atoms, could be used to create a much larger explosion based on fusion, the collision and combination of nuclei.

"Why buy a cow when powdered milk is so cheap?" Edward Teller had once replied in response to questions similar to those Henshaw was asking.

But Lauri didn't tell Henshaw what Teller had said.

"Well, the tritium used in nuclear weapons is produced from lithium-6," he said instead. "Boosted fission bombs and all hydrogen bombs use tritium. It has to be made from lithium-6 either in normal commercial nuclear reactors or in specially built breeders. At the moment we don't have the right kind of breeder reactors, so we buy it from power plants on the civilian side."

"And that's all?" Henshaw asked.

"Maybe now would be a good time for you to tell us what all this has to do with you?" Lauri replied to her question.

Katharine Henshaw hesitated. "I know I probably made a serious mistake coming here," she said. "But I think this might be important."

Then she looked Lauri straight in the eyes.

"You aren't going to get me into any trouble for coming here, are you?"

Lauri laughed.

"Just so long as you don't admit to killing anyone."

"What is this place?" Henshaw asked. "What does *NTU* mean?"

Lauri motioned to Andrews.

"NTU stands for *Nuclear Terrorism Unit*," Andrews explained. "We're a special division of the Department of Energy."

"I thought it might be something like that," Henshaw said. She drilled her gaze into Lauri, focusing on him as if Andrews no longer existed. "What do you do if you learn about lesser crimes than murder? Are you interested in that? Do you always have to report them?"

"Katharine—may I call you Katharine?—anything less than murder is up to our discretion if you have something important to tell," Lauri said. "We don't care if you're a cat burglar or a heroin addict. And to tell the truth, if what you have to say is important enough, we could even overlook a few murders. But don't tell that to the media."

"Yes, you may call me Katharine. So whatever I tell you, the only part you're going to pass on is what actually has bearing on your work?" Henshaw asked.

"Of course," Lauri assured her.

"Do you promise?"

Lauri smiled as reassuringly as possible. "I promise."

"I believe you," said Henshaw. "Even though I know I shouldn't."

"So what would you like to tell us?"

"A few days ago I was at a party thrown by a businessman named Timothy Washburn for some of his friends."

Lauri saw a dark cloud pass across Henshaw's face, but it quickly disappeared. What was she hiding, and would it decrease her credibility?

"Among Washburn's associates, there was a group that seemed tight knit," Henshaw continued. "Four men, two of whom spoke Arabic to each other. They definitely looked Arab. The other two were obviously South Asian."

"Where in South Asia do you think they were from?"

"They had relatively light skin, and they might have been speaking Punjabi, but I'm not a hundred percent sure about that. So my guess is they were Pakistani. Pakistani Punjabis are usually quite fair skinned. At least in my experience."

"Yes . . . and then?"

"They went upstairs and I was . . . Well, I was in the room next to them for a while. Once I was alone, I opened the window and smoked a cigarette. That was when I heard one of the Arabs talking on a phone, in English. I only heard three sentences, but I could make out his words perfectly. First he said, 'You have the lithium-6.'"

"'You have the lithium-6,'" Andrews repeated. "You heard him say it just like that?"

"Exactly," Henshaw said. "'You have the lithium-6.'"

"Was it a statement or a question?" Andrews asked as he walked over and stood next to Henshaw.

"A statement. Then he just said, 'Excellent.' And finally he asked, 'All six tons?' His companion said something in Arabic, but I didn't understand what. Though he might have said that it was dangerous talking next to an open window, because the next thing I heard was the window shutting, and no more of the phone call."

"What happened then?" Lauri asked.

"Suddenly I started getting a little scared. I had a feeling that something bad was going to happen, so I hid in the closet just before the door opened and the Arabs peeked in. When they saw the room was empty, they left. But I hid in there for almost half an hour before I went downstairs again. I was afraid I might attract attention if I reacted in the wrong way when I saw them, but luckily they were already gone."

"Would you recognize them if you saw them again?" Andrews asked. "Or if you saw their pictures?"

"Yes, I think so," Henshaw said. She looked back and forth between Lauri and Andrews. "You don't look convinced," she said. "But you're going to look into it now, aren't you? You're going to find out what the phone call was about?"

"To tell the truth, I'm not sure," Lauri said. "We get a lot of tips. And we don't have time to investigate them all."

"Whatever you decide," said Henshaw, while she stared at Lauri, "but I'm going to tell you one thing. These were not good people."

Andrews looked incredulous. Henshaw glanced at him in irritation and then turned her eyes back to Lauri.

"I've seen a lot in my life. But these guys . . . they sent shivers down my spine. And believe me, it takes a lot to do that."

Lauri nodded.

"OK, let's say we'll do a little digging around."

Henshaw looked Lauri up and down, measuring him.

"OK," she said. Then she stood up, turned around, and started to walk out of Lauri's office.

"Hold on. We have to call someone to escort you out," said Andrews.

Lauri waited until their visitor had disappeared, then he looked at Andrews.

"What do you think?"

"I think we should leave it alone," Andrews said.

"You wouldn't look into it at all?"

"Lauri, my boy, if we always jumped in feetfirst when some broad let her imagination get the better of her or whenever someone somewhere in the world said 'boo,' we'd never have time for anything but chasing our own tails. Don't you think we have better things to do?"

"But this broad just told us she heard some Arabs talking about lithium-6."

"Still. Lots of people are interested in nuclear power and fusion energy. Lots of people are even interested in nuclear weapons. But they don't go around building them."

"Hopefully you're right. If it were up to me, I would look into any tips we get about lithium-6. That's a pretty nasty isotope."

"As if I didn't know." Andrews snorted. "Maybe this is why I'm in charge of this circus, not you. You need *fingerspitzengefühl* in a job like this. You have to be able to separate the wheat from the chaff without thinking about it."

Later Lauri would remember these words.

6

Alice Little Hawk Donovan tied her horse Ayenwatha to a tree and sat on a large boulder with her legs crossed as her Iroquois mother's relatives traditionally did. Alice Donovan was a small woman with long, shiny jet-black hair and a slightly angular, boyish figure. Her face told of her Iroquois blood, but there were other genes mixed in that softened her features. As a teenager Alice had grown used to men thinking she was beautiful and "drooling" over her, as Lauri put it.

She was wearing a beat-up anorak and light blue jeans that were tattered at the ankles and had a hole in one knee. Alice was barefoot because she never wore shoes when she didn't have to. When she was a little girl, her parents had forced her to keep her feet covered and wear nice clothes, but she had always tossed her shoes aside as soon as she got far enough out in the wilderness.

The imposing view spread out before her as the gentle wind caressed her face and tousled her hair. Even as a little girl she had loved the towering sky, the wide-open spaces, the wind and rain on her bare skin, and the earth between her toes. She had spent two hours riding to this specific place in the hills behind Sierra Vera—the top of the last mountain, a lonely vanguard rising from an endless plain. The distance to the farthest extent of the horizon was at least a hundred miles.

Getting out in the country made her feel she could breathe again, and she was pleased that Lauri had decided to buy a place like Sierra Vera despite the fact that the transaction had shackled most of his financial resources to the sands of New Mexico. The same purpose had also tied down a small slice of Alice's own liquidity, which was much more significant than Lauri's worldly wealth.

As much as she loved it, Alice wasn't yet ready to move back to the country. Not at this point in her life. She had been forced to spend much of her youth with her father in Texas, far away from her mother's beloved forests in upstate New York, and that had made her immune to romanticizing country life. Although she didn't use the less poetic appellation for her father's home state of *Tex-ass* anymore, as she had done during her years of vulgar teenage rebellion, and although in theory she had made up with her father, she hadn't seriously considered the possibility of someday returning to her über-rich father's cattle-ranch fiefdom.

Even though her relationship with her parents had been distant and painful at times, they had paid for her college education at a good university, which Alice was thankful for. She genuinely missed her mother and was proud of being half-Onondaga. Alice also still maintained her soft Texas accent in deference to her father.

But she knew that despite her mother's company and support, she couldn't have tolerated too many days in a row in the same place with her ultraconservative father. And even now, much older and more experienced than when she left home, she couldn't completely understand what glue continued to bind her parents together. Her father was probably the only rich Texan who had ever officially married an Indian woman. Of course, Charlie Donovan hadn't yet inherited his fortune from his father when, to everyone's surprise, he married Little Tree, the

Onondaga activist he had met and fallen head over heels in love with when they were students in Virginia.

Alice was relatively satisfied with her own life, such as it was. As a respected member of an elite unit, she did work that was hard to dismiss. The only small minuses were the occasional dangers of her work and the fact that she and Lauri had been fighting more lately than ever before. But maybe that wasn't such a big deal either, once all was said and done. They had already gone through a lot together, so Alice had a hard time imagining that they might split up because of one little rough patch. Eventually they would work through their arguments and the differing goals and aspirations that were dividing them right now, and they would reach some compromise that satisfied both of them. A new state of equilibrium. Then everything would be good again.

Instinctively, Alice touched the long, thin scar that ran across her brow. It was much less noticeable than eight years earlier, and though it was slightly lighter than the rest of her skin, it was almost concealed by her deep tan. Alice had earned the scar in Waziristan, in a battle near the village of Dandar Kili, where it had seemed as if the entire mountainside in front of them had suddenly opened fire, with the muzzle flashes of first hundreds and then thousands of weapons blazing into life. A bullet from a Kalashnikov had gouged Alice's forehead, blinding her with blood. If Lauri hadn't dragged Alice to safety and then carried her on his shoulders to the helicopter, she never would have come back alive from Dandar Kili.

When the United States and Great Britain began bombing Afghanistan, tens of thousands of hotheaded Pashtun young men from North and South Waziristan rushed across the border of Pakistan to the aid of their kinsmen. Without a second thought, the United States Air Force bombed a few thousand of them along with the Afghani Taliban. Al-Qaeda guerillas watched all this from the sidelines, from the slopes of the nearby Safēd Kōh mountain range, probably chuckling in satisfaction.

Some estimates pegged the number of assault rifles in the Federally Administered Tribal Areas of northwest Pakistan at around eight million. Previously, following their common war against the Soviet Union, the rifle owners thought of the United States in positive terms. But in 2002, when they went with a group of Pakistani army units to see why all of the houses in Dandar Kili had suddenly gone up in flames, the owners of those eight million assault rifles switched sides. That was why fire and lead rained down on Alice and Lauri.

Alice gazed out at the landscape she loved so much. Then she returned to Ayenwatha. Untying his tether, she stroked the horse's brown, velvet back.

"Time to head home?" she whispered in the horse's ear. He turned his head toward Alice.

"It is, is it? Well, let's go then."

As Alice and Ayenwatha approached the buildings of Sierra Vera, she saw that Lauri was on horseback too. Once at the pasture, Alice dismounted and gave Ayenwatha some water and oats. Then she walked in Lauri's direction.

Lauri was holding a tall bow and six steel-tipped arrows as he sat on Orinoco, a large black stallion. Six targets of life-sized human silhouettes on a white background were set up on posts at ten-yard intervals, starting about forty yards away.

Alice waited for Lauri to start.

At Lauri's encouragement, Alice had tried shooting a bow from the back of a moving horse a few times, but so far she hadn't been able to get within two yards of the targets. It was actually fairly humiliating, since Alice had learned how to ride before she could read. During college she had twice won an intercollegiate archery championship—in addition to her ultratriathlon trophies. And yet when she tried shooting from the back of a moving horse, her arrows always flew awry.

The art of shooting from horseback had fallen into obscurity until Lajos Kassai began reviving it. Lauri had participated in three of Kassai's courses in Hungary. Between these he had practiced diligently at Sierra Vera. The first time Alice's parents visited them at the ranch, Lauri's ability to shoot from a moving horse made a deep impression on Alice's mother, Little Tree Donovan. Charlie Donovan had just snorted and muttered something about the superiority of machine guns compared to Stone Age toys.

In the seven and a half years Alice and Lauri had been a couple, Charlie Donovan had only visited Sierra Vera twice. The second time had been when Alice's appendix suddenly ruptured. Her father had come and whisked her away to the hospital in his small vertical-takeoff-and-landing jet.

Alice knew Lauri was holding a genuine Hun bow produced by the most skilled artisans in Hungary. An exact replica of models 1,700 years old, it was made out of the same materials the Huns had used. It looked like a normal bow, but it was a complicated and carefully designed instrument. In its own time it had been one of the most deadly weapons of war.

Hun bows were stronger and more lethal than any the world had seen before. They were made of a composite of bone, sinew, and wood that was at once strong and flexible. At either end was a small tip, or *siyah*, made of bone. The siyahs were the most unique characteristic of the Hun bows, giving them a slightly longer length and increased power without adding to the effort needed to draw them. Because of their bone tips, the bows could also handle greater stress. According to Lauri, wood alone would crack, because the highest forces were concentrated right at either end of the bow.

Of course Lauri emphasized that the Huns never actually accomplished anything useful. But even so, he clearly felt a sort of begrudging admiration for the ancient people, because he had a sideboard covered with genuine Hun jewelry and charms dug out of ancient graves.

Lauri had pointed out to Alice that in the 400s, the Great Hungarian Plain, which also extended into western Romania, couldn't have supported a particularly large group of nomads. And yet the Huns who had settled in that area drove a whole range of German and Iranian peoples out of the Eurasian Steppes, setting in motion a process that led to the destruction of the previously invulnerable-seeming Roman Empire.

Lauri and Orinoco exploded into motion. Alice watched spellbound, because even though she had seen the same display countless times, it was still just as impressive as it had ever been.

Lauri had said that the key was to empty your mind and switch off your conscious thoughts. When an archer aimed at a target on a firing range, it was possible to act consciously. There was time to seat the arrow, aim, and then wait for the right moment before shooting. But if you had to do the same thing from the back of a moving horse, that approach didn't work, because the horse was always in motion. The arrow had to be loosed at exactly the moment when all the hooves were in the air at once and the movement could be controlled. If you tried to aim, you always missed. The horse and the person had to become one and the same creature, almost like the centaurs of legend, a state the nomads of Mongolia still sought by tying their three-year-old children to horses' backs. Children remained tied until they learned to merge with the movements of the horse. Everything about riding and aiming and shooting had to become completely automatic, as reflexive as riding a bike, walking, or keeping your balance while standing or sitting.

Alice started the timer on her watch.

Orinoco galloped toward the nearest target, and Lauri loosed his first arrow. The black body of the horse obscured her view for a moment, so Alice didn't see whether Lauri had found his mark, but he had already nocked another arrow, and then it was in the air too, and Lauri was moving a third arrow from his fingers to the string in such a quick, fluid motion that Alice still couldn't comprehend how it was possible. And then the third arrow was in the air, and Alice saw that the first had struck between the nine and the ten, right in the middle of the target, and then Lauri was already shooting his fifth and sixth arrows. Orinoco turned and pivoted back.

Alice saw that all six arrows had hit home, on six different targets. Each one protruded from its post somewhere between eight and a perfect ten.

She didn't understand how he did it. Or she did, but even though she was a good shot, she couldn't do this. It was irritating, how easy he made it look.

Alice looked at the timer. Orinoco had galloped across the hundred-yard track in fourteen seconds, and Lauri had waited six seconds before loosing his first arrow. Six arrows in eight seconds, all in the center of their targets. It was an astonishing performance. And Lauri had only been practicing for five or six years. What of the Hun soldiers who studied the art from the time they were children?

On an open battlefield, the Huns would be rounding to make their second pass with six arrows and then another six. Lauri loved to emphasize that no battle force in the world had ever achieved such a rapid rate of fire until the repeating rifles of the early twentieth century, almost a thousand years later. The elite forces of the British Army outfitted with brand new Lee-Metford rifles at the Battle of Omdurman in 1898 had only shot twelve rounds a minute. English longbowmen during the Hundred Years' War had let fly one arrow every five or six seconds. Instead of holding bundles of arrows in their fingers, they took each one from their quivers singly and then stopped for a second to aim.

"It's actually a little frightening how quickly and easily world powers that had seemed invincible fell," Lauri had said to Alice. "A lot of times all it takes is one strategic or technological innovation. And just think of all the chaos and suffering the collapse of a great empire leaves behind!"

Lauri spun around and sped off again at full gallop toward the targets. Alice saw that another arrow was on the string and five more were at the ready in Lauri's fingers.

A moment later, six new arrows jutted from the center of the six targets. Lauri turned back and brought Orinoco to a halt next to Alice.

"How, little redskin," Lauri said, smiling at Alice.

Alice was surprised at the playful warmth that had returned to Lauri's voice. Things always went well for them when they were at the ranch. At Sierra Vera they were both usually happy. It was harder in the city, where there were other people around and constant reminders of everything that was painful about their lives.

Alice placed her hand on the flank of the great stallion slowly enough that it could see what she was doing. She didn't care to get kicked in the chest. Alice stroked his soft black hair.

"That went well," Alice said simply.

"Thanks."

"You're getting pretty good. You could think about the world championships."

"No one will ever beat Kassai," Lauri objected.

He didn't have the same competitive streak as Alice.

"Kassai is getting old," Alice said.

"Still."

"You could shoot for a silver medal."

"But that would be Pettra Engeländer."

Alice shook her head.

"You're better than Engeländer," she said with calm assurance. "You're obviously better than anyone other than Kassai. You could even beat him if you practiced more."

"Now you're exaggerating."

Alice looked at Lauri thoughtfully.

"You're almost as good as Kassai even though you only spend a fraction of the time that he does training. How do you do it?"

"I sort of practiced the same way when I was a little kid," Lauri said mysteriously.

Lauri's tone was suddenly hard. Alice waited for him to say something more, but he remained silent and Alice let it be. But she could see a distance in Lauri's expression as they led Orinoco toward the stable. *Where are you, my love?* Alice thought. *I want to know what you're thinking right now.*

After all the years they had been together, Alice was frequently surprised by how little they knew of each other. Was that a bad sign? Did it mean they weren't really interested enough in each other? Or was it just that people usually knew much less about other people, even about their spouses, than they assumed? Maybe no one could ever completely understand another person, the sum total of a lifetime of history and experience. Even shared experiences were never identical because of individual perspective. Maybe the greatest wisdom was to be satisfied with what was possible and not throw it away for an unattainable mirage.

And yet . . . it bothered her. Why did Lauri tell her so little about his childhood? Whenever she asked about it, he retreated into his concrete bunker of a shell. Suddenly Alice's good mood was gone. If things went badly for them, she would choose more carefully next time. She was tired of playing the mind reader.

7

As Lauri was leading Orinoco toward the stable, memories from half a lifetime ago began flashing through his mind. Early mornings of endless summer days when he would race through the forest along the lakeshore, while his mother and even the other boys in the neighborhood still slept. He had spent hours throwing fist-sized rocks at pieces of wood he had set up, again and again, hundreds of times until he could hit them without aiming. Over the years he had gradually increased the distances, the force of his throw, and size of the rocks. Later he had started practicing with his left arm too.

And then once when he was thirteen . . .

He saw in his mind the face of the older, bigger boy with his nose smashed, blood streaming down his jaw. He saw the expression of the bully go empty and his mouth fall open as he slowly fell forward, dropping to his knees and collapsing on the ground.

Lauri removed Orinoco's saddle and harness. He stroked his neck. The horse licked Lauri's face with its big tongue.

"So that's how it is," Alice said. "No wonder I've been feeling so jealous."

"Very funny."

After letting Orinoco out in the pasture with Ayenwatha, Lauri wiped the sweat from his face with a towel as they walked toward the ranch house.

Alice's black Tesla Roadster was parked on one side of the yard. On top of the ranch house roof was something that looked like a white satellite dish thirty feet across. But it was pointed straight at the sun, and if anyone had looked at the inside from above they would have seen that it was sheathed with a bright reflective surface.

Above the dish, a little below the focal point, an inquisitive observer would also have seen a cylinder three feet long and several inches across with two black plastic pipes diverging from its end. Alice had ordered the $30,000 concentrating photovoltaic system all the way from India. It produced forty-five kilowatts of electricity and ninety kilowatts of heat. In the winter the heat it produced was used for all of Sierra Vera's buildings and water. In the summer the heat was funneled through the plastic piping into the ground and stored deep in the rock for use in winter.

"Want a beer?" Alice asked.

"Why not?" Lauri replied as he picked up a science magazine sitting on the table. "Fusion Energy is Coming!" proclaimed the headline on the cover.

Alice saw the disgusted expression that spread over Lauri's face.

Lauri snorted. "Fusion power plants are religion, not science. They're churches. Prayer rooms. They don't have anything to do with anything practical like energy production."

"But these are just experimental generators," Alice joked. "You never know where it all might lead in the long term."

"Yeah, you never know," Lauri said, snorting again. "The whole thing is just another reincarnation of the old ridiculous 'Atoms for Peace' operation we're still cleaning up after. These atoms are just a little more dangerous than the earlier ones."

Alice thought Lauri sounded unusually bitter.

"Is this your usual weekly 'people are so stupid' outburst or is something else bothering you?" Alice asked. "What did I do this time? Or was it something I didn't do?"

"Come off it. There isn't anything specific bugging me. It's just that . . ."

Alice went to the refrigerator and took out two beers. Lauri thought it was probably best that he share the source of his irritation with Alice.

"Remember that woman I told you about who came into the office a few days ago?" he began.

Alice waited for Lauri to continue.

"She said she had heard some Pakistanis and Arab guys talking about lithium-6 arriving somewhere."

Alice's eyebrows went up just a bit.

"Andrews refused to investigate," Lauri added.

"Well, something like that doesn't necessarily mean anything," Alice said.

"You're right. It doesn't necessarily . . ."

"At least I can see now why fusion energy is so heavy on your mind. I mean, more heavy than normal."

Alice popped the caps off the beer bottles. She handed one to Lauri and took a long gulp from the other.

"Tomorrow is our last day off," Alice said.

"It sucks having to go back," Lauri muttered. "And a long weekend like this isn't even a real vacation. When was the last time we were here together longer than this?"

"Don't even get me started," Alice said. "We have to live with things the way they are. You can't always have everything you want."

"You have to decide what you want and make decisions accordingly."

"That's a selfish way to think about it. Our work just happens to be important. Even you've never disagreed with that. At least until now."

"You're such a workaholic! Can we get you into therapy for this? Life is passing us by while we're scribbling away in a sealed box surrounded by walls in the middle of the world's biggest concrete and asphalt desert. And besides, you're half-Iroquois. And Onondaga at that. Aren't you supposed to be more at home out in the wild than in New York City? I'm starting to feel like I got cheated. Maybe I should have read the packaging a little more closely before I started dating you."

"Yes, I enjoy it here. But New York also has its good sides."

"For example?"

"The pulse. The rhythm of the city. The warm asphalt. The culture is so much more diverse than here."

Lauri snorted. Alice had heard the same sound many times before.

"When was the last time we went to the theater together? Or dancing?" Alice asked. "Or just to a movie? Right now you'd probably prefer to live in a hut with a dirt floor, sitting on a log and sleeping in a hammock."

"Absolutely," Lauri said.

"Well, I think that would be nice too. Sometimes. And on a part-time basis. But I also happen to enjoy asphalt under my feet and some exhaust fumes in the air."

"OK, OK, OK," Lauri said. "You win. Let's go to the movies or a play when we get back to New York. What do you want to see?"

"I don't know yet. But we'll come up with something good."

"How about the new *Terminator*?"

Alice took her clothes off and went to shower. Lauri noticed how quick and efficient her movements were, as always. Alice left on only a small silver cross. Lauri was a fervent heathen and atheist himself, and Alice's Christian views irritated him. But he had decided to ignore the issue. And Alice wasn't a fanatic; she was more a Christian out of habit.

Realizing he was hungry, Lauri filled a saucepan half full of water and turned the induction burner on. Then he took a bag of spaghetti out of the cupboard. The cans and boxes of food were in neat rows, since Alice liked to keep things orderly. Lauri thought that sometimes—in some areas—she could be a little too orderly.

Lauri grabbed the remote and turned on the news. Huge flat icebergs appeared on the screen. The camera was in a helicopter or airplane. Guessing the scale of the picture was difficult since different sized pieces of floating ice often looked identical. The anchor's voice explained that the last strip of the Larsen C Ice Shelf had finally broken apart and was floating away as hundreds of icebergs. According to scientists, the enormous Ronne Ice Shelf had also started showing signs of instability. "A large number of small but relatively deep pools of freshwater have melted in it," the news anchor said. "The pools can act as wedges, like the ones the ancient Egyptians used for splitting slabs of stone from their quarries. And the Ronne Ice Shelf is almost the size of Spain."

Alice came out of the bathroom with an oversized white towel wrapped around her. She was drying her hair with a smaller one.

"Weren't you going to shower too?" Alice asked in an innocent tone. "You could trim your toenails while you're at it. You're on the verge of turning into a velociraptor, if you don't do something soon. And besides, you're getting holes in your socks."

"OK, OK," Lauri said and motioned at the TV. "Pretty bad stuff, huh?"

"Could be," Alice admitted. "If the Ronne Ice Shelf splinters too, the whole West Antarctic Ice Sheet will break up, probably pretty quickly. It's already melting fast on the Pine Island Bay side, and if it gets exposed to melting on the other side . . ."

Alice didn't bother finishing the sentence.

"That would raise sea level by twenty feet, wouldn't it?" Lauri asked.

"Roughly, yes. The Antarctic Peninsula has enough ice to lift sea level by about two feet, but the actual continental ice sheet has about ten times that. And then on the east side of course . . ."

"How fast could it happen?"

"If only we knew. Do you want another beer?"

8

Afterward, when they tried to remember when and how everything had actually started, finding the beginning of the chain of events was difficult. Things had crept forward, unnoticed, in small, slow increments. Lauri might have started everything from Katharine Henshaw's visit. But in reality he didn't begin worrying in earnest until a week later, after returning from New Mexico, when Kenneth Andrews barged into his office without knocking.

"Do you know what a Rapid-L is?" Andrews asked.

"Yeah," Lauri answered and continued typing.

"The Osaka police just announced that someone stole the emergency cooling system modules from a Rapid-L prototype."

"Excuse me, what did you say?" Lauri asked, looking at Andrews in surprise. He couldn't believe his ears.

"You heard right," Andrews said.

"Isn't the coolant in a Rapid-L . . . ?"

"You got it," Andrews replied.

Instantly Lauri remembered Henshaw.

"How much lithium-6 was in the reactor?"

"Six tons," Andrews replied.

"How much did the thieves steal?"

"All of it."

Now, suddenly, it was real. For the first time, it was really real. The thing he'd seen a thousand times in movies and on TV and read a hundred times in books. Now it was really happening.

"Are you OK?" Andrews asked. "You look a little pale."

"I'm fine," Lauri said. "Let me just get this straight though. Did the Japanese mention that amount themselves? Six tons?"

"Yes."

"Exactly six tons?"

"Yes."

"And Henshaw was also talking about six tons."

"Henshaw?"

"Katharine Henshaw. The woman who came in last week. She said she was at a party being thrown by a businessman named Washburn and overheard—"

"Shit, you're right," Andrews said, suddenly looking embarrassed.

"You have to admit that's one hell of a coincidence," Lauri said.

"Goddamn it, I think you were right. We should have looked into that."

"Maybe it isn't too late yet. Should I go visit Henshaw? Although I don't know how much more she'll be able to tell us," Lauri said.

"It's still worth checking. Look at her background too."

"Will do."

"But that isn't the most urgent item. First we need some information about this Washburn character and his business, including all his phone calls in the past few months. Incoming and outgoing. See if there are any security cameras that might have filmed his visitors. And then get information on all of their phone calls too."

"We're playing catch-up," Lauri pointed out.

"No use crying over spilled milk."

"Did the Japanese say when the theft occurred?" Lauri asked.

"Saturday before last. Between one and three thirty in the morning. They promised to send over all their information today."

"Good. Did they find any radiation trail?"

Andrews shook his head. "It was masked."

Lauri looked at him in astonishment. "What do you mean *masked*? How?"

"Apparently the thieves pulverized a little lithium, mixed it with some gas, and burned it at the bottom of a tall smokestack in an abandoned factory."

It took Lauri a few seconds before he realized what Andrews was saying.

"Now there are microscopic amounts of lithium-6 literally everywhere," Andrews explained. "All over south and central Japan."

"So much for a radiation trail then."

Andrews looked concerned. Lauri knew there was more coming.

"The Japanese also said that the heist was unusually violent," Andrews said. "There were eight guards in the building. All of them were killed. I don't know if anything comparable has happened in Japan since the war."

Andrews fell silent, waiting for Lauri to say something. Andrews's expression seemed to scream *OK, let me have it. Say it*. But Lauri just sat in silence, and Andrews left the room.

So much for his fingerspitzengefühl.

9

Could they really trust the ICBUW papers? Julia Noruz thought bitterly. The International Coalition to Ban Uranium Weapons was a single-issue lobbying group. It wasn't a serious scientific research center. Even so, some of the studies it published seemed reliable.

But she didn't know what to make of the one in her hand. Julia sighed. She had already smoked ten cigarettes that morning, and all she wanted was to go out on the balcony for yet another. Instead she held an unlit cigarette, inhaling imaginary smoke and tapping imaginary ash into her empty coffee cup. She was reading an article written by a Dr. Jawad Al-Ali, chief physician at the Iraqi Sadr Teaching Hospital. The paper detailed cancer mortality in Basra, southern Iraq. In 1990 the hospital had registered 488 cases of cancer, but in 2005 the figure was up to 1,375.

At first Julia thought it was probably just an illusion, a mirage caused by population growth or aging. But after she checked the demographic statistics, she wasn't so sure. According to Jawad Al-Ali, incidents of breast cancer rose significantly, along with lymphatic cancers, lung cancer, intestinal cancer, kidney cancer, and ovarian cancer. But stomach, skin, and uterine cancer hadn't increased at all. One more piece of evidence that didn't make any sense. And besides, there were significant statistical differences between neighborhoods that the population structure couldn't explain. How was it possible?

The ICBUW claimed the cause was dust from millions of depleted uranium rounds fired in the area during the war, but that couldn't be true. It was just propaganda for people who didn't know anything about physics. Depleted uranium was less radioactive than natural uranium. Spent nuclear fuel removed from a reactor was at least two billion times more radioactive. Depleted uranium ammunition couldn't have anything to do with the increased cancer morbidity in Basra.

So where were the area's problems coming from? Population growth and aging should have increased all cancers, not just the prevalence of certain ones.

Something didn't make sense. Something stank. Julia felt like a pattern was staring right at her, and yet she couldn't pinpoint it. It was the same thing with Chernobyl. She wondered if she had early-onset Alzheimer's or if she'd always been this stupid.

Julia glanced at her watch. Time to go. But she couldn't find her glasses. Or her keys. Or her phone. Julia quickly patted her pockets, but her keys weren't there. She lifted stacks of papers and files. Not finding any of the items she was looking for, she started to comb through the boxes on her desk, but then she saw Lauri Nurmi flash past the door.

"Wait, wait!" she shouted. Lauri stopped and turned back to Julia's door.

"You should maybe see these," Julia said and pushed a bundle of papers at Lauri. "I did a background check on Katharine Henshaw like you asked. She's a professional. A prostitute."

It was difficult to read Lauri's response. His expression was harder and colder than a moment earlier, but there was also something else there, like a hint of sadness or maybe even . . . pain? Julia didn't understand what Lauri was reacting to.

Lauri glanced over the papers.

"Is that so?" he said calmly. "That must be why she was worried about whether we would be interested in any minor crimes."

"Doesn't that reduce her credibility as a witness though?"

"Not necessarily," Lauri said sternly.

Julia looked at him in surprise. Where was his intensity coming from? She decided it was none of her business and turned back to digging through the piles on her desk.

"Missing something?" Lauri asked solicitously.

"I can't find my glasses anywhere."

"They're on your head."

Julia reached up. Lauri was right.

"Would you look at that? Now all I have to find are my keys and phone."

"They're in your coat pocket," Lauri said.

He pointed at Julia's long bright red coat, which hung from the coatrack a few feet away.

"They aren't there. I already looked."

"You didn't look hard enough."

Lauri removed the coat from the rack and reached into one of the pockets. He took the phone out and threw it to Julia. She caught it. In the other pocket Lauri found her key ring and threw it to Julia too.

"Well, I'll be," Julia said as she grabbed the keys out of the air. "How did you guess they were there?"

"In all the years we've known each other, you've lost your keys and phone about fourteen thousand times."

"Oh, come off it. I'm not that bad . . ."

"They're always in your coat pockets."

10

Lauri Nurmi climbed the stairs to the fifth floor of the Brooklyn apartment building where Katharine Henshaw lived. Graffiti covered the walls, except in places where the plaster was peeling. The bottoms of many of the doors had clearly been kicked at, and here and there signs of break-ins were visible around the locks. The building elevator didn't work, and by all appearances some time had passed since it had been used.

Lauri rang Henshaw's doorbell. Since he hadn't made an appointment, he hoped she was home.

When the door opened, Lauri found himself involuntarily holding his breath, because it was nearly impossible to recognize the woman standing in front of him as the same person who had visited his office. Henshaw was wearing a tight black dress that left her shoulders bare. She wore dramatic makeup, including bold lipstick and black eyeliner and mascara that made her eyes look as if they were painted on. Lauri noted a barely visible scar about two inches long on her neck, near the place of the carotid pulse.

Henshaw noticed Lauri's reaction, and her expression changed to one of mild amusement. *She's pure as New York snow,* thought Lauri. The lyrics of the Kim Carnes song suddenly popped into his head.

"I thought you might drop by," Henshaw said.

"Is now a bad time?"

"I have maybe an hour. Then I have to go. But come on in and have a seat."

Lauri thanked her and stepped in. Henshaw closed the door behind him.

"So you didn't exactly tell us everything," Lauri said calmly.

"Oh, you mean like what I do for work?"

"For example."

Henshaw shrugged. "Would you have?"

"I don't know. Probably not."

"I knew if you started digging, it would take about a nanosecond for you to figure out how I make a living. But if you didn't start digging . . . well, then I would have attracted undue attention and caused myself trouble without doing anyone else any good."

Lauri had to admit that Henshaw's words had a certain logic. He looked around. The apartment was small but comfortable, except for the tall stack of old newspapers in the entryway that Henshaw apparently couldn't be bothered to take out. On the floor were thick, plush rugs, blue and green and red. On the walls Scandinavian ryas hung alongside Indian and African batiks, and a collection of photographs was exhibited above a small chest of drawers.

"If you're worried about walking into a den of sin, don't worry—I don't work at home," Henshaw said sarcastically.

Lauri let his eyes wander around Henshaw's large bookcase. He noticed a few relatively new novels and a row of old classic romances. There wasn't anything particularly special, but a few shelves did seem to be devoted almost entirely to books about Armenia, Ukraine, the Armenian Genocide, and the world wars. Was there something behind that? Mixed in with the novels were also several popular science books and a few physics and chemistry texts. Henshaw had obviously been telling the truth when she said she had studied physics in college.

Lauri tore his gaze away from the bookshelves and turned.

"Can I ask one question?"

"How could I stop you?" Henshaw replied.

"Why do you . . . ?"

Henshaw sighed. "Everyone wants to know why. But there isn't anything interesting about it."

Lauri waited.

"You've heard the same story a million times before," Henshaw said.

"Could be."

"Something happened . . . and suddenly I needed four times more money than before. No one offered me a job as a top model or a CEO. And I couldn't go into politics because I didn't have the startup capital. I also wasn't beautiful or docile enough for millionaire bachelors to be lining up at my door. So what was I supposed to do?"

Henshaw smiled ironically at Lauri.

"Besides, nowadays a politician has to be willing to do anything with anyone. I get to choose my clients, and I decide which perversions I participate in. Politicians can't afford that luxury."

Lauri walked over to Henshaw's collection of photographs, which gave him the chance to glance at what was on top of the chest of drawers. There was a pile of letters from various organizations—the Amnesty International candle surrounded by barbed wire caught his eye, as did the Sierra Club logo. Under the letters were some magazines. Lauri turned his attention to the photographs hanging on the wall. In one was a very old woman with white hair in a beautifully embroidered dress. Lauri couldn't quite place what culture the dress belonged to.

Next to this was a newer portrait of a couple in their fifties. The man must have been handsome when he was younger, but here his face had a somewhat haggard expression and his gaze was haunted. The woman next to him had dark hair and was spectacularly beautiful.

"My mother was from Ukraine, if that's what you're wondering about," Henshaw said. "But my grandmother was Armenian."

Aha, thought Lauri. That was what was behind the books on Armenia and Ukraine.

A reproduction of an old painting also hung on the wall. It depicted a woman with black hair clothed in a white dress with a high collar. Based on the clothing, the painting was probably eighteenth century, or perhaps early nineteenth.

"Emma Hamilton," Henshaw said.

Lauri didn't know who Emma Hamilton was, and he didn't inquire.

"Would you like anything to eat?" Henshaw asked. "I could do with a bite myself."

"No, thank you," Lauri replied.

Henshaw went to the refrigerator and started moving its contents around. Then she turned to Lauri and handed him a half-eaten box of Chinese takeout. The leftovers were covered in a thick layer of fuzzy mold. Henshaw had also shoved two mummified apples in the box.

"You could take those out with you when you go," Henshaw said.

Henshaw's gaze landed on a vase containing a bunch of wilted flowers. Before Lauri managed to say anything, Henshaw shoved the dried-out bouquet into his hands.

"You can take these too."

"OK, OK," Lauri said submissively. "But in a minute."

He put the flowers and the take-out box down on the table.

"Why did you really come here?" Henshaw asked.

"Because we take your tip seriously and we're investigating."

Henshaw nodded. "Good. I'm pleased. To tell the truth, I thought you'd probably ignore me."

"I was hoping you could go over everything one more time with me. Everything you saw and heard, what kind of people were there, everything."

"Yes, I can do that. But I don't think I have anything very new or dramatic to tell you."

"You never know. You'd be surprised what details can be important sometimes."

Lauri pulled a notepad and pen out of his jacket.

"Isn't that a little old-fashioned?" Henshaw asked.

"I assumed you'd prefer it if I didn't tape anything."

A small smile lit up Henshaw's face. "Actually, you're right. That was very thoughtful of you. Thank you."

"First tell me one thing though. What were you doing at this Washburn's house? Were you working?"

"A while ago I received an offer from Washburn's assistant," Henshaw said. "I have his name and contact information if you're interested. Mr. Washburn was organizing a big party and wanted some girls there. To entertain the guests."

"And you went?"

"I went, although now I wish I hadn't."

"Why?"

"I'd prefer not to talk about that side of things, if that's OK," Henshaw said, her voice turning several degrees colder.

"Let's leave that alone then," Lauri said. "But can you say exactly when all of this happened?"

"Saturday two weeks ago," Henshaw said without hesitation.

"Do you know roughly what time it was?"

"Not exactly," Henshaw said. "But I'd say sometime between eleven and twelve at night."

The lithium had been stolen in Osaka between one and three thirty in the morning local time. What was the time difference between Osaka and New York? Fourteen hours? Or was it sixteen? Something like that.

Lithium-6

In any case, the phone call Henshaw had overheard in New York took place the same day as the robbery. That couldn't be an accident.

"That timing must mean something," Henshaw said.

"Unfortunately I can't comment," Lauri said.

Henshaw nodded. "OK. But I have one request. I told you what I know, so I think it would only be fair of you to tell me why you're concerned about the possibility that a large amount of lithium-6 has fallen into the wrong hands."

"We already told you," Lauri said.

Henshaw shook her head.

"Come off it. I don't want to hear any military secrets. But it would be nice if you would tell me what you can."

Lauri hesitated. Of course none of it was a secret anymore. It had stopped being a secret in 1954 when Joseph Rotblat deduced what had happened and revealed to the world that the United States government had lied. In an article for the *Bulletin of the Atomic Scientists*. Sixty years had passed since then, and now old *Bulletin* articles were online for anyone who was interested to read. Even so, NTU agents weren't exactly encouraged to go around spreading information about it.

Henshaw looked at him insistently.

Maybe it was fair. On a page of his notebook he wrote something and then tore it out and gave it to Henshaw. On the page were four words, on two lines. It said:

Castle Bravo
Lucky Dragon

"Put those words into Google and you'll find what you're looking for," Lauri said. "But don't tell anyone I pointed you in that direction."

Lauri stood up to go. He picked up the wilted flowers, rotten apples, and moldy Chinese food. Henshaw followed him to the door. Lauri saw where Henshaw's gaze went.

"Hey, come on," Lauri said. "I'm a federal agent, not a garbage man. And that's a big pile of newspapers."

"You could at least take some of them. Just as many as you can carry," Henshaw said. "You can get the rest next time you come."

11

A tall, dark-haired man leaned on a balcony railing and listened to the nocturnal sounds of the surrounding city. The city that never slept, thought the man. Traffic hummed in every direction like a distant cataract, and here and there from the sky came the whumping of helicopter blades or the roaring of an airplane higher up. Muffled music came from somewhere. The sky glowed with a dull light from the fog. No stars, no moon, just black space. One of the downsides of living in the city.

The night had a damp warmth, and the man took off his shirt. He let his eyes scan the white wall surrounding his house, the stands of trees in the yard and the well-trimmed grass, the swimming pool, and the statuary of the gazebo next to it. He saw the two guards at the gate and noted with satisfaction that neither allowed his vigilance to waver for a moment.

A house this close to Manhattan was priceless. His real estate agent had once estimated that the total value of the house and land would be at least $40 million. That had sounded like an exaggeration, but maybe it was true. He wasn't actually interested.

There had been a time when the value of a house might have been a preoccupation, but nowadays other things inspired him. He had decided to end his life, and in a circumstance like that, money had no significance. All that remained was the naked instrumental value of the wealth in terms of the things that did still mean something to him. There was one thing he wanted to do with his money before he closed his eyes for the last time.

The man's features were chiseled, but most of his upper body was covered in large white burn scars. No hair grew on the scarred areas, and none of them bore a single mole or birthmark. The skin appeared unnaturally smooth. He didn't want to see himself in the mirror ever again. He hated what he saw. Above all, he hated the voices he heard in his head whenever he remembered how he had received his burns.

He would never forget the screams, the shrill shrieks in his very own home as he lost everything he had ever loved in one hour of horror.

The man took a swig of whisky from his glass. Even though his mother had been a Muslim and even though he had later converted to the same religion to advance his own purposes, the sacred teachings of Islam had never really meant anything to him.

The man considered again whether everything he intended to do was right after all. Had he allowed his bitterness and desire for revenge to lead him astray? What right did he ultimately have to take the fate of so many people in his hands? The tired hands of one individual bored with living. Perhaps he should pull out of the undertaking now, while he still could. Perhaps he should be content to end his own time here and leave the rest alone. Simply let everyone and everything else lapse into oblivion along with the sandy flow of time.

Would that be a better choice? His own pain would end, but no one else would be forced to suffer. He no longer had anything to lose, but if he continued with the undertaking, many good people would suffer the pains of hell before everything was over. They would endure their pain on behalf of a good cause, perhaps the best cause in the world, but was it right to ask that of them? Even though he knew all too well that they were ready to sacrifice everything they already had or that they might someday have?

Perhaps it was precisely because they were ready to give their all that he should not ask it of them.

They were good people, the best of men, and if he carried out his plan, many of them would die. Those who survived would never be the same. What they would be forced to experience would destroy them in ways that no one could ever really recover from. They would be waking up in the middle of the night to their own screams for the rest of their lives. They would never be free of fear or anxiety even if the wounds to their bodies healed.

But on the other hand, they would be able to deal the enemy a crushing blow. To seriously injure it, maybe even fatally. To attack from an unexpected direction in a way that the enemy had never considered in all its calculations. Defending against this attack would be almost impossible.

So was he about to commit a great sin? Or was he doing the right thing?

The man sipped from his glass, feeling the hot burn of the alcohol on his lips and tongue. Perhaps it was already too late to turn back. Perhaps the decisions had already been made. Right or wrong, it would not concern him for long anymore. If there were a place where the dead could meet, he would be joining his loved ones there. In reality he didn't believe in that. Much more likely everything would simply end. To him that was also a perfectly acceptable option. He no longer knew how to hope for anything more.

An eye for an eye, a tooth for a tooth, the man thought. *A burnt offering for a burnt offering. Ashes for us, ashes for you. Then we will all be equally satisfied. Not perhaps actually satisfied, but at least equally satisfied.*

Exactly as happy, the man thought. *Square.*

TWO
URANIUM-237

"I greatly fear that forty years ago we overestimated the capacity of those in power to understand the implications of what we have created."

> —*Rudolf Peierls*
> *August 2, 1986*
> *German physicist who played a decisive role in the development of the English nuclear weapons program and through it the birth of similar programs in the United States and Soviet Union*

1

Lauri Nurmi, Alice Donovan, and Kenneth Andrews were reviewing the material on Timothy Washburn. With them were two other NTU agents, David Farley and George Robertson. Farley was young, a prodigy barely past twenty, a rising talent with high expectations placed on him from many quarters. He was meticulously dressed. He had blond curly hair and eyes with long lashes that many women found beautiful. Robertson was approaching sixty, a career civil servant with a beer belly. He would never reach any higher than his current position. Even so, Lauri knew that George was rock solid at his job, despite the questionable jokes he told a little too often.

Everyone had already read the stack of reports about Washburn, his company, and his business partners. They had also succeeded in identifying a significant portion of Washburn's guests using nearby security cameras and telephone metadata. Now they were sharing selected pieces and summaries of the information they had collected.

"Washburn's background is interesting," Andrews said. "His mother was part of the Iraqi upper class. His father was from here—New York, I mean. He was a pretty prominent businessman with large investments in Iraq."

"That doesn't necessarily mean anything," Alice said.

"After his father died, Timothy Washburn took over his business," Andrews continued. "He lived in Baghdad, he had a wellborn Iraqi wife like his father, and two children. He spoke frequently about building bridges between the Arab world and the West, and converted to Islam, probably more as a gesture to furthering peaceful dialogue between the cultures than because he had actually internalized the Prophet's teachings. Then one of our bombs accidentally hit his house during the Iraq War. Washburn received serious burns. Here it says there aren't burns on his face but that most of the rest of his body is covered in scars. His wife and children and mother were killed in the fire. For the past few years he's been very quiet, hiding from any publicity."

"So he would have motive," George observed.

"If we start automatically classifying everyone whose friends or relatives we happened to kill at one time or another as a terrorist, pretty soon we'll have the majority of the population of the planet listed as enemy combatants," Alice said. "With globalization running rampant, all kinds of perfectly respectable people have close friends in all sorts of D-grade developing countries. And yes, that was sarcasm I was using, if anyone didn't get that."

"So you mean we shouldn't interpret everything you say literally?" George asked, feigning astonishment. "I'm not sure if I understand."

"Shut up, George," Alice said good-naturedly. "I mean that we don't know who Washburn blames for what happened. Does he blame Saddam, or us, or anyone?"

George was unruffled by Alice's criticism.

"It's just that a lot of his acquaintances are a bit shady. Especially this Hassan Yussuf character," George said. "He could easily be the person Henshaw heard talking about lithium-6. Yussuf is suspected of having ties to at least three Islamic charities with terrorist sympathies."

"That isn't a direct connection though," Alice said.

"If Washburn is involved in this, the situation could get complicated," Andrews pointed out. "*Fortune* estimates his assets at two billion dollars minimum."

Lauri whistled. "That much?"

"Plus whatever he has squirreled away in offshore accounts," Andrews continued. "Creating tax havens like that is big business for KPMG and some of the other big auditing firms, so almost everyone with a lot of extra money sitting around is doing it. Multinational corporations, rich individuals, organized crime. But in any case, Washburn has significant holdings and board positions in a whole range of completely legal businesses. We can't bring him in for questioning without some serious evidence. Rumors are all it takes to send the stock markets sliding. We'd have millions of angry investors on our case."

"But Hassan Yussuf is fair game," Lauri said. "If he was talking about six tons of lithium, we have more than enough to put him under heightened surveillance. Or search his house. Do we have pictures of him?"

Lauri started riffling through his papers.

"We have something in there," Alice said. "But nothing very good. It came from one of the security cameras."

"I could ask Henshaw whether she recognizes him," Lauri suggested.

Andrews nodded. "Good idea. I could come along."

Lauri looked at him. "I can handle it just fine on my own."

"I have a proposition for her. She could go to Washburn's again," Andrews said.

Alice cleared her throat. "Based on what Lauri told us, Henshaw already said she wouldn't," Alice said, her voice openly cold and disapproving. "Rather clearly."

"I'm sure it wouldn't hurt to ask again," Andrews said.

"I seriously doubt she'll agree," Alice said.

"What if I ask really nicely?"

George Robertson scratched his stubble.

"Just speaking generally here, how worried do you all think we need to be?" he asked.

No one said anything. Robertson sighed and stretched his arms in the air, more than a little dramatically.

"Well then. I'm starting to get the munchies. Should we order in some hamburgers? Or a few pizzas? Anyone else interested?"

David Farley looked at him, genuinely appalled by the idea.

"Oh, don't pretend to be such a sour-faced snob," Robertson said mildly. "We can order you Chateaubriand à la Enchante de Castillo, flambéed in escargots."

"That doesn't mean anything," said Farley.

"How can you be so sure?" Robertson asked with a grin.

Food was one of his favorite topics of conversation.

2

Patricia Devereaux-Morgan stared in disbelief at the profusely sweating man standing before her. Devereaux-Morgan was the assistant director of the French nuclear power company Argeva. She led the corporation's unit responsible for nuclear fuel reprocessing. Within Argeva, Devereaux-Morgan was considered a stern and demanding boss. She was used to having a certain effect on her subordinates, but she had never seen Marcel Auvergeon in such an agitated state.

"Are you completely sure?" Devereaux-Morgan asked again.

Auvergeon swallowed dryly. "I've rechecked the calculations a dozen times. Pierre went through them too."

She didn't believe this was really happening. The security system was supposed to be airtight. There were radiation detectors at every gate.

"There are no errors in the figures," said Auvergeon. "We are missing one hundred and eighty grams of plutonium. That is a fact."

"How is it possible no one noticed this before?" Devereaux-Morgan demanded.

"It was all done very carefully," explained Auvergeon. "Apparently they only took ten or twenty milligrams of plutonium at a time. The problem only turned up when the cumulative amount grew large enough."

"Still," Devereaux-Morgan said. "One hundred and eighty grams is quite a lot."

Auvergeon wiped his brow with a handkerchief the size of a small towel.

"When I noticed the problem, at first I only extended the checks back about a year," he said in his defense. "That created a slight delay. But please take into consideration the indisputable fact that I am the first one reporting the issue, and without me no one would know anything yet. Don't shoot the messenger, as the saying goes."

"I will take that into consideration," Devereaux-Morgan said.

"For a long time I was unsure whether this was a real deficit or just the cumulative effect of decimal rounding and a miscalculation. But when I expanded the check back ten years . . . it became clear we are definitely talking about something that really happened."

Devereaux-Morgan rose from her chair. Walking to the window, she looked out over Paris and fingered the silver pendant that rested on her collarbone. Devereaux-Morgan was anything but satisfied. In the worst-case scenario, this problem could endanger her career within Argeva. So far she had exceeded the ever higher bars set for her, one after another. Breaking through all the invisible glass ceilings that usually cut short a woman's rise in the business world.

And now . . . it was just these sorts of little things that could undermine everything. Her malicious competitors and their cronies would take advantage of any weakness without a second thought. Business knew no rules of fair play.

"I don't see how we have any alternative but to notify the authorities," said Devereaux-Morgan.

But Devereaux-Morgan was well aware that the theft and smuggling of radioactive materials was much more common than people generally knew and that this had never led to any particularly serious consequences. Between 1993 and 2003 alone, the International Atomic Energy Agency had recorded 376 cases of radioactive material smuggling. However, only eighteen of the cases listed by the IAEA had to do with highly enriched uranium-235 or plutonium smuggling. In these cases, the amounts had always been so small that there wouldn't have been enough to build a real bomb, and the dangerous materials had always been successfully tracked down and confiscated.

Devereaux-Morgan returned to her desk. She picked up a pen and twirled it in her fingers.

"Wouldn't it take more than ten kilograms of plutonium to build a bomb though?" she asked, just to be sure.

"Well . . . in a way," Auvergeon said evasively.

Devereaux-Morgan could see that Auvergeon was starting to calm down.

Auvergeon had noticed that Devereaux-Morgan's restrained fury had subsided and turned to resigned irritation.

"What do you mean?" Devereaux-Morgan asked. Evasion annoyed her.

"It also depends somewhat on the purity of the material and what kind of bomb you're talking about," Auvergeon explained.

Devereaux-Morgan frowned, looking dissatisfied. "Explain."

"Let's say that a gun-type atom bomb like the one at Hiroshima takes about twenty kilos of nuclear weapons–grade uranium, meaning uranium with the content of uranium-235 enriched to ninety-three percent," Auvergeon began. "But you can also build it out of uranium that's less enriched. The bomb will just be bigger. To make the same kind of fifteen-kiloton bomb out of twenty percent enriched uranium-235 you'd need about four hundred kilos. Which would make the bomb pretty hard to handle."

Devereaux-Morgan looked at Auvergeon in surprise. She knew that natural uranium consisted of two different isotopes: the very common uranium-238 and the much rarer uranium-235, which appeared in nature 140 times less frequently than uranium-238. She also knew that for the uranium fuel to be used in a normal nuclear power reactor, the amount of uranium-235 had to be increased to 3 or 4 percent, and in breeder reactors to 15 or 30 percent, and in some cases even 60 percent. But she hadn't known that it would be possible to build a working nuclear weapon out of 20 percent uranium-235. She had always thought nuclear bombs required weapons-grade uranium.

"If the material is enriched beyond weapons grade, then you need correspondingly less of it," Auvergeon continued. "With something approaching one hundred percent uranium-235, you could build a weapon with two hundred and seventy grams. Highly enriched plutonium-239 requires even less."

"You're kidding," Devereaux-Morgan said.

"Actually, I'm not," Auvergeon said. "To tell the truth, I don't know exactly how small a nuclear bomb you could theoretically build with very highly enriched plutonium-239, because that information is still secret. But I'd wager we're talking about a few dozen grams at most. Plutonium-239 splits twice as easily as uranium-235 since it's so much less stable."

Devereaux-Morgan looked at Auvergeon in disbelief. "Do you actually expect me to believe that?" she snapped.

"Why would the United States Senate have debated so intensely about whether they should build nuclear weapons a thousand times smaller than the Hiroshima bomb if that wasn't even possible?" Auvergeon asked in his defense.

Yes, there was a certain logic to that, Devereaux-Morgan thought.

Auvergeon noticed that the pen Devereaux-Morgan was fiddling with was beginning to crack as her grip tightened.

"Are you trying to tell me that someone has stolen enough plutonium from us to build a small nuclear bomb?" Devereaux-Morgan asked in a treacherously calm voice.

"Yes, in a way," Auvergeon said.

Devereaux-Morgan noticed that he was starting to sweat again.

"I can't believe this," Devereaux-Morgan huffed, suddenly snapping the pen in half.

The two halves clattered to the floor.

Auvergeon looked at his boss dejectedly.

"I still don't think that we need to be too concerned," he said. "One hundred and eighty grams of ninety-nine percent plutonium-239 still wouldn't make a very powerful explosion. You could get that amount to explode, but very small nuclear bombs are basically duds. We're talking about an explosion equivalent to maybe one kiloton of TNT. At most."

"Only a thousand kilos?" Devereaux-Morgan said, her eyebrows going up. "Not even a kiloton? Let alone megatons?"

Auvergeon shook his head. "No, no, no," Auvergeon said. "Not at all. If the terrorists want to blow up something big, they'd do much more damage with a few tons of ammonium nitrate. Just your garden-variety fertilizer bomb."

Thank God, thought Devereaux-Morgan.

"What has happened is without question unfortunate, but not particularly concerning," Auvergeon confirmed.

"And . . . could they use the plutonium to make a hydrogen bomb? As an igniter for a thermonuclear reaction?"

Auvergeon shook his head decisively. "Impossible. Building a hydrogen bomb is extremely difficult. It is significantly more complicated than building a simple atomic bomb."

So we can probably forget this whole thing ever happened, Devereaux-Morgan decided. Maybe this wasn't so serious after all, she thought, gradually more content. She would make it through this. Her career wasn't over. Someday she would be the director of the entire company. Wait and tremble.

3

After a long search through its immense electronic archives, ECHELON, the signals intelligence network, had finally found the phone call to Hassan Yussuf that Katharine Henshaw had accidentally overheard. Alice Donovan had gone over every sentence in the short call more times than she could count. Again she returned to the beginning of the call:

"Mr. Yussuf?" The voice belonged to a man who spoke broken English. He could easily have been Japanese.

"Yes, this is me," Yussuf said. *"You have the lithium-6?"*

"Yes."

"Excellent. All six tons?"

"We have the entire shipment."

That was it. The call was short, with only twenty-one words said in all. She would send the tape down for closer analysis. Maybe someone would be able to find something new in it. Something that might help.

In reality she didn't believe they would find anything else important. The call had been made from a fresh burner phone, so tracking the owner would be impossible. It had come to New York through an operator in Osaka. But even the great ECHELON's abilities could not reach further than that.

Cell phone technology made life so easy for criminals. Alice heard her office door open. She turned to look.

"You aren't going to want to hear this," Julia Noruz warned her.

"Bad news?" Alice asked.

"That's putting it mildly," Julia said. "This message just came from French intelligence."

Julia handed Alice the printout she was carrying.

"One hundred and eighty grams?" Alice asked. "That much?"

Every previous theft of plutonium discovered had been much smaller. Usually just a few grams. Their biggest concern had always been the theft of highly enriched uranium from civilian research reactors.

"This could be really bad," Alice said, looking back up at Julia. "But I don't think you're done yet, are you?"

"Look at this," Julia said. "As soon as that message came in from France, I loaded all of the phone numbers we have related to Argeva, cells and landlines, and compared them to Yussuf's and Washburn's phone records."

Julia handed Alice another printout.

"Apparently the Argeva plutonium theft happened slowly, over eight or nine years. And it just so happens that eight years and four months ago two calls were made from Argeva to Yussuf and one to Washburn. After that Yussuf received two more calls from Argeva, and made three calls himself during the last eight years."

Alice glanced at the papers Julia had given her. Her expression didn't waver, but Julia knew her colleague well enough to sense that this information had rocked her to the core.

"This changes things," Alice said simply.

"Yes, you could say that."

The information Julia had found created a connection, at least a possible connection, between the Osaka lithium theft, the plutonium missing from Argeva, Hassan Yussuf, and Timothy Washburn. By themselves the Osaka and Argeva incidents were sufficiently unpleasant and worrisome. But when you added them together, the situation became much more dangerous. A thousand times more dangerous. Or, more precisely, a million times more dangerous, Julia thought. Literally.

"You understand what this means if these cases are connected, don't you?" Julia asked unnecessarily.

Alice glared back at Julia. "Really, you're asking me that?"

"OK, OK, calm down," Julia said. "I'm sorry. I didn't mean to . . ."

"Could you find the calls in the ECHELON archives?"

Julia shook her head.

"Unfortunately no. The system didn't work very well back then."

"But . . . wouldn't direct contacts like that be awfully careless?" Alice asked. "Is it really plausible that Washburn and Yussuf would be in contact with Argeva themselves? I mean, if they had something to do with these plutonium thefts?"

"Not necessarily. Maybe they thought the theft wouldn't come out for years, if ever, and that no one would save call information for that long. Back then not very many people knew ECHELON existed. Or maybe they thought nothing else could connect them to the crime. And sometimes there are just situations where you have to take a small risk to avoid a larger one."

"You might be right," Alice admitted.

"If there would have been dozens of phone calls, the credibility gap would be larger. But a few calls . . . I don't know. On the other hand, few people ever have any direct contact with companies like Argeva. They only make nuclear power plants and fuel for them after all. So if Washburn and Yussuf can't give a reasonable explanation for the calls, we've got them with their pants down. But even so . . . I can't shake the feeling there's something fishy about this."

"What do you mean?" Alice asked.

Julia paused for a moment to think how best to explain.

"The pattern this all makes is too clear," she finally said.

"Excuse me?"

"When scientific theory is working well, it produces patterns just like this. Everything falls neatly into place. But when you're looking for terrorists, things are usually much more complicated and murky. Everything is a chaotic fucking mess, a little like the research I've been looking at on the health effects of the Chernobyl meltdown. There are clues and blind alleys running in every possible direction, loads of them, and it usually takes a long time before things start to look clear. But in this case . . . we immediately ran smack-dab into the brightest, shiniest clues that seem to lead us right to our targets. It isn't normal."

"I'd think you'd be pleased," Alice said. "For once. We have to have a little luck sometimes. And not all terrorists are necessarily very good at what they do."

Julia still didn't look convinced.

"I've learned to trust my intuition," Julia said. "And the patterns I find. Trust me, something stinks here. I just don't know what yet."

4

Alice, Lauri, and George waited in a small diner for David Farley to give them the word that Hassan Yussuf was out of his apartment. According to the tracking report, Yussuf followed a very precise daily routine, so they predicted that he would head out within half an hour.

"I could do with some more grub," George said.

Alice shook her head, but George ignored her and walked to the counter. The young man working the register reminded George of someone he had met before. At first George couldn't place who it was, but then he recalled the lanky, absentminded physics student who had been in charge of guarding a research reactor at a certain university when George had visited to get acquainted with their setup. The reactor had contained several hundred kilograms of 20 percent enriched uranium, but the student in charge of security hadn't even noticed George when he walked in. The student had been far too focused on playing some kill-the-orcs type of computer game to notice what was happening at the door behind him.

George knew this sort of situation had been the rule rather than the exception for years. Many universities had programs related to developing new types of reactors, and they used TRIGAs or other research reactors containing relatively powerful materials. Nighttime security for the reactors was almost always a one-person job. The same guards usually also had responsibility for several other buildings at the same time.

"Could I have another hamburger?" George asked.

"Sure, just a minute," the young man said. "I'll bring it to your table."

George nodded appreciatively. He vividly remembered how the student "guarding" the reactor had jumped when he placed his hand on the kid's shoulder. He had thought that the young man had been a regular walking cliché, a stereotype come to life: round glasses, zits on his forehead, and a memory stick hanging from a string around his neck.

"Lucky for you I'm not an al-Qaeda terrorist," George had said. "You might think about staying more alert when you're on guard duty." But George had made this comment simply as a matter of form. In reality he didn't believe for a second that what the boy did or didn't do would have any significance when it came right down to it.

But really, in George's opinion, the stupidest thing was that the United States had delivered thirty-nine identical research reactors to various countries as part of their Atoms for Peace program aimed at encouraging the peaceful use of nuclear energy. After terrorist attacks in Washington and New York, the government bureaucrats in charge of security had suddenly realized that in all of those reactors scattered around the world there was enough plutonium and highly enriched uranium to build hundreds of nuclear bombs.

Cleaning up all these reactors loaded with highly enriched uranium became a race between the government and the terrorists. George himself had participated in operations that recovered fifteen kilos from Romania and seventeen kilos from Bulgaria of high-quality, highly enriched weapons-grade uranium. George was still horrified when he thought of the Romanian stockpile. Anyone could have walked in and started throwing uranium in the back of a station wagon. The door had just had a broken padlock hanging from it.

There were other times things had been just a little too close for comfort—for instance, when the United States started bombing Serbia and then remembered that the Serbs had enough uranium in the Vinča Nuclear Institute's research reactor to build at least three atom bombs. Or when the Italian police had helped the United States recover the TRIGA II reactor donated to Mobutu Sese Seko in Zaire and the 20 percent enriched uranium it contained. When rebels overthrew Mobutu, they tried to sell some of the uranium from the reactor through the Mafia, but Italian police managed to capture the uranium by posing as interested Egyptian businessmen.

The United States had a head start, enough time to collect most of the material before all the possibilities those reactors represented even crossed al-Qaeda's mind. Later the race had intensified, though, when the Bush administration started demanding that countries pay $5,000 for every kilogram of uranium and plutonium returned. Maybe that hadn't been the smartest place for belt-tightening. George would never forget how pissed off Kenneth Andrews had been when he heard about it.

At this same moment, David Farley was on the other side of the street watching Hassan Yussuf walk out of his building and look around for a taxi. The car they had situated around the corner, whose driver was really a unit employee, made the turn and pulled up in front of Yussuf. Yussuf opened the door and climbed in. The taxi drove off. Since the driver was one of their people, they would know exactly how far Yussuf went, and more or less the earliest he might return.

Farley called Alice. "You can go inside."

"OK," said Alice.

Alice snapped her cell phone shut and nodded to Lauri and George. "Let's go," said Alice.

A few minutes later, Alice, Lauri, and George were rummaging through Hassan Yussuf's apartment hoping to find something important. Or anything that would tell them something relevant. Alice knocked on the walls, looking for hollows, hidden cameras, or echoes that might indicate hidden compartments.

The linoleum on the floor seemed intact, and all of the edges and corners were securely fastened. There wasn't anything behind the living room furniture, and they didn't find any secret spaces in the desk. They also checked the kitchen cupboards, the closets in the entryway, and the few paintings hanging on the walls.

George unscrewed the vent grate in the living room and felt around for anything past the bend in the duct. All he found was dust, a thick gray mat of it. The vent in the bathroom was empty too.

George sighed. "There's nothing here. Let's go."

"Wait a second," said Alice, who had just moved to checking a new wall.

"There just aren't that many possible hiding places in an apartment this small."

"Maybe you're right," Alice said.

But her next knock produced a completely different sound, a muffled echo. George's and Lauri's eyes turned immediately. The bored expression evaporated from George's face.

Alice knocked on the wall again. Again the same hollow sound, like a badly rotted tree.

"There's something here," she said. "I think it might be a secret compartment."

"That's an awfully simple hiding place," Lauri said.

"Like George said, there aren't a lot of options in a small apartment," Alice said. "Maybe they weren't expecting a search."

"Can you get it open?"

Alice searched for a mechanism that would open the compartment. She felt along the wall, but she couldn't figure out how the compartment opened.

Lauri wondered if the wall was hollow. Or if there were termites or carpenter ants.

"Should we break open the wall if we can't get it open?" Lauri asked aloud.

George shook his head. "I'd recommend waiting. If Yussuf really is a terrorist, which we don't know yet, he could lead us to his accomplices if we tail him. If we start smashing holes in the walls and he figures out we're on to him, he definitely isn't going to be any help."

A moment later Alice found the latch for the secret compartment on the other side of the wall. She opened the compartment and found a thick bundle of photographs and papers, some of which had writing. There were also some drawings that depicted a round pipe or cylinder, while others showed a ball divided into numerous triangles.

"These look pretty interesting," George said. "I think we found something."

"Should we take it?" Alice asked.

"No. Take pictures and put it back," Lauri said.

"There are hundreds of pages here."

"We have three cameras, so divide the stack into thirds. We'll have time. Farley hasn't given any warning yet."

Alice gave part of the papers and pictures to George and part to Lauri. Getting down to work, they carefully photographed everything. It took them more than half an hour. Then Alice shoved the bundle back in the compartment and pressed it shut.

Checking to make sure no one was in the stairwell, they exited calmly and without incident.

5

George, Alice, and Lauri were gathered around a computer screen, reviewing the contents of the photographs they took in Hassan Yussuf's apartment. Many of the images depicted construction diagrams and blueprints that were simple yet anything but innocent.

"That is definitely the Nagasaki bomb," George said. "Fat Man. That diagram is actually one of the original blueprints for Fat Man."

In the drawing was a metal ball with an outer surface made up of pentagonal explosive plates. An implosion-type atomic bomb.

"Where did they get these drawings?" Alice asked.

"They haven't been secret for ages," George grumbled. "You can just download them off the Internet if you know where to look."

George pressed "Enter," and a diagram of the Hiroshima bomb—the simplest nuclear weapon ever built—appeared. Little Boy was just a metal tube installed inside a conventional bomb shell. On one end of the tube was a ten-kilogram lump of 93 percent enriched uranium; on the other end of the tube was a smaller uranium projectile and a small amount of conventional explosive. When the explosive charge detonated, it shot the uranium projectile toward the larger lump. The collision of the two subcritical uranium masses caused a nuclear explosion just over ten kilotons and razed the entire city of Hiroshima.

"This definitely gives us grounds for treating Mr. Yussuf with suspicion," Lauri said. "Even though you can find this material online or in any book on the subject. At the very least we know he's a hobbyist, if you want to put it that way."

The next drawing came up on the screen.

"Holy shit. I take it back. This is definitely more than a hobby."

This diagram was for a much more complicated three-stage nuclear weapon. In the corner of the drawing were words printed in Cyrillic.

"Is that what I think it is?" Alice asked.

"Yes. Tsar Bomba. Shit, shit, shit. Where did he get this? Not on the open Internet."

This was a nightmare. How far along were they? The question seared Alice's mind.

Tsar Bomba, the "Emperor Bomb," had been the largest nuclear bomb ever built. The Soviets detonated it in 1962 near Novaya Zemlya on the Barents Sea. The explosive power of Tsar Bomba had been well over one hundred megatons, but the Russians intentionally detonated it at a much lower power, around sixty megatons.

Then something even more frightening appeared on the computer screen. Another drawing accompanied by Cyrillic text.

"What . . . is that?" George asked. "That can't be . . ." His voice was suddenly strangely thick.

"Yes, it is. That's a plutonium initiator," Lauri said. "Like Tsar Bomba must have had. Alice, you know Russian. Does that say something about the amount of plutonium it needs?"

"Twenty grams," Alice said.

"Only twenty? So if Yussuf's gang took that one hundred and eighty grams of plutonium from Argeva, now they could make nine igniters like this."

George tapped the key to advance the image again. Lauri looked in amazement at a long cylinder divided with dotted lines into dozens of narrow slices. Every slice was numbered individually.

"Was there any explanation in the papers about what those numbers mean?" Lauri asked.

"I think there was something about it on the other side of the same page. It should be in the next photo," George said. "If I remember right."

George hit "Enter" again. He had remembered correctly. Numbered explanations appeared on the screen. The narrow slices were each marked with the code *U* or *C (grph)*.

"Do you understand what this is?" George asked.

"I think it's the Chicago Pile," Lauri said.

"You've got to be kidding me," George said.

The Chicago Pile was the first functioning nuclear reactor, Enrico Fermi's brainchild. Fermi's words echoed in Lauri's mind: "I give you the future."

The Chicago Pile was built out of simple unenriched natural uranium and carbon, in the form of graphite. Each in fifty-seven thin layers, alternating uranium and graphite. The graphite slowed the neutrons enough that they could split other nuclei. The experiment demonstrated that even natural uranium could reach critical mass if there was enough of it. The necessary amount turned out to be fifty-two tons. Actually, the experiment worked so well that the reactor could only be used for short periods of time, because it overheated so quickly. Building a cooling system hadn't occurred to them yet.

"I give you . . . the future," Enrico Fermi said when the cadmium control rods were withdrawn and the reactor started up. Later Fermi's wife, Laura, observed that the Chicago Pile was really the beginning of the atomic age. From there on everything else was just "diligent engineering."

But in retrospect, was setting up the world's first nuclear reactor in the middle of a major city under the stands of the University of Chicago football field really all that smart? What if they hadn't been able to get the control rods back into the pile and it had just continued heating up? What if the uranium in the reactor had ignited and started spewing radioactive contaminants into the sky? Avoiding unnecessary risks had never been one of the strongest traditions in the field. Anyone who wanted to unlock the deepest secrets of the universe and harness them for humanity's benefit had to gamble from time to time. And the gambles were usually high stakes.

"Why would they be interested in the Chicago Pile?" George asked.

"Why wouldn't they?" was Alice's response. "It's the simplest possible nuclear reactor."

"Wait a second . . . Could you make plutonium with it?"

"Of course," Alice said. "You can make plutonium with any nuclear reactor."

"Great," George grunted. "Then I understand."

However, the true depth of the nightmare did not become apparent to them until they saw the next diagram and accompanying photograph.

The drawing was the same one they had noticed first in Yussuf's apartment in the bundle of documents. In it was a rectangle, each end with a narrow strip delineated by a straight transverse line. In the center of each of these sections was a sphere with thick shell layers. At the center of each sphere was another much smaller circle. Each section, including the layers of the sphere, was labeled with a number, *1* through *9*.

"Is there a scale?" George asked. "Is it supposed to be half a meter or three meters long? It looks like some sort of variation on Little Boy, except that the structure is much more complicated."

Lauri shook his head.

"No, this is something else. Those balls look like implosion bombs. This is a pretty strange blueprint, almost like some sort of hybrid between Fat Man and Little Boy."

George zoomed in and navigated around the image.

"Bingo! There are the measurements. L for length and D for diameter—'60 m' and '4 m'? Sixty meters and four meters? That's enormous."

"It can't be that big," Lauri said. "Those have to be centimeters."

"But then it isn't a nuclear bomb," Alice pointed out. "Unless the material is really highly enriched."

"What about decimeters?"

"Maybe," Alice said uncertainly. "Were there any explanations for the numbers?" she asked George.

"Let's see."

George tapped another key and the explanations they were looking for appeared on the screen.

Number 3, referring to the large rectangle in the middle, was marked with the code "u238." The numbers on the shells of the balls, 4 and 5, corresponded to the code "TNT" and the interior circles to a chillingly simple, two-letter "pu."

Numbers 1 and 2 were just as brief: "li." L and I.

"Do you understand what the hell this is?" George asked.

"Wasn't there a photograph that went with this diagram?" Lauri asked. "Show us that too."

George thought Lauri's voice was strangely hoarse, but he did as instructed.

The photograph that popped up had obviously been taken in the hold of a large cargo ship. At the center of the picture was a huge metal pipe that filled a large part of the hold. Around the pipe were men in hard hats with welding torches. Bright showers of sparks cascaded from the welding guns. Black shadows with sharp edges fell on the walls.

The pipe was two times wider than the height of a man and very long. Perhaps sixty meters.

6

Kenneth Andrews looked at the printouts in disbelief. Even though the air-conditioning was on full blast, his office was sweltering, and Robertson had to wipe his brow every few minutes.

"So it's a hybrid," Lauri summarized. "Sort of a variant on Castle Bravo. But much simpler and obviously much larger."

"Could it work?" Andrews asked.

Neither Lauri nor Alice answered. Andrews turned to George, who shrugged.

"Let's just say that at the very least it wouldn't burn very clean," George said. "They've made up for quality with quantity. It's definitely not a suitcase bomb, I can tell you that."

"Great, thanks," Andrews grumbled. "Does anyone else have any good suggestions?"

Once again, Lauri and Alice said nothing, so Andrews looked to George, but this time he had no response. Andrews drummed the desk with his fingers as he considered next steps.

"Has the tail on Yussuf turned up anything?" he finally asked.

"Nothing," Alice replied. "He doesn't seem to meet with anyone or call anyone. Except that he goes to work at a little kebab shop. We've been following him for three weeks and so far the results have been a big fat zero. How long do we dare to wait?"

"We don't anymore. Bring him in and let's see what he knows," said Andrews.

Lauri nodded. "It's about time. Should Alice and I go get him?"

Andrews shook his head. "No, I'm going to give this to the professionals."

Lauri frowned. "Aren't we the professionals?"

"I mean a slightly different kind of professional. You might be a little too gentle for this job."

"Excuse me, but what kind of professionals do you mean?" Lauri asked incredulously.

"Believe me, you don't want to know," Andrews said. "Someone should also probably hop over to Japan and connect with our colleagues there. Volunteers?"

"I don't really have time," said Lauri.

"I can go," Alice said quickly.

"Good. Go as soon as you can," Andrews ordered. "I'll let them know you're coming. And don't look so happy. This isn't a vacation."

"I'll try to keep that in mind," Alice said with a grin. "But I do like the idea of visiting Japan."

She had no idea what would be waiting for her there.

7

Lauri Nurmi and Alice Donovan stood on the roof of a sixteen-story building in Staten Island and looked over the water toward New Jersey. Off to the northeast stood the skyscrapers of Manhattan.

The day was beautiful, the sky blue and dazzlingly bright. Only a few fluffy clouds hung above. The air was unbelievably calm, and the temperature was perfect. The surface of the ocean was as smooth as glass. Two large cargo ships steamed toward the strait between Staten Island and Jersey City.

Alice was turning to Lauri to say something, when a blazing light flared behind her over the Hudson River. For a moment the whole world was bathed in white. The glow was so bright that it burned the eyes and covered everything else. For a second Lauri couldn't see anything but the light and Alice's black silhouette flickering against the glow.

Then the light disappeared as quickly as it had come.

The landscape was visible again.

In place of the white light was a large red fireball with indistinct borders. At its center was a small unbearably bright shining point. The fireball grew gradually larger and was already much larger than the sun. It rose higher, but a small gray strand connected it to the ground. The bright center began to fade. The borders of the fireball grew even less distinct, and for a moment it was shaped like a giant raspberry or boysenberry rising into the sky. That roaring spherical mass was already miles in the air. The thread connecting it to the earth had swelled into a thick black trail.

The fireball faded, leaving only the dark cloud that continued rising and expanding, a long thin stem below and wide cap above. For a moment shades of purple flickered in the cloud, and then they were gone too and all that was left was the blackness.

Lauri had never seen an explosion column like this with his own eyes, but he recognized it instantly. Anyone would have. A mushroom cloud was probably the most recognizable symbol of the twentieth century. The most significant and simultaneously most horrific cultural icon of an entire age.

When Lauri looked toward Manhattan, he saw that some of its skyscrapers had disappeared, and the outlines of many other buildings had also become more . . . rough.

"Oh shit," Lauri said. "That was it. Where do you think it exploded?"

"On a freighter on the Hudson River," Alice said.

Lauri checked his watch.

"Shock wave," he said.

They rushed to the edge of the roof and crouched down behind the small lip for protection. Just then a trapdoor clanged open behind them, and Kenneth Andrews poked his head out. He climbed onto the roof and started toward them.

Lauri opened his mouth to warn Andrews, but the shock wave was already washing over them. The building's windows shattered in a rain of glittering glass shards, but the distance was enough that the force of the shock wave would not knock in the walls of the building, no matter what the size of the bomb. The blast wave weakened quickly with distance. As it swept over them, it couldn't be any stronger than the gusts of a normal hurricane, at most a hundred miles per hour. Strong but not catastrophic.

But Kenneth Andrews hadn't known to take cover. His windbreaker was open, and it billowed with the wave of air like a round spinnaker, and then the wind had him. Two seconds, and Andrews disappeared over the edge of the roof. There was nothing they could do for him.

The gust of air was gone as quickly as it had come. They moved to the other side of the building and waited for the return wave, again behind the lip of the roof's edge. The gust of wind coming back was much weaker.

Lauri stood up. Lifting his binoculars, he looked toward Manhattan. Dozens of thin, black pillars of smoke rose from where the buildings had once stood. Most of the skyscrapers remaining had also begun to smoke.

"How big was it?" Alice asked urgently. "How far do the fires reach?"

Lauri shifted his binoculars toward New Jersey. Dozens of smoke trails rose into the sky there as well, and it seemed as if more appeared as he looked. The first small breeze was already in the air, blowing toward the city, in the direction of ground zero.

When Lauri looked immediately around them, he didn't see smoke. By the time it reached Staten Island, the radiation wasn't strong enough to start fires.

"Are we inside the zone?" Alice asked.

"No, we're outside," Lauri said. "But Manhattan and Jersey City look like they're both in the burn zone. Completely."

Alice stared at Lauri in disbelief.

"That can't be true."

Lauri handed her the binoculars.

"Look for yourself if you don't believe me."

"I'm not sure I want to."

The wind intensified and blew toward the conflagrations raging in Manhattan and New Jersey. Forty miles per hour at least, thought Lauri. Already.

"The wind is really picking up," Alice said.

Lauri looked north again. There was much more smoke rising now, not just from hundreds of fires but at least a few thousand. As he watched, the individual trails of smoke quickly merged. A few more moments, and the whole view would disappear under a solid wall of smoke.

"That smoke will be highly radioactive," Lauri said. He was painfully aware that they did not have any protective clothing with them.

"The wind is blowing toward the fire," Alice said reassuringly. "Whatever goes up with the fire is going to come down somewhere much farther away."

The winds were getting even stronger, and it was becoming hard to stand upright. The gale-force current of air howled in the chasms between the buildings like a choir of deranged demons.

"How much can this building withstand?" Alice asked. "Are we safe here? I mean . . . the pressure of the wind could get pretty high. This building could . . ."

Lauri looked at Alice forlornly. "Yes, but where would we go? Where would we be safe?"

Alice had no answer.

Then Lauri felt something grab his shoulder and shake him. The outlines of the landscape blurred, and suddenly he was awake in his bedroom and Alice was looking into his eyes with concern.

8

"Where were you?" asked Alice. Her voice was tender, soothing.

Lauri rested his head in his hands for a few seconds. Then he went into the bathroom, rinsed his face with cold water, and looked at his watch. It was two thirty in the morning. The hum of traffic wafted through the open window.

"I had the dream again."

Alice didn't say anything.

"We were on Staten Island again, but this time the bomb exploded on the Hudson River. We were outside the burn zone, but the wind started picking up and . . . Then you woke me up."

"You've been having that nightmare a lot."

"Luckily there are slight variations, so it's never exactly the same. Otherwise I might get bored."

"Lucky it's only a dream," said Alice.

"But how much longer do we have? At what point is the nightmare going to become reality, and something that we never wake up from?"

"You want to try to sleep some more, or should I make coffee?" Alice asked.

"I'm not going to be able to go back to sleep."

"I maybe could."

"Well then, you should."

Alice sighed. "Not if you're going to be roaming around the house."

Alice started to make coffee. Lauri went out on the balcony and leaned against the railing as he looked out. The city glowed like a galaxy of millions of lights. Lines of cars flowed across the bridges and roads in unbroken streams. Lauri inhaled deeply and tried to relax. It didn't go well. In his mind's eye he kept seeing the picture of Ted Taylor smiling when his cigarette started to smoke, when Taylor put it to his lips and drew the nicotine smoke into his lungs. Atomic high.

"I give you the future"—that was what Enrico Fermi had said. He developed the first nuclear reactor and was the first to suggest using an implosion to create a hydrogen bomb. But when he said he was giving us the future, which did he mean, the hydrogen bomb or the nuclear reactor? Or both at the same time?

Lauri had seen nuclear reactor prototypes developed for airplanes. Some of them were still classified. Those plans had been abandoned in 1973 when the famous physicist R. W. Bussard calculated that a reactor in an airplane would melt down within thirty seconds if its cooling system stopped working.

Another initiative, the aptly named United States Air Force Project Kiwi, also turned out to be a dud that would never fly. In theory it was possible to build an open-core nuclear-powered rocket you could refuel midflight like the boilers of an old steamship, but in practice it was just as bad an idea as the nuclear jet engines or the "Davy Crockett" atomic bazooka developed by American physicists to launch small nuclear weapons at targets a hundred meters away.

Some future. Lauri went back inside to talk to Alice.

"When we dropped those bombs on Hiroshima and Nagasaki, we said they would shorten the war and save hundreds of thousands of lives. But this war against terrorism . . . everyone knows we've lost. At least in Iraq and Afghanistan. How would we feel now if someone were to detonate a nuclear bomb in New York to save the lives of innocent Muslims, to shorten the war? Or if they destroyed Los Angeles the same way four days later?" Lauri asked, his voice rising.

"Don't yell. And besides, that isn't a very good analogy," Alice protested.

"Really? Why not? We've never admitted that it was wrong to burn hundreds of thousands of civilians alive with nuclear bombs, or with firebombs for that matter. The Germans have apologized, over and over again. A lot of others have apologized too. We focused on explaining why what we did was right and reasonable."

Paul Tibbets even named the *Enola Gay* after his mother! How could anyone name a bomber after his mother and then burn alive a hundred and forty thousand civilians? Lauri wondered.

What did the name Tibbets gave his plane say about Americans? What did it say about the human species? Americans weren't any better than other humans, and humans weren't any better than other animals.

"Guess what scares me the most about all of this?" Lauri said.

"OK, what?"

"When those fucking maniacs flew those jets into the Twin Towers and three thousand people died, we went completely nuts. We killed a hundred thousand innocent people in Afghanistan and a million innocent people in Iraq. More than three hundred civilians for every one of our dead. If we hadn't been as lucky as we were in Afghanistan, the results would have been even worse. We knew that eight million people were threatened with starvation, and we knew that our bombing would cut off food deliveries to the mountains. But we were too angry to care. If the winter hadn't been late, millions of people would have starved to death."

"You know I agree with you, right?" Alice pointed out calmly. "So what exactly are you trying to say?"

"I want to say that if we went so berserk that we were willing to kill millions of innocent people because three thousand Americans died, what would we do if someone incinerated twenty million of us with a nuclear bomb? I've got to tell you I'm afraid even to think about what we might be capable of. I'm much more afraid of that than I am of New York being destroyed or dying myself along with everyone else. Although it would be horrible if you died."

Alice nodded, slightly. "I understand what you mean."

"Just think. We could become some sort of super-Nazis," Lauri ranted. "Nazis who still have ten thousand nuclear bombs. What if an American Hitler comes to power and we decide to carry out some kind of Final Solution for the Muslim problem, all over the planet? Just think! Before Hitler, Germany had about the same position in the world as the United States after the Second World War, didn't it? Germany was the obvious world leader in science and culture. Fully a third of Nobel prizes for science went to Germany. But when push came to shove, cultural and scientific leadership didn't protect Germany from sliding into collective madness."

"Maybe it actually made it worse," Alice suggested.

"If we don't think these things through ahead of time and decide what we should do if we ever face the possibility, then they definitely will come true when Manhattan burns," Lauri said. "I mean, if that happens someday. If we aren't emotionally prepared for something like that, then we probably will turn into a new Third Reich. Don't you think? And how many Muslims would we kill then? A hundred million? A billion? A billion and a half? We certainly have the means to kill them all if we decided to. Actually, I kind of hope that Iran has its own nuclear weapon at that point and that the Saudis have bought more bombs from Pakistan. And that all of the North African and Middle Eastern countries that suddenly decided after the last Iraq war started that they needed to build nuclear power plants to desalinate water will have built those reactors and gotten their plutonium from them."

Lauri ended his parade of horrors. He leaned on the balcony doorjamb, breathing heavily.

"Aren't you exaggerating a bit?" Alice asked cautiously.

"About what?"

"I don't think we have the resources to kill that many people these days without nuclear weapons. No matter what the terrorists do. And we can't actually kill anyone with nuclear bombs without the fallout coming back here like a boomerang and killing us too. The atmosphere has a nasty habit of collecting radioactive fallout in the northern latitudes."

"I hope you're right," Lauri said.

Alice looked out the window, toward the small strip of water just barely visible between the tall buildings. She looked sad.

"How did this happen to us?" Alice asked. "We started out so well. Better than anyone else."

Lauri could see tears glistening in Alice's eyes and on her cheeks.

He guessed that Alice was thinking about the Iroquois Confederacy and her Onondaga roots. Alice was emphatically proud of being half-Iroquois, sometimes irritatingly so. Though there were reasons to be proud. It was nearly a thousand years ago that the Iroquois had created one of the first constitutions, the Great Law of Peace, which limited the power of the state and its rulers in dozens of ways. The Iroquois also started the world's second-oldest continuously functioning democratic system of representation, only about a hundred years after the Icelandic Althing. And no other government that historians knew about had ever distributed power as equally and successfully between men and women as the Iroquois Confederacy.

Next to the accomplishments of the Iroquois, the much later US Constitution was actually quite old-fashioned, racist, chauvinistic, and reactionary. But it had still signified a step beyond the way almost every country in Europe was governed at the time. Lauri knew that Alice was convinced that all of the most beautiful parts of the US Constitution were at least indirectly inspired by the spirit of the Iroquois Confederacy's Great Law of Peace. He suspected she was at least partially right. While the Iroquois hadn't had direct contact with the individuals who wrote the US Constitution, the authors of the Constitution had definitely plucked ideas from the Iroquois and other American Indians. So Alice's ancestors had almost certainly left indelible marks on everything that had always been good and noble about the United States.

At what point did this country lose all of those beautiful ideas? Lauri wondered. At what point did the United States turn from the torch of freedom and source of inspiration for oppressed peoples everywhere into a military power that most of the world thinks of as an oppressor? When did those roles change?

"So you're leaving today?"

Alice nodded. She glanced at her watch. "My flight leaves in five hours."

"How are you getting to Osaka?"

"I'm going to have to kill a couple of hours at the Tokyo airport. But that isn't a very bad layover."

"Remember that Andrews told you to keep a low profile," Lauri said.

Alice smiled. "I always keep a very low profile. At this height I don't have any option!"

9

The next day Kenneth Andrews and Lauri Nurmi were in a taxi on their way to Brooklyn. They were slated to meet with Katharine Henshaw. Unlatching his briefcase, Andrews handed Lauri a report.

"You should have a look at this," Andrews said. "I had a psychological profile done on Henshaw."

Lauri grabbed the report and started leafing through it.

> *Henshaw went to Berkeley to study physics. Her older brother, Michael Henshaw, was an assistant professor in astrophysics there at the time.*

So Henshaw was telling the truth about her education, Lauri thought.

> *Henshaw was forced to drop out after a car accident in which her brother was paralyzed from the neck down. When the accident occurred, Henshaw, who was driving the car, was under the influence of alcohol.*

> *While in prison, Henshaw lost custody of her daughter, Rheya Bergman, to former boyfriend Ritchie Bergman, who moved in with another woman. Rheya Bergman refuses to see Henshaw, apparently because of her profession.*

Heavy stuff. Lauri couldn't have had anything but sympathy for her.

> *By temperament Henshaw is impatient and reactive, but she is also extremely intelligent and articulate. Personality fragile. Harbors strong feelings of guilt about her brother's accident and the subsequent situation with her daughter. Loses temper easily due to feelings of guilt. Most fits of anger probably projections. The flip side is an overdeveloped sense of duty. Despite this, Henshaw's suitability is decreased by her suspicion, hostility, and mild bitterness toward police and other government representatives, probably because she did not receive significant economic assistance from the government when she needed it for her brother's and parents' hospital care. Henshaw does not have documented addictions, except possible emerging alcoholism.*

Lauri didn't like the sound of the word *suitability*. He wondered why Andrews had asked for such a thorough evaluation of Henshaw's traits and personality.

> *Henshaw's attitude about her current work seems contradictory. On the one hand, she obviously hates what she does and it causes her periodic feelings of deep self-loathing. Apparently she protects herself from this personal contempt mostly by rationalizing her prostitution as a necessary evil. However, it may be that she also uses the sale of sexual services as a way to punish herself and through that to moderate her constant*

feelings of guilt. This may be partially conscious and partially unconscious.

"Where the hell did you get this?" Lauri asked.

"Most of the information is public record, at least for us. And I assigned one of our people to approach Henshaw."

"'Approach?' How?"

"As a customer, of course."

"Come off it. Are we paying employees to visit whores now?"

"Only sometimes. When there's a good reason. In this case it was the only option. Henshaw doesn't let people close to her."

Fifteen minutes later they were ringing Henshaw's doorbell.

"Oh, hello again," Henshaw said. "I was thinking you might turn into regulars."

Lauri noted the sarcasm in her voice. Henshaw undid the chain and let them in.

"I imagine you do just fine," Andrews said. "And I mean that as a compliment."

"You could say that," Henshaw said.

"How much per time, roughly?" Andrews asked.

Lauri looked at Andrews in surprise—the question was so abrupt and clumsy, almost crude. Why was Andrews being so insulting? Andrews's blue eyes were even icier than usual. Lauri sensed something bad; perhaps Andrews was planning something he hadn't told Lauri about.

Henshaw didn't flinch at Andrews's question. She looked at him slowly, appraisingly.

"I didn't think you were supposed to be interested in that," Henshaw said coldly. "And I'm not at work now. Call me tomorrow. In the evening, if you really are interested."

Andrews turned a deep red and closed his mouth.

Henshaw looked at Lauri.

"You aren't going to break your promise and report me to the IRS, are you?"

"No," Lauri assured her.

"Good."

Henshaw looked them up and down. Lauri could see she didn't like Andrews, and that she looked as apprehensive as he felt. Not knowing what Andrews had in mind irritated Lauri.

"By the way, I heard a funny joke yesterday you might like," Henshaw said suddenly. "Why does the United States have three presidents?"

"Excuse me?" Andrews asked.

"It's because one knows how to read, one knows how to write, and the third one guards those first two damn French intellectuals."

"As far as I understand, the United States still only has one president," Andrews said.

Lauri thought his tone was a little too humorless.

"Oh," Henshaw said in surprise. "Really? Well, that would definitely explain a lot. Do you happen to know which one of the three is on duty right now?"

"Very funny," Andrews said, glowering, but Lauri couldn't keep a slight smile off his lips. He found himself enjoying Henshaw's sense of humor.

Henshaw turned serious.

"OK, what do you want this time?"

"Has Washburn's assistant contacted you again?" Andrews asked.

"Yes," Henshaw said. Her mouth tensed into a tight line.

"How did you respond?" Lauri inquired.

"I said no. And that he shouldn't call back."

"Why?" Andrews demanded. "I assume they paid you well."

"That isn't actually any of your business."

"Something new has come up," Andrews said. "Something serious."

"What?" Henshaw asked.

"We can't tell you," Andrews said. "But it may have a connection to what you told us about Washburn's guests."

"Aha."

"Do you think this is the Arab you saw at Washburn's party?" Lauri asked. He showed Henshaw Hassan Yussuf's picture. "The one you heard talking about lithium-6?"

Henshaw did not hesitate for a second.

"That's him."

"Are you sure?" Lauri asked.

"Positive. No doubt in my mind."

"Well . . . we were hoping you might be willing to go to Washburn's house again, to a party, that is, if the opportunity came along," Kenneth Andrews said. "If you could keep your ears open, you might hear something important. You also might be able to take a couple of listening devices in."

"Come on, guys, that's too much to ask," Henshaw said.

"Don't you even want to think about it?" Lauri asked. "We would pay you well, in addition to what you get from Washburn."

Henshaw grimaced.

"You would have to pay me an awful lot to get me to even consider it."

"How much, roughly?" Andrews asked. "Would ten grand do it?"

Henshaw shook her head. "I'd say roughly, oh . . . three million dollars."

"Be serious," Andrews said angrily. "That's a lot of money."

"But it still means that I'm not going there," Henshaw said. "My job isn't particularly pleasant in general, but what Washburn and some of his friends want to do . . . Well, I don't want to talk about it, and under no circumstances am I ever going back there again. Ten grand is definitely a lot of money, but in this case that doesn't matter. Believe it or not, everyone has their limits."

Andrews looked at Henshaw, and his expression turned hard. Threatening.

"We could have done this the nice way, but because you didn't want to, now we'll do it your way," Andrews said.

Henshaw's expression grew cold as well.

"Either you go there and get ten thousand dollars from us or you go somewhere else," Andrews snapped. "As you know, what you do isn't exactly what we call legal in this state."

Henshaw said nothing. But she looked at Lauri accusingly. Lauri wished he could have melted into the wall.

"Kenneth, don't . . . ," Lauri said.

"Don't get in my way."

"Kenneth, this is a mistake."

"Who's in charge here?"

Andrews opened his briefcase and set a thick brown envelope in front of Henshaw. Henshaw glanced inside. The envelope was full of photographs. The first shots confirmed they were what Lauri thought.

"What the hell did you do?" Lauri asked angrily.

"Oh, so you're playing good cop, bad cop," Henshaw said icily. "Don't bother. You're amateurs. As if I didn't know what you're trying to do."

"There is enough evidence here to put you away for a long time," Andrews said. "I think I'd probably call that hard-core porn. The prosecutor wouldn't have the slightest problem using those to send you up the river for practicing prostitution and tax evasion, among other things."

"Don't play around, Kenneth," Lauri tried.

"Go ahead," Henshaw said expressionlessly. "If you don't have anything better to do, then go ahead. Give them to whoever you want. But how legal is that? Isn't it trespassing or voyeurism or something?"

"There are a lot of things we can do nowadays in the name of national security that might have been off-limits before," Andrews explained. "And besides, I happen to know that you use heroin and sell it to the customers from your other business. We have witness statements to that effect."

Henshaw's eyes went wide in surprise.

"That's a lie. I've never used anything but alcohol and tobacco in my life. Let alone selling anything."

"Our information says different. I suspect that if we let the police search your apartment with a drug-sniffing dog, they'll find something. Maybe a considerable amount. Regardless of how well it's hidden."

The look that Henshaw gave Andrews was lethal.

"You fucking bastard," said Henshaw. "Even I never imagined there were bastards as sick as you in this world."

"Thank you. Coming from you that's a compliment. So what do you say? Do you want your mother and your brother to learn what you do for work? We can easily send them copies of these pictures too. I'm sure they'd be delighted to hear that you're a whore and a drug dealer. Few things warm the heart of a mother or a paralyzed brother as much as that. Or a daughter's. Except that she already knows, doesn't she?"

"Ken, please don't do this," Lauri begged.

"How can you live with yourself?" Henshaw asked Andrews. "I came and told you about Washburn out of simple decency. I didn't have to do that. You never would have heard anything about it if I hadn't come."

"I admit it. We owe you for that," Andrews said. "I acknowledge the debt, and we can certainly do you a favor in return if you tell us what you want. But the time for that is later. Here and now we've got enough on the line that I don't have any option but to order you to go to that party so Washburn and his friends can screw you. You make your living on your back anyway, so does it really matter that much in the end exactly who's on top?"

The look Henshaw shot Andrews could have cut through steel. Then she turned to Lauri. Lauri had never felt so sordid before.

"And you . . . I never would have believed that you would have told him how to blackmail me."

"Believe me, I didn't."

"Eat shit."

"Hey, you didn't even tell me anything," Lauri said. "I had no idea he was going to do this. And I don't like it."

Lauri turned to Andrews. "Goddamn it, couldn't we try something else?"

Andrews looked at Lauri expressionlessly. "I'm sorry, but we have to get more information about Washburn," he said.

Andrews looked at Henshaw threateningly.

"So what do you say? Are you going to delight your mother and brother by becoming the most notorious public whore in the country or would you rather do us a little favor? You get ten grand plus whatever Washburn pays. How about it?"

"As if I could say no," Henshaw said.

10

The Osaka airport was even more crowded than Alice Donovan had imagined. Droves of black-haired Japanese rushed purposefully in every direction, with the occasional European or North American tourist or businessman here or there. Flight numbers and schedules changed rapidly on the large display boards, and announcements in Japanese echoed in the concourses and corridors. Alice wondered how she could ever find anyone in these throngs.

But then a young woman in light blue jeans, a denim jacket, and running shoes walked up to her and bowed. She looked at Alice inquisitively.

"Excuse me, but are you Alice Donovan?"

"Yes," Alice said. "And you must be Akiko Nobura?"

Alice felt overdressed in her official-looking dark pantsuit. She had assumed the Japanese would be very formal, especially when dealing with a foreign government agency.

Akiko noticed her confusion. She smiled and bowed slightly, touching one sleeve of her jacket with her other hand.

"Hopefully my dress does not offend you," Akiko said. "I came here straight from a field assignment. My superior, Chief Inspector Niori, would be angry if he were to see us right now. But to tell the truth, I feel most comfortable in these clothes."

"You took the words right out of my mouth," Alice said quickly. "I mean, I would feel more at home if I were dressed the same way you are. The person you see here right now isn't really me."

Akiko grinned happily and bowed again. Alice immediately liked her feisty Japanese colleague, and she thought this might turn out to be a pleasant little trip.

"What would you like to see first, Ms. Donovan?" Akiko asked.

"Oh, please call me Alice," Alice said. "Otherwise you make me feel so old."

Akiko laughed.

"Very well, Alice-san. But you still need to answer my question."

"What would you recommend?"

"The crime scene. The headquarters of the Yoshikawa Corporation."

"Sounds good," Alice said.

Taking the elevator down into the parking area, they went to Akiko's car, a red Mitsubishi that had long since seen its best days.

"Is this your own car?" Alice asked.

"Yep, I mean, yes. I receive a little reimbursement in addition to my salary when I use it instead of an official vehicle. Osaka is quite expensive. My apartment loan payments are killing me."

"Same thing in New York. I should probably move out in the country."

"But how long could you stand it there?"

"Actually, I love the country. My boyfriend and I have a little place in New Mexico," Alice said. "We have horses. And guest rooms. Come visit sometime, if you're interested."

"We only just met, so don't be so rash if you don't really mean it," Akiko said with a smile. "I might just take you up on that someday."

Akiko hefted Alice's suitcases into the trunk and then climbed into the driver's seat.

As soon as Alice sat in the passenger seat, Akiko handed her a holster with a Japanese police pistol.

"I was ordered to give this to you," said Akiko. "This is quite irregular, but I just do as I am told."

"Thank you," Alice said and began fastening the holster to her waist under her jacket.

Akiko started the car.

***

The Yoshikawa Corporation headquarters were located about halfway between the airport and downtown Osaka. Within half an hour they were in the basement of the building next to the offline Rapid-L reactor. Alice looked thoughtfully at the state-of-the-art thermoelectric cells installed on the reactor. From the background memos in her folder, she had read that an Estonian scientist named Thomas Johann Seebeck had first invented the concept in 1821. When two different semiconductors were combined in a U shape it could create a cell that converted temperature gradients directly into electric current.

"Did you say the normal operating temperature of a reactor like this is only five hundred and thirty degrees?" Alice asked.

"That's what they tell me," Akiko said.

"And it really produces electricity just with the thermoelectric cells and no turbine?"

"Yes."

"Can I ask a stupid question, then?"

"Go ahead," Akiko said.

"Developing more efficient thermoelectric cells is a really big deal," she began. "This is a significant technological advance. But lithium-6 is one of the most dangerous isotopes in existence. So . . . why do the Yoshikawa Corporation engineers insist on producing the heat they need with a small nuclear reactor using highly enriched uranium-235 and lithium-6 rather than any of the other possible options? Five hundred and thirty degrees isn't even a very high temperature—you could easily produce that all kinds of ways. Like with sunlight, for example."

"I don't know whether that's a stupid question at all," Akiko said. "But to answer it . . . Perhaps they're simply repeating what they've always done. What they're used to doing."

"Probably. But isn't that a depressing thought?"

"A lot of things are," Akiko said.

11

Lauri knocked on Katharine Henshaw's door for the eighth time.

"Open up. I know you're in there. I heard you walking around."

Still no answer.

"Do you want me to break down the door?" Lauri asked.

Henshaw relented. Lauri heard her unfasten the chain and unlock the dead bolt.

"Can't you leave me alone already?" Henshaw asked once she opened the door. "I don't have anything more to tell you. This is the third time you've been here. I already promised to put myself through the wringer again for you. Isn't that enough?"

"I'm sorry," Lauri said. "I'm very sorry."

Henshaw looked at Lauri coldly. "Apologies don't help much at this point. Or at least they don't help me any."

"You're right," Lauri said. "You can punch me in the mouth if that helps."

"What if I kicked you in the balls instead?"

Lauri had to admit Henshaw had good reason to be angry. He couldn't think of anything that would help.

Maybe there weren't any simple solutions in this situation, Lauri thought dejectedly. But then he noticed the way she was looking at him—thoughtfully and with a frown.

"Actually we might have a lot in common," she said. "I mean, in terms of our work. We both dance with death. I'm surrounded by AIDS and hepatitis and all kinds of other viruses, and you play with pyromaniacs, murderers, and suicide bombers."

Lauri looked at Henshaw in confusion.

"Except that I kill for money and you make love for money," he pointed out.

"Yeah . . . I think I'd use a different word than *love*." Henshaw snorted.

"You probably want to come in," she said.

"If you're not in a hurry."

Henshaw hesitated, then gestured for him to enter.

"Alright then."

Lauri stepped inside and, after standing for a moment in the doorway to the living room, sat down on the sofa.

Henshaw took out a cigarette and lit it. "I made a mistake coming to your office with the information, didn't I?"

"Depends on how you look at it. It's a complicated question. I wouldn't necessarily say so, but maybe in a way. I never would have believed Kenneth would have come at you so hard. I'd read most of it in the report he had written up about you, but the lie about the drugs and then trying to blackmail you was over the line."

"Report, what report?"

Henshaw stubbed out her cigarette in a crystal ashtray.

"Working with you bastards is such a pleasant experience."

"I'm sorry."

"So you know everything?"

"Yes," said Lauri.

"But you didn't know before?"

Lauri shook his head.

"Your boss didn't give me any option," Henshaw said. "If Michael found out where my money comes from, it would break him."

Lauri felt uncomfortable. He let his gaze wander around the room. On the desk were two stacks of new books. They were all on the same subject.

Standing up, he went over to the desk and picked up the first book. Lynn Eden's splendid but shocking *Whole World on Fire*. He knew it all too well.

Lauri looked at what else was in the pile: popular books on nuclear terrorism, such as *Weapons of Mass Destruction* and *Nuclear Terrorism*. At the bottom of the pile was a book with a 1950s-era picture of some sort of rocket approaching the Moon. "*Project Orion, The Atomic Spaceship 1957–1965*," Lauri read aloud. He didn't know the work, but it seemed interesting.

In the other pile were several memoirs from Nobel prize–winning or otherwise famous scientists: *Racing for the Bomb, Disturbing the Universe, Atoms in the Family,* and Linus Pauling's *General Chemistry*.

Volume 10, LEP-MES, of the classic McGraw-Hill *Encyclopedia of Science & Technology* was also on the desk. Of course, that was the volume that would give her the headwords dealing with lithium. On top of the encyclopedia was a photocopy of "Thwarting Nuclear Terrorism," an article from *Scientific American* about uranium enrichment.

"Looks like you've been doing a little studying," Lauri said.

"Your powers of observation are astounding," Henshaw said dryly. "This lithium thing has been bothering me. To tell the truth, I'm a little terrified about what I've got myself mixed up in."

Taking out another cigarette, Henshaw lit it and blew smoke at Lauri.

"You didn't actually tell me much," she said accusingly. "And there isn't much interesting online unless you already know a lot. You have to know exactly the right search terms to use."

"So you've been looking for the search terms in these books?" Lauri asked a little incredulously. "So you could look up information online?"

"Bingo!" Henshaw said. "I already had a few books, and Michael had even more. I ordered some more that looked interesting."

Lauri's expression was still one of disbelief.

"What, do you think I'm illiterate?" Henshaw asked angrily. "Just because I'm a woman? Or because I got myself into a situation like this?"

"I didn't mean that," Lauri said.

"Yes, you did," Henshaw said. "And it's really offensive. Especially since I was studying physics before . . ."

"I'm sorry," Lauri said.

Henshaw looked at him coldly.

"Is lithium-6 used for anything besides breeder reactors or fusion power?" she asked suddenly. "And creating tritium for nuclear bombs?"

Lauri didn't respond immediately, thinking about what he should say.

Henshaw sensed where his thoughts were going.

"Come off it," she said. "I put my head on the chopping block just to help you, and as thanks you dumped me up to my neck in a pile of shit. I think it's only fair you give me some idea what it's all for."

"I just think you don't really want to know."

"I hate it when people say that," Henshaw huffed, casting another deprecating glance at Lauri. "Don't be so condescending. I'm allergic."

You don't want to know—one of nuclear physicists' favorite phrases, thought Lauri. How often was it actually true though?

Lauri thought of Edward Teller again, who together with Stanislaw Ulam had invented the hydrogen bomb. Thanks to the Teller-Ulam work, the United States Army was suddenly able to build an explosive more than a thousand times more powerful than Little Boy. "Here we were not bound by the known conditions in a given star," Teller had proclaimed at the height of his hubris, "but were free within considerable limits to choose our own conditions. We were embarking on astrophysical engineering."

Whimsically named Ivy Mike, the first hydrogen bomb was quite crude and relatively small, an eighty-two-ton refrigerator. In order to reach sufficient density, a mixture of liquid deuterium and liquid tritium was used as the second stage of the bomb. In order for the mixture not to melt, it had to be kept very cold, only a few degrees above absolute zero.

Of course Mike had been plenty powerful enough to blow the entire island of Elugelab sky high. But the key to more powerful hydrogen bombs had been lithium deuteride, a mixture of lithium-6 and deuterium. Lithium deuteride was solid at room temperature, so no refrigeration was necessary. "Why buy a cow when powdered milk is so cheap?" Edward Teller said.

In the early 1950s, loading an extra kiloton of power into a nuclear weapon by adding deuterium and lithium-6 had only cost sixty cents. Zero point six dollars. Seven dollars per Hiroshima.

And on March 1, 1954, Ivy Mike was followed by Castle Bravo.

Perhaps Henshaw should get to know what was really going on, Lauri thought. Maybe it really was only fair in this case.

"OK, fine," Lauri finally said. "We'll do it your way. But first tell me how much you've figured out yourself. There's no point repeating things you already know."

"Sounds reasonable."

Henshaw thought for a moment about where to start.

"According to those books, the second stage of a hydrogen bomb is always made up of heavy isotopes of hydrogen," she finally said. "In practice that either means deuterium and lithium-6 or deuterium and tritium. Getting deuterium is probably the easiest part of it all. All you do is distill a bunch of seawater and, voilà, heavy water. But to get tritium, first you need lithium-6."

"True," he said, in a terse tone.

"And if I understand correctly, lithium-6—or tritium—and deuterium can also be used as boosters in normal single-stage fission devices," Henshaw continued. "So if a small amount of lithium-6 and deuterium or tritium and deuterium is added to a normal plutonium bomb, the result is a spectacular increase in explosive power. The yield can go from tens to hundreds of kilotons."

Lauri nodded in agreement. "I'm impressed."

"But is it really true that only a few grams will do it?" Henshaw asked.

"Unfortunately."

"I think I need a drink," Henshaw said and went in the kitchen. "Do you want one?"

"I'm working, but maybe just this once."

Henshaw brought a silver box and took a bottle of whisky out of it. She poured the richly colored liquid into two glasses.

"Ice?"

"No thanks."

Henshaw handed one of the glasses to Lauri and took a big swig of her own.

"At first I thought you were just afraid that someone would use the lithium to boost the yield of a normal nuclear bomb," Henshaw continued. "But then I decided that wasn't plausible. Because building a normal nuclear bomb would take at least ten kilograms of weapons-grade uranium or plutonium. And I'm sure that's all guarded pretty closely."

Lauri remembered what Andrews's report had said about Henshaw's education.

"Then I thought someone was trying to build a hydrogen bomb and needed the lithium-6 for that," Henshaw continued. "Igniting that would probably only take a small amount of plutonium."

Lauri tasted his whisky. Not bad. The aftertaste was smoky. He picked up the package and looked at the brand: Glengoyne. Single Malt. Scotch. He would have to remember that.

"But then I started wondering what anyone would need six tons of lithium for," Henshaw said, increasingly engrossed in her narrative. "According to Linus Pauling, a hydrogen bomb two thousand times more powerful than Hiroshima would only take ninety kilograms of deuterium and one hundred thirty-five kilograms of lithium-6. So why would anyone steal six tons of the same element? And besides, when I dug into it more, I started doubting the whole hydrogen bomb theory. Cobbling something like that together isn't exactly simple—all these beryllium reflectors and stuff are pretty complicated-looking gizmos. To tell the truth, I'm having a hard time believing we're dealing with a normal hydrogen bomb."

Holy shit, thought Lauri.

"So I'd like to know what you haven't told me yet," Henshaw said.

Setting her glass on the table, Henshaw picked up her pack of cigarettes again. She offered one to Lauri, but he shook his head.

"You're right," Lauri said. "The greatest danger has nothing to do with normal hydrogen bombs."

"What then?"

"You always have to think these things through to their logical conclusion. If you have a few dozen grams of plutonium, a big pile of lithium-6, and a really large amount of completely unenriched natural uranium, you can build as big a nuclear bomb as you want. Without any beryllium neutron reflectors."

12

Kenneth Andrews turned to Julia Noruz and looked at her uncertainly. They were in a long underground corridor located far outside the city in a large building Julia had never known existed. An electrified fence with a tall spool of razor wire on top surrounded the building. At the gate there had been four soldiers armed with assault rifles.

"Julia, I still think you shouldn't come," Andrews said.

"If Yussuf has started talking, I want to hear with my own ears what he's saying," Julia argued. "And besides, you know I'm fluent in Arabic."

Andrews didn't look convinced.

"You don't know Arabic," Julia added.

Andrews looked at her sullenly.

"And besides, I'm a Muslim," Julia continued. "Which you aren't. That might help too. Maybe."

"OK, fine," Andrews said. "But you might regret you came. Remember I said that."

Julia thought Andrews sounded strangely ominous. What did he mean?

She understood immediately when she saw Hassan Yussuf in the interrogation room, through the one-way glass. Andrews had been right. She shouldn't have come—she was going to be having nightmares for the rest of her life. Hassan Yussuf's face . . .

Could that mutilated face with the skeletal smile really belong . . . to a person? To a living human being? His mouth . . . where were his teeth? And when Julia moved her eyes down, to Yussuf's hands and naked body . . .

Julia turned away and vomited violently. Andrews and the three other men in the room looked at her expressionlessly.

"I told you," Andrews said.

One of the men brought Julia some paper towels. Julia wiped her mouth and turned toward Andrews with accusation in her eyes.

"Ken, that's wrong!"

"You know how much is at stake."

"Things like that are always wrong! That can never be right. If we start doing this . . . where will it end? This is a Pandora's box. You can't close it once it's open."

"Would it be better to let millions die without doing anything?"

"Maybe it really would be better," Julia said angrily. "Better than this."

"You can't be serious."

Julia stopped wiping her mouth and dropped the foul-smelling paper towels in the trash.

"Kenneth, have you thought that if word of this gets out, no one will be able to sleep in peace at night? Every US citizen will be afraid of being detained. Of being tortured. All the time. For their entire lives."

"You're exaggerating. Just stay away from terrorist organizations, and you're safe."

"And what if the government decides to change the definition of terrorism?" Julia shot back.

"Why would we do that?"

"And what if at some point the official interpretation starts changing every week, or every day, without anyone knowing for sure anymore what is terrorism and what isn't?"

Andrews sighed. "You've been reading too much George Orwell."

"And what if in the future we end up having to avoid committing terrorism by guessing what's acceptable each day? Like in Stalin's Soviet Union?"

"You can always move back to Iran if you feel that way," Andrews pointed out. "The mullahs will welcome you back with open arms."

"Very funny, Ken."

"OK, that was a low blow."

"And what if someone sets me up, accidentally or on purpose?" Julia continued. "Slips some dangerous documents into my briefcase? Hides them in my apartment when I'm gone?"

"Julia," Andrews said icily. "Don't let's get hysterical now."

"And what if someone I know is set up and then he breaks under interrogation when he's tortured and gives up my name? Since he can't think of anyone else to denounce?"

"Your puke really stinks," Andrews pointed out. "Would you mind going and finding a custodian who could clean up a bit?"

13

In a secluded corner of a quiet restaurant, Akiko Nobura and Alice Donovan sat on large pillows around a low table. The restaurant was divided into sections by shoji screens. Skillfully grown bonsai trees sat on the windowsills, and the walls and ceiling were covered with delicate paintings of a bamboo forest, which created an interesting illusion that they really were in the shade of an enchanted bamboo forest straight from a fairy tale.

It was no wonder this was Akiko's favorite restaurant, thought Alice.

The windows gave a view of a heavily trafficked street. On the sidewalks people passed by in an unbroken stream in both directions. On the other side of the street was an illuminated sign covering an entire wall; its images shifted shapes like a kaleidoscope. In the darkness of the evening, it flashed in every color of the rainbow, alternating between Japanese characters and moving pictures.

They had just finished their dinner of prawns, clams, and mushrooms dipped in *donabe* broth and were moving on to green tea served in delicate, beautifully patterned porcelain cups.

"You said the modules were probably carried out on a small boat," Alice said, continuing their conversation.

"That seems like the most likely possibility. Or, well, the boat couldn't have been terribly small. But not one you would cross an ocean in."

"So it looks like they took the modules to a larger ship?"

"Yes, I think so."

"Is there any hope in tracking it?"

"Theoretically we should have a very good chance of seeing the boats meet on the satellite imagery," Akiko said. "We've been through our own satellite pictures and haven't found anything. Which is definitely a little strange. We're sifting and analyzing your images now, along with some from other sources. We have so many pictures from different satellites that the meeting of the boats will have to show up in some of them."

"What happened to the first boat?"

"It continued on to Hokkaido and landed at a small marina."

"So you've found it?"

"We found a fishing boat that was mildly radioactive but not enough so to prove anything in these conditions. The boat had been abandoned, and none of the local fishermen recognized it or knew anything about it. The LR modules were not in the boat."

"So it could be the right one?"

"There are other possibilities," Akiko said. "But I think this is the right one. If it is, the satellite pictures will definitely show us the ship they transferred the modules to. If it's a surface vessel anyway."

"And if it's a submarine?"

"In that case the modules could be anywhere and we won't necessarily find them ever."

"Let's not focus on that option then. What about the Yoshikawa headquarters? Have you found any clues there?"

Akiko nodded.

"Very many. The security camera tapes were destroyed, and we didn't find any fingerprints in the reactor room. The van at the port was stolen, so naturally it was full of fingerprints. Of course most of them belonged to the legal owner of the vehicle, but a few were genuinely interesting. It turns out they belong to a member of the Red Dragon yakuza who we've arrested several times on suspicion of various violent crimes."

"Red Dragon," Alice sighed. "Sounds pretty clichéd."

"I agree," Akiko admitted. "You should go tell the yakuza bosses. Maybe they'll listen to you."

Akiko was silent for a moment.

"Well, on second thought, maybe they won't. Probably not worth your time," Akiko said, cracking a crooked smile.

"Red Dragon is a semi-independent criminal gang," Akiko explained. "As we understand it, they're loosely affiliated with the Yamaguchi-gumi, which is our biggest criminal organization in Japan. Actually, it's more of a coalition of criminal organizations. And it also controls thousands of perfectly legal businesses."

"We have the same kinds of problems in the United States," Alice said.

"We know," Akiko said tersely.

"I'm sorry."

"Well, in any case, we also found fingerprints from this same person, Eiji Nishishava, on one of the smashed video cameras in the Yoshikawa building."

"Which is a clear indication that Red Dragon was behind the break-in," Alice said excitedly.

Akiko looked dubious. "I think that's going a little too far. I'd be more likely to guess that they stole the modules on someone else's orders. What would they do with the modules themselves? This is Japan, after all. This has to be a contract job. Now we just have to find out whose payroll they were on."

"Shouldn't we ask them directly?" Alice suggested.

"We've meant to do exactly that," Akiko said. "I just don't think it will be much benefit. Getting yakuza members to talk is very difficult, and besides that, I don't believe they would even know who made the order. Believe me: they have their ways of handling these things and making their tracks disappear. But with any luck we'll be able to figure out where the modules were taken. Assuming that boat did belong to the yakuza. If someone else entirely was at the controls, we might not get very far."

Akiko didn't seem particularly hopeful in that regard.

"What do you think?" Alice asked directly.

"They always operate in a certain way," Akiko said. "Very calculated, very deliberate. I don't think the yakuza who stole the modules would have known who was in the boat."

"So the satellite pictures are our only hope," Alice said.

Alice found herself fervently hoping that the modules were carried off in a surface vessel and not a submarine. Previously only national governments could afford submarines, but now almost anyone could buy a small submersible meant for recreational use. Anyone who had a couple of million dollars lying around anyway.

"But do you want to hear what I really think?" Akiko suddenly asked.

Alice looked at her in astonishment. "Please, yes."

"I think something stinks about this whole thing."

"What do you mean?"

"My boss, Chief Inspector Niori, has been saying the whole time that everything about this is too tidy. He thinks . . . he thinks in patterns, and he doesn't like the pattern this makes. Everything is too clear and easy. He says this is a show. A theatrical performance. Someone is leaving clues they want us to find. For example, why would they take the body of the eighth guard to the harbor? Without that it would have been much more difficult for us to find the boat."

"But what do you think?" Alice asked.

"I think Chief Inspector Niori is right," said Akiko.

"Interesting," Alice said. "One of my colleagues, Julia Noruz, has been saying the same thing. She also thinks intuitively and looks for patterns, a little like your boss. Julia keeps arguing that something about this case feels . . . wrong."

"If both my boss and your colleague are thinking the same thing, shouldn't we take it seriously?" Akiko asked.

"But if they're right, what are we dealing with?"

Akiko spread her hands in a sign of uncertainty.

"I don't know," she said. "To tell the truth, I don't have the faintest clue. But maybe the answer will come to us if we start looking at it from a slightly different perspective."

The waiter brought the bill. They paid, exchanged bows all around, and then walked toward the small side street a couple of blocks away where Akiko had parked her Mitsubishi. Two men stood smoking on the corner. Something about them made small alarm bells go off in Alice's head. The men looked at them when they came out of the restaurant, but then turned the other direction and continued their conversation.

Alice was suddenly sure the men were carrying weapons. Somehow they looked dangerous, accustomed to violence. On the other hand, so what? Osaka was full of gangsters. Japan had at least one hundred and fifty thousand people directly employed by the yakuza, mostly members of the *burakumin*, the outcast Japanese underclass. Statistically there would have to be yakuza thugs in this area. But Alice and Akiko didn't have anything to do with them, and—as Akiko had repeatedly emphasized—the yakuza had their own clearly spelled-out methods, based on strict agreements.

Alice didn't even know that they were armed, and even if they were, what good was she as an agent if armed criminals sent her into a panic? Her paranoia was over the top, but she couldn't help that all her instincts were screaming at her to run.

Akiko clicked the car doors open.

"Would you like to drive?" she asked on the spur of the moment.

"Why not?" Alice replied. "It might be a good idea to practice driving here. On the opposite side, I mean."

Akiko threw Alice the keys.

"Just so long as you don't put any dents in my beloved bucket of bolts," she said, laughing.

"I promise to be good," Alice assured her, grabbing the keys out of the air. "I always drive very carefully."

Alice fastened her seat belt and waited for Akiko to do the same. Then she started the engine and drove to the end of the street. On the left was a black Toyota with two people visible inside, but it appeared to be parked on the side of the road. No other cars were coming, so Alice turned right, lining up behind a large SUV stopped at a traffic light.

She saw in the rearview mirror that the Toyota rolled into motion at the same instant the back doors of the SUV flew open and two men jumped out onto the street.

"No!" Akiko screamed.

The men were holding submachine guns, and they were pointing them straight at the women.

Cold fear lodged in Alice's stomach. She should have trusted her instincts. If they shot now, Alice and Akiko wouldn't be able to do anything.

She glanced at the rearview mirror and saw the Toyota ease up to their rear bumper.

"Do you know what this is?" she asked Akiko.

Akiko looked pale.

"I don't understand," Akiko managed to say. "This isn't good. They never do things like this. Not to the police. Ever. This could be . . . bad."

"Do you think they're going to kill us?"

"I don't know," whispered Akiko. "But it's possible. This is very unusual."

Alice saw that the men from the corner were rapidly approaching the car. Each had a pistol in his hand. A thought flashed that she should try to get her gun out, that she might not have another chance to do so.

She decided to wait—the smallest threatening gesture, and two submachine guns would rip them to shreds.

"We walked right into a trap," she said just as the men from the street flung open both front doors of the Mitsubishi simultaneously.

"If I were you, I wouldn't try anything," one of the men said in heavily accented English and nodded toward the men with the machine guns.

With efficiency that suggested significant practice, the men first grabbed each woman's pistol. Having a man come that close and touch her as if he owned her nauseated Alice. She just managed to catch a glimpse of a large, reddish tattoo of some sort of dragon visible under the man's collar.

How stupid to die at the hands of a ridiculous cliché. Alice also noticed that the other man was missing the first joint of his little finger on one hand. *Yubitsume* was the word that came to mind, a traditional ritual in which a yakuza who had failed at a task begged forgiveness by cutting off a piece of his finger and handing it to his *oyabun*, his godfather.

The yakuza jumped in the backseat behind them. Alice saw one of them place the confiscated pistols on the floor of the car.

The men with the submachine guns retreated into the SUV, but the men sitting in the backseat kept their weapons trained on Alice's and Akiko's necks. The men's attention did not flag for a moment. They did not even stop to fasten their seat belts.

They were professionals. Alice was sure.

I'm so sorry, Lauri. I may never see you again. I'm so sorry I screwed up, thought Alice.

"Follow that SUV," said one of the men.

14

Katharine Henshaw looked at Lauri Nurmi suspiciously. Her eyes narrowed. Her dark brown hair and dark skin suddenly made Lauri think she appeared almost South Asian.

"I don't follow you," Henshaw said and stubbed her cigarette out in the crystal ashtray.

"Did you do a search for *Lucky Dragon*?" Lauri asked.

Henshaw nodded. "I did."

"What did you find?" Lauri asked, genuinely interested in how much Henshaw had figured out.

"Apparently our government did some sort of a nuclear test on March 1, 1954 on the Bikini Atoll in the Marshall Islands," Henshaw began.

"Castle Bravo," Lauri said. "*Castle* is the name of the series of tests, and *Bravo* is the code name of that particular detonation."

"Fun names," Henshaw observed. "For nuclear bombs."

Lauri knew that Castle Bravo had been a twelve-megaton bomb. The wind had been blowing from Bikini toward two other Marshall Islands atolls, Rongelap and Utrik. They were about one hundred and three hundred miles from ground zero. The Japanese fishing vessel

Daigo Fukuryū Maru, the *Lucky Dragon No. 5*, had also been about a hundred miles away. Radioactive waste rained down on it in large flakes, covering the deck. The whole crew fell violently ill with burns, vomiting, vertigo, and severe pain. All the symptoms of radioactive exposure. The inhabitants of Rongelap and Utrik also grew sick.

Eight hundred and fifty other Japanese fishing boats received smaller doses of fallout and had to throw their catches into the sea. The incident inspired a long series of Godzilla monster movies. The *Lucky Dragon*'s radio operator died, but the rest of the crewmembers recovered. When the Japanese government protested, the US Atomic Energy Commission declared their fears groundless. According to the commission's statement, the fallout had faded to safe levels within a few miles and was completely undetectable with any existing instrumentation at five hundred miles.

Within a year, the Japanese had collected thirty million names on a petition opposing further nuclear testing. For a while the *Lucky Dragon* was decommissioned and used as a training boat under the name *Dark Falcon*. Later it became a star attraction at a popular museum.

Lauri took another sip from his glass. Not bad, he had to admit.

Henshaw poured herself more, then raised the bottle and looked at Lauri inquiringly, but he raised his hand.

"This was nice, but I've probably had enough, thank you," Lauri said.

Henshaw capped the bottle.

"By all means. I couldn't figure out one thing though," Henshaw continued. "Why was the fallout from Castle Bravo so dangerous? None of the other nuclear tests had nearly the same effects. What made Castle Bravo special?"

That was the rub. The sixty-four-thousand-dollar question. Or . . . maybe sixty-four thousand dollars wasn't the right order of magnitude in this case. What would be? Maybe it would be better to talk about the sixty-four-trillion-dollar question. What was the value of all the property on the North American continent?

"Castle Bravo was designed in a particularly unpleasant way," Lauri said.

The government did everything it could to keep it secret. But then the famous physicist Joseph Rotblat was able to use the Castle Bravo fallout to deduce what kind of bomb it must have been, more or less.

"Do you know what a cobalt bomb is?" Lauri asked.

"I might have heard the term before, but I don't remember what it means."

"Leó Szilárd once calculated that if you wanted to make a doomsday weapon, a bomb that would kill everyone on the planet, you could use radioactive cobalt-60 to do it. Cobalt-60 is extremely radioactive, but only for a few years. Before decaying, it would have plenty of time to spread all across the globe though, getting into the lungs of every man, woman, and child alive."

Henshaw's eyes went wide with shock and restrained rage.

"You don't mean Castle Bravo . . ."

"No, not quite. But according to Joseph Rotblat, in a certain sense it was an even nastier contraption than a cobalt bomb of the same size. Because the fallout contained a lot of uranium-237, along with everything else."

"I only remember uranium-238 and uranium-235."

"Uranium-237 doesn't appear naturally," Lauri said. "It's about two hundred billion times more radioactive than uranium-238, so it disappears quickly."

"Two . . . hundred . . . billion?" Henshaw asked. "Wouldn't a little less have been enough? What a nice world you've all built for us! I guess I'm lucky I didn't turn into a physicist!" she said, snickering.

Henshaw saw Lauri's expression and fell silent.

"There's something else," he said. "In addition to the uranium-237."

Henshaw opened the whisky bottle and poured Lauri more, without asking.

"Do you know what ITER is?" Lauri asked.

"No."

"It's an acronym for International Experimental Thermonuclear Reactor. A joint fusion reactor trial between the United States, the European Union, and Japan. A lot of people hope it might be the solution to the world's energy problems."

"I can see from your expression you don't share their optimism," Henshaw said.

"A trenchant observation," Lauri replied. "ITER would be a deuterium-tritium reactor. Sort of a controlled hydrogen bomb. Usually in public they say it would only use seawater as fuel. Of course that's partially true. But more precisely, it requires deuterium and lithium-6 to run."

Lauri took a long pull from his glass and let the full-bodied malt whisky burn his lips and palate.

"The important point is that using lithium-6 you can basically burn wet wood," he said. "Wet wood that's been lying in a ditch soaking for years. Even if the wood has spent billions of years rotting away."

15

Alice and Akiko had been forced to follow the SUV far outside of Osaka. The crazy sea of city lights had fallen behind them, and Alice didn't have a clue where they were. She had just followed the orders that came from the yakuza in the backseat, always turning when told to. They hadn't gone north though, on the road to Kyoto, but west, toward Kobe and Hiroshima, based on what she could gather from the signage. They had left the main road at a large intersection with lanes leading off in every direction.

Alice felt as if they had been gradually gaining altitude, because there had been more uphill than downhill. On their right side were tall hills with small clutches of light in the darkness, indicating villages and the individual lights of isolated homes. On the left there was only blackness at first, but then a wide, jagged strip of sparse lights appeared. Behind it were only a few dim lights, most likely ships or lighted buoys. At the horizon a distant light shone—as if the sunset had stuck in place.

Probably Shikoku. If Alice was right, then they were getting closer to Hiroshima, and she was struck by how ironic it would be if she died there. Although, she didn't know that Kyoto would have been any better. Alice was always horrified when she thought how it was only at the last minute that Kyoto was removed from the top of the target list for the first nuclear strikes. The whole world definitely would hate the United States now if it had burned Kyoto as the military leadership of the Manhattan Project wanted to do.

It was quiet in the car, and other traffic was almost nonexistent. Ten minutes had probably passed since the last oncoming car, and Alice couldn't see any cars behind them other than the black Toyota that the yakuza drove.

"What is this about?" Alice had asked the men in the backseat after she started driving.

The men did not respond, simply staring with stony faces.

"You aren't going to kill us, are you?" Alice had asked.

The yakuza sitting behind her laughed, almost playfully.

"Of course not. A certain person just wants to ask you a few questions," the man said.

"Don't worry. We'll return you to the city safe and sound. This won't take long."

Alice didn't believe a word of it, because every time she looked at him in the rearview mirror, he averted his eyes, which was a bad sign. They were hard men, killers, at least some of them, if not all. But they didn't want to kill young women. It made them uncomfortable. That's why they wouldn't look at Akiko and Alice. They didn't want to see them as people before they did what they had been ordered to do.

It was possible she was exaggerating. Maybe they really wanted to ask something. Maybe she and Akiko weren't in any real danger.

But when Alice glanced at Akiko out of the corner of her eye, she saw that her Japanese colleague was stiff with fear. From time to time Akiko also yawned, as many people do to try to mask their fear when they're genuinely terrified. Akiko knew all the cultural codes and messages Alice couldn't see or understand.

No, Alice wasn't imagining anything. The yakuza were intending to kill them.

But even as she became convinced of the reality of the danger, other questions burned even more brightly: Why? Why right now?

She would ponder these questions later, assuming she could somehow extend their lifespan beyond how abbreviated it appeared it might now be. Alice needed to focus on the problem at hand. So here they were, with two yakuza sitting behind them, both with their guns out and safeties off. One of the men had his gun pointed at her neck, and the other was aiming at Akiko. Even if she could figure out some way to escape, Alice was sure the yakuza would not hesitate for an instant to shoot her and Akiko. She had to come up with something.

Alice guessed there were four or five yakuza in the car in front of them and two in the Toyota behind. With the two in the backseat, there were at least eight gangsters, possibly nine. That was a lot, especially because the yakuza had taken their pistols. This time things could go really badly, Alice thought uneasily.

The road was starting up the hillside again, which was obvious from the tight turns. Suddenly a lone pair of headlights appeared in the oncoming lane. They grew dazzlingly bright, but then the car had passed them, and its taillights shone in the mirror as quickly dying tiny red fireflies. Then they were gone, and Alice felt very alone. Even more so than a moment before. If she intended to do something, she would have to do it soon. Before they reached wherever the yakuza were taking them.

Alice straightened up slightly to get a better look in the rearview mirror of the men in back. In the blink of an eye, the yakuza sitting behind her shoved the cold, metal barrel of the pistol into her neck.

"No tricks," the man said coldly. "Stay where you are."

"My leg was cramping up," Alice complained.

"Do we need to change drivers?" asked the yakuza.

"No, it's passed already," Alice said.

She was satisfied with what she had seen. As satisfied as she could be given the circumstances. Out of the corner of her eye, Alice glanced at Akiko and verified that the other key fact was still true too. There was still one thing that might cause a problem. Alice looked at the dashboard. Most of the lights and buttons looked the same as in her car, but some were more difficult to recognize. And all of the words were in Japanese, so she didn't understand any of them. *Why did I study Chinese?* she asked herself, annoyed. The chances of survival can depend on such unexpected things sometimes.

Alice couldn't ask Akiko to translate the words on the dash without arousing the suspicion of the yakuza. So she couldn't know the state of things. But she didn't have any better alternative plan. And besides, Akiko's car was quite old—maybe the whole system that formed the potential problem hadn't even been invented when her Mitsubishi came off the factory assembly line.

Alice noted that the hillside was more sparsely populated. They had passed the last full village quite some time ago, and single houses only came along infrequently, miles apart. The lights along the coast disappeared from sight. Now there was nothing but deep darkness on their left side. They were probably in some sort of valley surrounded by hills. Alice could see, from the lights of the SUV ahead of them, that the road became almost straight and relatively flat.

Farther off in the darkness flashed a small red warning light. As they approached it, Alice saw that it was some sort of road construction zone. A line of concrete barriers in the middle of the road appeared in the light of the SUV. The remaining usable lane was very narrow.

Alice made her decision and braked hard. The Mitsubishi stopped almost as if it had hit a wall. The lights of the Toyota behind them brightened blindingly. The driver braked too late, and the Toyota turned half-sideways on the road. The SUV didn't notice they had stopped, and so it continued on. Its taillights glowed in the darkness.

"What's the problem?" yelled the gangster sitting behind Alice.

"Some kind of construction zone," Alice said, trying to sound uncertain.

"Forget it. Keep driving."

Alice watched as the SUV's taillights receded and grew smaller.

"Drive!" ordered the yakuza behind her, now much more harshly.

The SUV would soon notice that something was going on, so Alice pressed on the gas, but only a little. The Mitsubishi moved forward, slowly.

"Drive faster," the yakuza said coldly, poking Alice's earlobe with the gun.

Alice inhaled sharply, trying to sound frightened. It was easy, since she was.

"O . . . OK," she stuttered and floored the gas pedal. "Watch your neck," she whispered to Akiko as quietly as she could.

Alice thought Akiko looked as if even more color had drained from her face, but she could have just been imagining it. It was hard to tell in the dark.

"What did you say?" the gangster demanded.

"My leg is cramping again," Alice said, feigning pain.

The first concrete barrier was only a couple of hundred yards ahead now.

The speedometer needle pointed to ninety kilometers per hour, then one hundred. The Toyota had gotten back on the road and was quickly gaining on them.

"Now you're going too fast," said the yakuza sitting behind Alice. "Slow down a little."

Alice turned her head partially back, toward the man.

"Could we trade drivers?" she asked. "My leg is really cramping badly."

The man looked at her uncertainly. Alice saw that the gun wasn't pointed straight at her neck anymore but a little to the side. Good.

As she spoke, Alice let up on the gas pedal so their speed fell to eighty kilometers per hour, then seventy. The first concrete barrier was getting closer, and the Toyota was gaining on them. She hoped it was going fast enough. Otherwise her plan wouldn't work. And hopefully Akiko's car didn't have air bags.

"I have to stop," Alice said, and an instant later she turned right and slammed into the concrete barrier at sixty-seven kilometers per hour.

16

When Lauri returned to his office at the NTU, he had barely managed to sit down before Julia Noruz barged in. She was clutching two sheets of paper in her hand, and Lauri could see instantly that she was worried.

"Lauri, something is very wrong."

"I could name quite a few things that are completely fucked up. How have you chosen the focus of our attention today?"

Julia shook her head. "Don't make jokes. Something isn't right. The pieces don't fit together. Not the way we're trying to make them fit. I'm worried that we don't seem to care that the pieces don't fit but we keep charging ahead anyway."

"Stop saying that! We always do things this way," Lauri said.

"Now might be more dangerous than usual though," Julia shot back.

"OK, OK. You obviously have some point to make."

"Two things in particular bother me. First, I don't know if you've heard yet, but Andrews and the big shots above him allowed Yussuf to be tortured. In a very unpleasant and brutal way."

Lauri swiveled in his chair. "Goddamn it. I was afraid of that. We're starting to get awfully medieval."

"They said this was an exceptional case. What they did is chilling, and I'm even more afraid of what those methods could lead to in the long run. But there's something else too."

"Such as?"

"Apparently Yussuf broke once they'd tortured him for a week and a half. After that he was willing to admit that he belongs to an organization planning a nuclear bomb attack against the United States."

"A confession like that doesn't necessarily mean anything," Lauri said.

Julia nodded.

When a person was tortured, often he just said whatever the torturers wanted to hear. His best guess about what the torturers wanted to hear. Anything to make the pain stop.

"Yussuf knows a lot of details, so he can't be completely innocent," Julia said. "Apparently he said that his friends have built a big nuclear bomb including several tons of lithium-6. He also said they had procured small amounts of plutonium from Argeva. But he doesn't seem to know the real name of the contact person there or any details about how the plutonium was stolen."

Lauri whistled loudly. "So they really do have both the Argeva plutonium and the lithium-6 from Osaka."

"So far everything fits more or less," Julia admitted. "But Yussuf also gave a list of the people he knows are involved in the organization in one way or another. He knew a few operators and several fund-raisers."

"Excellent. That could help us find them before it's too late."

Julia didn't seem as satisfied as Lauri.

"Something is really bothering you," he said. "What is it?"

Julia handed Lauri the sheets of paper she was holding. "Look at Yussuf's list. You'll probably recognize most of the names. Something really smells here. I mean stinks!"

Lauri reviewed the papers. There were forty names. Reading through the list, Lauri groaned in astonishment.

"This is a complete bombshell. The biggest coup in years."

"Well, maybe," said Julia. "But only maybe. I actually have a hard time believing that list is real."

"How so?" Lauri asked.

"A lot of those people Yussuf claims are fund-raisers for his organization are prominent American Muslim leaders. Extremely influential. And they are all moderate Muslim leaders. Millions of American Muslims listen to them. Literally millions—I'm not exaggerating at all. I can't believe they would be involved in something like this. I just can't. They've always been on our side, always supporting us and trying to calm the situation. And they've succeeded really well. We would be in a real mess without them."

"But isn't that the perfect cover story if you want to raise money for Al-Qaeda?"

Julia hesitated.

"But they would have to raise billions of dollars to balance their accounts," she argued. "For them to be more help than harm to the terrorists. They've damaged Al-Qaeda more than almost anyone else."

"And what if we've only thought they were helping us? How can we know everything that's really happening in the mosques and Koran schools? Even you don't know since you never go to mosque."

Julia lifted her glasses onto her forehead and rubbed her neck.

"Lauri, believe me, this whole thing stinks to high heaven," she said.

"What do you suspect? Intentional disinformation?"

"Yeah."

"But if Yussuf took a week and a half to break under torture . . ."

"They said at the beginning he didn't say anything, or just fed them complete BS. But then, once he had finally broken, he rattled off all those names on that list. I guess in a way it's perfectly credible, but . . . I don't know."

Lauri looked at the list again.

"Some of these names on Yussuf's list are people our intel says do have contacts with Al-Qaeda," Lauri pointed out. "We've already picked some of them up, and some of them are on our terrorist watch lists. Doesn't that increase the credibility of the list?"

Julia shook her head.

"Not necessarily. What if somehow they know who we have on our lists? Then giving us the same names wouldn't cause any harm."

"They can't have access to our files," Lauri protested.

"Well, at least they know who has already been caught."

"I think you're being pretty paranoid now."

"We all are. So much so that it's going to mean our downfall someday. Mark my words. I just don't know which of us is being more paranoid. In times like these, the line between paranoia and clear-headedness seems to overlap easily."

"Julia, the blueprints are real. We found them in Yussuf's apartment. Along with that photograph. They exist. We didn't imagine them. We can touch them."

Julia's expression was difficult to read.

"Except that's the other thing I needed to talk to you about. First, why did Yussuf have the drawings and that photo in his apartment at all? Why store evidence at home? We have the Internet after all. It doesn't make any sense."

"Did anyone ask Yussuf?"

"Yes. He claimed he needed the photograph and drawings to convince his Muslim brothers that they were serious."

"Isn't that a perfectly good explanation?" Lauri asked.

Julia asked Lauri to wait for a minute and then returned with a portfolio under her arm. Opening the portfolio, she searched in it for the photograph of the large metal pipe they had studied so much already. She pointed to the center of the image.

"Look at these shadows," Julia said. "Here. And here. Look at the directions of the shadows."

Lauri looked at the places Julia was indicating and understood what she was getting at. The shadows fell in different directions.

"You're right," Lauri said. "That's an interesting detail. But we don't know what kinds of lights were in the hold. If there were several different light sources, and we can't see all of them in the picture, the directions of the shadows could easily be confusing."

"But look at the shades," Julia insisted. "Look how they get darker here, from light to gray and then finally totally black. Do you see how the range of shades goes here, on the other side of the pipe?"

Lauri had to admit that Julia might be right. The darkening and lightening in some places in the photograph were strange.

"The explanation could be the same," Lauri said.

"No, it can't. Look how the shadows darken as they move toward the light source. That can't happen. It can't be darker nearer to a light than farther away from it."

"Are you claiming the picture was doctored?"

"I'm not claiming anything yet," Julia said. "But I think we should take the possibility into consideration."

17

When an automobile collides with an immovable obstacle, its momentum stops in a split second. If the speed of the vehicle exceeds one hundred kilometers per hour at the time of impact, the human aorta ruptures. A seat belt does not change this, and an air bag barely alters the outcome. When the aorta ruptures, the person dies quickly, unless she is extremely lucky. Alice Donovan didn't want her aorta to rupture.

That was why she slowed the Mitsubishi just before the crash.

A significantly higher speed also would have been enough to send the Mitsubishi flying in a high arc over the concrete barricade. Alice didn't want that either, because the results of such a flight were unpredictable. And she didn't know how much the front end of the Mitsubishi could take before it crumpled and smashed her legs into a bloody mess.

Besides, Alice didn't need that much speed, because when a car collides with a fixed obstacle, a person holding on to her seat with both hands at the moment of impact can only stay in place if the car's velocity doesn't exceed thirty kilometers per hour. Neither of the gangsters in the back was holding on to his seat. In fact, they were leaning forward. And neither of the yakuza had fastened his seat belt, unlike Alice and Akiko.

In any case, they had been traveling sixty-seven kilometers per hour. Sixty-seven kilometers per hour—forty-two miles per hour—does not sound particularly fast, but in reality it was significantly more than Alice needed to deal with the yakuza.

When Alice Donovan stopped Akiko Nobura's Mitsubishi by driving it into a concrete barricade, the car didn't fly over it or even flip over on its roof. It stopped as if it had hit a wall, but its rear end bounced into the air a good three feet.

The crash and the screeching of crumpling sheet metal made Alice's ears ring. The seat belt dug painfully into her stomach, chest, and neck. However, it also did its job by stopping her forward motion before she could hit the windshield.

The yakuza sitting in the back were left to the mercy of the laws of physics defined by Galileo and Newton. One of the yakuza flew forward between the seats, the other over Akiko's head, who was folded like a jackknife. The men struck the windshield head-on with terrible force, and Alice thought she heard a nasty crunch, but it was instantly drowned out by the squeal of grinding steel.

Hopefully the car wouldn't crumple so badly that she would end up with the dashboard in her lap.

The windshield shattered, and two large spiderweb patterns instantly appeared. However, the safety glass did not splinter into pieces. Only now Alice realized that a split second earlier she had also heard the spit of a silenced pistol and felt a small sting on her skin where the muzzle flash had singed her forehead and hair. A tiny hole had appeared in the side window, but Alice could tell that she hadn't been hit, and her hair wasn't on fire.

The car wasn't crumpling completely. Her legs were safe. Alice felt relief course through her, but everything was happening so slowly, as if in a dream.

Where was the Toyota? Had it managed to brake in time? What if it did brake and stop before . . .

The rear of the Mitsubishi continued rising, and now the car also slid sideways from the force of the impact. It blocked the entire road. Then the car stopped, and it froze in place for less than a second before the rear began falling back down.

Alice just had time to throw both of her hands up to protect her neck and bend her head down before the black Toyota slammed into the left rear corner of the Mitsubishi.

18

At Kenneth Andrews's request, Katharine Henshaw came to the offices of the NTU two days after Timothy Washburn's next party. Andrews had also asked Lauri, Julia, and George Robertson to attend. Lauri was somewhat distracted by his concern that he hadn't received any messages from Alice all day. Alice also hadn't answered any of his calls.

Henshaw looked with disdain at the people in the room and refused to shake any hands.

"Well, here I am," she said. "What do you want to know?"

"Did you hear anything interesting?" Andrews asked.

"Nothing," Henshaw replied.

"Nothing?"

"Nothing. Nothing about lithium. And not anything else I could imagine might interest you."

"OK, even so, tell us word for word everything they did and said. Everything."

"You can't really mean that," Henshaw said in disbelief.

"You never know what might be important," Andrews growled. "Start talking."

An hour later Henshaw had repeated everything she could remember.

"Is that all?" Andrews asked. "I don't know if there was anything useful there."

"I told you," Henshaw said.

Henshaw's face was red with humiliation and suppressed rage. She seemed on the verge of bursting into tears. It definitely wasn't one of their finest moments, thought Lauri. Julia and Robertson looked embarrassed too.

"Is there anything else, or can I go now?" Henshaw asked.

"Yeah, go ahead and get out of here," Andrews said.

Henshaw stood up to leave.

"At least you probably made some good money," Andrews said.

Henshaw turned back to Andrews and looked at him with disgust.

Lifting one of her arms, she pulled up the sleeve of her blouse. A nasty-looking abrasion circled her wrist. In places the skin was scabbed over; other areas still looked raw and were an angry red.

Lauri closed his eyes. *Jesus Christ*, he thought.

Henshaw didn't say anything—she just stared Andrews straight in the eyes until he couldn't bear her gaze and lowered his head. Henshaw pulled her sleeve back down to cover the abrasion. Without a word she turned her back on them and started walking out the door.

Andrews stood up too. "Let us know when they invite you again," he called after Henshaw. "Hopefully you'll hear something next time."

Lauri saw Henshaw flinch. Her shoulders trembled and she almost tripped.

Something in Lauri's mind snapped, and suddenly the fingers of his left hand stiffened into a sharp wedge, which lashed out like a piston and struck Andrews in the solar plexus. Andrews's mouth went wide in shock, and he doubled over. Robertson sprang up and rushed Lauri from behind, but Lauri saw him coming in the reflection in the window and without even turning swung his right hand backward in an arc.

The blade of his hand struck Robertson in the neck, and he fell to the ground without making a sound.

He did move beautifully, Julia thought as she sat firmly in her chair. Not for an instant did she consider intervening, not until Lauri had switched out of fighting mode, because even though he was purposefully controlling the power of his blows, accidents happened.

Besides, Kenneth had earned that. Julia was just sorry Lauri was probably going to get fired. Maybe he didn't care, at least not right now. But why had Lauri reacted so strongly?

Andrews sprawled on the floor hopelessly struggling to catch his breath.

"Do you think he's OK?" Julia asked calmly.

Lauri snapped back to reality. Julia saw how his muscles started to relax and his breathing began to even out. Lauri looked at Andrews coldly.

"Yes, he'll recover," Lauri said. "Unfortunately."

Julia saw that Henshaw had turned to watch what was happening behind her. Her face wore a curious, confused expression.

"Lauri, you should really start training again," Julia said disapprovingly.

"Meaning?"

"You took almost two seconds to lay out Ken and George. What if you'd been facing someone serious?"

THREE
FIRE LOADING

"This new phenomenon would also lead to the construction of bombs, and it is conceivable—though much less certain—that extremely powerful bombs of a new type may thus be constructed. A single bomb of this type, carried by boat and exploded in a port, might very well destroy the whole port together with some of the surrounding territory."

>   —*Albert Einstein*
>   *August 2, 1939*
>   *From a letter to President Franklin Delano Roosevelt, written by Leó Szilárd and signed by Albert Einstein*

1

Lauri woke up in a dream. Was he awake or asleep? he thought. He'd been here before.

The place was familiar. It was the same sixteen-story Staten Island apartment building he had visited so many times in his dreams, with Alice and Kenneth Andrews. For some reason unknown to himself, this particular roof had become the stage for his recurring nightmares. But this dream wasn't normal, because this time in an odd way he was simultaneously awake and asleep. A lucid dream. He was having a dream but understood he was dreaming and could decide what he did in the dream.

Interesting.

Lauri turned toward the horizon to see whether Manhattan and Jersey City were already burning. Yes, they were on fire. So the bomb had already gone off. Soon the wind would start. But where was Alice? And what about Andrews? Lauri turned to look behind him.

There she was.

"Hi, Alice," Lauri said.

"What do you mean 'hi'?" Alice asked, confused. "I've been here the whole time. Do you have a fever?"

"What about Kenneth?"

Alice looked at him as if he were a half-wit. The wind was tugging at the sleeves of her shirt and her long black hair.

"You saw yourself how he went over the edge. He didn't have a chance."

"Oh, so this is that version."

"What are you talking about?" Alice asked.

The wind picked up and blew Alice's hair wildly all around her head. *Alice certainly is beautiful*, Lauri thought. *When was the last time I told her that? I should tell her that one of these days. Maybe that will make her happy, since things have been a little tangled up for us lately. Of course I could say it right now, but that wouldn't be as helpful because this is all just happening in my own head and the real Alice wouldn't hear what I say to her now.*

"We should get out of here," Alice yelled. "The wind is getting stronger. I don't think this building is going to stay standing."

"How bad do you think the wind will get?"

Alice shrugged.

"All of Manhattan is burning. And Jersey City and a lot of Brooklyn. That was a pretty big bomb."

"Let's go," said Lauri. "We need to get underground. Into a subway tunnel or a deep basement."

"Are the elevators working?"

"No way. We'll have to take the stairs."

Isn't it nice this is just a dream? thought Lauri as they went down the stairs. *Otherwise we'd be really screwed.*

"Why are you grinning?" Alice asked almost angrily.

"It's a little hard to explain."

"Do you find something funny about any of this?"

"No, not really."

By the time they got downstairs and opened the door, the wind was already at gale force. Lauri hadn't known there could be wind like that on earth.

"We have to find someplace to take cover," Lauri said.

They heard a muffled noise and watched as the roof of a building at the end of the street tore off and joined a stream of metal sheets and shingles. There were cars and people on the street, but then suddenly the people weren't standing anymore; they were whipped upward, shrieking into the air. The wind lifted some of the cars, and one slammed into the wall of a building next to them and exploded in flames. Burning fuel flew through the windows, and the buildings immediately caught fire despite the wind.

Cars and motorcycles shot by like missiles, crashing into the building behind them, and they fled, holding the sidewalk railing, struggling to reach the wall of a short warehouse building so they wouldn't end up under a pile of flaming gasoline and scrap iron. The wind was so strong that they wouldn't have been able to make any progress at all if the warehouse hadn't sheltered them from the worst of the hellish fury of the wind.

Both buildings behind them were in flames two or three stories up. The wind tossed cars like giant Molotov cocktails, and one gas tank after another ruptured, sending fuel running along the walls of the buildings. In a few seconds the gas would catch fire, and the blaze would spread even farther. There were no sounds of sprinklers coming from anywhere. The supermassive electromagnetic pulse caused by the nuclear blast had probably fried beyond all repair every electronic system within its radius.

Lauri wouldn't have believed the strength of the wind could still increase, but the pitch of its demonic howl continued to grow.

"Lauri!" shouted Alice.

Lauri realized that in the real world he probably wouldn't be able to hear Alice's voice anymore at this point. But in a lucid dream, anything could happen.

"Lauri! Are there any gas lines here?" Alice yelled through the wind. Lauri didn't want to tell Alice that all of the buildings around them used natural gas. She would probably notice soon enough.

Without warning, a gaping black hole opened up in the bottom of the apartment building they had been in, and the whole place simply toppled on its side, collapsing astonishingly fast into a huge confusion of concrete blocks and stairways and pipes and rebar. Long tongues of flame licked out in every direction from the chaos, with pipes splitting and gas burning in the open air. Lauri watched as the wind flung detritus away from them, toward the center of the conflagration. Only a few hundred meters behind them was another inferno.

Alice looked at the warehouse wall that was currently shielding them from the worst of the wind.

"This building is going to go soon too," she yelled.

Lauri knew Alice was right, but he didn't have a clue what they could do since methane was shooting out of the rubble low to the ground, with flames hundreds of feet long constantly moving and shifting shape. Smaller tongues of flame came from every cleft in the rubble, and there was no way they could cross the area without being burned to death. Lauri knew that if too many fires started, they might strengthen the main firestorm and the superhurricane it was feeding. Flanking blazes wouldn't necessarily decrease the strength of the firestorm. They were too close to ground zero, so there would be no competition between the fires.

The warehouse began to shake. At any second the hurricane would collapse the walls and raze the whole building—with them under it.

"There it goes!" yelled Alice.

The building began to collapse. A large block of cement fell at Alice's feet, and they fled . . . where?

Lithium-6

Lauri didn't know. The last thing he saw was something coming whirling straight toward them through the fire. *No*, thought Lauri when he recognized the object. *Not this, not this again. I've seen this too many times.* Before his eyes the bale tumbling through the fire disintegrated into a thousand individual pieces of straw. They spread in every direction but then organized in an instant into a hail of tiny spears all pointed in exactly the same direction, horizontally toward them. Alice looked right at them, and then all the blades of straw . . .

2

In the shower, Lauri let the ice-cold water wash over him as he tried to shake off the remnants of the nightmare. Then with a towel wrapped around his waist, he walked to the living room and checked again whether any messages had come from Alice. There weren't any, not in his voice mail or his e-mail inbox. More than twenty-four hours had passed now since Alice's last communication. That was unusual, but not completely unheard of. There were a million different perfectly rational explanations for it.

Lauri checked his watch. He still had more than enough time to call Alice. Dialing the number from his favorites, he waited. Still no answer. Lauri left a message:

"Hi, honey. It's me. Call me when you get a chance. But don't call at two in the afternoon, here time. I have an important meeting in Washington right then."

***

A couple of hours later, Kenneth Andrews picked Lauri up in a black Ford Expedition.

"Good. At least you took the effort to put on a suit," Andrews said.

"You only reminded me a dozen times."

"You're welcome. Though I didn't mean the cheapest thing you could find in the bottom of the bargain bin at the Salvation Army."

"I don't have any other suits."

"Oh, don't we pay you enough? I'll have to bring that up with Janet."

"I've had other things to do with my money."

"Is that so?" grunted Andrews.

"If you want a fashion model instead of an expert, ask Farley," Lauri replied. Andrews's pettiness disgusted him.

Minutes later they pulled up to the Downtown Manhattan Heliport, where an unmarked Black Hawk idled.

As they lifted off, the buildings of Staten Island and the narrow strait separating it from the mainland came into view off to the left. *Hey there, Staten Island. I'll come visit again some night soon*, thought Lauri.

Half an hour later the landscape below had changed. Now the scenery was dominated by a coastal plain with a patchwork of thick brush and sparse deciduous forest.

For some reason a strange nursery rhyme started echoing in Lauri's head: *Rockabye catsy, in the tree top.* He felt like the rhyme had some connection to something important. *When the wind blows, the cray-dull will rock.* But what?

"Remember, this is a very exceptional situation," Andrews said for about the thirtieth time.

After passing south of Philadelphia, they followed the Delaware River. Below Lauri saw fields interspersed with thick forest and sand dunes covered by vegetation.

. . . If the bough breaks, the cray-dull will fall . . .

"It isn't at all normal for the president to meet with lower-level advisers in such an intimate way."

. . . down will come cray-dull . . .

"It shows she really understands the significance of this."

. . . catsy, and all . . .

Lauri suddenly remembered where the stupid rhyme was from.

"Ice-nine," Lauri said.

"Excuse me?" Andrews asked.

"The book by Kurt Vonnegut, *Cat's Cradle*. Ice-nine."

"Explain."

"Often we only see what we want to see."

"What a unique, original idea," Andrews said mockingly. "I'm stunned."

"We have a tendency to get stuck on the one detail that we find we like the most and that best fits our purposes. Forget the big picture. That's too complicated. Visualizing that in all its complexity takes too much time and patience."

"So?"

Out the window, Lauri saw the Delaware shore, with more wetlands bordered by reeds in among the dunes and coastal lowlands.

"Vonnegut's scientist character is irritated that the Marines had to slog around in the mud during the Second World War," said Lauri. "So he invents a substance called ice-nine that makes water freeze at a significantly higher temperature than normal. His big idea is that if they dump ice-nine on a tropical swamp before the Marines land, the swamp will freeze and the Marines won't sink into the mud."

"Sounds like a useful substance." Andrews grunted. "Definitely an idea worth investigating. Does something like that exist, or is it just speculation?"

Lauri ignored his question.

"Vonnegut's scientist leaves the idea unfinished, not following the logical chain past the first link. Let alone the second and third."

"So?" asked Andrews again.

"See, the streams that start in the swamp, they freeze too. And the rivers the streams empty into, they also freeze. And when the river reaches the ocean, the ocean freezes, and you have the end of the world."

Andrews looked at Lauri indignantly.

"If this is some kind of joke, I didn't catch the point when I was supposed to laugh."

"Forget it," said Lauri. "Except . . . have you ever heard of Project Orion?"

"What does that have to do with . . . ?"

"With ice-nine research."

"Excuse me?"

"Project Orion was supposed to develop spacecraft that were propelled by the force of nuclear explosions," Lauri explained.

"Didn't they actually test it?" Andrews asked. "Didn't the tests prove the concept? That you could use a spaceship like that to fly to Alpha Centauri if you wanted to? Or am I remembering wrong?"

Andrews was right, in a way. Lauri had heard the same urban legends. In reality the Orion prototype had only been a meter long though, and instead of atomic bombs, it used normal C-4 plastic explosive. And it only went fifty meters in the air. Did shooting off a rocket packed with gunpowder on the Fourth of July prove that man could fly to the stars using nuclear bombs?

On paper they had developed versions intended for interstellar space flight. But to accelerate the Super-Orion, it would have taken millions of megaton-sized nuclear bombs, several thousand times more than the total nuclear weapon arsenals of mankind. A later version of the same idea, Daedalus, would have required thirty billion very small atomic bombs.

At some point the Orion and Daedalus developers started thinking about the fallout from the bombs. But they didn't consider it a serious problem. Space was big. Then they realized that the wake of radioactive particles hurled off by the bombs would be pointed straight at Earth.

But maybe that wasn't so serious after all, they had thought, and focused on more important things, like destroying Moscow and Kiev with nuclear-tipped missiles.

Then they finally realized that the stream of particles left by the nuclear bombs would have been entirely in the form of ionized plasma. In other words, Earth's magnetic field would have sucked up most of it like a vacuum cleaner and returned it right where it had originally come from. In the atmosphere the atoms would have stuck to each other and drifted down as a light rain of tiny nanoparticles. Everyone on earth would inhale them. *Ice-nine*, thought Lauri.

Lauri glanced out to the southeast, and down toward the open water of Delaware Bay, glittering blue on the horizon.

"Ice-nine is fiction," Lauri said to Andrews. "But think about fusion research."

"Yeah?"

"How have they made everyone believe that a fusion reactor would be safer than a normal nuclear power plant?" Lauri asked. "Or that it would produce less radioactive waste. Why does everyone want to believe that fusion plants would produce endless supplies of clean energy on nothing but seawater?"

So often people only saw what they wanted to see. That was *Homo sapiens'* most dangerous trait. If the species couldn't get past that, the rapid development of technology would almost certainly lead to self-annihilation. In times like these there wasn't actually much room for fooling around anymore. These toys were dangerous enough that somehow the world needed to find the courage—now, not sometime in the future—to see them for what they were with all their attributes. To take a good look into the black abyss and face the truth about what humanity had done.

People believed—or wanted to believe—that they were rational, cool, and unemotionally logical, focused on the cold, hard facts. In a way that was probably true. Except that there just happened to be an awful lot of facts. They formed a sea with no shores, and people had a tendency toward getting sentimental and choosing what they wanted to believe from that infinitude. People found what they wanted to find and wanted to know. What they already decided to know. The latent a priori solution, the scientist's worst disease.

"Ice-nine, is it?" Andrews said, sounding slightly concerned. "Hopefully you aren't thinking of repeating that to the president."

Yes, Lauri was thinking he would tell the president the ice-nine story. Actually, he thought they'd already agreed to tell the story together, though it was pretty likely they'd tell it in a different form than Lauri just had.

But he did not share this idea with Kenneth Andrews.

3

The collision threw the Mitsubishi forward, and Alice Little Hawk Donovan felt a stabbing pain in her neck even though she had pulled her head forward and tried to slow its whiplash with both hands. Then the motion stopped.

Alice waited for the back of the car to crash down, but then she realized that the Toyota had driven under them and wedged the Mitsubishi into a semivertical position.

Suddenly everything was quiet, but there was a strong stench of gasoline in the air, and Alice could hear liquid dripping. Drip, drip, drip. Hopefully it wasn't gas.

Alice saw that the neck of the yakuza who had been sitting behind Akiko was contorted against the windshield, and he wasn't moving. They wouldn't have to worry about him anymore. The other yakuza was moving and moaning faintly. His face was smashed almost beyond recognition. Alice saw that he was still holding his pistol. Could he see enough to shoot? The stench of gasoline was very strong, and the muzzle flash of the pistol could ignite the fumes.

Managing to unfasten her seat belt, Alice eased her legs onto the steering wheel and dashboard and then, with all her might, kicked the yakuza in the face. There was a crunching sound, and he stopped moving. The man's fingers loosened, and Alice extracted the pistol from his hand.

That was that. They needed to get out of there, fast. There probably wasn't much time left.

Alice looked at Akiko. She was feeling her forehead but didn't look badly hurt. She was obviously dazed though.

Alice pushed on the door, but it didn't budge.

"Akiko, can you try the door on your side?" she asked calmly, but she was counting the seconds.

"I . . . I'm a little dizzy," Akiko said. Her voice was slurred. She fumbled for the door handle, but her movements were feeble.

Alice kicked the upper edge of the windshield with both feet as hard as she could. It collapsed as a single mat of broken glass. A few shards remained on the edges of the frame, and Alice took care not to cut herself on them as she dropped out onto the badly crumpled hood of the Mitsubishi. Even so, she felt a shooting pain and something warm and wet on one of her hands, but she pushed that out of her mind.

Her heart was pounding.

How long had passed since the collisions? Fifteen seconds? Twenty? Where was the SUV? Was it possible the men still hadn't noticed what happened? They had at least two submachine guns, and maybe other weapons. If they came back, Alice and Akiko wouldn't stand a chance. Right now, they had no choice but to flee to the other side of the road. But would Akiko even be able to do that in her state? It helped that some of their opponents were out of the game, but the situation was far from under control.

Alice looked up the road, perhaps six or seven hundred yards away, and noticed that the red fireflies glowing in the dark slowed down and then stopped.

At least twenty seconds, thought Alice, so first the two from behind, then Akiko, and then you little darlings in your nice little SUV.

Alice moved quickly to the smashed Toyota. She saw out of the corner of her eye that the SUV tried to turn around but had to stop at the concrete barrier and back up toward the outer edge of the lane.

Good. A few extra seconds.

The back corner of the Mitsubishi had gone straight through the Toyota's windshield. A car was one of the most lethal weapons ever invented, Alice thought. One of the men moaned, and Alice shot him three times in the head and upper torso. She might have been going overboard, but they were in no position for her to be tenderhearted. She didn't want any more functional yakuza to deal with than she had to.

The spits of the pistol were pleasantly muffled. Alice hoped the yakuza in the SUV weren't noticing the muzzle flashes. Walking around to the other side of the Toyota, she opened the door, confirmed that the other yakuza was as dead as he appeared, and took the pistol from the holster under his jacket. She glanced in the direction of the SUV. The driver had backed up as far as he dared and was trying to turn around again, but there still wasn't enough room. He was forced to back up again.

Akiko got the door open and floundered out. She stumbled and would have fallen flat on her face if Alice hadn't grabbed her.

The SUV lurched forward again—and succeeded in turning. The engine whined as the vehicle started toward them. So that was how it was going to be. Go ahead and press that accelerator, Alice thought with satisfaction. The less time he had to change his tactic, the better.

Alice lowered Akiko to the ground.

"You stay here," she said, hoping that the heap of automobile would protect them if the other side opened fire.

The whining SUV was about three hundred yards away now.

Alice grabbed her pistol and Akiko's from the floor of the Mitsubishi. She kept her own weapon but placed Akiko's gun and the two pistols from the dead men at her feet. Crouching, she leaned against the car, hoping the yakuza would assume she was in shock or unconscious. Her heart was drumming in her chest, its quick beats thudding in her ears.

Alice could tell by the sound that the SUV slowed down. But the driver didn't brake; he only downshifted. Alice had her back to them and hoped that the SUV would come close before the men climbed out. If it stopped two hundred or even a hundred yards away, she would be in a bad position. One pistol would have no chance against two submachine guns at that distance.

Alice closed her eyes and listened. The SUV slowed again but didn't stop. It was getting close. But how close?

With her left hand, Alice clasped the wrist of her right—her pistol hand. Then she turned.

The SUV was coming like a meteor through the darkness, its headlights blazing like the eyes of some prehistoric animal as it screamed. One blink, and then Alice opened fire. She emptied the magazine of the first pistol into the windshield above the lights. The weapon bucked and kicked in her hands, the barrel flashing in the night. Hopefully it wasn't bulletproof glass.

The monster swerved, but Alice didn't know whether she had hit the driver or if he was just avoiding debris in the road. She dropped the spent pistol and picked up another. The SUV had almost reached them when it accelerated, and Alice realized the driver had decided to drive past. Or maybe he was injured and his leg was convulsed against the gas pedal. Alice shot three rounds through the front door and four through the back, then grabbed the third pistol and emptied it into the rear. At least some of the shots penetrated the back window.

The SUV ran off the road, and there was a loud crash. Alice picked up the last weapon and ran across the road. They still had two machine guns. Alice couldn't take any risks. She pulled the door open and emptied the clip of the fourth pistol into the rear and front seats.

Was this too much? she thought. Her heart was pounding so hard it felt like it was coming out of her ears.

Alice dropped the gun. She heard it clatter to the ground.

We survived, she thought. *I nailed you bastards. All of you.*

Alice slumped to her knees, a vast feeling of relief washing through her. All the extra adrenaline was suddenly gone, and the strength drained from her limbs like water from a bathtub. Tears burned her eyes and started dripping onto her hands.

Alice heard Akiko's steps behind her but didn't have the energy to react.

"I thought we were going to be fish food soon," Akiko said in a hushed voice.

Alice turned, wiping her face. She noticed that one of her own hands was covered in blood.

Akiko was holding her head. "Are you OK?" she asked Akiko.

"My neck hurts, but that's about all."

"I'm sorry."

"Don't be. Better mildly hurt than permanently dead."

"I think I scratched up your car a little," Alice said, suddenly feeling guilty. "Even though I promised I wouldn't."

"Don't worry about it," Akiko said. "It wasn't going to last much longer anyway," she said, laughing and sitting down next to Alice.

The wrecked heaps of metal creaked and sighed in the darkness, puncturing the otherwise perfectly quiet night. The smell of fuel running from the ruptured gas tanks was strong in the air.

Alice felt a delicate breeze on her cheek. Being alive was nice. That she could still feel the wind on her skin was nice. She looked up and saw the dazzling array of stars and the Milky Way, which was clearly visible so far from any major city.

"Do you know what?" Akiko asked, breaking the silence.

Alice didn't say anything.

"I always thought all the action in those American movies and TV shows was fiction," Akiko said nonchalantly. "But maybe not. Maybe where you come from it's really like it was here tonight."

4

"Mathematical Background and Programming Aids for the Physical Vulnerability System for Nuclear Weapons." "A Classification of Structures Based on Vulnerability to Blast from Atomic Bombs." "Rand Study on Redefining Basic Overpressure-Damage Curves."

Over the years Lauri had waded through hundreds of research reports on the estimated effects of nuclear bombs. American scientists had built whole artificial towns at nuclear test sites to understand the pressure effects of atomic explosions and to estimate the damage the shock waves of variously sized explosions would do to buildings and other structures.

The houses in the test area had been built out of stone and metal. Inside them there was nothing flammable—no paper, no wood, no plastic, no gas. Even the window shades were made of metal.

Scientists had carefully measured down to the millimeter how far a nail would penetrate a board under the pressure of the shock wave at one mile, two miles, and five miles away from a nuclear detonation. The results were carefully recorded, and the understanding of the effects of nuclear bombs increased with each test.

Of course in order for the studies to produce scientifically conclusive results, the models had to be made as simple as possible. Ambiguous results were not an option.

The conference room was small and spare. Plain concrete walls and a large map of the United States. No paintings or other works of art. The only furniture was a desk, a few chairs, and bookshelves. On top of the room were two hundred feet of custom-built reinforced concrete and then the Pentagon.

Only five people were present. A woman of about sixty, with gray hair, sat behind the desk. She radiated authority and political charisma, which was no wonder since she was the president of the United States of America. However much US influence might have waned in recent years, this was still the most powerful person on the planet.

Kenneth Andrews and Lauri Nurmi sat in simple armchairs opposite the president. On either side of the door stood a large stony-faced Secret Service agent. Outside were more armed guards.

The president placed the last memo on the desk. Taking off her glasses, she folded them and laid them on top of the memo. Her movements were emphatically slow, seemingly intended to give the president a few extra seconds to think. Then she turned to Andrews.

"So, based on these memos, you believe that the terrorists have in their possession a small amount of highly enriched plutonium and six tons of lithium-6."

"Exactly," said Andrews.

"In other words, they could build one or more very large nuclear bombs?"

"Yes, Madam President."

"If they really used these against us, what would be the worst-case scenario?"

Lauri looked at Andrews. They had agreed that Andrews would do most of the talking. If he wanted Lauri to respond, he would signal him.

Lithium-6

"The worst-case scenario . . ." Andrews began, but stopped himself midsentence. "No, we need to back up before we go there."

The president nodded. "Very well, Colonel Andrews. Where do we begin then?"

Andrews blinked toward Lauri, in the way they had agreed.

"Let's assume they can build a nuclear device the size of Tsar Bomba," Lauri began. "If they detonate it in an airplane at a high enough altitude in the middle of the Atlantic Ocean . . ."

The president looked at Lauri narrowly, and he shut his mouth. The president turned to Andrews.

"The electromagnetic pulse would fry every computer and sensitive electronic device in North America and Europe?" the president asked.

"Unfortunately, yes," said Andrews. "Electronics are everywhere, so everything would stop working. Water systems, heating, cooling, cars, trains, airplanes, hospital equipment, phones, computers, Internet, radio, and television. Low-orbit satellites."

"How high would they have to get?" She picked up one of the memos again and scanned through it. "It was in here somewhere."

"Twelve to fifteen miles would be enough to do a lot of damage."

"Is that possible?" asked the president. "With a normal jet? Without rocket motors?"

"Yes, if they build enough speed and fly straight up. At some point the engines would stall and the plane would start falling, but if it's a suicide attack . . . And installing rockets on the wings of a plane isn't actually all that complicated. Plenty of amateurs have done it."

The president looked thoughtful. She pursed her lips.

"If they already have a nuclear bomb, what can we do to prevent this sort of attack?"

"Nothing," Andrews replied. "Unless we find them."

"I see," the president said quietly.

There was a knock on the door. The Secret Service agents stiffened, and one opened the door. A young woman came in pushing a cart with coffee and baskets of sandwiches and pastries. As soon as she'd placed the food and coffee on the desk and left the room, they resumed the conversation.

"We're actually much more worried that they'll load the bomb in a cargo freighter and sail it into a harbor in New York or Los Angeles," Lauri said.

"And inspecting every incoming shipping container is impossible," the president said. "Isn't it?"

When J. Robert Oppenheimer was asked whether malicious people could smuggle an atomic bomb into New York, Oppenheimer responded that it was absolutely possible and that a small group of people could destroy a whole city with a nuclear device. When Oppenheimer was questioned about how to prevent this kind of catastrophe, he simply said: "With a screwdriver." Of course, in practice the problem was much more complicated than that.

Fifty thousand shipping containers entered the United States each day. That was an average of 140 ships, 6,500 train cars, and 30,000 semitrailers. Every day. Government officers could inspect only a small fraction, less than 10 percent. Many containers were filled with smaller boxes. If they were lined with the right materials, it was very difficult to see what was inside them. Inspecting every container would require a massive amount of man power. In addition, there were the borders with Canada and Mexico, as well as the coastline. Constant monitoring of every foot of shore was impossible, and inspecting every piece of cargo would clog the ports to such an extent that world trade would come to a standstill.

"If the bomb is very large, it will have to be on a ship. That's the only option," Andrews said. "We have some evidence that the terrorists are trying to build a bomb in the hold of a ship, which is significantly larger than a shipping container. We are requesting permission to inspect any suspicious freighters while they're still at sea."

Lithium-6

"Why not in port?" asked the president. "That would be an easier solution politically and diplomatically."

Lauri served himself a Danish and then passed the pastry basket to Andrews.

"If they have a big enough bomb, they don't have to get through customs," Lauri said. "For fifty years the Nuclear Security Administration thought about nuclear bombs as if they were just abnormally large conventional bombs that mostly broke things with pressure effects. But the pressure effect isn't a terribly important aspect of nuclear bombs when you get right down to it."

The president sipped her coffee. She looked skeptical.

"I've always understood it the other way," she said. "The shock wave of a nuclear explosion can obliterate a skyscraper like a house of cards."

"True, but the firestorm always destroys a much larger area," Andrews said, backing Lauri up. "Any area exposed to more than ten calories per square centimeter bursts into flames. Curtains burn, plastics burn, books burn. A nuclear bomb creates a firestorm that can be twenty-five times larger than the area hit by the shock wave."

Lauri and Andrews both knew that with very large bombs the difference could be even more dramatic. The pressure of the explosion always discharged in a three-dimensional space. It dissipated quickly, more or less with the cubic root of the distance. However, more than half of the energy of a nuclear bomb was released as electromagnetic and thermal radiation. The radiation only stopped when it hit a surface that could block it. The strength of the radiation dissipated with the square root of the distance, much more slowly than the strength of the pressure wave.

"Wait a second," said the president. "Did I understand correctly? Are you trying to tell me that if they have a big enough bomb, they can detonate it out at sea and still burn Manhattan to the ground?"

The fingers of her left hand drummed the surface of the desk in an impatient staccato.

"Yes, Madam President, you understood correctly," said Andrews.

"How big a bomb would they need?"

Andrews signaled to Lauri to explain.

"The bigger the bomb, the farther out they could set it off," said Lauri. "If they get the bomb into the harbor, they only need one the size of the Hiroshima device. That would destroy all of Manhattan."

With a quick motion the president rubbed her temples, a gesture that was familiar from her television appearances.

"But that can't be true," said the president. "At least that isn't what I've been told. The Hiroshima bomb would only destroy a small part of Manhattan."

"With all due respect, Madam President, the old models left out the effects of the firestorm. They only focused on the shock wave."

"You're telling me we've used six trillion dollars on nuclear weapons and related research and development, more than we've ever spent on health care and education combined, and we still don't understand their effects? Come on, give me a break!"

"When enough fires start in a given area, it creates an extremely strong updraft," Andrews said. "This starts sucking new air in from the periphery. If the updraft created by the fires is powerful enough, the wind blowing in toward the center can reach hurricane force. That feeds the fires, which feed the wind. The result is even more fires, spreading uncontrollably. The whole area turns to a lake of fire where no one can survive."

"And this is what wasn't taken into consideration in our models?"

"Correct," said Lauri. "They just focus on the pressure effects."

"Why?" asked the president.

"That's a long story," said Lauri. "But organizations have a bad habit of focusing on doing what they already know how to do."

The president poured herself more coffee, without saying anything. Lauri and Andrews understood that she needed a moment to digest what she had heard. They waited.

There were firestorms in Dresden and Hamburg. Hiroshima was destroyed by a firestorm, as was Nagasaki. But we only see what we want to see.

"So the casualties would be much higher than a few hundred thousand," the president said after a full minute. "Even if the explosion wasn't any larger than Hiroshima?"

"The fire load per square meter of modern cities is significantly higher than during the Second World War," Lauri said. "The buildings are taller and there are enormous amounts of hydrocarbons everywhere—in plastics and asphalt and transportation fuel and natural gas. The fires would be much hotter, so the wind would blow much stronger."

"How strong could the wind be?" asked the president.

"The Dresden and Hiroshima firestorms caused winds of at least one hundred miles per hour," said Lauri.

"If a bomb the size of Hiroshima was detonated in Manhattan, the latest models suggest the winds could reach more than three hundred and fifty miles per hour. If the bomb is bigger . . . I don't know."

"What are winds that strong capable of?" asked the president.

"A very powerful hurricane with winds of a hundred and fifty miles per hour creates a pressure equal to the weight of three hundred pounds per square foot," explained Lauri. "That's more than enough to pick up a person. It can tear off roofs and collapse normal walls."

"Why am I only hearing about this now?" asked the president.

"A superhurricane with winds of three hundred and fifty miles per hour would be five times more powerful," Lauri continued. "Well beyond the design specifications of any skyscraper. In fact, I think it would break them off at the base using the whole building as a big lever."

The president blinked quickly, but otherwise her face remained perfectly impassive.

"An F5 tornado sometimes causes winds of three hundred miles per hour," Lauri added. "That's enough to shoot a piece of straw through a tree. And the human body is much softer than the trunk of a tree."

The president shook her head. Lauri could see she was still having a hard time believing everything she was hearing. But the president's cool composure did not break, despite all the bad news she had heard. A considerable feat, thought Lauri. But a person had to go through quite a meat grinder before becoming the leader of the greatest military power in the world.

"How wide an area would winds like that cover?" asked the president.

"We don't have any good models," said Andrews. "But hurricane-force winds would definitely affect an area ten or twenty times larger than the firestorm."

The president shook her head.

"Do the two of you have any more good news, or is that all?" she asked, a sarcastic smile flitting across her face. Suddenly she seemed very tired, and to Lauri she looked much older now than she had half an hour earlier. Lauri and Andrews exchanged a quick glance. The president noticed it.

"Let me have it," she said. "What haven't you told me yet? Out with it."

"Not much," Andrews said evasively, "except that . . . we don't have a clue what would happen next."

5

Alice Donovan shivered under a blanket and watched the lights of the police cars and ambulances flash. Her forehead stung, and when she touched it, she came away with some blood on her hand. She hadn't noticed a wound there until now, but it couldn't be too deep since blood wasn't reaching her eyes. Her hand stung too, but the pain reminded her that she was still alive. The police walked by, carrying a large plastic bag with a zipper closure. Alice knew all too well what was in it.

"Here," said Akiko, handing her a large cup of delicious-smelling hot tea. "Drink this. It will help you feel better."

"Thank you," Alice said.

Sipping from the cup, she instantly burned her tongue. How did they have such hot drinks so far out here? Alice looked at the bags that had been carried to the ambulances.

"I think I overdid it a little," she said regretfully.

"Maybe you didn't have any options," said Akiko.

"What do you think? Am I going to be in trouble?" Alice asked.

Akiko shook her head. "No. They intended to kill us. I'm sure of it. I don't understand why, but they were taking us for execution."

"That's what I thought too."

"And besides, you're the official representative of a foreign country and an armed kidnapping was perpetrated against you, which is a serious enough crime in itself."

For a moment Akiko went silent and pursed her lips.

"Although you didn't exactly do anything for our annual statistics," she said. "We normally have fewer than twenty people killed each year by firearms in Japan. You may have just made a forty percent increase in this year's total."

Alice sighed. She wasn't doing a very good job of keeping a low profile.

"Do you know who they are?" Alice asked. "Or were? Or . . . did any of them survive?"

"Three are still hanging on, but one of them doesn't really have a chance. The other two aren't in particularly good shape either. You really did a number on them. But they are definitely Red Dragon members. And one of them belongs to the fingerprints we found in the truck and on the Yoshikawa Corporation surveillance equipment."

"Which one?"

"He was in the SUV. You shot him."

"There were four or five of them in the SUV. I didn't have time to tell them apart."

Alice sipped her tea and tried to clear her thoughts. Why had they been attacked? Why did someone want them out of the way?

"We've both been investigating this case for weeks," Akiko pointed out.

Alice saw that Akiko's thoughts were running along the same lines as her own.

"They haven't done anything like this before," Akiko said. "So why now? We must have discovered something new, something they see as especially threatening. So dangerous that even the murder of an American agent seemed like an acceptable risk."

"Yes, it must be something new," Alice said. "Something we just barely figured out. And then it also has to be something they believe they can solve by killing us. You and me specifically."

"Which means it has to be something we said or did together. Something the others don't know about yet . . . Damn it, they must have been listening to us," Akiko said.

"Probably," Alice said. "But even if they had heard every word we said, I still don't understand. What the hell are we supposed to have figured out? All we've been doing is groping around in the dark."

Alice tried to remember everything they had talked about.

"It has to be something we haven't realized is important yet," Alice said.

"We need to go back in time and think about everything we've talked about," Akiko said. "We have to reconstruct our conversations as precisely as possible, word for word."

Then she grinned mischievously.

"The yakuza might have tapes of our conversations. I wonder if they'd lend them to us if we asked nicely."

6

Julia Noruz stood on the balcony smoking her umpteenth cigarette of the day. Lauri and Alice were right, she thought glumly.

I should quit. Or at least smoke less. How many times have I given it up already today? On the plus side, smoking doesn't have anything to do with radioactivity. Because it's clear now that . . .

. . . that . . .

. . . because it was unthinkable that . . .

And then the pieces clicked into place. In a split second the jagged, formless mass of junk organized itself into an astonishingly coherent pattern. It became a smooth, shiny spherical surface with neither seam nor edge.

Julia felt dizzy, and for safety she took hold of the balcony railing.

"Are you feeling alright?" asked Robertson from the doorway. Julia waved her hand at him impatiently.

"Is everything OK?" he asked again.

"Hush, I'm fine. I just need to think."

Could that be right? Julia thought feverishly. No, it couldn't be. There was no way.

But on the other hand . . . it would explain everything. Patterns this beautiful usually aren't random. Actually, she didn't think they were ever random. Not when so many apparently unconnected, unpleasant pieces suddenly decide to fit together. Without the slightest hint of respect for the old paradigms.

Julia walked back to her desk as if in a dream.

"Julia?"

She heard David Farley's voice from somewhere far away.

South Asians had been smoking their damned beedies for centuries. Maybe longer. Some people smoked them constantly. And what about marijuana and hash? Or opium? People hooked on hash or opium usually didn't do much of anything but sit around and smoke. They were much more strung out on their garbage than she was on nicotine.

And what about wood and dung smoke from fires? In houses where people cook their food over wood but don't have a chimney or even a window open during the monsoon season? The fine particle exposure must have been unimaginably high, thousands of times higher than that of people in wealthy industrialized countries.

If all of that is true, how could it be possible, even in theory that . . . ?

Julia went through every link in her chain of logic again. Every one of them held. God, this had to be it.

Certain human tissues, such as the skin but also to a lesser degree the entire digestive system, could withstand small doses of radioactivity without any problems. Gamma radiation wasn't dangerous to the skin unless there was a lot of it. Really a lot of it. Skin tissues didn't even notice alpha particle bombardment. Radioactive material that entered the body with food and water usually wasn't any more dangerous than the radiation the skin encountered. It didn't absorb into the body very well, so whatever went into the stomach through the mouth generally exited the body within a few hours, a couple of days at most.

That was the only way to explain the contradictory observations. The cancer epidemics in southern Iraq and the effects of Chernobyl. The catch was that the becquerel levels measured in certain areas shouldn't correlate with morbidity. Actually, in most cases, the correlation should have been negative.

We have misunderstood everything, thought Julia. Because if we turn our assumptions upside down and look at the picture the other way, then . . .

"Julia?" Farley asked for at least the third time, now much more loudly and indignantly.

Julia turned to look at him.

"Jablokov is right," she blurted out.

"Excuse me?" Farley asked.

"Jablokov is right," Julia repeated.

Farley shook his head.

"I'll bite. What's the punch line? And who is Jablokov?"

"There isn't one. I'm not telling a joke. Jablokov is a Russian scientist who thinks atmospheric bomb tests caused a worldwide spike in cancer."

"Sounds like bullshit," Farley said. "Where's Andrews?"

Then Julia noticed that Farley seemed strange somehow. He was breathing more heavily than normal, and his face had a strangely frightened, almost spooked expression. Normally Farley was cool and controlled, pointedly steady. Julia had never seen him so on edge. And beyond that, this was the first time she had ever heard Farley use bad language. Decorum was his rule.

"Kenneth is meeting with the president," Julia said. "With Lauri."

"The president of the United States?"

"Yeah."

"That's pretty shitty timing."

Uh-oh, there was number two, thought Julia. They must really be up the creek.

"They absolutely have to hear what I just found out," said Farley. "Before they decide anything."

"I'm sure it can wait a while. I doubt they're taking any phone calls right now."

"No, goddamn it! We have to try at least."

"What's wrong with you, Dave?" Julia asked. "Are you OK?"

"No, no, I'm not. Hassan Yussuf . . . told more."

"Let me hear it," Julia said.

"Do you remember those pictures of the big metal cylinder?"

"Yeah?"

"We were right. They've been building a bomb in the hold of a ship."

"Yeah, we did guess that much."

Except she had never quite believed it. Apparently now she was going to have to learn to accept that she could be wrong.

"But that isn't all," Farley continued. "Yussuf said the bomb is already built. He doesn't know where it is, and he doesn't know the name of the ship."

"What else did he say?" Julia said, interrupting.

"He said the bomb is already on its way."

"Damn it, no!"

"But the worst thing is what Yussuf told them next. He said they have three men stationed at the trigger and that on top of the bomb they've loaded . . ."

7

The president of the United States of America stared at Lauri and Andrews, impatient for an explanation.

"The hurricane wind caused by the firestorm blows the flames inward," Lauri began. "But if the fire loading is large enough, the fire can also grow outward. That is if the thermal radiation is enough to ignite the surroundings even though the wind is blowing inward. Wind can't stop infrared radiation."

The president shook her head in disbelief.

"What is your projection?" she asked Andrews.

"We can't say anything certain, Madam President," Andrews replied, not meeting her eyes. "This has never been studied."

"How is it possible this hasn't ever been studied?"

"Large forest fires can have one hundred and fifty thousand kilowatts of thermal energy per meter of flame front," Lauri continued. "Nothing but a heavy rain can put out a fire like that."

"And in a large city?"

"Well, what would it be? A few hundred thousand, maybe a million kilowatts per meter," Lauri said. "Probably not much more than that. But the fire could only spread out as long as the fire loading was sufficient. When the population density dropped off, propagation of the fire would probably slow. Then it would stop. So it couldn't spread indefinitely."

The president walked to the large map on the wall and stared at it. She moved her index finger across the large population centers and their environs. Lauri guessed she was remembering what each place looked like and thinking about what each place's fire loading might be. She would have traveled the country extensively during her election campaign.

"Does it seem that we overdid it a bit during the Cold War?" the president asked. "That we didn't need to build quite so many thousands of nuclear weapons?"

"You could say that, Madam President," Lauri said.

Andrews raised his hand for a chance to interject.

"Is there something more?" the president asked. She didn't turn her gaze away from the map.

"As I said, these large fires are a little difficult to model," Andrews began.

The president moved her finger from San Francisco to Oakland, from there to Berkeley, and on to Concord and Stockton.

"Yes?" the president said absentmindedly.

"We are able to model what we call the firebrand effect in the actual firestorm area," said Andrews. "Various burning objects flying through the air greatly increase the speed of the fire's spread in this area. But we can't predict events in the area surrounding the firestorm. Hurricane-force winds would sweep over very large areas. Buildings would fall, gas lines would rupture. Cars and motorcycles would fly through the air and strike other hard objects, rupturing their gas tanks and dumping out gasoline."

The president moved her finger to the other side of the country. Now she started at Boston and traveled to Providence, then Worcester.

"There would be a lot of metal in the air, plus a large amount of sand, dust, and dirt," Andrews continued. "But it won't rain. The wind will be dry and hot. So static electricity will also be a factor to take into consideration but which, I fear, hasn't been so far. Wind blowing at that speed produces a lot of frictional electricity. It electrifies everything."

Springfield. Hartford. Waterbury.

"If there are a lot of gas leaks and spills, there could be a large number of secondary fires in the hurricane wind area," Andrews said. "Thousands, tens of thousands, finally millions. Even in the Sahara sandstorms create enough static electricity to ignite gasoline if you try to fill your tank in a strong wind."

Bridgeport. Stamford. New York.

As a few drops of sweat appeared on the president's forehead, Lauri realized her composure was beginning to fracture.

"Of course the winds would also blow a lot of the fires out. But if they got going, as natural gas or gasoline or hydrogen fires easily would, then the oxygen brought by the wind would start feeding the fire at some point. At least when the wind died down a little."

Trenton. Philadelphia. Baltimore. Washington, DC.

"We don't really know how this would go. That hasn't been studied either."

Richmond. Hampton.

The president lifted her finger from the map and turned to Andrews. "Ah," she said, and sighed before turning back to the map.

"Hiroshima and Nagasaki had very low fire loadings," Andrews said. "The buildings were one story and partially constructed of paper. There were no plastics and almost no cars."

The president looked increasingly tired. She had heard a lot, and Lauri was beginning to pity her. Nevertheless, there was more she should know.

"Madam President?" Lauri asked.

"Yes?"

Lithium-6

"Well . . . do you want to hear the very worst-case scenario given this theory? Even though it probably doesn't have any real chance of happening?"

8

For Julia Noruz, the situation was strangely unreal. Believing that all of it was really happening was difficult. For a moment she gazed out at the thin strip of blue sky visible through the window. There was a single white fluffy cloud. She would have liked to watch its leisurely, peaceful trek over their city, which throbbed with haste and stress.

"David, that can't be true," Julia objected.

Julia wondered why her own voice was echoing so strangely in her ears—as if it was coming from somewhere very distant. She knew that she must have heard Farley's words correctly. Farley had enunciated them clearly and slowly enough that there wasn't actually any room for misinterpretation. Still Julia asked Farley to repeat his sentence, hoping against all hope that she had somehow misunderstood and that Farley hadn't really said what Julia knew he had.

Because when something bad was happening, something too bad to contemplate, it was preferable to put it off. Even just for a moment. Sometimes a few seconds felt like such a long time that it was worth trying. Because with good luck maybe, just maybe, everything would turn around. The chance was small, but it might be greater than zero.

"Yussuf said that . . ."

Lithium-6

This was it, Julia thought.

". . . they've loaded . . . twelve thousand tons of uranium on top of the bomb."

Julia closed her eyes for a second. She knew that lithium-6 had many interesting applications. But this was probably the single most unpleasant.

"Boss?" Farley asked. "Are you still here?"

You couldn't build a very large nuclear bomb out of plutonium-239 or uranium-235. Physics set limits on its size. If the amount was too large, it just set itself on fire. Or exploded.

"He also said that the ship is already on its way," said Farley.

"But you didn't get the name of the ship?" Julia asked.

If you had enough lithium-6 at your disposal, there wasn't any theoretical upper limit to the size of the bomb anymore. In principle you could collect all the uranium on the planet into one enormous nuclear bomb.

"No," Farley said. "Yussuf said he doesn't know it, and he probably doesn't. As you know, he doesn't exactly . . . look human anymore. So I think he's gotten to the point where he's told us everything he can."

If a few dozen grams of plutonium were compressed using a conventional explosive inside a mixture of lithium-6 and deuterium, at first, within the initial microsecond, the result was a very small nuclear explosion. A little heat, but nothing more than what a thousand kilograms of conventional explosive would produce. Plus some neutrons.

"There was one more important thing Yussuf said," Farley continued.

But when the neutrons hit the lithium-6 atoms, many different atomic reactions ensued.

"If anyone attacks the ship, apparently they can detonate the bomb at a second's notice," Farley said.

Each reaction released a lot of energy.

"Yussuf said that in the hold there are three men near the trigger," Farley continued.

Lithium-6 split, forming tritium.

"So if we intend to do something, we have to do it very carefully."

Tritium and deuterium fused.

"Otherwise they'll have time to set off the bomb."

Deuterium fused with other deuterium.

"At least then it wouldn't explode in a harbor," Julia said.

When the lithium-6 split, energy was released.

Farley shook his head and barked, "Who are you kidding, Julia."

When the tritium fused with deuterium, energy was released.

"You know as well as I do it doesn't make a fly shit's bit of difference in this case . . ."

When the deuterium fused with other deuterium, energy was released.

". . . where the bomb explodes," Farley ranted.

With each microsecond reaction more neutrons were released. Lots and lots of neutrons.

"We're all already dead," screamed Farley.

9

The president suddenly looked ten years older. Lauri felt sure she hoped he would stop, but he also knew that they needed to continue this conversation. There wouldn't necessarily be another chance like this. Ever.

"The very worst scenario is that the terrorists hijack a ship carrying natural uranium or depleted uranium and detonate a bomb containing lithium deuteride in its hold," Lauri said.

"Why would that be the worst possibility?" the president asked. "How could anything be worse than what you've already told me?"

"It would be the most unpleasant scenario because with a mixture of lithium-6 or lithium and deuterium it's also possible to detonate common uranium-238," said Lauri.

"Excuse me?"

"Lithium-6 makes it possible to create an enormous nuclear bomb out of perfectly normal unenriched uranium dug out of the ground," Lauri continued. "Or out of depleted uranium, which we sell as uranium-tipped projectiles to basically anyone who wants to buy them. Because for us it's just mildly radioactive hazardous waste."

"But uranium-238 can't explode," exclaimed the president.

Was it possible she really didn't know? Of course all the public information always said that uranium-238 couldn't be used for making nuclear weapons. But shouldn't the president of the United States know the truth?

"You can't have real chain reactions in uranium-238," Andrews said, taking Lauri's explanation further. "When a uranium-238 atom splits, the neutrons released aren't able to split other nuclei anymore. But if a large amount of lithium-6 and deuterium is detonated within a jacket of uranium-238, the initial neutron release is so massive that a relatively large portion of the uranium-238 nuclei split and release energy."

"Really?" asked the president. "Are you absolutely sure?"

"The largest nuclear weapons built during the Cold War were three-stage devices," Andrews replied. "Fission-fusion-fission bombs. Hydrogen-uranium bombs. Like Castle Bravo. A small plutonium-239 or uranium-235 trigger. Then lithium deuteride, and around it a massive natural uranium jacket. In the same way, you could make a much larger bomb, at least in theory."

"Let's assume that the ship's hold has ten thousand tons of yellowcake," Lauri said. "That's just natural, unenriched uranium that's been prepared for processing. Uranium shipments are pretty big nowadays since they've been concentrated to give terrorists fewer chances to get at them. If the terrorists detonated a large hydrogen-uranium bomb with a few tons of deuterium and lithium-6 in the hold of a ship like that, a significant percentage of the uranium nuclei in the yellowcake could split."

"How large a percentage?" the president asked.

"I wouldn't want to guess," Lauri said. "We don't have any good models. And they wouldn't be terribly accurate anyway. But it would definitely be the largest nuclear explosion ever seen. If the explosion happened near shore, it would instantly ignite a large area. More importantly though, it would produce radioactive fallout across the entire continent."

The president's eyes moved to the map again. "The fallout would cover most of the United States. That's what you're saying?"

"Yes," said Lauri.

"How many people would die?"

"What's our population right now?" Lauri asked. "About three hundred and fifteen million, plus illegal immigrants. Some of the fallout would reach as far as Eurasia. And not everyone would survive there either. I suppose the total deaths could reach well past half a billion."

"Don't play with me!" snapped the president.

"I wouldn't dream of it, Madam President," Lauri assured her. "The fallout from a hydrogen-uranium bomb is always extremely lethal because there is so much uranium-237 in it, especially if a lot of the fallout spreads into the lower atmosphere instead of rising high enough for the uranium-237 to decay before living creatures inhale the particles. We're talking about an unusually dirty, unusually large nuclear bomb. A little like if someone were to detonate ten thousand Castle Bravos at the same time."

"Of course this scenario is highly theoretical," Andrews quickly pointed out. "The terrorists would have to get their hands on a large shipment of uranium. They would have to hijack a freighter coming from Australia, Canada, Namibia, or the Congo without anyone noticing. And they would have to be able to move their own bomb into the hold, to the middle of the yellowcake. We can definitely prevent any strikes like that. Easily."

"I hope so," said the president. "I really hope so." The president went to her desk again and sat down. She poured her third cup of coffee.

"I always thought it was enough if we were able to control all the weapons-grade uranium," she said.

Lauri watched as the president began loading her cup with sugar again. Four cubes and a splash of milk.

"If we really want to be safe, we would also have to prevent uranium ore from being processed into yellowcake," said Lauri. "Once the ore has been concentrated into pure uranium, the damage is already done. If we only focus on preventing our opponents from changing the ratios of the uranium isotopes, we make things a little more difficult for the terrorists. But not that much more difficult."

"And the nuclear power plants?" asked the president.

"With all due respect, we should just forget them, Madam President," said Lauri.

"Forget nuclear power plants?"

Opening the top drawer of her desk, the president took out a copy of the previous day's *New York Times* and spread it out.

"And what about this?" the president asked angrily. "RONNE ICE SHELF THREATENS TO BREAK APART," screamed the banner headline.

The subtitle read: "West Antarctic Ice Sheet in Danger."

"This is a bad thing too, isn't it?" demanded the president.

10

Julia struggled against the panic welling inside of her. She had to think clearly. But a voice inside her head drummed—*Game Over Game Over Game Over*—with the certainty that—*Game Over Game Over Game Over*—they had already lost, that all hope was gone, that this time they couldn't do anything—*Game Over Game Over Game Over*. That now things would just drift inexorably toward the tragic final act. *Do something!* Julia silently screamed at herself. *Get a grip!*

"OK, first we have to find the ship," she said. She was surprised how calm and collected she suddenly sounded. "Then we can start thinking about how to attack it," she added.

"Attacking it won't be easy," Farley pointed out. "Assuming Yussuf was telling the truth."

"We'll worry about that next," Julia said. "First we have to find that ship and get satellite imagery of it. That shouldn't be too hard."

"You think so?"

"There aren't that many yellowcake shipments. First it has to go somewhere that makes fuel for our power plants. And besides, it's coming from the west, so Namibia and the Congo are off the table. Canada is also out. So it's most likely coming from Australia. Or are there other possibilities?"

"You might be right," Farley admitted.

Julia was already sitting at her computer, her fingers flying across the keyboard.

"Actually, here it is," she said, motioning for Farley to look. "The MS *Bristol* out of Australia."

"That was fast," Farley said. "Are you sure?"

"Now that we know what to look for, it's simple. According to this, the *Bristol* is loaded with . . . eleven thousand tons of yellowcake."

Farley whistled. "It has to be that same ship."

Julia nodded. "I think so too. But let's check in case there's another big shipment of uranium coming in from somewhere else. By some other route, I mean."

Julia opened some new files and quickly scanned them.

"No . . . there isn't anything else like this moving now. Anywhere. Not even on the Atlantic side. The *Bristol* has to be our ship."

"That was amazing," Farley said. "How did you find it so fast?"

"That's not hard to do. Next we have to find out where that boat is right now. We need to know how much time we have left."

Opening an online service for tracking ship movements, she typed in the ship's name.

A satellite image of the *Bristol* quickly appeared. It was small for an ocean freighter, but still well over four hundred feet long. A large command bridge sat astern. On the foredeck there were two long rows of steel containers set so close together they were nearly touching. Where they ended on the bow side, there were hatches leading into the hold, and between the hatches and the bow there were four smaller containers.

A moment later the rest of the information Julia had requested also began flashing onto the screen. Julia looked at it, not understanding what she was seeing.

Then she realized what part of the world the map represented, but she didn't want to believe it was true.

"Well, what?" Farley asked.

"The *Bristol* passed Hawaii the day before yesterday. It's already approaching Los Angeles."

Julia and Farley heard the door open behind them. Alice Donovan walked in. Both of her hands were wrapped in bandages, her nose was mildly burned, and there was also a wide white wrap around her forehead.

"Don't ask," Alice said. "I'll tell you once I catch my breath."

"Must have been a rough job," Julia said needlessly.

"You could say that."

"Want to go on another one?" Farley asked.

"Not particularly," said Alice.

11

Alice and Lauri lay in the darkness of the hot night, wet with sweat. Lauri had his leg wrapped around Alice and squeezed tight against her.

It was four in the morning. They had only arrived home an hour earlier, tired and hopeless, because even though they had spent hours reviewing ways to attack the *Bristol*, none of them had felt satisfactory. In every scenario they came up with, the terrorists always had time to detonate the gigantic hydrogen-uranium bomb in the hold of the ship.

Every exercise had ended the same way, leaving the entire continent of North America under a cloud of lethal radioactive fallout. Within a few hours a narrower tongue of the death cloud reached Europe.

Finally they had decided to give up for the day, or, more accurately, for the night, even though they knew they didn't have any time to spare. Every hour brought the *Bristol* inexorably closer to Los Angeles. They would have to think of a new approach and make their move soon.

Lauri knew that he had to get at least a few hours of sleep, but he didn't believe he would be able to. Alice was awake too. If they didn't find some way to stop the terrorists in the next couple of days, the *Bristol* would seed the skies over North America with thousands of tons of uranium-237.

Lauri glanced at Alice. He noticed a familiar expression on her face, one of extreme concentration. He knew that she was about to make some sort of breakthrough, or already had, so he remained quiet.

In her mind's eye, Alice was traveling in a helicopter above the permafrost of Western Siberia, with thousands of meltwater lakes sliding past below. She remembered how Russian oceanographers had taken her close to the North Pole on a massive icebreaker ship. They had gone to see how far the floating ice pack of the Arctic Ocean had already receded from the Siberian shore. She remembered how the icebreaker had suddenly received a distress call from a fishing vessel whose side had been ripped open by a completely submersed and nearly transparent block of ice. The ship was one of many fishing vessels unsuited to the environment, which the melting of the ice pack had lured to the area. By the time they reached the fishing boat, it had already been half sunk, and the fishermen in their rescue suits frantically waved at them from the stern.

Why had her subconscious brought it to the surface right now? The answer lit up like a neon sign the instant Alice asked herself the question.

Of course, thought Alice. Why wouldn't we do the same?

Even in the dark, Lauri could see Alice's eyes were shining with excitement.

"What now?"

"You aren't going to like this," Alice warned. Then she explained her idea.

"That could work," said Lauri, with some reluctance. "At least it's the best idea anyone has suggested so far. But who would we send to do it?"

Alice didn't respond. Lauri's expression was one of disbelief.

"No, Alice. No way. Not in a million years. You just almost died in Japan."

Alice still didn't say anything.

"Don't even try," said Lauri. "Someone else will have to go."

"OK, fine," Alice said. "But let's get started on the plan."

Lauri had to suppress a slight feeling of discomfort. It wasn't like Alice to give up so easily.

12

"Still nothing," Lauri huffed impatiently.

He lowered himself from the listing, half-submerged sailboat and swam to the other side to climb into their tiny life raft next to Alice.

"We just have to wait," Alice said calmly.

Alice was wearing a small, bright red bikini, and Lauri had on swim trunks. They had to look as harmless and as badly sunburned as possible so they could pass as credible castaways. At this rate, though, they would end up a little too credible. Lauri thought they were starting to look like boiled lobsters. And if they burned really badly, there'd be no getting out of bed without morphine.

Despite the fact that they had spent some of their time protected from the rays of the sun under the sail that hung slack, half on the boat and half in the water, they had still received a hefty dose of ultraviolet radiation.

"And what if they don't stop?" Lauri asked Alice.

"Oh, they'll stop," Alice said. "They don't want to seem suspicious."

"But what if they don't."

"Well, then we'll have to come up with something else."

Lauri suddenly felt a deep tenderness toward Alice. Looking at Alice's face, he regretted every fight and disagreement he had caused at home over the previous months. He would make it all up to her and would stop being so selfish and only dwelling on his own bad moods. Or whatever he thought Alice was doing wrong. Or what he thought was missing from their relationship. He would do his best so Alice would be happy. He would focus on listening to her hopes and dreams. He would go all-in like he should have done years ago.

"What?" Alice asked. "Why do you look so lovey-dovey?"

He just shook his head and smiled back at her.

Lauri's gaze fell on Alice's shoulders, slid across her breasts, and then down along the curve of her hips. With his eyes he caressed Alice's body, which right now was strangely blotchy with the purposefully acquired sunburns. On her forehead was a long red cut, which, only a few days after the run-in with the yakuza, was healing surprisingly quickly.

Lauri admired the hollows of Alice's knees, and he marveled at her graceful fingers and the exceptionally elegant shape of her hands. At the same time he was afraid, because he knew all too well how quickly that physical splendor could be destroyed, how easily the body of a young, vigorous woman could be turned into nothing more than rotting meat.

But he also knew very well how surprisingly strong this particular body was and what it was capable of when necessary. In Afghanistan and Iraq and Chad and many other places, Alice had shown time after time what a deadly, ruthless opponent she could be. Lauri had heard what Alice had just done to nine yakuza. But now, in his eyes, this same woman looked delicate, even fragile.

They would make it through this, Lauri assured himself.

In reality he wasn't nearly as sure as he wanted to be. Because according to the satellite pictures, the *Bristol* had at least eighteen armed men aboard. From the images, they had seen that most of them had at least a submachine gun, and some of them might have even more dangerous armaments. He and Alice didn't have any weapons with them since they were stuck in their tiny life raft, waiting for the cargo ship to get closer and pluck them out of the ocean.

Lauri didn't want to be there. But most of all he didn't want Alice there. He could accept it if something bad happened to him, but if Alice was harmed in some way, he would have a hard time forgiving himself for agreeing to this.

Of course Alice had volunteered as soon as the operation was approved. She steamrolled Andrews's objections in three seconds. Lauri was irritated that Alice hadn't talked the matter over with him, and that she was always so goddamn responsible and ambitious.

Lauri's irritation had passed, as it always did, and he volunteered as his "wife's sailing partner."

Three hours earlier a Coast Guard airplane had made radio contact with the *Bristol*, reporting a capsized sailboat with at least two survivors. The Coast Guard noted that the sailboat was more or less on the ship's route and requested that the *Bristol* rescue the castaways, because the plane was too low on fuel for a sea landing and takeoff. The captain of the MS *Bristol* responded in the affirmative.

And there they were. They had been dragged to their current location eleven hours earlier, as soon as the route plan of the *Bristol* became clear enough.

"I think I see smoke on the horizon," Alice said. "Should we fire the flares?"

"Wait a little while. We should pretend to be out of it enough that we don't see their smoke immediately."

The light gray trail of smoke and steam rising from the stacks of the *Bristol* grew larger.

"Now?" Alice asked.

"Go ahead."

Alice shot a flare high into the air. It exploded into a ball of red that then fell slowly.

"One more," Lauri said.

Alice shot another flare. This one was still burning when they saw the *Bristol*'s answer go up.

"Yippee, we're saved," Lauri said.

"Don't joke," Alice said. "We don't know what's coming."

"But at least we're going to make it onto the ship. Try to look as pathetic as possible. If you can squeeze out some tears too, that might help. They have to think we'd lost all hope and they just saved our lives."

"Should we get some more sun?"

"No, I think we're burned enough already. Let's just stay here by the sail until they get closer."

A moment later they saw the freighter on the horizon.

"It's coming straight toward us," Lauri said. "Here we go, little redskin."

"For the first time ever that name actually makes some sense," Alice replied. "My shoulders really sting."

Twenty minutes later the cargo ship was next to them. Lauri shaded his eyes with his hand and tried to see onto the deck. On the bridge he could make out a line of black silhouettes, and some of the men appeared to be armed. More armed men were situated on the main deck. Behind them were rust-brown, red, and gray containers fixed with heavy metal cables.

A breeches buoy began lowering from the ship. Along with it came a large man dressed in a wet suit. As soon as it reached the water, the man jumped in and swam toward the sailboat, towing a rope.

"Are you alright?" asked the man in a thick Australian accent.

Goddamn traitors, thought Lauri, but he didn't let what was going through his mind show on the outside. *How much did they pay you? Or do you even know what you're mixed up in?*

"Thank God you came!" Alice cried.

Her tears were convincing. *Nice acting,* thought Lauri.

Ten minutes later Lauri and Alice stood on the deck of the *Bristol*. The captain came to shake their hands.

"Captain Marcus Hamilton," the captain said. "Nice to have you aboard. I recommend that you see our ship's doctor first. Then he can show you to your cabin. You must be exhausted."

"We really can't thank you enough," Lauri said. "You saved our lives. We thought we were goners."

"Oh, we didn't do so much. A Coast Guard airplane noticed you. They're the ones you should thank."

"Lots of guns," Lauri said, indicating the two guards behind the captain. Each held a submachine gun.

Hamilton's expression turned grim.

"These days we don't have much choice. Our cargo is concentrated uranium ore. Yellowcake. They use it to make fuel for nuclear power plants."

Lauri watched as the rescue diver who had helped them affixed a small radio buoy to the sailboat. Then he detached the rope and set the sailboat adrift. A moment later Lauri and Alice heard as the *Bristol*'s engines accelerated from idle. The ship began to move again, toward Los Angeles, which was only one thousand miles away now.

The ship's doctor, Desmond Clarke, seemed competent. He immediately gave Alice and Lauri electrolyte drinks and handed them large bottles of the same for later. He also gave them ointment and painkillers for the sunburns, which had already started smarting badly.

Damn, I think we overdid it a little, Lauri thought. At the same time he started wondering about who on the ship was actually in league with the terrorists. Were some of the crew innocent, or were they all on the wrong side of the law?

The doctor led them along a series of corridors and down a flight of stairs to the ship's guest cabin, which was located to the aft, just under the main deck.

Lauri and Alice had memorized the layout of the MS *Bristol*, down to the smallest detail. According to the diagrams, the crew quarters were mostly on the two levels that made up the bridge, but below decks, there were also two rows of cabins. The engine room was in the stern, significantly below the cabins. The steady, muffled throbbing of the main engine echoed from somewhere beneath their feet. According to the drawings, the whole front of the ship, all the way back to the bridge, formed a single cargo hold with access through three different hatches. The ship had a radio on the bridge and another in a separate radio room on the main deck level.

"Are you a couple?" Clarke asked. "That was the captain's impression, but if you need a second cabin . . ."

"No. We don't. Happily married," Alice said, flashing Clarke her most radiant smile.

"Well, I'll leave you here to rest. There's clothing in the cabinets. You should be able to find something to fit you."

Clarke left the cabin, closing the door behind him. A moment later Alice and Lauri heard a latch slide closed on the other side of the door. Lauri waited for a few minutes and then carefully tried the door. The lock opened, but the exterior latch wouldn't let the door open all the way.

The cabin was clean and spacious, apparently intended for paying passengers. It included a bathroom, coffeemaker, and a small refrigerator that was stocked with a little food and beer. Foster's, of course. But nothing about these amenities changed the fact that they were prisoners in their own cabin.

Lauri opened the cabinets and did a quick inventory of their contents. He also tried surreptitiously to look for any cameras or microphones. He didn't find anything, but of course that didn't mean there weren't any. He was hoping to find rope in the cabinets—a long shot, he knew—but there was only a reasonable selection of men's and women's clothing. However, some of them hung from hangers made of stiff metal wire. Lauri thought those might be of use later.

"Nice the ship is prepared for situations like this," Lauri said.

"The cabin is nice too."

Lauri chose to wear all black—trousers, shirt, and shoes. Alice settled on a dark red skirt and black shirt. It wasn't perfect, but the dark red wouldn't stand out much in the dark.

Lauri mouthed, "There might be microphones."

"And guns? Why the locked door? Suspicious?" Alice mouthed back.

Lauri nodded.

"Can you open the latch?" Alice asked soundlessly.

"Yes, but they'll notice," Lauri mouthed.

"Window?" Alice asked.

"Let's try," Lauri said silently.

Lauri pushed the cabin's round porthole open and looked out. He estimated the window was twenty-five feet above the waterline. It was large enough that he could just squeeze through, and Alice could more easily. Lauri peered up. The deck railing was about ten feet above. Between the window and the railing was nothing to hold on to.

"We'll need about ten feet of cord," Lauri whispered. "By tonight."

Alice gave him a thumbs-up. Taking off her bikini, she traded it for the underwear she had found in the cabinets. Who did these clothes belong to? Lauri wondered. The captain's wife?

"Let's sleep for a bit. I'm beat," Alice said aloud.

"That works for me."

Lauri bent down to kiss Alice.

"Should we fool around a little?" Alice whispered in his ear. "Just in case they have a camera or microphones. That way they'll see we don't suspect them."

"You're such an exhibitionist," Lauri said, whispering back in her ear. "But I'm game."

13

A large US Navy seaplane floated thirty miles from the MS *Bristol*. In addition to the crew, the plane carried thirty-four passengers: thirty special ops commandos, plus Kenneth Andrews, George Robertson, Julia Noruz, and David Farley.

The commandos waited for their orders, while the others watched satellite images of the *Bristol* on a video monitor.

"The ship will be within range of this bird's camera for another ten minutes," said Julia. "Then we go another fifteen before the next satellite comes into view."

"They aren't going to do anything yet," Andrews said. "At night the breaks in visual communication will be much more of a problem. But the *Oregon* is following them underwater from just a couple miles away. They'll hear instantly if there's any shooting onboard."

"I don't like this operation," Farley said, interrupting. "There are too many things that could go wrong."

"You didn't have any better suggestions when we were talking about it," Julia said. "The situation is difficult, and the risks are unusually large no matter what we do."

But guilt weighed on her like lead. It was so easy for them to speculate, sitting here in safety.

"If anyone can handle this job, it's those two," Andrews said. "Either of them alone is dangerous enough. Alice just took out nine yakuza single-handedly. Nine. When they're working together . . . I wouldn't necessarily want to be on the other side when things start going down on that ship."

"I'm going to go out for a smoke," Julia said.

"Just so long as you don't fall in the ocean if we have to take off in a hurry," Andrews said.

Julia opened the hatch and climbed onto one of the plane's large pontoons. She lit her cigarette and greedily sucked smoke into her lungs. *I'm an addict*, Julia thought with self-loathing. *This is the fastest, most direct way of getting a drug into the brain. That's why they do it with crack and heroin. But right now I really need this.*

Actually, Julia suspected the risks might be even greater than anyone had guessed.

The largest amounts of radiation from the Chernobyl disaster were measured in areas where it rained as the fallout passed over. When it rained, the hot particles came down inside raindrops. They didn't come down as micro- or nanoparticles, as an aerosol that was easy to breathe in. Where it didn't rain, there were fewer becquerels of radioactivity, but they were in a more dangerous form. Particles coming in through the digestive system only stayed in the body for a few hours or days, but tiny particles that entered the lungs could park in the alveoli or other internal organs for decades.

Looking for connections between the areas that were most badly contaminated by aerial nuclear tests and increased cancer morbidity was a waste of time, because you wouldn't find any. Jablokov had long argued that a large percentage of the worldwide increase in cancer mortality could be a result of atmospheric nuclear tests. Maybe he was right, Julia thought. They'd just been looking for spikes in the background noise, but maybe they needed to look more carefully at the background noise itself.

And what if most of the cancer and heart disease caused by smoking was actually a result of radioactivity? Before the Second World War, medical students and doctors jammed the morgue whenever there was a patient who died from lung cancer. It was that rare. The increase in lung cancer wasn't just a result of modern cigarettes or demographic change—South Asians had been smoking those nasty rolled leaves of theirs for centuries.

What if tobacco plants, which greedily suck trace elements from the soil, had been vacuuming up more radioactive particles from the ground than before? Particles from the nuclear tests, from Chernobyl and Sellafield? Tiny uranium particles spewed into the environment by coal power plants? Concrete and crushed granite from roadways and the radon and polonium they gave off? What if a burning cigarette deposited those particles permanently in the lung tissues? And what if every one of those tiny particles exposed exactly those same cells to long-term radioactive bombardment? Damaging them over and over again? Maybe the cells could repair the damage a certain number of times, but ultimately something would break.

And what if radioactive particles were constantly creating new cancer genes, along with all the other kinds of mutations? New cancers with novel genetic codes that would be passed down endlessly from one generation to another?

Julia hoped more than anything that she was wrong. It was frightening that they didn't know—even generally—how many people would die if Alice and Lauri failed to prevent this terror attack.

They just didn't know. They didn't know what the immediate effects of a nuclear blast would be, and they didn't know what the long-term consequences of the fallout would be. But did they not know because finding the truth would have been difficult? Or did they not know because no one ever really wanted to know?

14

Later that night, Alice huddled under the blanket and unstitched the seams of her bikini top. She pulled out the specially designed padding and unraveled it into two twenty-foot pieces of thin nylon cord, which she then knotted at one-foot intervals. Though it was so thin it was undetectable in her tiny bikini, the cord could hold several hundred pounds. But without the knots it would be hard to climb and would cut their hands. To make the knots bigger, she shoved in bits of sheet Lauri had ripped. The knots shortened the cord, but they were still left with more than enough.

While Alice was doing this, Lauri disassembled the hangers and then twisted them together. Then he bent them into a hook that was now strong enough to bear his weight without unbending immediately.

"Ready?" Alice whispered in his ear.

Lauri nodded. The cabin was perfectly dark. Lauri opened the window and stuck his head out. Constellations shone in the sky, but the moon would not rise for a while yet. In the darkness he could just barely make out the gray water below, its swells constantly changing shape.

The ship's engines throbbed, and the impacts of the waves against the bow came in slaps and crashes. The water sliding along against the side of the ship foamed a little. But no sound came from the deck. Weren't there any guards up there?

Then Lauri heard steps. They approached at a steady, leisurely pace. The steps passed them. They waited. Fifteen minutes. The steps went by and then receded in the direction of the bow. Fifteen minutes. If the guard maintained the same pace, they would have fifteen minutes, a generous amount of time for the simple operation they had planned.

Lauri reached up and threw the wire hook toward the main deck railing. The first throw went a hair past, and the hook just clinked on the rail and came falling back. They waited, holding their breaths, to see if anyone had heard. Nothing happened, so Lauri threw again. This time the hook snagged the rail, and Lauri tugged it hard a few times to make sure it was secure. Then he grabbed the cord and started climbing up. Alice followed behind.

Lauri removed the hook from the end of the cord and tied the cord to the base of the railing, in as inconspicuous a place as possible. Now they could quickly get back down into the cabin. Through the dark Lauri could see that the cord hanging next to the ship reached all the way to the water. It dragged in the swell, sending little cascades of droplets into the air, but he didn't believe anyone would notice it. At least not until the sun came up. And by morning everything would be over. One way or another.

"What now?" Alice whispered. "The hold?"

Lauri nodded. Hassan Yussuf had said that three men guarded the bomb trigger in the hold, ready to detonate it if any attack came on the ship.

Lauri and Alice knew that Kenneth Andrews and the strike team were monitoring the ship by satellite and through the periscope of the submarine. They had to take out the three men at the bomb trigger. Then somehow they had to send a message to the strike team that they had completed their mission. Once Lauri and Alice neutralized the men and the immediate danger of an explosion was eliminated, they would only have to keep themselves alive for three or four minutes until the heavy guns moved in. And as soon as they did, Alice and Lauri would be home free.

Of course even three minutes could be a very long time, thought Lauri. It could be much longer than the difference between living and dying. On the other hand, he also knew that Alice was at least as lethal as he was, and she was a much better shot. They didn't have any firearms yet, but they would get some.

Lauri checked his watch. Their first weapon would arrive in five minutes.

"Let's wait for the guard," Lauri whispered to Alice.

A few minutes later the guard's steps echoed on the deck of the dark ship.

They waited until the guard passed, and then Lauri stepped out from behind a lifeboat and struck him behind the ear. The blow was hard. The man lost consciousness instantly and would have fallen to the deck if Alice hadn't caught him. He didn't have a machine gun, just a pistol.

"Take it," Lauri whispered. "You're the better shot."

They hid the guard under the cover of the lifeboat. They had no way of knowing how long it would take for someone to notice he was missing, and they didn't have a clue how often the guard was changed. But in any case, they needed to handle their primary task as quickly as possible.

They peeked around the corner of the wall below the bridge, in the direction of the bow. Several feet in front of them the rectangular black outlines of the shipping containers interrupted the starry sky. The deck was deserted. Directly above them light shone from the angled and recessed windows of the bridge. On the radio and radar masts there were small warning lights, and near a door beneath the bridge shone a single lamp. Otherwise the whole deck was covered in dark shadows.

Staying low, they sneaked to the nearest containers. Lauri admired Alice's ability to move quickly but silently. They jumped into the space between the rows of containers. The large steel boxes were close together, so there was no view to either side. The sound of the *Bristol*'s engines grew fainter as they proceeded toward the bow.

The containers ended, and they stopped to wait. No one.

The foredeck hatchway was wide open. Beyond it were the smaller containers and then the bow.

Lauri pointed at the open hatch and whispered "Why?" at Alice.

"Radon," Alice said. "Uranium produces radon—they're venting it."

"Let's go," he said.

Cautiously, they peered into the hold. It was pitch-black. Steps led down from the hatch, ending a couple of feet above the surface of the pile of yellowcake. Holding their breaths, they listened, but they didn't hear any sounds indicating human presence below.

"Strange," Alice whispered. "This isn't exactly what Yussuf described."

"Or they're sitting quietly in the dark. In case someone like us shows up."

They took damp scarves from their pockets and tied them around their faces to cover their mouths and noses. Although the concentrated uranium ore wasn't terribly radioactive, breathing uranium dust still had its risks.

Then Alice started descending the stairs, as quietly as she could. Every so often she stopped to listen, but no sound of any kind came from the hold. Alice had a hard time imagining that three men were really sitting somewhere in the hold day after day, week after week, maintaining perfect silence. Without speaking, breathing, coughing, sneezing, sniffing . . .

The last step. With catlike grace, Alice dropped down onto the heap of uranium. The lumps of yellowcake were jagged under her hands and feet.

Alice stood up and sneaked deeper into the hold. Lauri waited a moment and then followed her. A little light entered the hold from the open hatch, but the deeper they went, the harder it was to see.

Alice's hand reached the side wall of the hold. She crept along it, stepping as slowly and silently as she could. Half an hour later they had circled the hold without encountering anything but uranium. Huge piles of uranium.

"They aren't in the hold," Lauri whispered to Alice. "They must be somewhere else, maybe in the radio room. But the bomb has to be here. With a wire leading to wherever they are. If we sever it . . ."

"What if cutting the wire sets off the bomb?"

"I doubt it."

"Are you sure?"

Lauri sighed. "No. Maybe we should find the wire and then see where it leads."

But they didn't find any kind of wire or any other signs of an atomic bomb built in an enormous pipe, even though they quietly searched in the dark for nearly two hours.

"This is going nowhere," Lauri whispered. "It's too dark in here."

"What do you suggest?"

"We need light. Let's see if we can find a flashlight in the lifeboats."

"And what if the wire is under the uranium?"

"Then we'll have to come up with something else."

"How much time do we have before sunrise?"

"Not much. Two and a half hours, maybe. And the moon is going to rise first. That will make things harder."

They climbed back on deck. They could just make out the first hints of the dim glow of the rising moon. They were running out of time. Alice was just turning toward Lauri to say something, when a bright light appeared in the darkness and focused on them.

"I guessed there was something—"

The discharge of Alice's pistol cut off Captain Hamilton's voice. Her bullet hit the spotlight dead center and blew it to smithereens, throwing them into darkness again. Alice didn't have a chance to take another shot before a burst of ammo from a submachine gun cut her down.

Lauri heard the chatter of the gun and saw the muzzle flashes in the darkness. In front of him, protecting him from the bullets with her body, Alice doubled over, holding her stomach.

15

Katharine Henshaw awoke to her own screams, damp with sweat. A while passed before she realized she was in her own bed and not on a quiet nighttime highway next to a Mercedes that was turned over on its roof and smashed into a tree. It all kept coming back, over and over again, in the same vivid detail as if it had just happened. The trees along the side of the road, the acrid stench of the gasoline leaking from the tank. Her knees caked with mud, her hands, knees, and forehead stabbing with pain.

Katharine tried to calm down and waited for the nightmare to loosen its grip, though that wouldn't ever entirely happen. Though she wished it were only a bad dream, in reality this was something she would never wake up from.

How many times had she wished that they hadn't driven to Michael's apartment but had done something else instead? Or that Michael had driven? Michael had wanted to drive, but he had been even more drunk than she—so it hadn't been completely the wrong thing to grab the keys from him.

In retrospect of course it was obvious she should have been smarter, stopping Michael from going *and* not offering to be his slightly less drunk driver.

But I was under so much pressure, Katharine thought. We both were, and I wanted to get wasted, so we did.

But then . . .

Everything happened so fast. The lights that turned into their lane without warning, the blinding brightness. She had reacted to the situation more than half blind, trying to avoid the oncoming car.

In a way it wasn't even my fault, thought Katharine. *Except that I shouldn't have been driving.* In retrospect, so many things were clear. Crystal clear.

If I hadn't driven, thought Katharine, *Michael still might be able to walk and run and swim, and he would probably have a wife and children, and I would be able to live with myself without all this self-loathing. I would be doing something else. Rheya would probably still be living with me, and maybe Ritchie and I would still be together.*

Katharine stood up, wrapping her robe around herself and walking into the kitchen. She poured herself a stiff shot of whisky and then looked at it.

"Hell no!"

She grabbed the glass and poured the liquid down the sink.

Then she went out on the balcony. Squeezing the railing with both hands, she breathed in the cool night air. It smelled strongly of smoke and felt as clean and fresh as a poorly ventilated bar. A little like inhaling exhaust straight out of a tailpipe, thought Katharine. The air grated her lungs like sandpaper.

It would be nice to live somewhere different, thought Katharine. Somewhere where life was simpler. With a yard, a dog, and maybe some other pets. A few apple trees and one cherry tree with white blossoms in the spring, covering the ground in a blanket of petals.

She tried to focus, but something else was bothering her—something more than everything that normally did.

Katharine let her thoughts wander aimlessly. What had actually been happening lately? Washburn's party, the NTU, Lauri Nurmi, and Kenneth Washburn. No, it was Kenneth Andrews—sometimes keeping him and Timothy Washburn straight was difficult. The second, even more ghastly job at Washburn's house. But at the NTU office Lauri Nurmi had defended her and laid his boss out flat. That had been . . . unexpected. To put it mildly.

She was starting to feel as if whatever it was had something to do with Lauri Nurmi. As if something was telling her Nurmi was in danger. That he might die, right now, tonight.

She wondered if she should call and warn him. What could she say other than that she had a bad feeling? Why would he believe her? And what would it make him think?

What did it matter? thought Katharine.

Katharine picked up her phone and searched for Lauri Nurmi's number.

"Kenneth Andrews," replied a voice on the other end of the line.

"Oh, it's you." Katharine sighed.

"Who is this?"

"You probably don't want to know. I was trying to reach Lauri Nurmi. Why are you answering his phone?"

"Why are you trying to call him?"

"Well . . . I just had this feeling he's in danger. That . . . God, I know how stupid this sounds. But I just wanted to warn him."

"Excuse me, but what exactly has he told you?" Andrews asked suspiciously.

16

"I'm hit," Alice sputtered. "It's bad."

Her voice trembled with pain. Lauri dragged Alice behind a container. *Why aren't they shooting anymore?* he wondered. *Maybe they want us alive.*

Lauri took the pistol from Alice's half-limp hand and shoved it in his belt by his right hip.

"This is bullshit," Alice panted. "I should have changed jobs . . . while I had the time."

"Don't worry. Let me take a look," Lauri whispered, trying to make his voice sound calm.

But the whole time he was fighting the panic welling inside. *Not you!* a silent voice screamed in his mind. *Not you, Alice, not you!*

When he carefully turned Alice onto her back, he saw how serious her wounds were. There were three hits, and at least one of them was in her stomach. Her lower body was already covered in blood, and more was gushing out. Lauri knew he couldn't do much to stanch the flow of blood, but he still started ripping his shirt into strips.

"It hurts," Alice said. "A lot."

"Try to hold on," Lauri said. "We're going to make it through this."

Alice shook her head. A quick, forced smile flitted across her lips.

"No . . . I definitely bought . . . the farm."

"Don't give up. You can't give up."

"Are you going to come out with your hands up, or should we throw in a grenade?" yelled one of the terrorists.

"Could I have some time to think about it?" Lauri yelled back.

If the terrorists threw a grenade between the containers, Alice would die too.

Lauri shoved pieces of fabric into Alice's wounds and tried to stop the hemorrhaging. It only helped a little.

"It sucks that . . . but please remember that I . . . loved you."

"We still have our whole lives ahead of us. We can get married if you still want to," Lauri said quickly. "We can have children. As many as you want."

Alice smiled tiredly. Lauri could see the pain was getting worse. The bullet that hit her stomach must have really torn her up inside.

"It's so easy to make promises . . . to a dying woman."

"You're wrong. You aren't dying."

Alice didn't have the strength to argue. "OK," she sighed.

Lauri saw her strength was waning.

"Lauri . . . one more thing . . ."

"We can talk about it later."

"If . . . I don't . . ."

"Alice, no."

"But if . . ."

"Try to hold on just a few more seconds. I'll take care of them and then come back."

"Good . . . OK . . ."

Lauri didn't have much time. He had to get Alice medical attention. He had to call for help and in the meantime see if he could find anything in the ship's first aid locker that would do any good. But that all had to happen very fast, and he couldn't do anything before he had dealt with the rest of the terrorists. There were at least eighteen of them, and he was trapped between two heavily armed groups. Not good.

What options did he have other than surrender? That wasn't possible, though, given the plutonium and lithium-6 thefts they were dealing with. There were too many lives at stake.

"Time's up," shouted the same terrorist.

Lauri had to act, now. The cord down to their cabin was on the other side of the ship, near the stern, and he was more than thirty feet from the bow. How long was the ship again? The exact number mentioned in the blueprints was four hundred and forty-six feet. The ship was about sixty-five feet wide, wasn't it? And its speed? That wasn't terribly fast right now. The captain must have given a command to slow down. At most five or six knots—seven miles an hour, maybe even a little less. So it might be possible, at least if . . . But would he see anything when he came up?

Lauri glanced at the night sky. The crescent moon had just begun rising from the sea. A delicate pillar of light rippled on the waves in front of it. The conditions could have been better, but it might be alright. It had to be alright.

"Well, are you coming out?" shouted a voice to his left.

"OK, you win. I'm coming out," Lauri replied.

"Alice, I love you," whispered Lauri.

Backing up right against the container, he took a running jump and dove headfirst over the railing toward the black water waiting thirty feet below.

17

Lauri dove toward the bow of the ship. He heard angry shouts and a few shots, but he didn't hear bullets whizzing by. He was probably already safe below the side of the ship. But how low an angle did he dare to come down at? The drop was quite high, so the surface of the water would be rock hard. On the other hand, the more severe the angle, the deeper he would sink, and he would lose precious seconds swimming up. And he didn't have very many extra seconds. Maybe not any.

Lauri splashed through the surface. A thick cloud of air bubbles erupted around him but disappeared quickly, gyrating upward and vanishing from sight. The water was black, and he couldn't see anything anymore. His descent stopped, and he started swimming hard. He turned sideways and began rising but simultaneously tried to get as far under the ship as possible.

Impenetrable darkness lay above and below and all around. The entire world had disappeared. He hoped he was going in the right direction. What if he was swimming out to sea? How could he know without seeing anything? And what if he was moving straight toward the propellers? Just then his arm hit the bottom of the boat, and the barnacles attached to the metal sliced his fingertips open. The massive black hull of the freighter slid by above him, and to avoid touching the bottom of the ship, he dove deeper.

My kingdom for fins, was the thought that went through his mind. He wished he had fins. People were so incredibly slow and awkward underwater. He needed to be moving almost three feet per second.

The hull thumped over him. The turbulence in the water was intense, slowing his swimming.

The ship was moving too fast. He was going to end up in the prop, Lauri thought hopelessly.

Then he was at the deepest part of the hull and went under the keel. The large barnacles stuck to the hull cut a few angry red scrapes on his arm.

How far away were the propellers? He couldn't see them in the dark water. Would he see them even if they were close? Or would they just suddenly slice him into pieces without warning? The ship was moving many times faster than he could swim. If only Alice were there. She was a much better swimmer.

The side of the ship rose more steeply. The blackness of the water seemed to fade. Was he just imagining it?

But then, in the midst of the blackness, he began to make out the white roiling of the water caused by the propellers. His mind screamed with terror. The stern of the ship was too close. He was going into the propellers! That wasn't the kind of end he would have hoped for himself, and then there was Alice . . .

His head broke the surface next to the *Bristol,* and he gasped for breath. In the dim light of the moon, he saw the knotted cord a few feet in front of him . . . he was going to miss it . . . desperate, he stretched out his arm as far as possible and . . . caught hold of the cord.

Lauri grabbed the cord with his other hand and hung on tight as he caught his breath. As the ship dragged him along, his waist and thighs cut through the surface, spraying water into the air as if he were practicing some strange variation on waterskiing. Droplets sparkled in the faint luster of the crescent moon.

Lauri glanced up. The side of the ship rose high above him like a grim black wall. How long did he have before the terrorists thought to check this side of the ship? Probably not very long.

Lauri started climbing. Thirty feet to the deck. Luckily Alice had tied knots all the way to the end of the cord. And luckily they had lowered the whole cord down. You never knew what would be useful.

Then Lauri was over the railing and on the deck. He was relieved to have made it up there, but he still had to face at least eighteen terrorists who were armed to the teeth and seemed to know their craft. They hadn't left Alice any chance.

The pistol was still in Lauri's belt. Taking it out, he shook water from the barrel. Alice had only shot it once, so the magazine still had seven rounds. That was much more than none at all.

He heard footsteps from around the corner of the bridge tower. How many terrorists were coming? One? More? Lauri froze in place and strained to listen but only heard one set of footsteps. The captain must have sent only one of his men to check the other side of the ship. Wouldn't he have sent more if he'd known about the cord? *Excellent,* thought Lauri. The man would surely have a firearm, hopefully a submachine gun.

Lauri pressed himself flat against the wall. The terrorist ran around the corner, and he had a submachine gun. *Perfect.* Lauri couldn't have wished for a better present right now. *Thank you very much.*

The man was looking straight ahead, so he didn't notice Lauri until he was right on him. The man froze, and Lauri hit him first in the larynx and then hard in the back of the neck. The man fell to the ground without making a sound, but the submachine gun slipped from his hands and flew toward the railing. Lauri tried to grab it but was too late, and the weapon clattered into the railing and slipped over the edge and into the water. Lauri didn't stop to bemoan the loss. That kind of thinking was pointless and would just break his concentration. He didn't even glance at the man on the ground, because he knew all too well the terrorist wouldn't be getting up. Ever.

One down. Seventeen more to go. He was badly outmanned and outgunned, but he did have two significant factors on his side. The terrorists weren't expecting him. If he managed to capitalize fully on the element of surprise, he might be able to take several of them out of the game before it even really started. And, given the situation, he would know that everyone he encountered was an enemy combatant. He could shoot without hesitation, but the terrorists had to be careful to avoid friendly fire. The more chaotic the situation became, the better his chances would be.

Silently and quickly, Lauri sneaked to the stairs leading to the bridge and started up them.

Time was of the essence. Below, around the corner, he heard more footsteps, and the beams of flashlights danced through the darkness, swinging from side to side. It occurred to him that they would see the water that had dripped from his clothing onto the deck, but he couldn't do anything about that. Alice would die if he didn't act fast. He had to hit the main group without delay and eliminate them.

As Lauri stepped onto the bridge, he heard a surprised shout from below. More shouts and curses and running. The terrorists had found their dead comrade. Within a few moments they would see the puddles. A few seconds more, and they would find the rope and realize that he was back. He would lose the element of surprise, and without that his chances would be close to zero. He had to get down to business. From the bow side of the bridge, he would have a direct line of sight onto the place where the terrorists had surprised him and Alice.

Lauri stepped out from around the corner of the bridge, right under an electric light. Only a few feet away stood four men armed with submachine guns.

18

If Lauri Nurmi had stopped for even an instant to think about it, he would have understood that the situation was hopeless, that he didn't have a chance. He would have realized that he would never have time to kill four men before they had shot him full of lead, especially since he only had seven bullets left.

During the Second World War, only one soldier out of six had actually been willing to shoot at enemy soldiers, to wound or to kill. Five men out of six intentionally shot wide.

At the Battle of Gettysburg, during the US Civil War, most of the soldiers on both sides had loaded their weapons over and over again without firing them in order to avoid killing or hurting other people.

Time slowed. It almost stopped.

Lauri's eyes locked with the first terrorist. The man hesitated, looking confused. He turned his head, unable to meet Lauri's gaze, and lowered his gun. Nothing about the man made it seem as if he was an experienced professional.

The second man pulled his trigger, releasing a short burst of shots. But at the last instant, he jerked the barrel of the gun to the side, which sent the bullets whizzing past Lauri's head, into the wall. The sparks disappeared with shrill screeches, and chips of paint and tiny splinters of metal showered over Lauri. The muzzle of the submachine gun flashed so near his hands and face that he could feel its heat.

Lauri's hand moved as if it wasn't part of him. The first thing his conscious mind registered of its movements was a small jolt in his shoulder, the kick of the gunshot, and the appearance of a small round hole in the center of the forehead of the man who had shot at him. Then he felt another kick in his shoulder and arm, and the crown of the head of the terrorist who had lowered his weapon exploded. Blood and bone sprayed over the other terrorists, who hadn't had time to react at all.

As if in slow motion, Lauri saw how the eyes of the first enemy he had shot went fuzzy and glazed over, how the strength drained from his limbs and body, and how he started collapsing to the ground as the terrorist next to him, whose head was smashed, fell hard into the man behind, preventing him from raising his gun.

Lauri saw the fourth opponent look at him. He saw the fear in the man's eyes as he dropped his flashlight and grabbed his submachine gun, starting to aim it at Lauri, but he moved so slowly, so impossibly slowly, that Lauri almost laughed when he realized that in two seconds the situation had actually turned into a victory for him. Again, his hand moved as if of its own accord. This time he felt two kicks, and the terrorist jerked twice as the bullets pierced his heart and lung. Lauri understood instinctively that his hand was already pointing at the last enemy.

The last terrorist tried hopelessly to shove his dead comrade off himself in order to raise his own weapon and shoot, but he didn't have enough time. Lauri shot him right between the eyes.

From somewhere far away came shouts and curses and then dull thuds and metallic clangs. Lauri stepped over the dead men and dropped his pistol to the ground. He peeked through a side window into the bridge. No one was there; apparently the ship was on autopilot.

Lauri glanced at the sky. The crescent moon was already higher, providing slightly better light. But the black shadows it cast here and there on the deck did not yet significantly reduce his chances.

A clattering echoed up from the stairs that Lauri had just climbed, which led from the main deck to the bridge. At least three or four terrorists were coming, maybe more.

Lauri picked up a submachine gun and switched it to single fire. How many seconds would he have before the first attacker poked his head topside? Five? Ten? Fifteen? Fewer than ten seconds, his internal calculator said. He pointed the submachine gun toward the top of the stairs and waited.

Time passed painfully slowly. Lauri knew that his own sense of time had changed, that it was stretched out for him. But still he was impatient. He didn't want to wait. He was in a hurry.

Finally the first of the men rushed to the top of the stairs. Lauri saw him clearly silhouetted by the moonlight. The man looked to the left, noticed Lauri, and froze in place.

Idiot, thought Lauri.

The terrorist recovered from his surprise and began turning his submachine gun toward Lauri. But the barrel banged into the railing and got caught. *Go to hell, you bastard*, Lauri thought and pulled the trigger three times. The bullets slammed into the man like a sledgehammer, and Lauri saw as the black silhouette flipped over the rail.

The clattering on the stairs stopped. There was a thump and a nasty crunch. Then nothing.

His attackers stopped on the stairs, seemingly uncertain about what they should do next.

Lauri grabbed another submachine gun and threw its strap over his shoulder. Then he slowly slid closer to the top of the stairs. The terrorists remained paralyzed. Lauri couldn't believe his luck. They should either attack or retreat, as fast as they could. That's what he would have done, but he wasn't going to complain if they stayed right where they were. It worked perfectly for him.

Lauri switched his gun to automatic fire.

"Let's attack before he gets away," yelled one of the men on the stairs.

"Bugger that," hissed another voice. "I don't want a bullet in my brain."

I'm sorry, but life is hard, Lauri replied in his mind. You should have thought about that before you sold the material for a superbomb to a bunch of terrorists.

He pushed the barrel of the machine gun out over the top of the stairs, keeping himself hidden. Then he pressed the trigger and fired blind, following the angle of the stairs. The weapon thundered, and long yellow-and-orange flashes lit up the darkness.

He heard shouts of pain, but ignored them. The submachine gun bucked in his hand and made his ears ring, while burning hot shell casings cascaded from the breech and pinged off the railing and metal deck of the ship—one grazed his cheek and burned it.

Silently, Lauri switched the empty weapon for the one hanging from his shoulder and moved forward, careful to maintain the cover of the bridge wall and deck. Then he glanced down. In the light of the moon, he saw that four men lay on the stairs, two of them not moving or making any sound. The wounds of the other two seemed less serious. At the bottom of the stairs was a fifth mildly hysterical but otherwise uninjured terrorist. He was sobbing loudly, and tears were running down his cheeks.

Find a new job, Lauri thought and with a short burst executed the man crying at the bottom of the stairs. Then he switched the submachine gun to single fire and shot, quickly but methodically, two or three bullets into each of the bloody heaps on the stairs. None of them moved anymore.

Lauri heard shouts of rage from farther along the deck. At least two guns opened fire toward him. The muzzles flashed in the darkness like fireworks. He wasn't in the line of fire but still retreated, because he knew the wrong ricochet could also do a lot of damage. He didn't have any room for an injury. That would be the end of Alice.

One below, four on the bridge, and six on the stairs—that made eleven altogether, Lauri thought. Not many more to go.

He returned to the four men he had shot with the pistol. From the stairs behind him, he heard shouts and a long burst from a submachine gun. *Go ahead and shoot. I'm not there anymore*, thought Lauri. The more shooting they did, the more they would draw the others out of his way.

Grabbing a new machine gun, he threw it over his shoulder and continued to the other side of the bridge without wasting another moment.

He couldn't see anyone on the main deck below. All the noise must have lured the rest of the terrorists to the other side of the ship.

Lauri sneaked down the stairs. Still no one. A stupid enemy was worth his weight in gold, thought Lauri as he continued around the corner at a jog.

Before him were four enemies, with their backs to Lauri. They were rushing toward the stairs where their comrades had died just moments before. The din of their own steps and voices, plus the shots from the stairs, drowned out the sound of Lauri's movements, so the terrorists didn't hear or see him until he opened fire and dropped the rear three with a short burst in each one's back. All three collapsed. Their companion spun around, but he didn't have a chance. Lauri cut the man down before he could return fire.

Fifteen, said the counter in Lauri's mind.

Where were the other three? Probably around the next corner, where he had killed six. Shots and bursts were still coming from the stairs. Lauri picked up a new machine gun and continued on, slipping on the big puddles of blood on the deck. *What a mess,* he thought.

Lauri rushed around the corner, and the two terrorists at the stairs firing wildly died before they even understood they were being attacked. The third turned to run, and Lauri shot him in the back. There was one more, and Lauri shot him in the head and torso.

Then there were no more.

Lauri rushed to the radio room and clubbed the radio operator with the butt of his gun. But there weren't any extra cables running from the radio room, and there weren't three men there—not even one with his finger on a button ready to detonate a huge nuclear bomb in the hold.

Where were they? Had he already gotten them?

Three or four unarmed men peered out of the kitchen, two of them in white cook's hats and uniforms, but they quickly retreated when Lauri fired two shots into the wall next to them. Lauri knew there would be a few men in the engine room, but they might not have heard anything yet because of the noise of the engines. They might be a problem later, though. Lauri ran to the door leading down to the engine room and bolted it from the outside. *Stay there.*

But then all he saw were the dead or mortally wounded, and no one was shooting at him. A few of the injured moaned, but most of them were still. The engines continued thumping as the ship plowed forward on autopilot as if nothing had happened. The deck was sticky and slick with the blood trickling into the ocean.

There wasn't anyone else, Lauri thought, his brain still in overdrive. There weren't three terrorists waiting to blow up the bomb. Maybe he'd already gotten them. There weren't any others, so he had to get to Alice. There wouldn't be any danger with Alice. Why didn't any of the terrorists look Arabic? He had assumed . . . but where was Alice?

Lauri ran to the place where he'd left Alice. Quickly he glanced at his watch. Only a few minutes had passed since he dove over the rail into the ocean. Andrews and the others would show up soon with the strike team. There'd be a medic. Alice still had a chance.

Then he saw her.

Alice had fallen to her knees, with her head and hair and face against the steel deck of the ship. She was very still, and her posture looked unnatural.

"Alice . . . ?"

But Alice didn't answer. And she didn't move when Lauri touched her hand.

19

When Kenneth Andrews, Julia Noruz, and the special ops team arrived, Lauri Nurmi was sitting on the deck of the MS *Bristol* holding Alice Little Hawk Donovan in his lap and stroking her hair.

"Lauri, she's dead," Andrews said.

"No, Ken. I think she's just sleeping."

"Lauri, she's gone," said Julia. "You have to let go."

Lauri whimpered.

"Lauri," Julia pleaded.

Lauri nodded.

"Wait . . . just a second . . . let me hold her . . . for a few more seconds. Just . . . a few seconds. Then I'll come with you."

A few minutes later Lauri let go, and Julia led him toward the rope ladder the strike team had attached to the side of the ship.

"I think a few of the terrorists survived," Lauri explained. "At least three, maybe four."

His face looks dead, Julia thought.

"There are a few men in the kitchen and a few more in the engine room. All unarmed. I don't know if they're guilty of anything. I didn't do anything to them."

"We counted twelve dead," Julia said. "The rest are alive. Just barely. But don't worry. The others will take care of things from here on out."

Julia helped Lauri climb down onto the deck of a patrol boat, where Farley and Robertson greeted them.

"Where is Ken?" Lauri asked after a while.

Julia looked at her watch. "I was wondering the same thing."

Ten or fifteen minutes passed. Then Andrews came down the rope ladder with two commandos following him. A few moments later they were on their way to Los Angeles.

"But at least we . . . succeeded," Lauri said. "At least the danger is passed. What?"

He couldn't interpret the expression on Andrews's face.

Lauri turned to look at the *Bristol* receding in the distance. Then the rear of the ship suddenly exploded. Huge flames erupted into the air, and a thundering shock wave washed over them. Pieces of metal rained down on the ocean, but none of the pieces came close enough to endanger them. Lauri saw black smoke rising from the back of the ship, which was beginning to sink aft first.

"What the hell?" Lauri choked. "They had a bomb set after all?"

Andrews shook his head.

"Not exactly. We sank it ourselves."

"Why!" Lauri screamed.

"I don't know how to tell you this, but . . . Well, they weren't terrorists."

Lauri reeled. His vision went black, and he had to grab the side of the boat to stop himself from falling overboard. He must have heard wrong.

"What did you just say?"

Andrews looked at him. There was pity in his gaze, perhaps even a sort of tenderness, and seeing that completely foreign expression on Andrews's face made the world spin in Lauri's eyes.

"They weren't terrorists," Andrews repeated.

"What?" Lauri shouted. "What do you mean they weren't terrorists?"

"We made a mistake. I'm sorry."

"Ken, you're full of shit. Of course they were . . ."

"This was a normal, completely legal uranium shipment for our own nuclear power plants."

"But they had guns, submachine guns."

"Those were the Australian mining company's security guards. Their job was protecting the ship from terrorists to keep nuclear fuel shipments to the United States safe." Andrews's expression hardened again. "This time that didn't work out so well, but what are you going to do?"

"No, that can't be true . . . it can't be."

"I'm sorry, but mistakes happen. We can try to minimize them, but we can't avoid them completely. Collateral damage is just part of the game. You know that."

"Collateral damage? Was Alice collateral damage?"

"I'm sorry about Alice. I really am. You won't be held responsible. Don't worry about that."

"I don't give a shit what happens to me. Do you hear what you're saying, Ken? If those were Australians . . . this is going to be a huge mess. Next to Britain, Australia has been our most important ally in the war against terrorism."

"We can't do anything about it if Al-Qaeda sinks an Australian ore freighter. I think that will only increase Australia's motivation to support us."

"But it wasn't Al-Qaeda."

"No one will be able to prove that, and we already sent a message to Al Jazeera from a previously unknown Al-Qaeda cell, taking responsibility for the attack."

"But the survivors will tell what happened."

"What survivors?"

"Excuse me, but what did you say?"

Kenneth Andrews shrugged.

"You heard me."

"Kenneth, no. *No.* You can't mean . . ."

"We didn't have any choice. And this isn't the biggest sacrifice ever made. This is war, and in war people die. Do you think it would be better to lose Australia's support?"

FOUR
HOT ASH

"I have often wondered about the inner attitude of Werner [Heisenberg] and Carl Friedrich [von Weizsäcker], but I believe I understand their psychology. Many people, especially young ones, cannot reconcile themselves with the great irrationality of the present, and so in their imagination they construct castles in the air. It is an enormous task they have undertaken, to find a good side in things they can do nothing about."

> *—Nuclear physicist Max von Laue*
> *April 26, 1942*
> *From a letter to Lise Meitner, the "German Marie Curie" (who was the first to realize that Otto Hahn and Fritz Strassmann had succeeded in splitting uranium atoms)*

1

Lauri Nurmi sat, naked, in a high-backed upholstered armchair at the Sierra Vera ranch house. Two weeks had passed since the strike on the *Bristol*. He was drinking whisky right from the bottle, his second bottle of the day.

Fortunately he had a good supply—more than enough.

A loaded pistol and a pile of news articles he'd printed off the Internet were on the table in front of him. The articles were from American and Australian newspapers and magazines, and they all dealt with Al-Qaeda's latest terror attack, this time on an Australian ship carrying uranium ore. The stories did mention that the amount of uranium that went to the bottom in the strike would have supplied US power plants for six months. But without exception the focus was on the victims and their families. Twenty-nine people had been brutally murdered, eighteen of them armed guards and then eleven crew members. No one survived.

Many of the news outlets had pictures of all of the dead. Lauri had also read the interviews with their wives and parents. Some of them had adult children who spoke openly with the press about how deeply the incident altered their lives. The worst were the kids, little kids crying in their mother's arms or holding their hands, little kids whose eyes were dull with shock and sadness and for whom life would never be the same.

Lauri Nurmi still hadn't decided when he would shoot himself, but he wasn't in any hurry. It wouldn't change anything for anyone else, because no one would ever know everything that had happened. This was just a question about himself and his own ability—or rather inability—to live with himself and face what he had done. And besides, it didn't seem right for him to leave too soon, too quickly. The bereaved would have to live with his actions for years, decades, until the ends of their lives. Maybe he should suffer a little longer. But what was a reasonable time? A week? Two weeks? How long could he stand this?

The loaded Beretta smiled enticingly at him from the table, his dear and faithful friend. His only friend in the whole world. He could always trust it even if everyone else betrayed him. Fortunately freedom from everything was so close, just on the other side of a quick, gentle kiss from this violent but decisive friend. Within arm's reach, only a few short movements away.

But not yet. Soon. But not yet.

Lauri took another swig from the whisky bottle. The alcohol burned his mouth and warmed his belly, but not like it had a week ago. His body was going numb. Soon he would need something harder to keep the nightmares and demons away.

The sun had set behind the mountains, and the landscape was wrapping itself in the cocoon of the thickening darkness. Lauri hadn't turned on any lights, and darkness was engulfing the house.

Then . . . he thought he heard something.

Lauri strained to hear. Yes, he was right. It was the sound of an approaching car. The road out here only led to Sierra Vera, so the car was coming to the ranch.

What was going on?

Maybe . . . of course, thought Lauri. What had he said to Andrews the last time he called? He had been pretty drunk and threatened to expose everything, to go to the media. Maybe after thinking about it for a while, Andrews had decided to take him seriously. Or maybe he had thought it his duty to report Lauri, and someone higher up had decided to take him seriously. They knew how irresponsible he was, given that he had hit Andrews and Robertson—never mind that it had been on Katharine Henshaw's behalf. Now he had gone off the rails entirely and might do anything. That was probably the best explanation. They were coming to deal with him.

Well, they were going to be in for a big surprise, Lauri thought, grinning mirthlessly. They would be expecting a hard job and serious casualties. Very serious casualties.

Lauri grabbed the Beretta and removed the magazine. He shoved it under the pad of the armchair and set the empty gun on the table, where it had been before, within easy reach.

There wouldn't be any casualties.

Not anymore. Not by my hand. Not one more death by my hand.

The sound of the car grew closer. Soon it would turn into the driveway. But there was something strange. There was only one car. That meant four, five men, tops. Unless it was a van, but it didn't sound like one. Kenneth Andrews would never send such a small group against Lauri, not on his home turf. Not to Sierra Vera, where Lauri knew every square inch and had set up . . . well, things. There wasn't any sense to it, not even if Andrews knew Lauri had been trying to drink himself to death for a week now—starting the very first day after Alice's funeral.

Thoughts of Alice's funeral stabbed at his stomach and heart. He pictured the faces of Alice's parents, twisted with sorrow, and he heard the voice of her mother, Little Tree Donovan, when she said he shouldn't blame himself, that what had happened wasn't his fault, that Alice had been happy with him. Lauri shoved aside the image of Little Tree and focused on the problem at hand.

Andrews would have played this kind of situation safe. Lauri was sure of that. Andrews never took needless risks unless he had to. Maybe the others were parachuting in or coming cross-country. But why would they give him such a clear warning by sending a car too? Was it some sort of ruse? Lauri had a hard time understanding the logic of the attack.

The headlights of the car flashed through the windows of the house, momentarily blinding Lauri. Then the headlights went out, and the engine switched off.

Bring it on, Lauri thought.

He sat in the dark and waited.

A knock came at the door. Lauri didn't answer. *Come on already*, he thought, suddenly impatient. *Don't waste my time.* Though, really, he wasn't in a hurry to get anywhere. He could wait a few more seconds.

Whoever was out there tested the door and found that it was unlocked. *Hurry up*, Lauri thought. The door squeaked as it swung wide open.

"Is anyone here?" a voice asked in the dark. A woman's voice. Odd.

"It's pretty dark in here," said the woman.

The voice was vaguely familiar. She seemed to have come alone. What was going on? He wondered about pointing the empty Beretta at her so she would have to react and shoot him full of holes.

As she stepped farther into the room, she appeared as a fuzzy silhouette in the darkness.

"It is you, isn't it?" asked the voice. "I'm going to turn on a light."

The woman fumbled with a floor lamp and clicked it on. The light stung Lauri's eyes, and it took a few seconds until his eyes adjusted and he could see anything.

The woman stood a few yards away. She looked at Lauri with an expression that was difficult to interpret. As her gaze touched on the Beretta, she flinched slightly. She was wearing all black—a sleeveless T-shirt and tight jeans.

"Hi," said Katharine Henshaw.

"How did you get here?"

"It wasn't hard. Actually, your friend Julia asked me to visit you. She gave me directions."

"Julia?"

"She said you weren't letting anyone near you and that she was worried about you."

"She shouldn't be."

"She thought you might treat me differently than them. Apparently you and I have a lot in common."

Lauri rubbed his jaw and tried to collect his thoughts, which weren't all that clear.

"You have beautiful horses," said Katharine. "I saw them under the light by the barn."

Lauri grabbed the whisky bottle and took a stiff gulp from it.

"Would you like to get dressed?" asked Katharine. "Not that I mind what you're wearing now. I'm used to naked men, you know. But if you want . . ."

Lauri stood up and pulled on the jeans he had dropped in a heap on the floor.

"If you came here to chew me out, go ahead and do it," he said. "I probably deserve whatever you have to say."

Katharine shook her head. "I heard what happened. That you failed to stop the attack and that . . . that your girlfriend died."

Yes indeed, that was the whole truth, thought Lauri. He knew he couldn't tell any more. If Katharine knew everything . . . In the worst-case scenario, he would be putting her life in danger by filling in the missing parts of the story.

Katharine watched as Lauri quickly drank several gulps of whisky.

"Would you like to offer me some too?" she asked. "Drinking alone is impolite."

Lauri stood up. He retrieved another bottle and grabbed a glass from the cupboard. He poured the glass full to the brim and then handed it to Katharine. Despite how drunk he was, not a drop spilled.

"That's quite a shot," she said. "A little less would have been fine."

"There's plenty more."

"Cheers to that." Katharine took a sip. "Based on what Julia told me, I thought you might need some company," Katharine said. "Someone you could talk to."

Lauri took another big gulp from the bottle.

"You're going to be pretty plastered if you keep going like that."

"I'm already pretty plastered. Drunk as a skunk. But not as drunk as I want to be."

"Do you think that's going to help?"

"Yes. At least for a while."

Katharine noticed that while Lauri was looking at her thoughtfully, he was also swaying a little.

"That daughter of yours. Rheya?" Lauri blurted out.

Lauri saw how Katharine shuddered and seemed to curl up in a ball when he mentioned Rheya's name.

"Yes?"

"In our files I saw that her whole name is Rheya Bergman and that she lives with her father, Ritchie Bergman."

"True," said Katharine.

Her voice was flat and colorless.

"Is that painful for you?"

Katharine was silent for a long time. She glanced at the door, and for a moment Lauri thought she would get up and leave as unexpectedly as she had come.

"Yes, it is very painful for me."

"Do you want to talk about it?"

"Not particularly," Katharine said, turning away so Lauri couldn't see her face.

"OK, let's leave it alone then. But . . . you might be interested to know that . . . Well, never mind."

Katharine turned to Lauri again.

"Who are you?" she suddenly asked.

"What do you mean?" Lauri replied.

"You're a strange bird. Your last name is weird. You only smile when something genuinely amuses you, which doesn't seem to be very often. And you can go so long without saying anything. It's odd. Almost un-American. You're like some eighteenth-century frontiersman who just fell out of a time machine."

Lauri stood up.

"Should we go outside?" he suggested. "We could make some food over a fire."

"Are you sure you could actually start one right now?"

"Hey, I could light a campfire even if I was so drunk I had to crawl on all fours. I spent half my time in the forest when I was a kid."

"OK then," Katharine said. "But I need to change into something a little warmer. And you might even want to put on a shirt to go with those jeans."

Katharine fetched a small suitcase from the car.

"You're going to offer me a place to sleep, right?" she asked Lauri.

"You can take the guest room. First door on your left down the hallway."

"Thanks."

A few minutes later Katharine came back. She had changed into a white turtleneck sweater, blue jeans that were faded and ripped, and simple black moccasins that were well worn in. Lauri thought Katharine looked strangely at ease. For a while Lauri considered, as a theoretical thought experiment, whether it would be possible to find clothing that wouldn't look good on Katharine Henshaw. He came to the conclusion that it was probably impossible.

At the fire pit, Katharine discovered that Lauri hadn't exaggerated. In less than a minute, he had a fire started, and soon the first tongues of flames were beginning to lick the sides of the logs.

As soon as there were hot coals at the bottom of the fire, Lauri started to walk toward the house.

"Wait here a sec," he said.

"Where are you going?" Katharine asked.

"I promised to make food. You aren't going to be afraid sitting alone in the dark for a little while, are you? Don't worry, the fire keeps the wolves away. Usually. Unless they're really hungry."

"Just so long as you don't pass out somewhere and choke on your own vomit."

Lauri staggered into the house. Moments later he returned with a bag of large onions and two forks.

"Right now I don't think I'm going to be able to whip up anything more gourmet than this," he muttered and shook the onions out of the bag so they rolled into the hot coals.

"Hey . . . don't we need to wrap tinfoil around them?"

"If you insist on wasting electricity and other natural resources."

"But they'll burn."

"Just a little on the outside. They have a lot of layers. Like many things. Truth, for example."

Katharine gave Lauri a bored look.

"See, when you start peeling away all the layers, looking for the one ultimate truth in the center, all you end up with is nothing. It's all layers, all the way down. Like an onion. Or anything else."

About a half hour later, Lauri fished a big onion out of the fire with a fork and offered it to Katharine.

"This is completely black," Katharine said.

"That's just the outside that's burned. Peel it off."

Katharine followed his instructions and then tasted the remaining onion.

"Delicious," she said with surprise in her voice. "So juicy. It melts in your mouth. Wow. This is better than roasted in foil."

"I told you. This recipe is a bit too complicated though. You have to go get the onions and dump them in the fire. By the way, are you a good cook?"

Katharine laughed out loud.

"Terrible. If I don't eat out, I usually just heat something up in the microwave or order pizza or call the Chinese place around the corner and ask them to bring something. I'm going to have to remember this onion recipe of yours, though."

"You can't make campfire onions in New York. Even if you have a balcony."

"I can try. Someday when I have a penthouse."

"They'll fine you."

"If I ever have the money for a penthouse, then I can pay the occasional fine for lighting a fire," Katharine said.

She wiped her hands on her jeans. Transfixed, she stared at the flames.

"Better than TV, isn't it?" Lauri said.

Katharine laughed, and Lauri thought she sounded content in that moment, if not actually happy.

The fire started to die down, though the coals were still magnificently alive, and faint glows and shadows ran across the cinders. Lauri went to get two more logs. The fire started burning more vigorously again, and sparks shot toward the sky. In the darkness they drew thin red streaks that died almost instantly but remained for a moment as afterimages on Lauri's retinas.

Katharine stared at the embers. "By the way, thanks for sticking up for me that time at your office," she said.

"No problem."

"Did you have any trouble?"

Lauri shrugged.

"My fingers were sore for a couple of days. And I jammed the knuckle in my middle finger. A couple of times I had to take something for the pain. But nothing broke."

"I meant trouble with your job."

"I handed in my resignation the same day. Andrews didn't accept it. But he won't bother you anymore—I promise you that. I told him I'd give him a real beatdown if he didn't leave you alone."

"You're lying."

Lauri smiled. "I don't lie. Of course he thought I was bluffing, but he isn't completely sure. So I think he'll play it safe."

"Were you bluffing?"

"To tell you the truth, I don't know. I've been feeling pretty self-destructive lately."

"You're too aggressive. If you act that way, you aren't any better than Washburn or Andrews. Or at least not much better."

Lauri didn't answer.

"You probably wanted me to thank you right away," Katharine said. "But I don't actually like anyone protecting me that way. With violence. If I did, I would have hired myself a big gangster as my pimp. I don't like violence. And I detest violent men."

"I understand. What can I say? You're probably right."

"Anyway, thanks. Really," said Katharine.

2

The next morning Lauri Nurmi woke up next to Katharine Henshaw. His clothes were on. The back of his head and his temples throbbed. His mouth tasted foul.

"Don't worry, nothing happened," Katharine assured him. "Your virtue is still intact."

Struggling to his feet, he went into the bathroom and swallowed three ibuprofen. The water quickly triggered a wave of nausea, and for a moment he was afraid he was going to vomit. Then the queasiness passed.

"Do you want some?" he asked Katharine and showed her the bottle.

Katharine shook her head.

"No need. I didn't drink like you did."

Katharine walked into the living room, where her gaze fell on the Beretta lying on the table.

"By the way, what were you planning to do with that? Shoot me? Shoot someone else?"

"More like shoot myself," Lauri replied honestly.

"I kind of thought so. And are you still thinking of doing something like that to brighten my day? As a little thank-you for coming to see how you were doing?"

Katharine's voice bit like a whip. Lauri rubbed his jaw, suddenly embarrassed, and didn't say anything.

"Good, then we can get rid of this." Katharine picked up the Beretta with two fingers. Her expression was one of disgust, and Lauri thought she looked like she was dangling a decomposing rat. Katharine went over to the compost bin and dropped the pistol in on top of the coffee grounds, eggshells, and fish bones.

Lauri dove after it. "Hey, you can't do that," he said. "You can't treat a firearm like that . . ."

Completely ignoring Lauri's protestations, she started opening cupboards until she found the coffee. She spooned what in Lauri's opinion was far too much coffee into the coffeemaker's filter.

"Coffee that strong messes up your stomach," Lauri said.

"I think in your case the problem may be something other than coffee."

"But . . ."

"Coffee isn't strong until a spoon stands up in it. If you want to drink weak swill, then go boil a bucket of ditch water. I need some proper poison to get me moving in the morning."

"And what if it gives me an arrhythmia?"

"Does that matter? You aren't going to live very long the way you've been going anyway."

Female empathy is the most overadvertised thing in the world, Lauri thought bitterly, but he didn't say it out loud.

After breakfast they went to let Orinoco out in the pasture. Katharine took her shoes off.

"There might be stickers on the ground," Lauri said.

"I think my feet can take it," Katharine said.

"Have it your way. But they can swell up pretty nastily."

"I always go barefoot when I can," Katharine explained. "I enjoy the feeling of freedom. My life can get a little claustrophobic sometimes."

Just like Alice, thought Lauri, and he felt as if a small circular saw had just started up in his stomach.

Katharine looked at him, frowning.

"I'm fine," Lauri said.

When they approached the enclosure, Orinoco trotted toward them. He looked at Katharine suspiciously. Lauri dug some sugar cubes out of his pocket and dropped them into Katharine's hand.

"This is a really bad habit, not good for the teeth, but just this one time. Give him these."

Katharine offered the sugar cubes to Orinoco. After only a second's hesitation, the horse stretched out his muzzle and started to munch the sugar cubes out of Katharine's palm.

"There you go. You may have a new friend," Lauri said.

Katharine let her gaze scan around the yard, the large main ranch house, and the barns and other outbuildings surrounding it in a wide half circle.

"You must be rich," Katharine said. "That Tesla in front of the house wasn't cheap."

"Less than a third the cost of a Lamborghini," Lauri said. "Although it does go zero to sixty in four seconds. Three seconds faster than a Lambo."

"So you're in a hurry to get somewhere?"

"It's Alice's. Or, I mean, it was. Actually, I don't know who owns it right now."

Katharine stroked Orinoco's neck, and the large stallion whinnied with pleasure.

"He likes you," Lauri said. "Yeah, I guess I have accumulated quite a bit. Hazard pay. I wish I could say I'd earned it with honest work like you do. Adults buying and selling sex doesn't necessarily hurt anyone.

But this is blood money. I'm not an American by birth, so I guess technically I'm a mercenary. A war whore."

"But at least you've always been with the good guys against the bad guys, right?"

"That's what I thought. But now . . . I don't know anymore. Everything is kind of blurry these days. Confusing."

Lauri was aware of how thoughtfully Katharine was looking at him.

"We're the soldiers of a crumbling world power," Lauri said. "Someone might think there was something romantic about that. But there isn't. The might of a great empire is like a picture drawn on water. But there isn't any glory to its collapse. It's just shit. Nothing more, nothing less."

"If only all choices were so simple," said Katharine. "But those lithium thefts and Washburn . . . Have they gotten the lithium back?"

Lauri shook his head.

"One terrorist we interrogated said they have lithium and plutonium igniters. And we found a picture of an enormous hydrogen-uranium bomb being built in the hold of a ship. But that's all. We can't find the lithium or the plutonium or the bomb."

"Have you made any progress?"

"We're going around in circles. We're back at square one. Actually, everyone is getting pretty hopeless."

"So what do you intend to do?"

"We don't have very many options. And I don't know how long we dare to wait anymore. We'll probably have to arrest Washburn and all of his friends and interrogate them soon. Maybe they know where the lithium is."

"And if they don't know?"

"Then we don't have anything."

"And then what happens?" Katharine asked.

"Good question," Lauri said. "How will people react when a nuclear bomb turns a whole city to ash for the first time? I mean, all the residents of all the other big cities? Or even if that never happens, what will people do if information about the danger leaks to the media?"

It was possible they were living the final moments of modern urban culture. Its last weeks. Worst-case scenario, its last days.

"Right now I might not put all my savings into apartment real estate," Lauri said.

"Well, then I'll have to put off buying that penthouse until next year," said Katharine.

3

In the afternoon wind, melancholy squadrons of gray, tattered clouds wandered the sky over Sierra Vera. The air was growing cooler and smelled of approaching rain.

Katharine and Lauri had climbed the slope of a nearby mountain. Before them spread a wide view over Sierra Vera and the surrounding plains. They saw Orinoco as a tiny black dot in the farthest corner of the pasture. Next to him was a second, slightly smaller brown dot. Ayenwatha.

Dried golden-yellow grasses covered the mountainside in a thin but soft carpet. Here and there among the shorter grasses were areas covered by burro-weed, thorny velvet mesquite, and cacti. Behind them was a line of gray and red sandstone cliffs, low mountains climbing several hundred feet high. In many places the slopes were perfectly bare, nothing but rock and sand.

"So you didn't actually tell me anything about yourself," Katharine said. "Back when I asked."

"When was that? What do you want to know?"

"Just what you want to tell me."

They sat on the mountainside. Lauri let his eyes scan the landscape.

"I'm originally from Finland," Lauri finally said. "It's the country between Sweden and Russia."

"Yes, I believe I know where Finland is," said Katharine. "The land of Lordi, Santa Claus, and the Moomins. What I didn't know is that people live there too."

"Very funny," Lauri said.

"How did you end up here?"

"It's a long story," said Lauri.

Lauri heard his own voice from long ago, his own determination. "*This is the last time you chase me and beat me up. It ends now, one way or another.*"

"OK, never mind then," Katharine said.

Lauri watched the clouds moving, faster now, across the sky.

"I guess my past is a little like yours," Lauri said suddenly.

"What do you mean?"

"I read in your file that your grandmother was from Ukraine. I know what happened to her."

"You have a lot of information about me."

"Apparently my grandfather was from East Prussia. That was probably the only place that suffered worse than Ukraine in the war."

"Is that so?" Katharine's tone was dry, but Lauri also sensed a new interest that she wasn't trying hard to hide.

War didn't end when the battles were over, Lauri thought. Every war left mounds of flotsam drifting back and forth in the waves. People whose bodies were alive but who were dead otherwise. A war didn't even end when the people who survived it had died. People passed down their wounds and scars. They encapsulated their untreated traumas as big, solid lumps of silence whose muteness made them something even worse for their children. What chance did children or teenagers have to understand or deal with something that didn't even have a name? Especially if they didn't have even a vague idea of the horrors that had shattered their parents' souls.

Katharine waited for Lauri to answer. She sensed that he wanted to say something important.

"When my mother was young . . ." Lauri let his sentence trail off.

"You aren't getting out of here alive." The voice of the biggest boy flashed in Lauri's mind. He saw it all again. The bright blue, cloudless sky. The boy many years older and much larger, seeming almost as tall as a mountain, coming straight for him. *"You're going to die now. You never should have done that!"* When the mountain had approached, Lauri's hand had moved automatically, as if it weren't a part of him at all, and suddenly the mountain stopped and fell heavily to its knees. The four other bullies looked in shock at the mountain who had attacked Lauri, whose nose Lauri had broken with the first stone he threw. He remembered how somewhere in the background there had been a dull thud when the stone thumped right into the mountain's forehead. Blood gushed from a face contorted in pain.

And then, a little later, the worst moment of all, when he realized that . . .

Lauri snapped out of his memories.

"Let me guess," Katharine said quietly. "Your mother did something similar to what I do now?"

Lauri nodded.

"That was why you defended me?"

"I don't know."

Katharine waited.

"Maybe. Could be. It's possible."

"Is your mother still alive?" Katharine asked.

"Yes. But I haven't seen her for a long time."

"Why not?" Katharine asked.

Her voice was quiet, but the intensity of the question was palpable.

"I . . . don't know."

"No, of course not," Katharine said dryly.

"It isn't that easy. But . . . you're right. I should . . . before it's too late."

"Do you have siblings?" Katharine asked.

"No."

They sat for a while in silence. More than half the sky was covered in deep gray now, and at the horizon, thick masses of cloud were accumulating. When Lauri watched them closely, he thought he could see dim flashes of lightning, but the front was still so far away that the thunder didn't reach them. Two turkey vultures circled, dizzyingly high in the sky.

"We'll get wet if we stay here much longer," Lauri said.

Katharine nodded absentmindedly.

"There's one more thing I should ask," she said.

"Go ahead."

"You said we have to think things all the way through. That you can't stop at the first link in a logical chain. That you always have to follow the whole chain to the end."

"Yeah, that's what I think."

"What if we thought one thing through? I mean . . . to the very end?"

Lauri looked at Katharine in confusion. What was she getting at?

4

A single raindrop slapped against Lauri's forehead. It wouldn't be long before it was pouring. Lauri stood up, and Katharine followed his example. They began descending the hillside toward the ranch house.

"My brother suggested I ask you what would happen if the terrorists used the lithium to blow up nuclear power plants," Katharine said. "If someone launched a lithium-deuteride grenade into a nuclear reactor."

"I don't think the explosion would be very large," Lauri answered evasively.

But a small voice at the edge of his consciousness tried to tell him something.

Katharine nodded. A strong gust of wind fanned her hair and made a few thin, dark strands dance on her face and lips.

"That's what Michael guessed," Katharine said, pulling her hair away from her face. "But did you say that if we started using nuclear power to fight climate change, we would need breeder reactors? Or fusion?"

"Yes. Otherwise there would only be enough fuel for the reactors for a few years."

Lauri knew that in theory all the energy humanity would need could be produced with thirty thousand large nuclear reactors, because the nuclear fuel reserves of the Earth could be multiplied a thousandfold using a combination of fast breeder reactors producing plutonium and converting thorium to uranium. But five reactors out of six would have to be breeders. In addition to what they consumed, five breeder reactors also produced enough fuel for one more regular power plant.

They stopped for a moment, as Katharine tied her tangled hair into a tight ponytail, and then continued their descent.

"Breeder reactors either use liquid sodium or lithium as their coolant, right?" Katharine asked.

"Yes," Lauri said. "Water doesn't work. It slows the neutrons down too much. Slow neutrons are good for splitting atoms, but if you want to turn a lot of uranium into plutonium, you need fast neutrons. They have to come in really hard to penetrate the nuclei and get trapped there."

A few more drops fell from the sky. One of them hit Lauri's lips, another his nose. He saw small droplets glistening in Katharine's hair. Niels Bohr had compared atomic nuclei to drops of water and the force that held the nuclei together to the surface tension of the drops.

"Michael said the fuel in breeder reactors has to be stronger than in normal nuclear power plants. At least fifteen but preferably thirty percent plutonium-239 or uranium-235."

"I don't think Michael's the only one who's been doing his homework," said Lauri. "Rapid-series breeder reactors, which the lighter Rapid-Ls were developed from, use up to sixty percent uranium-235 in the outer edges of the reactor. The interior parts have fifty-two percent material."

"Doesn't that get awfully close to weapons-grade concentrations?"

"It does," Lauri said. "And I know what you're going to ask next, and the answer is yes. You can also make the first stage of a uranium bomb with breeder reactor fuel. But only if the bomb can be really large."

"Michael said I should ask what would happen if someone shoved lithium deuteride into a sodium-cooled breeder reactor," Katharine said.

"Jesus H. Christ!" he exclaimed, genuinely shocked at the idea Katharine had presented.

"What exactly does 'Jesus H. Christ' mean in this case?" Katharine asked, making air quotes.

"No one knows. I don't think anyone has ever researched that possibility. No one's wanted to think about something like that."

Ice-nine, thought Lauri.

A strong gust of wind came at them. Large raindrops fell, and they disappeared in the ground, absorbed instantly by the bone-dry dust.

"Ballpark?" Katharine insisted.

"I can't say without some computer model runs."

"Try. Guess."

"The reactor would explode, like a large nuclear bomb," Lauri said, slowly and thoughtfully. "Ten Tsar Bombas, at least. Maybe a hundred. Even if it was a normal breeder reactor, not a Rapid-series contraption. The force of the blast would depend on the amount of lithium deuteride."

"But the explosion would be big?"

"The more fissile material, the larger amount of it that generally splits. As a rule of thumb. Larger nuclear bombs are always relatively more efficient than smaller ones. The larger the nuclear bomb, the easier it is to build. With very small nuclear weapons, you have to be very precise to avoid a dud, but with really massive bombs it doesn't really matter what you do. The material will explode anyway."

"Wouldn't the explosion destroy the reactor and prevent a chain reaction from starting?" Katharine asked.

Lauri shook his head.

Lithium-6

"That's a common misconception. A large number of the neutrons come at relativistic speeds, millions of miles per hour, at least a thousand times faster than a shock wave. The shock wave only matters if the bomb is very small, the size of a pea or a human fist. If it's bigger, the pressure of the radiation forms condensates in the explosion cloud that the neutrons run into. It's a little like a supernova."

"What kind of fallout would it cause?" Katharine asked.

Lauri didn't bother answering.

"Oh," Katharine said. "So that's how it is."

An even stronger wind began howling around them, and they heard the distant roll of thunder. The slope was so steep in places that they slid down among a cascade of gravel and small rocks.

"And what if the breeder reactor was lithium cooled?" Katharine asked innocently.

Ice-nine, thought Lauri. And then he had a strangely absurd, unreal feeling because his and Katharine's roles had just changed, upending what they had been when they first talked about these same things.

"I assume your brother suggested you ask." Lauri grunted.

"He's had time to think about a lot of things," Katharine said. "And you haven't answered yet."

Lauri sighed.

"If you surrounded the reactor with a few tons of lithium-6 . . ." Lauri trailed off. "I don't even dare guess. Not without a computer model."

A furious gust of wind hit, nearly knocking them over.

For a moment its noise filled the world, and then rain began pouring down.

Katharine's face wore a hard expression of mixed anger and disdain.

"Michael said that in La Hague in France there are about seventy-five hundred tons of used fuel rods in cooling ponds near each other," she continued mercilessly. "Basically out in the open."

"True, but I didn't pile them there."

"I didn't say you did."

Raindrops beat down on their backs, and their clothing stuck to their skin. The surface of the ground was dark and wet now.

"If we start using breeder reactors to fight climate change, there would probably be cooling ponds like that near them?"

"Absolutely." *Ice-nine*, thought Lauri.

"All of those breeder reactors and cooling ponds would be located in big clusters?"

"I suppose so. I don't think people would like them scattered all over everywhere."

"So at one complex like that there could be many more spent fuel rods cooling than at La Hague now?" Katharine asked.

"Definitely." *Ice-nine.*

They were soaked from head to toe. Enormous raindrops pounded the ground like minuscule grenades, sending tiny bits of mud flying into the air. Their pant legs were filthy up to their calves. The rumble of thunder grew louder, and small, brown rivulets began running down the slope.

"How many more than at La Hague? Ten, twenty times more?"

Ice-nine.

"Maybe. That sounds reasonable. Something like that. About. At least. If we assume somewhere in the neighborhood of twenty percent of our power coming from nuclear in the future."

"Michael suggested that I ask what would happen to all of those fuel rods . . ."

Ice-nine.

". . . if a lithium-cooled breeder reactor blew up in the middle of them?" Katharine said.

Lauri's expression was her answer.

"The spent fuel rods in the cooling ponds would explode? Like the third stage of a thermonuclear bomb?"

"Yes, if there are enough neutrons," Lauri said reluctantly.

"And if we were talking about a fusion reactor?"

Ice-nine.

"Or a hybrid reactor, a fusion power plant that also works as a breeder reactor?"

Ice-nine Ice-nine Ice-nine.

"Michael said building that kind would be the most economical."

Lauri didn't reply.

"The explosion would probably start a large area on fire?"

"Yes," Lauri said. "That it would."

"How large?"

Bright lightning flashed across the sky almost directly above them, and a second later a thundering crash filled the world and made them instinctively duck.

"That was close," said Lauri.

"You're avoiding the question again," Katharine said. "Give me your best estimate."

"I can't. There are too many factors that would influence the final result. Like whether the sky was cloudy or not. Clouds could reflect radiation back, even making areas over the horizon ignite."

Katharine stopped. She was completely soaked; rivulets of rain ran down her forehead into her eyes. But she looked at Lauri seriously.

Another lightning strike split the sky.

"So there's the possibility that . . ." The roar of thunder buried Lauri's words.

Lightning flashed regularly now, and the thunder was constant, so loud that Lauri had to shout so Katharine could hear him.

". . . that the breeder reactor explosion would act a little like a gigantic Casaba-Howitzer," Lauri finished.

The sounds of the crashing thunder and the words pounding in his head—*Ice-nine Ice-nine Ice-nine*—combined as a terrible, nightmarish thrum.

"Excuse me, what?" Katharine asked.

"A plasma cannon. A directed nuclear explosion."

"I'm not sure I want to hear this anymore." Katharine's face was twisted in disgust. "Maybe you're right now. This time I don't want to know any more."

Katharine shook her head in disbelief.

"A couple more days of listening to you and I'm going to start feeling like Mother Teresa teaching Sunday school," Katharine said.

The whole slope was now a confused mix of mud and water, and they had no choice but to slide down it, each of them completely bathed in mud once they reached the ranch yard.

Bright branches of lightning splintered the black clouds. Trees bent over sideways in the wind. Darkness had almost fallen.

5

Lauri opened the door for Katharine and held it firm against the wind so she could slip inside. Inside, the sounds of the storm became fainter, but thunder shook the house.

In the illumination from the flashes of bright white lightning, Lauri could see that Katharine was shaking with cold. He brought her a large towel and a thick bathrobe.

"Go dry off and put this robe on so you don't catch cold. I'll make you a hot toddy."

A couple of minutes later, Katharine joined Lauri in the kitchen. She looked at the induction cooktop in amazement. The water pot was already heating up, and the moisture between it and the burner hissed and spat as steam escaped. Lauri flipped a switch on the wall, and the lights came on.

"I thought a storm like this would knock the power out," Katharine said.

"I don't use grid power. Power lines are ugly."

"Where does the electricity come from then? I mean, right now? Do you have big batteries?"

"The photovoltaic system is water-cooled, and the cooling system stores heat underground," Lauri explained. "Then when the sun isn't shining, the thermoelectric cells turn some of the heat stored in the rock into electricity."

"Sounds smart," said Katharine. "But aren't thermoelectric cells awfully expensive?"

"Not anymore. You get ten times as many watts out of the newer ones."

"Ah. Interesting. Shouldn't you put on something dry too so you don't get sick?"

"That would be smart."

"I can tend the water," Katharine said.

Lauri hung his clothes up to dry, put on a bathrobe, and went back to the kitchen. Once the water was boiling, he poured it into two mugs with sugar and rum.

Katharine sat on the couch, relaxing and sipping the rum toddy. Then her body suddenly stiffened.

"No, let's follow this all the way through," she said. "That's what we agreed, so don't go back on me now."

She stared at Lauri, challenging him. "Well?" Katharine demanded.

"Well what?" Lauri asked evasively.

"You said that with new technologies we should always follow the whole chain of consequences to its logical conclusion. So back to the last point: tell me what the hell you were just saying. A Casaba-Howitzer? What's a Casaba-Howitzer? You said it was a directed nuclear explosion, but I don't know what that means. I've never read about anything like that."

Lauri rubbed his chin, looking pained. While Freeman Dyson and the other Project Orion researchers were designing their civilian reactors and nuclear-powered spaceships, they also developed an entirely new kind of nuclear weapon.

"The Casaba-Howitzer would have projected million-degree plasma from a nuclear explosion toward any enemies. According to the general principle sketched out by Dyson, a nuclear explosion that started out in the shape of a cigar would spread into a pancake, but a nuclear explosion that started as a pancake shape would create a narrow plasma jet shaped like a cigar. Because the pressure gradient of the explosion in the latter example would be highest along the axis, the plasma around it would shoot forward in a narrow jet. I'm afraid inventing that idea wasn't exactly the most clear-headed moment in the history of the human race," Lauri said.

"But how does that connect to breeder reactors?" Katharine asked.

"I don't even know if it does. No one has ever studied it."

"You say that a lot."

"That isn't my fault."

Another bright strike of lightning flashed. The house shook with the power of the thunder, and glasses jangled against each other in the cupboard.

"If no one has ever studied it, you'll have to give me your best guess again," Katharine said.

"The explosion of a lithium-cooled breeder reactor or a hybrid reactor would probably be closer to Dyson's pancake than his cigar," Lauri said.

"How far would the plasma arcs reach?" Katharine asked.

"Nuclear tests have only ever produced spherical explosions. Symmetrical plasma balls. But theoretically, I think they could reach pretty far. Everything they touched would ignite. The fire storms would be huge."

"And what if nuclear power plants ended up in the middle of those firestorms? Or if a plasma arc hit another breeder reactor?"

Lauri didn't bother answering.

"OK," said Katharine. "So what you're trying to tell me is that if our governments let the world get filled up with reactor complexes, some sort of chain reaction would be a real possibility?"

"I'm not trying to say anything of the sort," Lauri protested.

"But you're the one who said we have to think things all the way through."

The lightning flickered like a television left on in a dark room. Lauri glanced out the window. The eye of the storm had passed.

"And what if in the future we have big reactor complexes with breeder reactors and cooling ponds next to fusion power plants and their fuel reserves?" Katharine continued. "And what if a tsunami hits a breeder reactor? Or a missile battery protecting a nuclear power plant from terrorists explodes by accident? Soldiers are always blowing things up—that's what we pay them for."

"Well, I don't know if that's exactly right, but . . ."

"So if we have breeder reactors, we don't actually need terrorists at all anymore?" Katharine summarized. "Great. Awesome."

Lauri watched Katharine's face as a mixture of emotions—loathing, frustration, sadness—made their way across it. Katharine set her empty mug on the table and walked to the window. For several minutes she stood in front of the window, silent and almost motionless, watching the trees driven by the storm, the flashes of lightning in the sky, the rain-battered yard. Katharine's body tensed like the string of a bow. Then she sighed deeply, and her muscles relaxed. She turned. Lauri feared what she would say next.

"Dyson, Washburn's assistant, called me again," Katharine said. "I refused. But . . . I don't know. Maybe I could find something out this time. To tell the truth, I didn't even try last time. I wasn't exactly motivated."

"I don't know if that would be a very good idea," Lauri said.

Katharine frowned. "You certainly have gone soft now."

Lauri sighed. "I don't need anything else on my conscience."

Katharine looked at him accusingly.

"You can go ahead and wallow in self-pity if you want. But you might not be the only person with a problem like that."

Lauri looked miserable.

"I can talk to Andrews directly," Katharine said.

Lauri realized she had already made her decision. He shook his head in resignation.

"You're just as stubborn as Alice," he said. "Fine, but I'm coming too. We've infiltrated their circle, at least a little bit. Washburn invited one of our agents to his next house party, and our agent also has permission to bring a couple of friends. David Farley and Gus Taylor were supposed to go, but I could go instead of Gus."

Katharine's brow furrowed deeply. Clearly she didn't like this idea.

"I want to be there in case things get too dangerous," Lauri said. "But you don't have to go. We can get along without you."

"You don't seem to be getting along very well at all. If you'll pardon me saying so."

"Well then . . . at least let me teach you a few things."

Katharine looked wary. "A few things? Such as?"

6

Katharine and Lauri were in the shooting range in the basement of the main ranch house. Lauri had rescued the 9 mm Beretta from the compost bin, and he showed Katharine how it loaded and where the safety was. Then he handed the pistol to Katharine, grip first.

"Go ahead," he said.

Katharine stared at the gun with disgust.

"Go on, take it," said Lauri.

Reluctantly Katharine took the gun.

"This will be the one and only time. When this job is over, I'm never going to touch one of these again."

"We have a deal."

"I know. But I already regret it."

"Well, shoot toward the target and try to hit something. But first put on the hearing protection. It's pretty loud even though those panels absorb some of the noise."

"Yes, father."

"Remember, it kicks pretty hard."

Katharine put on the ear protectors, pointed the Beretta at the target, and pulled the trigger. Nothing happened. The safety was on. She sighed and switched the safety off. Then she aimed again and emptied the Beretta into the target.

The gunshots boomed like thunder in the closed space of the basement, and the cordite smoke stung their noses. Katharine pulled off her ear protection and handed the pistol to Lauri with the slide still locked back.

"OK, can I go now?" she asked.

"You have to practice a little more than that," Lauri protested.

"I didn't shoot that poorly, did I?"

Lauri went to look at the target. Every hole was within the eight or nine rings, and the grouping was tight.

"You haven't practiced shooting before?" Lauri asked in amazement.

"I already said no. Are you deaf? I don't like guns."

"But . . . you shoot ridiculously well. For a beginner, I mean. You're a natural."

"What can I say? Can we stop now?"

"Don't be so impatient. That might just have been luck. Let's try again."

Katharine sighed. With Lauri's instruction, she took new rounds out of the box and loaded them in the magazine. Then she clicked the magazine into place, released the slide, turned toward the target, and immediately opened fire.

Again all the holes were nearly touching, but now they were even closer to the center of the target. Including two right in the middle, in the ten ring.

"Well, well . . . so you're a KGB sleeper agent or something?" Lauri asked.

"Come on. I want to get out of here."

Lauri shook his head.

"Not yet. You still need to learn a few things."

"Well, what now?"

"I really hope you won't have to use these, but . . . if things get out of hand, it will be good that . . . Well, you'll understand what I mean."

Lauri pulled a small transparent plastic bottle out of his pocket. In it were ten white pills.

"Take one of these."

"Absolutely not. At least not unless you tell me what's in them."

"They are . . . well, battle drugs. They're technically illegal these days."

"Sounds great. And you want to feed them to me?"

"They used to be quite common, especially in Vietnam. They work perfectly well, but they were outlawed because . . . well, there were too many civilian casualties. Officially we don't use them anymore, but in practice . . ."

"Fuck no! There's no way I'm taking those. Pardon my French. But . . . how do they work?"

"They change your perception of time. They slow things down. And they also make you use your subconscious reflexes more than your conscious mind, which makes you faster. You can get to the same place through the right kind of practice, but that's harder and takes much more time. I use horseback archery to achieve the same result."

"I'll just stick to yoga. No drugs for me, thank you very much."

"They also remove . . . inhibitions. So you can hurt another person if you need to."

"And you want me to take something like that? Really, thanks but no thanks!"

"They don't work for very long. Maybe a day."

"That's one day too many."

"Without them you probably won't be able to do anything no matter how bad the situation gets. Without the right training, most people can't kill another human being even if they need to—unless they're seriously emotionally impaired."

People's reluctance to kill other people had always been a huge issue for armies. One of the easiest solutions to the problem was battle drugs. Earlier in history, soldiers were given large amounts of liquor before combat, partially so they wouldn't be too afraid but also at least as much so they would be able to shoot an enemy in the head or shove a bayonet in his stomach.

Lauri hoped Katharine would refuse so he could call off the whole plan.

But still he said, "Take one now so you can see how it works. And if you go to Washburn's place again, you'll take one beforehand. An hour or two before."

"I don't want to."

Lauri pointed at some human dummies at the back of the room.

"Then I want to teach you a stabbing attack. You can do it with any edged weapon, and it kills quickly. You can use a knife or scissors, or even knitting needles if you really have to."

"Stabbing? No. No. I don't want to know anything like that. The shooting was bad enough."

"You can't carry a firearm with you there. So if something happens, you'll have to find a weapon, and the only way you'll be able to get one is by taking it from one of Washburn's men. It's unlikely they'll give you one voluntarily . . ."

"So you're a comedian too?"

"You'll have to do something to one of them. At least in the kitchen you should be able to find a knife if you have to."

"Lauri. No. No."

"OK, no it is. We'll just forget the whole thing then. We can do it without you too."

Katharine saw the relief in Lauri's expression, and anger started boiling inside her. Grabbing the pill bottle from him, she shook one out into her hand. Lauri felt his mood fall again as Katharine rotated the little pill in her fingers, looking at it with disgust.

Katharine put the pill in her mouth and swallowed loudly.

"OK, are you satisfied?" she snapped. "Now tell me what fun thing have you cooked up in that dirty little mind of yours for us to do next."

7

Three days later Julia Noruz did a double take when she saw Lauri Nurmi walking into the offices of the NTU. A lump formed in her throat, and her pulse sped up.

"Hi, Julia," Lauri said quietly.

Julia stared at Lauri. He looked emaciated. His face was gaunt, he had dark bags under his eyes, and suddenly there were strands of gray in his hair. But at least he was alive, Julia thought in relief.

"I was worried," she said.

"No need," Lauri said, "I'm fine."

I'm never going to get into heaven if I keep lying like this, thought Lauri.

"Did she come . . . ? Katharine?"

Lauri nodded. "Yes. Thank you."

Julia looked sad.

"I thought she might be your type. Regardless of what she's been doing for work lately. I suspected you might let her in."

Lauri said nothing.

"Are you . . . I mean . . ." Julia swallowed her question.

Lauri noted that Julia's eyes were wet.

"No," Lauri said and shook his head. "Not at all. Nothing like that. I don't feel anything right now. Not anything at all. For anyone."

Julia swallowed hard. Lauri felt a lump in his own throat. Damn it, he thought. Poor Julia. Damn it all to hell. What was he doing here?

"I'm sorry," Lauri said.

"Don't be," Julia sighed. "It isn't your fault."

"I don't know. In a way it is."

"You can't help it," Julia said, drying her eyes. "Let's talk about something else."

"Have you made any progress?" Lauri asked hopefully. "Have you found the lithium?"

Julia shook her head.

"It's a needle in a haystack," she said.

Lauri looked at the world map hanging on the wall.

"The bomb could be almost anywhere," Julia said. "Every big nuclear power plant produces five hundred tons of depleted uranium every year. And we've been selling depleted uranium–tipped rounds all over the place. To dozens of countries."

"Yes, that's definitely a problem."

"The government wants to start inspecting every ship coming to our ports while they're still six hundred miles from shore," Julia said.

Lauri whistled. "That would be quite an operation."

"We'd have everyone on our case. Europe, Russia, China, everyone. It would be like Christmas came early for everyone who hates us."

"When do they want to start?" Lauri asked.

Julia shrugged.

"I don't know. It won't be an easy decision. But probably pretty soon. The president is worried."

"A six-hundred-mile buffer zone won't be enough if they have six tons of lithium-6," Lauri said. "We have to try something else. We can't just wait until they make their move and kill us all."

8

Lauri looked at his watch. It was 6:30 p.m. He turned to David Farley.

"Should we go?" asked Farley.

"Might as well," Lauri said.

"OK then," Farley said, standing up. Andrews and Julia walked Lauri and Farley out of the office.

"As soon as you give the signal, we'll be inside in thirty seconds," Andrews assured them.

Lauri knew that more than two hundred special ops forces had been assigned to the operation. Whether they would actually be of any help was another matter entirely.

Julia looked intensely at Lauri.

"Be careful," she said. "I have a bad feeling about this job."

"You always do," Lauri said with a laugh.

As the taxi headed off toward Timothy Washburn's house, Lauri thought once again of where everything had started, the Manhattan Project. What terrible irony was concealed behind that innocent-sounding name. Because now their greatest fear was that the Manhattan Project would return home. All the monsters that tormented his dreams and those of so many others were originally born from the ashes of the Second World War.

For at least ten thousand years, the primary fear people held was that someone might hit them in the head with a stone ax. Had our tendency to paranoia come from that, from stone axes splitting cavemen's heads? Is that why we tend to see conspiracies everywhere, without understanding that really we're just seeing our own fears? And what about what seemed to be our constant need to divide people into *us* and *them*? As if the "other" were a different species.

Everyone has fears. But when one group acts on its fears, it turns the imagined fears of other groups into reality. Attacking someone who speaks a different language or has a different skin color gives that person a real reason to fear you and seek revenge.

The taxi turned onto Riverside Drive. Oppenheimer was from here, from Riverside Drive in Manhattan, Lauri remembered. He looked at the steel gray surface of the Hudson River. In his final years, "Oppie" had been pale, almost a ghost. He had faded into a withered shadow of his former boundlessly self-confident and spirited self as his understanding increased in regard to what they had really done. Those quotations he so revered from the Bhagavad Gita probably didn't bring him much comfort, thought Lauri. In his mind he saw a photograph of Oppenheimer. The suffering on his face. The agonized, hopeless look in his eyes.

Einstein and Szilárd hated the idea of the atom bomb, which was why they wrote to Roosevelt. Still, in spite of their reservations, they initiated the Manhattan Project. Because they were afraid.

And in a way they had reason to worry, Lauri thought. Germans or Austrians laid most of the early groundwork in nuclear physics. Many, like Einstein, fled their homelands to avoid Hitler's persecutions. But the Germans still had their supergenius, the brilliant Werner Heisenberg, whom they dragged from a hideout in the mountains of

Bavaria to lead Hitler's nuclear weapons program. So it had probably been pretty frightening.

Except that Heisenberg didn't want to build the atom bomb for Hitler either. He drew up a budget for a laughably small $82,000 for the nuclear weapons program of the German Reich, as if he didn't understand that creating atomic bombs would require a massive industrial effort. Later a total of six hundred thousand people would work for the Manhattan Project, and the yearly salaries of individual scientists reached as high as $10,000. That was nearly $150,000 in today's money. So maybe Heisenberg decided the result of the whole damn war by himself, thought Lauri. Heisenberg tried to explain his trick with the budget to Niels Bohr when they met in Copenhagen. But Bohr was never what you might call a good listener. All he heard was the part about Germany having a nuclear weapons program.

Traffic was heavy, and the taxi slowed to a crawl. Lauri looked out the window to the sidewalks. Men, women, and children. Young and old. From different cultures and ethnicities and countries. From the riverbank, a few hopeful fishermen floated their lines in the Hudson River.

Why was history always such a chaotic mess? Lauri wondered. Why couldn't it have obvious grand arcs and clear red lines like in old-fashioned nationalistic historiography, like Grimberg or Herodotus? Why couldn't there be obvious good guys and bad guys? What did we do when we destroyed Hiroshima and Nagasaki? That may be the only thing we're really remembered for two thousand years from now. Like the Mongols are eternally remembered for what they did in Baghdad. Of course the reason was to scare the Russians. And they were definitely scared. They just got a little bit too scared, and see what came of that. They got so scared we all ended up minutes from obliteration. And Perimeter still exists, thought Lauri, even today. Dr. Strangelove's dead man's switch.

"How I learned to stop worrying and learned to love the bomb," Lauri said out loud.

"Excuse me?" Farley asked.

"Have you ever seen *Dr. Strangelove*?"

"The movie? Who hasn't? What about it?"

"Well, in it the Russians have this doomsday device that explodes automatically if any ICBMs are launched at the Soviet Union. It was a little like Perimeter. The system the Russians put online when NATO stationed tactical nukes in Europe in the early eighties in spite of the peace marches. After that, the Perimeter computers would automatically launch missiles if nuclear weapons were used against the USSR, even if the command centers were destroyed."

"So?"

"I was just thinking that maybe the whole system was unnecessary," Lauri said. "That the Russians built it for no reason. Because in a way something similar already existed. It was just that no one realized it. Think about the report by Nichelson, Medlin, and Stafford."

"You certainly are in a philosophical mood today," Farley said.

So much happened because we were afraid, mostly for no reason, thought Lauri. But this time the fears weren't in vain. No. This time it was real. No threat could ever be more real than this.

9

Akiko Nobura, Kenzaburo Niori, and their colleagues sat in front of a large table full of satellite pictures. There were thousands of them, and they all showed the same subject: the fishing boat. The command room walls were also plastered with copies of the pictures.

"The yakuza that Donovan killed have been identified," said Niori. "We've interrogated the survivors and all of the members of the same organization we've been able to round up. The interrogations have not produced anything useful, at least not yet."

Akiko had heard that Alice was dead. This caused her great sorrow, because she had genuinely liked Alice.

"Then we have the lithium shipment out of Osaka," Niori continued.

Akiko glanced at the satellite pictures on the walls and table. The problem was that not a single one of the photographs showed any ship other than the fishing boat.

"I think we can say we proved that the modules were moved with this specific fishing boat," said Niori. "All of the experts agree, and the radiation traces confirm it beyond dispute."

They had also gone through all of the other boats, small and large, that had left Osaka Harbor at more or less the right time. None of their holds had contained appropriate amounts of radioactivity. So it was clear the modules hadn't been transported in them. Even if the modules were packed at the harbor in a container lined with lead, the traces of radioactivity still should have been stronger.

"When the fishing boat leaves the harbor, it heads straight out to sea," Niori said. "More or less at the deepest part of the Japan Trench, it turns northeast. It continues past Tokyo, still more or less following the trench. At the southern tip of Hokkaido, it changes course again toward the east. Finally it makes a turn back toward the southern tip of Hokkaido and lands in a small fishing village."

Akiko had never seen her boss this tired. The pressure and expectations that had been heaped on him in the past weeks must have been crushing, and she felt sorry for him.

"Let's go over everything one more time," Niori said wearily. "Maybe that will help."

Everyone could see he didn't believe that. Niori went to the map on the wall and ran his finger along it.

"Based on the satellite images various countries have given us, we've been able to reconstruct the fishing boat's path from here in Osaka to the tip of Hokkaido."

Akiko looked at the picture collage on the wall. There were no holes in it. Not one single break. The fishing boat had not met any another surface vessels.

"The satellite pictures don't show the meeting we're looking for," Niori summed up. He tapped his finger on a black cross drawn in marker on the coast of Hokkaido.

"When the fishing boat arrives here in the village, the modules aren't on it anymore."

They had conducted hundreds of interviews in the village. At least twenty eyewitnesses had confirmed the same story. When the fishing boat landed, four men got out. They moored the fishing boat to the dock. Then they just left, walking briskly to some cars waiting for them nearby.

"They weren't carrying anything with them," Niori continued.

At least not six tons of lithium, thought Akiko.

"So, what's left?" asked Niori.

They must have dumped the modules in the ocean, thought Akiko. Most likely through some sort of bottom hatch. That wouldn't have been hard.

"We might be dealing with a submarine," said Niori. "A second, more likely option is that they set the modules adrift in a sea current leading in a direction where a surface vessel could pick them up. Floats designed the right way would have prevented the modules from sinking to the bottom but kept them below the surface."

There was a third possibility, and Akiko believed it because she knew that if she had been one of the terrorists, it was what she would have done. It would also explain why they wanted to kill her and Alice, and why no one had been able to think of any other logical explanation for the attempt on their lives. Akiko thought she was right, but she didn't know if anyone would believe her. Particularly in Japan. Except maybe Niori.

When it came to the Americans, though, Akiko was 100 percent sure no one would listen to her theory.

10

Lauri snapped out of his musings when David Farley nudged him in the shoulder.

"We're almost there."

"Good," said Lauri. "I sort of drifted off there for a second."

"It seemed like it," Farley said. "But I don't think there's much to talk about anymore. At this stage."

Moments later, as they walked toward the main entrance of Timothy Washburn's enormous house, a strong feeling of foreboding hit Lauri.

"Are you alright?" Farley asked.

Do I look worried? Lauri wondered.

"Never mind," he said. "Let's go."

Except that the last time I felt this way, Alice died, Lauri thought darkly. *Maybe I shouldn't be here. Katharine definitely shouldn't be here. She helped me. She may have even saved my life. I never should have let her come here.*

Washburn stood at the door, shaking hands. Lauri recognized him from photographs. He was a dark-haired handsome man with a faint bitterness in his eyes and on his lips. Even his brilliant smile didn't quite conceal that edge.

Washburn didn't seem to Lauri like a terribly happy person. On the other hand, why would he be? A US bomb had killed everyone he loved.

"Tim, this is John Mitchell," said one of the men standing with Washburn at the door. "Remember, I told you about him."

"Excellent. Nice to meet you, Mr. Mitchell," Washburn said, extending his hand to Farley. "Come in and enjoy everything my house has to offer. Consider everything you see at your disposal. Make yourselves at home."

"Thank you, Mr. Washburn," said Farley. "I'm pleased you invited me. And may I introduce my business partner, Arthur Hall."

On cue, Lauri nodded to Washburn.

David Farley/John Mitchell and Lauri Nurmi/Arthur Hall walked inside, past the two guards Washburn had posted at the door. Loud rock music played inside the house. Lauri noted that it was coming from large loudspeakers suspended from the ceiling. He could feel the drums and bass guitar in his gut. They went to get hors d'oeuvres from a lavish buffet that offered everything from caviar and oysters to shrimp and cold cuts. They picked up drinks at the next table.

Lauri looked around and tried to count how many men Washburn had. Fifteen minutes later he was convinced there were at least twenty men who were probably armed. They were either guards on Washburn's payroll or his shady business associates. Or both.

The unarmed guests numbered well over one hundred, and all of them were men. The only women were the prostitutes Washburn's assistants had hired. There were about thirty of them, some very scantily clad. Every once in a while one of them would disappear up the stairs with one of Washburn's guests. Lauri tried not to look for Katharine. He had seen her last the previous evening, and she had promised to take a battle-drug pill. Just in case.

Lauri finished his Scotch and went for a refill. He thought he would arouse suspicion if he didn't drink along with the others. He didn't see Farley anywhere. Where had David disappeared to?

"Would you like to go upstairs with me, hon?" Katharine's voice asked from beside him.

Lauri jumped and turned toward Katharine. At first all he saw were her eyes, which were made up to look unnaturally large.

Then he saw that Katharine was wearing next to nothing but the red-and-black henna tattoos that covered her from neck to toes.

"Jesus, Katharine," Lauri whispered.

"Don't overreact," Katharine said. "This won't attract any attention if you don't react to me too strongly. I'm supposed to talk to the guests and invite them up."

"But what you're wearing . . . I mean not wearing . . ."

"This is how they wanted me," Katharine said, a sudden tinge of bitterness in her voice. "Don't get all sanctimonious on me. I couldn't stand that now. You were the ones who sent me here."

"I've been trying not to notice you," Lauri muttered.

"I saw. That was why I thought I'd come talk to you. I didn't want you to suddenly catch sight of me and be startled enough for Washburn and his men to start wondering."

"I don't know if I would have wanted to see you in that outfit. I mean in that outfit, here."

"We'll have to talk about that later sometime. But remember, I charge premium rates."

Lauri blushed.

"The worst things are always the ones you can only imagine," said Katharine. "Don't worry about me too much. I've been doing this for years. Business is booming, so I'll be sore tomorrow, but I'm not going to die from it. Don't you worry about that. I probably took that battle pill for no reason."

Lauri didn't look particularly happy, despite Katharine's reassurances.

"OK, now I believe that you don't want to come up. You obviously have work to do, and I'm going to leave you here. Just a little kiss on the cheek."

Pressing her lips lightly to Lauri's cheek, Katharine continued her rounds. Lauri noticed that his hands were sweating and his forehead felt damp too. Holy hell, that was a dangerous stunt, he thought. An unnecessary risk. Except that . . . of course everything she had said was perfectly true.

Lauri noticed that Timothy Washburn was looking at him from the front door. Lauri lifted his hand holding the wine glass in greeting, and Washburn walked over.

"Mr. Hall," Washburn said.

"Nice party," Lauri replied. "Good lookin' chicks, and the food is fantastic."

Washburn nodded absentmindedly.

"You and I seem to have quite a bit in common," Washburn suddenly said. "I mean, in light of your recent accomplishments."

"Excuse me, but I'm not sure I get your meaning. What are you referring to?"

Washburn smiled knowingly.

Shit, does he know who I am? Lauri thought.

"You see, Mr. Hall, when you hear your children and your wife and your mother shrieking as they burn to death, you burn too," Washburn continued. "All that remains of you is ash. But it is a strange ash because it never cools. It smolders eternally. A little like radioactive fallout."

Why was Washburn telling him all of this? Lauri wondered. But at the same time, he had to admit that in a certain sense Washburn was right when he said that he and Lauri had a great deal in common now. They had both lost everything they had once truly cared about. Neither of them had anything anymore, not their loved ones, not their homeland, not their ideals, to say nothing of their hopes and dreams.

They were nothing but hot, smoldering ash. The same ash that falls as snowflakes in hell. They were walking corpses.

"Do you know what is the most unique specialty of this great and wonderful land of ours?" Washburn asked.

"Well, there are so many," Lauri said vaguely.

"Of course, but I believe one outstrips all the others: we are extremely good at burning people alive," said Washburn, his voice chilling. "Even the Nazis went to the trouble of gassing the Jews to death before they burned them. The Inquisition strangled their victims before lighting the pyre. But our badge of honor is burning people alive. We're really good at that. Just think of the thermite incendiary bombs in World War II. White phosphorous. Napalm, nuclear bombs, Hiroshima and Nagasaki. Fuel-air bombs. Thermobaric bombs. Uranium ammunition. Excellent. Superb pyrotechnics. No pointless weeping and wailing. No futile questions. The Inquisition always went through the formality of asking women if they were coupling with Satan before burning them. But we don't need to waste time on formalities. Because we're defending democracy, our bombs can't make mistakes. By definition our bombs are always democratic and just. With us everything is simpler. Just a brief flash and then you're ash. If you get in our way, you're automatically an enemy combatant or at least some sort of terrorist. So it's your own fault."

Lauri laughed, somewhat coldly, because Washburn's outburst was as black as hell.

"Some might call that cynicism," he pointed out.

"Be that as it may," said Washburn. "But isn't it also true?"

Lauri saw that one of Washburn's men was motioning to Washburn from the stairs leading to the second floor.

"I'm sorry, but I have to go see to the comfort of my other guests," Washburn said. "But it was very pleasant and interesting to meet you, Mr. Hall. I hope we will be able to enjoy each other's company again soon."

Washburn climbed the stairs, as Lauri stared after him in astonishment. Had he found out anything new from that conversation? No, not really. Except that he had the feeling that Washburn knew precisely what they were doing. But how could he have found out their plans? Unless someone in the NTU was a traitor. Lauri didn't believe that was possible. Maybe he had just read too much into Washburn's comments. Or maybe there were things in Arthur Hall's background he hadn't been briefed on. Maybe he had forgotten to commit one of the memos to memory. He would have to be more careful in the future!

Lauri decided to ask Farley, but he didn't see him anywhere. Strange. He circled the whole downstairs and looked out in the yard, but there was no sign of him. Could Farley have taken a fancy to one of Washburn's prostitutes and gone upstairs?

That didn't seem probable. So where was he? This was bad.

Then Lauri heard a quiet cough behind him. When he turned to look, he met the gaze of one of Washburn's security guards. The plastic name tag pinned to his jacket only had a last name: Collins.

"You must be looking for your friend," Collins said. "Actually, he'd like to talk to you about something. He says it's important."

"John?" Lauri asked.

A red warning light was going off in his head.

"Exactly," Collins said. "Mr. Mitchell."

"Where is he?"

"Upstairs. I can show you the way."

What the hell had Farley done now? Something stank.

Lauri started up the stairs, following Collins. His heart was pounding. Collins opened the first door and motioned for Lauri to enter.

Lauri walked through the door and into a corridor that led to a large living room. As soon as he stepped in, he noticed two things simultaneously.

David Farley lay spread-eagle on his back on the floor. He wasn't moving, and his eyes were glassed over. Under him was a large puddle of blood, and his throat had been sliced open. Next to the body was what looked like a fish-filleting knife. The long, thin blade was covered in gore.

And there stood Tim Washburn and his two men. All three were holding pistols, and all of them were pointed directly at Lauri. *Oh shit* flashed through his mind. Behind him he also heard a faint click as Collins removed the safety on his weapon.

"Please, come in," Washburn said, smiling sweetly.

Lauri turned to his left, just a few degrees, so he could see exactly where Collins was standing. No chance, he thought. Collins was too far away—in the doorway, ten feet back. Lauri was unarmed in case he had been searched upon arrival, and he wouldn't have had time to draw a weapon in any case.

They had walked straight into a trap. But he and Farley hadn't expected Washburn's men to attack them in Washburn's own house. That was insane. Weren't they afraid of getting caught? Didn't they know the house was being watched?

"Sit down, in that chair there," Washburn said.

"Hey, if you have some beef with John, that has nothing to do with me," Lauri tried, even though he didn't really believe it would help. "I just do business with him. I'm not going to make any trouble about this. I'm sure you had a good reason for it."

"If we could please dispense with the needless prattle, Mr. Nurmi," said Washburn. "I know who you are and who the unfortunately departed Mr. Farley was. So if you could please do as I asked, we'll proceed."

Lauri opened his mouth to protest, but Washburn shook his head.

"You can save me the tedious display and simply believe that I know everything you've been up to lately."

Lauri's expression was one of open disbelief. Washburn laughed.

"Guess whose company makes the very best state-of-the-art listening devices?" Washburn said. "But, could you please sit to save me from having to put a hole in your stomach?"

Lauri sat in the seat indicated. Washburn and his men kept their weapons carefully trained on him. Still no chinks in the armor, thought Lauri.

Washburn owned a company that made high-tech listening devices. Goddamn it. Why hadn't they known that? Maybe the company's ownership status was hidden too well, behind too many subsidiaries and holding companies. And what about Katharine? Was she in danger? Lauri tried to think what Washburn would know about Katharine if he had microphones in their offices. What had they talked about at the office and what only happened at Sierra Vera and Katharine's apartment?

"Then you can start taking off your clothing," Washburn said.

"What?" Lauri asked.

"I don't want to take any risks. You might be wearing a wire or hiding something else. Take your clothes off, now."

"But . . ."

"Would it help if I shot you in the foot?"

Lauri realized he had no choice but to comply. He took off his jacket, shoes, and socks. Then he unbuttoned his shirt and dropped it on the ground.

"Stand up and take off your trousers," Washburn ordered. "No sudden movements."

Lauri stood up and pulled off his pants.

"Underwear too," Washburn said.

Lauri complied.

"And now?" Lauri asked, standing stark naked before Washburn and his men.

"Next you bring the pile of clothes over here and return to your chair," Washburn said. "Go ahead and try to throw them at my face, if you want. But we're aiming at your stomach right now, so it might hurt a little."

Lauri carried his clothing to the middle of the room and dropped them where Washburn had indicated.

"Fine, now go back," Washburn said.

Lauri returned to his chair and sat down.

Collins, who had still been standing at the door, came and inspected Lauri's clothing with a metal detector and some other device Lauri didn't recognize. Then he threw the pile of clothes back at Lauri's feet.

"You may dress, if you like," Washburn said.

Lauri pulled his clothes back on. Two men came in and picked up Farley's body, while Collins retrieved the fillet knife next to the corpse. Then he went out and closed the door behind him.

"I was beginning to wonder a little that I hadn't heard from you," Washburn said. "I'm not necessarily surprised that none of our businessman guests told you anything; after all I am wealthy enough that they probably decided to think with their calculators rather than their brains and managed to explain away everything suspicious. But I did find it strange that your famous ECHELON hadn't found anything yet and none of the whores we dragged in had gone to the police. We did treat some of them with quite a heavy hand, after all. Bloody hell, we were loose lipped. We were getting worried it might look too much like a setup if we made it any more obvious."

Lauri had a terrible, dizzying feeling that things weren't like they were supposed to be, that they were once again going off the rails, this time even worse than when they attacked the *Bristol*. It was as if he were playing chess against a grand master—who was several moves ahead of him and who was also somehow dictating how the game would be played by the opposing side.

11

A mocking smile appeared on Timothy Washburn's face.

"You still don't understand any of this, do you?" Washburn asked.

The whole situation was feeling increasingly unreal to Lauri.

Where was this going? he wondered.

Washburn hesitated.

"Maybe you deserve to know," he said to Lauri. "First of all, just for your information, what's going to happen next is that I'm going to shoot you and then we're going to drag your body and Mr. Farley's outside. I assume the rest of your associates will see and rush in here. Then a few men will die in the ensuing firefight. For example, me and everyone else around me who knows too much. The others will be taken prisoner. So this is actually a sort of suicide mission, although it may not look like it."

Lauri looked at Washburn, genuinely confused, still not understanding what he was talking about.

"You see, Mr. Nurmi, as soon as you start using the methods of the Inquisition, you also necessarily begin experiencing the same problems as the Inquisition."

"I don't understand what you mean."

"At first there were only a few witches in Europe, but when they started squeezing confessions out of people with torture, they found more. Millions. So many that for a few centuries Europe became the only continent where there was no knowledge of painkillers. Since all of the herbalists had been burned at the stake. For centuries the Catholics and Protestants concentrated with admirable enthusiasm on little more than killing each other. Which, in terms of the rest of the world, may have been the most intelligent thing the Europeans ever did. Too bad those grand traditions have faded as of late—hopefully they can be revived someday."

And then Lauri suddenly understood what Washburn was saying. Washburn looked at him in amusement. He had clearly taken note of Lauri's downcast expression.

Washburn sneered. "Yes, exactly. Before, your government fought against torture, at least to some degree. Now you have become the greatest apologists for it in the world, a veritable torturers' PR machine. Even Hollywood has been enlisted to explain to the good people of the world why torture is really a perfectly appropriate form of entertainment. All of our men who are taken prisoner know what will happen to them. They are prepared for it."

"You can't really mean that . . ."

"Yes, I mean precisely that. They have learned to withstand severe, unrelenting pain. Practice does wonders, especially since pain is largely a psychological thing. They won't say anything for a long time. But when they start to talk, they will reveal a long list of names, some the same, some different. Some will be invented. People who never existed."

Washburn gave a joyless laugh.

"I hope your friends have fun looking for our ghosts," he said. "Some of the real names will be brothers you've already caught. Some will be brothers whose names you know but who are not in the United States at the moment. And then, the sugar at the bottom: a small number will be your strongest allies. Carefully chosen American Muslim leaders who work against us and have large networks of followers we find bothersome. But you can handle that problem for us now."

Lauri closed his eyes. *This can't be true,* he thought. No one could ever plan and execute such an insanely devious plan.

"I have an inkling that what you do to these important allies of yours will turn a large number of their supporters against you," said Washburn.

Washburn watched Lauri with a tense, bitter smile.

"But they don't live in Iraq or Afghanistan or Vietnam," continued Washburn. "They are US citizens. Your neighbors. Soon you will be forced to brutally repress all US Muslims. But I digress. We should be getting down to business."

Completely without warning, without even any change of expression, Washburn shot Lauri in the right thigh. At first Lauri only felt a blunt force that struck like a hammer and a numbness that spread through his leg. Then came the pain, which started from his thigh but instantly spread through his whole body, concentrating in the back of his skull. Lauri knew the bullet must have broken his femur. When he looked down, he saw blood gushing from his leg. The bullet must have damaged one of the arteries in his thigh. Immediately Lauri knew this was a life-threatening wound. He had seen a lot of people die this way.

Washburn looked at Lauri appraisingly.

"What do you think? Is that enough to do it?" he asked Lauri.

"Yes, I think that should do it," Lauri panted.

"Well, just for good measure, let's add one more." Washburn shot Lauri again, this time in the shoulder.

Lauri's arm swung violently to the side, and he spun out of the chair, onto the floor. When he slammed into the tile, the pain hit his brain like a jolt of electricity and he nearly lost consciousness.

"This job didn't quite go the way you'd hoped, did it?" laughed Washburn. "Or what do you say?"

Lauri tried to move his left hand, but it didn't obey, and a stabbing pain ripped through his shoulder. Blood was also coursing from it, but not quite as much as from his thigh.

"Sometime when you're bored, ask someone at your office why they added small amounts of mercury to some of the weapons used in the nuclear tests. I don't think they'll tell you, but if they do, I think you may be amused. Oh yes, I'm sorry, I forgot for a moment that you won't ever have that chance."

"Just out of . . . curiosity: How much . . . plutonium . . . did you manage . . . to steal?" Lauri spluttered from the floor, gasping with pain.

He felt the rapidly growing pool beneath him, wet and sticky. The pain was at once stabbing and throbbing, and almost unbearable.

Washburn looked at Lauri strangely.

"Plutonium?" he asked. "None. Why would we?"

12

Katharine Henshaw held the hand of one of Washburn's business partners, a man of about sixty, and led him upstairs. One of the hall doors opened. Katharine watched two of Washburn's men carry David Farley's body out and close the door behind them. Katharine froze.

Ten minutes earlier she had seen Lauri go into the same room.

Something was very wrong.

The gangsters hauled Farley's body to the end of the hall, leaving a thick trail of blood.

"You're not supposed to see this," a third man who exited the room said to Katharine. "Get lost!"

Katharine read the man's name badge: Collins. It seemed as if he barked his command for show, like it didn't really have any significance. How was that possible? Washburn's men had just committed murder. They had killed a federal agent. Katharine and her companion were witnesses. By all rights this should have concerned Collins a great deal.

Katharine watched as her companion ran down the stairs in a panic. But no one tried to stop him. Why not?

A bang came from the room. The space must have been sound insulated, because the noise was muffled. But there was no doubt that it had been a gunshot.

Before she could turn around, Katharine saw that some of Washburn's bodyguards downstairs also heard the gunshot—their expressions immediately turned nervous, expectant.

There could only be one explanation. Something was going to happen soon that would change the order of things. That would make small details like allegations of murder inconsequential. Should she do something? What could she do?

As she turned toward the door, another shot echoed in the room. Katharine trembled as if the bullet had struck her.

What was happening in there? Who was being shot? No, it couldn't be . . .

Collins looked at Katharine in amusement. Katharine saw that he was holding a knife with a long, narrow blade in his left hand. The blade was bloody.

"I told you to get lost, baby," Collins said again. "Go."

Katharine smiled back.

"It's embarrassing to admit it, but . . . this kind of thing turns me on," Katharine said in a husky voice.

Katharine noticed that the battle-drug pill was really starting to kick in. She felt strangely light as she walked toward Collins. As if she were gliding in the air, her feet not touching the ground. It seemed to take a small eternity to reach Collins. She moved in very close to him and stroked his cheek.

"I like your kind of men," Katharine whispered. "Real men."

Katharine breathed slowly and heavily, making her breasts heave and fall with each inhalation and each exhalation.

"Real men who can kill weaker men," Katharine murmured in Collins's ear. "Who can crush any pathetic worms who get in their way."

Collins's gaze moved down, resting on Katharine's barely veiled breasts.

"Some other time, baby," Collins said coldly.

"It would only take a minute," Katharine said.

Katharine lightly brushed her hand against Collins's lower stomach and then his upper thigh.

"Come off it," Collins said.

But his insistence that Katharine stop was not as determined as before. She gently tried to remove the long knife from his fingers. Katharine noticed that she no longer had normal feeling in her hands. She felt increasingly unreal. As if she were in a dream.

Maybe it was just a dream. Maybe she would wake up soon. Maybe none of this was real. Maybe no one was going to get hurt. No matter what she was about to do.

Collins's grip on the knife weakened slightly.

I don't believe this is really happening, Katharine thought distantly. *I don't believe I am doing this.*

13

Lauri looked at Washburn, dumbfounded. The warm, wet pool of blood under him kept getting bigger.

"What did you mean when . . . that you didn't . . . plutonium?"

Washburn laughed smugly.

"Why would we have stolen it?"

"But . . ."

"Plutonium is terribly radioactive. It's nasty stuff to handle. You get blisters on your hands. Your balls fall off."

"But . . ."

"We paid a French scientist a million dollars to record an extra one hundred and eighty milligrams of plutonium in his company's figures. In many tiny batches. Material that never existed, that is. Then when he 'noticed' the issue and reported it to his supervisor, and the missing plutonium was nowhere to be found, a minor panic ensued. Actually it was pretty funny. And then we paid the yakuza to steal us a nice big pile of lithium and dump it five miles down in the ocean. We asked them to splash a little blood around while they were at it to make the job attract attention. So everyone's brains would get locked into just the right grooves."

And they certainly delivered, Lauri thought, his heart breaking.

"See, once people decide to think about something a certain way, they aren't able to change their opinions about it later," Washburn said. "There are rare exceptions, but mostly people's behavior is quite predictable."

Lauri couldn't stand listening to Washburn.

"We thought this might poke the hornet's nest, as it were," Washburn said with a chuckle. "The yakuza enjoyed the prank just as much as we did. You're mistaken if you believe the Japs have forgotten what you did to Hiroshima and Nagasaki. That your government so casually decided to blast a few hundred thousand more civilians to ash even though Japan wanted nothing more at that point than to surrender. These sorts of things always come back to haunt you, sooner or later. There's no escaping them. They fade, but only a little. They never actually disappear. I think it might have been a good idea for the United States to apologize at some point. Would it have been so hard to say 'Sorry, we shouldn't have done that'? But you've just continued on in that same conceited way you always do."

"So you don't have . . . plutonium initiators?"

Lauri tried to force the simultaneously stabbing and throbbing pain away in order to think clearly.

Washburn laughed.

"No. It's much easier to make things look as if you've stolen plutonium than to actually steal it. It's also much cheaper. Do you know what it costs to build or buy a nuclear weapon? Pakistan has been bleeding the Saudis for a billion dollars a year for decades. And the Saudis fork out whatever the Pakis ask because they want our enthusiasm for nation-building to stay focused on the crude in Iraq and Iran instead of their own oil reserves. Our virtual nuclear bomb cost six million dollars, one millionth of the US nuclear weapons program's price tag. Five million to the yakuza and one million to that greedy French shit. Who, by the way, is going to be fish food soon. Just for safety's sake."

"And . . . the pictures . . . of the ship's hold?"

The pain was more distant now. He could still feel it, but it was like an intensely pulsating lump somewhere an arm's length away, something that wasn't entirely his anymore.

Washburn snorted. "Photoshop. You can do anything with a computer these days."

"Julia thought . . . the same thing . . . that they were faked."

"You probably should have believed her. A nuclear bomb that exists only in your opponent's mind is always much more useful and effective than a bomb that really exists."

"How . . . so?"

"Do you really still want to chat with me? I mean . . . do you want to leave now or in a few minutes? As far as I'm concerned, you can choose."

Lauri gave an exhausted smile. The pain was no longer unbearable, but the strength was draining from his limbs. The world began to turn blurry and dim in his eyes. Lauri knew he couldn't do anything. Soon he would lose consciousness due to the loss of blood and go into shock. He would die even if Washburn didn't do anything else to him.

"You're a very noble person," Lauri said. "If I get . . . to choose . . . I'd love to hear . . . what this is about. Why I'm . . . dying."

Washburn looked at Lauri suspiciously.

"Won't that just make you feel more bitter?"

"Maybe I'm playing for time . . . and will try . . . to take you . . . by surprise."

Where was Andrews with the cavalry? Lauri thought desperately.

Washburn shook his head.

"You certainly have grit. I'll give you that. Two slugs in you and still full of bravado. But with that blood loss, you aren't going to stay conscious very long."

"You're probably . . . right," Lauri said.

"Maybe you deserve an explanation," Washburn said, and there was grudging respect in his voice. "You see, a bomb that only exists in your opponent's mind is the perfect deterrent, because it exists everywhere at once. It is simultaneously with every known and unknown terrorist organization and in every enemy country. It is in every container coming in on every truck, train, and ship, and in the belly of every plane approaching the United States. You can't find it, you can't dismantle it, and you can't destroy it, for the simple reason that it doesn't exist. Even if in the future we claim a thousand times that the whole thing was just a ruse, your government will never believe us. Never. So now that we've convinced you that we have several plutonium igniters and six tons of lithium-6, all we have to do is wait and watch as the United States of America tears itself apart. As it bullies and harasses its allies and tortures their citizens and its own citizens and alienates one country after another until the coalitions it built with such effort during the Cold War are all irretrievably damaged and it doesn't have any real friends in the world except for Israel."

The perfect plan, thought Lauri. He had to admit that Washburn's logic approached a sort of genius in its devious simplicity.

"Martin Luther King Jr. said that all of the bombs dropped on Vietnam actually exploded on American men, women, children," Washburn said. "Modern weapons systems are even more expensive. Only a small part of the bombs and cruise missiles used in Iraq and Afghanistan do any real damage there, but every one of them blows another hole in US public health care, education, and social security."

"Could you please . . . not quote . . . Martin Luther King Jr.," Lauri said. "Just . . . to humor me."

"Right now in the United States any number of people die prematurely every year who would have lived if they would have had the sense to be born in Europe," Washburn continued. "I remember how that used to make me sad, but now I mostly just find it amusing. Actually, it's pretty damn funny. Your perspective changes so much as you gain life experience."

Washburn reached toward a glass of cognac on the table, but he kept his gun trained on Lauri the whole time, just as his men did.

Lauri knew he wouldn't have a chance even if the men lowered their weapons or, for that matter, put them away in a cabinet. He didn't have the strength to kill a fly anymore.

Washburn sipped his cognac.

"Well, how did you like it?" he asked Lauri.

"I have to admit . . . it was a . . . very interesting . . . plan," he said.

The world lurched and spun as if he were drunk. He didn't hurt much anymore. But now his fingers and toes were cold, and the chill was moving slowly upward, toward his wrists and ankles.

"Of course an imaginary nuclear bomb does have the drawback that you can never detonate it even if you want to," Washburn said. "But in reality, the same thing applies to all nuclear bombs. They are weapons that cannot be used. And why would we want to use a nuclear bomb against the United States anyway? After that everyone would hate us for the next thousand years. The US would get all its old allies back. We don't want to be marginalized, we want our own men in power in Iraq, Iran, Saudi Arabia, Pakistan."

The spinning motion stopped. But the cold, chilling sensation moved up his arms and legs, and Lauri couldn't feel his fingers or toes at all anymore. He tried to move his thumb, but it didn't respond. His index finger wouldn't react to his brain's signals either. Lauri tried to move his hand, but that was even more hopeless. His arm weighed at least a ton. That's that, thought Lauri, his time here was up.

Washburn glanced at his watch and stood up.

"It would be lovely to stay and chat longer, but I have the feeling you're on your way out anyway, so what do you say? I have other things I could be doing downstairs."

Washburn and his men walked around Lauri toward the door.

Lauri swiveled his head to follow them, which was as much motion as he could still manage.

"OK," he spluttered. "We had . . . a good . . . talk." His voice was rough and congested. "Just . . . between us," Lauri said. "Have you ever heard . . . of . . . empathy?"

"Nowadays I only subscribe to the American version of empathy," Washburn shot back. "This is war, and in war people die. These aren't terribly big sacrifices anyway."

How strange. Lauri thought he'd heard those same words somewhere before, coming out of someone else's mouth.

Washburn curled his finger around the trigger.

"Too bad we're on different sides," Washburn said begrudgingly. "I would have liked to watch you take out those Australians. Eighteen ex-military security guards. That was quite a stunt. Such a pity that incident won't be staying secret for too much longer. Your boss may not be very pleased when certain recordings end up in the hands of the Australian media."

"Come on . . . do it," Lauri hissed. "Do it."

He wanted to die now, while he was still conscious.

Washburn raised his pistol so the barrel was pointed straight at Lauri's forehead.

Lauri was sure he was about to die. That this was it.

But Washburn uncurled his trigger finger. He looked as if he had just thought of something more he wanted to ask or say.

The hall door opened, so slowly and quietly that Washburn and his men didn't notice. At first Lauri thought he was just imagining it, but then he saw Katharine, and she was pointing something shiny and black at the back of Washburn's head. Collins was sprawled out behind Katharine. Something protruded from his neck. There were red splatters all over Katharine's face.

Red splatters . . . Was it . . . ?

Washburn was opening his mouth to say something when Katharine's hand flashed and Washburn's head exploded. Blood and something else shot all around, but the bang itself seemed very distant.

Washburn fell toward Lauri without making a sound, and Lauri saw that the back half of his skull was missing and that where his forehead had been a second before was now only a big, ragged hole. *Man, I bet that surprised him.*

He saw Washburn's men turn toward Katharine, but their movements were so slow, even more unhurried than a slow-motion film. Lauri didn't bother being worried, because he could see they didn't have a chance. An adult human turns around surprisingly slowly; a 180-degree turn takes far more time than it does to aim a pistol . . .

Somewhere very far away there was a second bang and then a third. One of Washburn's men jerked twice, and his clothing and hair fluttered as the bullets Katharine had shot pierced him. *Excellent,* thought Lauri. *Good girl. Well done.* Then he felt a quick prick in his heart and was sorry for Katharine, because he knew more or less how she would feel when the effects of the battle drug wore off and she realized she had actually killed real people. Of course that assumed Katharine would live long enough for the drug to be filtered out of her blood. It didn't seem particularly likely.

The remaining man had his gun out but hadn't managed to turn all the way around when Katharine shot a fourth time. The man dropped to the ground.

They were falling like pins on a bowling lane, Lauri thought with admiration.

Katharine held the pistol with both hands and pointed it at each man in turn. Lauri saw that one of the men looked very dead but that the other one was still moving and trying to point his gun.

I'm history, thought Lauri.

Somewhere in the distance there were two more explosions, and then the man stopped moving.

"Just another second." Katharine's voice was a murmur, a whisper.

Strange, Katharine's mouth was wide open, as though she was shouting, so why was her voice only a whisper? Did Katharine have laryngitis?

Katharine grabbed the gun one of Washburn's men had dropped, and she rushed to the door. Lauri saw her empty the pistol down the stairs. The shots were dull and muffled. Lauri thought he might have heard indignant shouts and screams of pain, but maybe he was imagining them. Katharine slammed the door and locked it. Click! Katharine grabbed Washburn's gun and came over to Lauri.

"Stay awake," Katharine yelled at him. "Just for a few more seconds."

Easy for you to say, Lauri thought bitterly. Katharine inspected his wounds. She removed Washburn's belt from his half-headless body, wrapped the belt around Lauri's thigh, and tightened it. The serious bleeding was in the lower part of his thigh, so the tourniquet was in just the right place. The bleeding from the hole in his shoulder had already begun slowing under a black mass of coagulation, but a compress should have been applied ages ago in order to do any real good.

Katharine turned Lauri on his side, and he remembered dimly that this was the right thing to do. He would go into shock less quickly. Katharine must have taken a first aid course. Could he get his legs higher so there would be more blood for his brain? No, his legs weren't listening anymore. Too late, he thought.

A knock came at the door, and a distant voice yelled something. Katharine grabbed the gun she had laid on the floor and fired twice through the door without a moment's thought. Lauri heard the cracks as the bullets penetrated the door and something collapsed to the ground on the other side.

Katharine was giving them their money's worth this time. That thought was suddenly ridiculously funny. But Lauri should probably tell her what Washburn had told him. That might be pretty important so innocent people wouldn't have to suffer. Would Katharine listen? She seemed quite impatient and busy at the moment. And how could he tell her if he couldn't get any words out of his mouth?

Katharine started to drag him along the floor. Why couldn't she leave him in peace? Katharine hauled him behind a corner, out of the line of fire, just before shots came flying through the door. The shotgun pellets hit the walls, shattering picture frames and glass. Sheetrock came off in big chunks and fell on the floor. The boys were going to town. *Time to remodel,* Lauri thought . . . first the stairs and now the walls.

He figured there were at least twenty more of Washburn's men downstairs. Katharine couldn't take on all of them herself. And there were probably even more than that—it was likely that most of Washburn's guests were also gangsters.

"Go," Lauri spluttered.

"Fuck that," Katharine replied.

What an intelligent conversation, thought Lauri.

Katharine waited for the men to come through the door. This time a barrage of shots from pump guns splintered the door. The whole lock mechanism was almost free, now hanging only by a few thin slats of wood. All they would have to do now was kick the door in.

At any second.

Katharine had a rare natural talent. If she shot as well as she had on the range in the basement at Sierra Vera, she would get at least one of the men about to rush in, and with any luck, she'd get two or three. They couldn't really hope for more than that, not now that Katharine no longer had the element of surprise on her side. If Katharine didn't leave now, they would both die within seconds of the door giving way.

The shotgun blasts had stopped. Katharine waited for the assault. Supporting her wrist with her other hand, she kept her gun trained on the door.

EPILOGUE

New York

Leaning on his cane, Lauri Nurmi hobbled toward a table in a French restaurant in SoHo where Katharine Henshaw was waiting.

"You're walking pretty well already. It's only been a month," Katharine said.

"Thanks. But the doctor says I'm going to have to miss this year's horseback archery world championships," Lauri said sarcastically.

He sank down in the chair and let the cane rest against the edge of the table.

"Maybe that isn't the most important thing in the world," Katharine said.

Lauri took a quick look at the menu and closed it.

"What will you have?" Lauri asked. "I'm buying."

Katharine shook her head. "No, it's my turn. I'm leaving if you don't let me pay."

Lauri sighed. "You don't leave me much option, do you? But I don't understand this menu. Do they have campfire onions here?"

Katharine grinned. "I can help you order."

They both ordered the catch of the day, with a bottle of sauvignon blanc to go with it. Once the waitress had gone, Katharine looked at Lauri.

"So they were stringing me along from the very beginning," Katharine said. "And through me they suckered you too."

"That isn't quite how it went. They actually succeeded in fooling us in a number of ways. We were already panicking because we had swallowed the plutonium story and knew about the lithium theft. And you remember—you don't know anything about any of this, right?"

"I remember, I remember," Katharine said impatiently. "You learn to keep secrets in my job."

"If you hadn't come to my rescue, no one would have ever known the truth. Washburn and his inner circle would have taken the secret with them to their graves, and his other cronies would have only known what they were told. We would have been chasing ghosts, and the more desperate we got the more our actions would have turned against us."

Lauri paused. "I'm sorry you had to pay such a high price for saving my life," he said.

"Let's talk about something else," Katharine said. "And besides, everything is OK now. The danger has passed."

Lauri looked at Katharine and smiled, though he grimaced mentally. Everything was OK now? The danger had passed?

The waitress brought the bottle of wine and began pouring a taste for Lauri. Instead he shook his head and indicated Katharine. As soon as she nodded in approval, the waitress finished pouring.

Lauri raised his glass. "What should we toast to?"

"Maybe spring," Katharine suggested. "Or the fact that the world as we know it still exists."

They clinked glasses and sipped their wine.

"Good," Lauri said. "Very good. Oh yeah, I have something for you."

Lauri took out a small brown envelope and handed it to Katharine. "I said I would pay you for your time."

"And I said just as clearly that I'm not working right now," Katharine protested.

"I didn't mean for tonight. For the work you did before," Lauri said.

Lauri pressed the envelope into Katharine's hand. She took it, but then gave Lauri a thoughtful look and handed the envelope back, shaking her head.

"No, I don't want money from you."

"It isn't my money," Lauri said.

"Whose is it then?"

"Well, not anyone's really. It's a little complicated to explain. It's sort of virtual money. Fiat money is the technical term. Created out of thin air. Like all money is, actually. So in a way it's just as real as any other money in the world. This money just didn't materialize out of nothing at a bank as a result of someone taking out a mortgage. It . . . well . . . it just came from somewhere."

"Wow, that really clears things up."

"Well, it isn't that important."

Katharine shook her head. She pushed the envelope even closer to Lauri. "Thanks, but no thanks."

Lauri looked dissatisfied. He didn't touch the envelope.

"Would you please just open it?"

"Why?"

"Because I had a feeling you would refuse."

"So?"

"So there's a bank statement in the envelope, not the money itself. That's already in your account."

Katharine frowned.

"How did you get a statement from an account that belongs to me?"

Lauri sighed. "Don't get angry now."

Little sparks flashed in Katharine's eyes.

"I don't particularly like when people—"

"Come on, at least see what's in it."

Katharine gave Lauri a narrow look. Then she opened the envelope and took out the bank statement. Her eyes went wide with shock.

"This has to be a joke."

"No. It's your freedom."

Katharine shook her head. "I can't accept this."

"Do whatever you want with it. Give the money to charity. Or a home for orphaned owls. Or burn it and keep doing what you're doing. That's fine with me if it's what you really want to do with your life. But if you change your mind, it's there, and it isn't any loss for me."

"But . . . three million dollars?"

"As I remember, that's how much you asked for originally. Now you can buy that penthouse in Manhattan. And invest the rest sensibly."

"But . . ."

"Take it. After all that's happened, my conscience will feel better if you do. Or, to be more precise, I won't feel like quite as big of a bastard."

"I'll go to prison if the IRS finds out about this."

Lauri grinned. "As I recall, you've already paid all your taxes on it. I bet you might even receive a refund at some point."

Katharine had to laugh. "OK fine," she said. "Thank you."

An hour later Julia Noruz showed up at the restaurant. A small wave of warmth washed through Lauri when he saw his old friend. Julia was madly chewing on what Lauri imagined was nicotine gum. He noticed her red coat had gotten a bit too tight on her. He hoped this meant she'd finally managed to quit smoking—at least for more than five minutes.

"I'm not too early, am I?" Julia asked.

"Actually, you're right on time," Lauri said, setting his napkin on the table.

Julia nodded to Katharine.

"Hi," she said.

"Came to chaperon, did you?" Katharine asked.

"Lauri asked me to be his designated driver, since he can't hold his liquor. But hey, listen . . ."

"Yes?"

"I just want to say . . . I think I may have misjudged you a little," Julia said. "That time at the office. I'm sorry. I was being stupid."

"Don't worry about it."

"And besides, what Andrews did to you was wrong."

"The end result was good," Katharine said calmly.

"At least you should have been compensated better for your work," Julia muttered.

Katharine and Lauri laughed.

"What? Did I say something funny?"

***

Lauri and Julia stopped to buy flowers, and then they drove to the cemetery and parked just inside the gates. Lauri placed the flowers on Alice's grave, and then they stood in silence for a long time.

Lauri remembered the time he had spent with Alice, how they fell in love and when they first moved in together, and everything they did at Sierra Vera. The big safari they took near Lake Chad. The mesas built up over a million years from the shells of sea creatures living and dying. The bones of ancient animals protruding from the sands of the Sahara. Their visit to the Serengeti and Lake Nakuru, their shared assignments to Afghanistan, Pakistan, and Iraq. He thought about everything that could have been but never would be.

Julia quickly touched Lauri's hand, lightly but consolingly.

"It wasn't your fault," Julia said.

Julia knew Lauri didn't believe her. She would never be able to convince him he wasn't responsible for what happened.

"What now?" Julia asked once they were back at the car. "You said there was somewhere else you wanted to go."

"If you have time," said Lauri.

"I've got the whole day reserved just for you."

Lauri was carrying a small cloth bag. He pulled out a folded map and a stack of printed pages that were stapled at the corner.

Julia picked up the papers: "Nichelson, Medlin, and Stafford," she read. "Radiological Weapons of Terror."

"This is a classic," Julia said as she handed the report back to Lauri.

"You could say that."

"Aren't all three of them Air Force generals now?"

According to the three generals, the explosion in Manhattan of a dirty bomb containing two curies of radioactive material would force authorities to evacuate everyone in a one-mile radius. Permanently.

Curie. A unit of radioactivity. Thirty-seven billion radioactive decays per second. One gram of radium.

Lauri opened the map and spread it out over the steering wheel. Julia's car had GPS, but Lauri liked maps. He showed Julia the place he had marked with a small *x* in ballpoint pen.

"Indian Point is here, twenty miles north of the city," Lauri said. "Here at the *x* is a tall hill with a good view of New York. I want to go there. To the top of the hill."

Katharine's words echoed in Lauri's mind: *"Everything is OK now."*

Julia didn't ask Lauri's reasons. She just inspected the map for the most convenient route.

"I think I can get there, but keep the map out anyway. Just to be safe."

Now the danger had passed, Lauri thought.

"Indian Point. What a terrible name," Lauri said. "Alice's mother is Iroquois, and nothing could be further from their traditional values and ways of shaping their environment."

Julia turned from the intersection by the cemetery onto the highway, and soon they were weaving through the brisk traffic north of New York City.

"You were supposed to turn there!" Lauri said.

"Thanks," Julia said. "You could have warned me earlier."

Abruptly Julia crossed two lanes of traffic and received a chorus of honks in return.

Half an hour later they arrived at the outer perimeter of Indian Point. Across the road were two concrete barricades with a dozen soldiers armed with M16s. In either direction from the barricades, a tall fence with a spool of razor wire on top ran through the forest. Lauri could see a few anti-aircraft guns a little way inside the fence.

One of the soldiers waved for them to stop and walked up to the car. Julia rolled down the window.

"I need your papers," the soldier said. "We don't have your license plate on file."

Julia showed the soldier her ID. He examined it and then handed it back, signaling for the gate at the barricade to be opened.

"You can go through."

Julia drove through the checkpoint. They passed more soldiers in small squads. Next to the road there were also two tanks and a few other armored vehicles outfitted with anti-aircraft guns and rockets.

"Quite a bit of hardware," Julia said.

"It's better this way," Lauri grumbled.

After driving for ten minutes, they reached the second perimeter. The fence was even more robust than the first. Behind it they could see the sleek outlines of the first large anti-aircraft missiles. The metal barrier across the road was so massive that even a heavy tank charging at full speed couldn't have broken through.

This time four soldiers approached, all pointing their assault rifles straight at Julia and Lauri. Julia rolled down her window.

"This is a restricted area. You need to turn back now."

Julia handed the soldier her ID card. He inspected it carefully.

"Do you have one of these too?" he asked Lauri. "If you don't, you'll have to remain here."

Lauri handed the soldier his own card. Retreating to the guard shack, the soldier placed the cards on a scanner and waited for what the computer would say.

Nichelson, Medlin, and Stafford, thought Lauri. Blowing up a dirty bomb containing three hundred curies of radioactivity would cause two hundred thousand cases of cancer unless the whole island of Manhattan was evacuated.

The soldier returned the cards.

"Everything seems to be in order," he said.

The heavy barricade began slowly retracting into the ground. As soon as it was flush with the road, Julia drove over. They passed more squads of soldiers, tanks, and anti-aircraft batteries.

"There must be a whole division here," Julia said.

"Well, not quite. But they sure have concentrated a lot of firepower. Indian Point is . . . well, it's in a very strategic location."

That was one way of putting it, thought Julia. Thirty miles from Manhattan.

"We'll be at the third fence soon," Lauri said. "Just before it is a parking lot at the base of a hill. Stop there. We'll continue on foot."

"How many of these fences are there?"

"Four or five. I don't remember exactly."

Julia stopped the car in the place Lauri indicated and locked the doors. A few soldiers walked over from the third fence to check their IDs again. Behind the parking lot was a tall hill covered in a thick scrub forest.

A narrow serpentine trail wound up the hill. They started hiking. Even though Lauri was still limping badly, he moved faster than Julia, who quickly started panting and sweating.

"I don't seem . . . to be . . . in very good shape," Julia said. "Maybe I should have kept smoking."

"Give it time," said Lauri.

Finally they reached the top of the hill, where there were twelve anti-aircraft missiles and six four-barrel anti-aircraft cannons. Approximately forty soldiers were being commanded by a surprisingly young-looking captain. Lauri and Julia had an expansive view over the Indian Point Energy Center. There were three large nuclear reactors with their containment domes and cooling towers, and next to them were the buildings that contained the spent fuel rod cooling ponds. Right around the power plant were two fences with additional soldiers and anti-aircraft weapons. In the distance were even more cannons and missiles. Outside the fourth fence were small roads only accessible to local residents, and outside the fifth fence was the freeway, along which traffic streamed endlessly in four lanes.

Nichelson, Medlin, and Stafford. According to the generals, with the right wind, ten kilograms of nuclear fuel fresh from a reactor could expose much of the population of the East Coast to a fatal dose of radiation—if it were pulverized by a conventional explosive.

"Everything is OK now," Lauri heard Katharine say again in his mind. *"The danger has passed."*

Each reactor at Indian Point had more than one hundred tons of uranium that had been exposed to long-term neutron bombardment. The whole complex contained at least two hundred billion curies of radioactive material. The fallout of four thousand Chernobyls, one hundred billion two-curie dirty bombs.

Was there any point to their work at the NTU when it really came down to it? They tried to prevent terrorists from enriching uranium and building nuclear bombs, but all the terrorists really needed to do was blow up a few nuclear power plants, and that would be that. The country would thrash around a bit, and then they'd be done for.

Farther to the south Lauri and Julia could see the skyscrapers of Manhattan. Seen from that distance they were tiny, but Lauri knew that at this time of day each of them was swarming with life. Tens of thousands of living, breathing, feeling, and thinking human beings. People with friends and relatives. Parents and siblings. Many with spouses and their own children. Each with their own hopes and dreams and goals, their own ideas about what the world was like and what it should be like. Twenty million parallel realities, each the center of its own miniature universe.

And they were all just as vulnerable, just as terribly fragile, able to live and thrive only in a zone of heat the width of a single hair from the perspective of the universe. Raise the temperature by a hundred degrees, and they would bake. Lower it by a hundred, and they would freeze, thought Lauri. The human habitat was so small. No one should ever bring the heat of a star—actually a supernova—to where people lived. Humans weren't meant for that.

"I've heard about this place, but I've never seen it before," said Lauri.

He looked at the landscape spread out below them.

"I wanted so see this because . . . Well, because I think I'm going to be coming here a lot in the future. In my dreams."

"Excuse me?" Julia said.

"In my nightmares. Before I was usually with Alice on Staten Island or in New Jersey when a nuclear bomb exploded in Manhattan. But a conversation with Katharine in Sierra Vera changed my perspective."

"Ah. I see."

Julia didn't inquire any further. Lauri would tell her if he wanted to.

Lauri thought of Dr. Strangelove and the real Perimeter system again. In reality Dr. Strangelove's automatically retaliating superbomb had existed ever since people built the first nuclear power plant. It was just that no one understood it. Launching nuclear weapons at an enemy would set off widespread firestorms. Those would destroy so many nuclear power plants that the radioactive fallout wouldn't leave anyone alive on either side. In reality it didn't matter whether the other side had time to launch their own missiles or if they were destroyed in their silos. The end result was always the same either way. For everyone.

Julia stared at the containment domes of the Indian Point reactors.

"I have to admit, it's awfully close to the city," she said. "At least those cooling ponds should be protected a little better."

How could they be so sure that frightening other people was the best way to increase their own security? thought Lauri. Once again he remembered the burning Twin Towers and the cloud of smoke and dust that covered all of Manhattan. He looked at the containment domes and wondered whether he would ever see radioactive smoke rising from them.

"Those Al-Qaeda idiots were originally supposed to attack here," Lauri said. "They didn't because they were worried about doing too much damage. See, with their own twisted logic, they thought they only had the right to kill six million Americans—one for every Muslim who had died because of us, according to their arithmetic. So they were acting a little like Hitler, who approved the Holocaust and Operation Barbarossa but who didn't want to use chemical weapons and dirty bombs against the Allies."

"Yeah?" Julia asked. "So what?"

"Somehow we succeeded in interpreting those Al-Qaeda imbeciles' messages in a pretty strange way. They didn't attack any nuclear power plants when they had the chance. But we somehow saw that as evidence that they would attack our nuclear power plants the instant they had the ability. But that isn't really true, and we can't really defend them. So just to be sure, shouldn't we concentrate on explaining to everyone that Mecca and Medina will also be contaminated if some rabid maniac attacks our nuclear plants? Shouldn't we use Al Jazeera to tell everyone that five times more Muslims would die than the entire population of the United States simply because there are five times more of them on Earth than us?"

"We couldn't only do that."

"Well, no, but should we *also* do it? Wouldn't it be beyond frustrating to die just because some idiotic terrorist didn't understand what a nuclear power plant is and why it really isn't such a good idea to attack one?"

It wasn't possible to make any progress just by building newer, more monstrous weapons. That was what humans had always done, but that road was blocked now. There wasn't anything worse to develop. And even if there were, what would it change? There was only one planet to live on. Even if someone developed more effective weapons, what would they destroy with them?

Lauri glanced at the anti-aircraft missiles surrounding him. How many missiles and anti-aircraft guns were concentrated around Indian Point now? Every increase in tensions had gradually swelled their numbers.

Lauri walked over to the captain commanding the soldiers on the hill.

"Excuse me, may I ask you a question?" Lauri asked.

"Of course, sir," said the captain.

"Do you know . . . If a three- or four-hundred-mile-per-hour windstorm picked up those missiles and tossed them at that nuclear power plant, would they detonate?"

"Sir?" the captain asked in astonishment.

"Oh, never mind," Lauri said and returned to Julia.

"I doubt he knows things like that," Julia said.

"Maybe he should, though."

"Well, put it down on the list of things to figure out," Julia suggested practically. "Item number twenty thousand four hundred and eighteen."

Lithium-6

I give you the future, thought Lauri. *Why buy a cow when powdered milk is so cheap. A seven-dollar Hiroshima. We are not bound by the known conditions in a given star. We are free within considerable limits to choose our own conditions. We are embarking on astrophysical engineering.*

Once again, in his mind's eye, Lauri watched as Ted Taylor carefully adjusted his small parabolic mirror. As Taylor looked at his watch and took a packet of cigarettes out of his pocket, opening it and tapping out a cigarette. As he placed the tip of the cigarette at the point where he thought the focus of the mirror would be, and waited. As the artificial star human technology had momentarily created on the surface of the earth made the world burst first with brilliant light and then, as the atmosphere burned, with orange, red, and yellow flames, Taylor waited for the end of his cigarette to begin to glow. Then he lifted the cigarette to his lips and drew the nicotine smoke into his lungs, smiling triumphantly.

Afterword

Thousands of nuclear technology documents became public following the end of the Cold War, and many of the facts I mention in *Lithium-6* were closely held secrets until recently. I have read everything I could get my hands on that was written by the scientists who originally developed the first nuclear reactors and nuclear bombs. These scientists—many of whom won Nobel prizes for physics or chemistry—understood more about nuclear technology than later generations, because they had the opportunity to probe its limits directly through nuclear tests.

In *Lithium-6*, I have tried to keep fact and speculation as separate as possible. It seems important to note that I haven't been able to obtain any precise information about the amount of lithium-6 contained in a Rapid-L reactor or the minimum amount of plutonium necessary to detonate a two- or three-stage nuclear weapon. This latter piece of information in particular is kept strictly secret. The estimate presented in this book ("a few dozen grams") is a guess, but it is a reasonable one. The description of the consequences of a nuclear explosion occurring in a big city is also largely speculative, but new models do suggest that an explosion in Manhattan similar to the Hiroshima bomb really would cause a firestorm with winds up to 375 miles per hour.

The scenes that outline possible methods for carrying out terrorist attacks involving nuclear technology contain a certain amount of intentional disinformation. Several much easier approaches exist, but for obvious reasons I didn't want to call attention to them.

If we want to continue producing electricity with nuclear power, the most important thing is to ensure that no accidents or terrorist attacks of any kind could release significant radioactive aerosol emissions into the atmosphere under any circumstances. Even though small amounts of radioactive material occur naturally all over the earth, nuclear power plants produce unusually large amounts of them. One cubic meter of spent nuclear fuel just removed from a reactor contains as much radioactivity as all the uranium in the outer meter of the Earth's crust. As two-time Nobel Prize–winner Linus Pauling explained in 1956, one nuclear reactor contained thirty million times more radioactivity than all of the radium extracted by the human race up to that point. For these reasons it is important that any nuclear power plants built in the future be installed directly into subterranean bedrock. This solution increases initial investments, but when the entire life cycle of the power plant is taken into consideration, there would be long-term savings. A power plant built underground in bedrock would never need to be dismantled. In addition, guarding underground nuclear power plants would be significantly easier and cheaper than aboveground stations. Building nuclear power plants deep underground could offer a significant compromise between the views of the opponents and supporters of nuclear power, allowing development to proceed but minimizing risks of containment leaks.

Nuclear power plants built aboveground will never be unequivocally safe. Based on our experience so far, the risk of a serious accident seems relatively small, but in recent years several terrorist groups have made it clear they have been considering attacks against nuclear installations. The containment domes, vents, pipes, and other parts of a nuclear power plant cannot be built to withstand an explosion within the reactor. A comparison to a firecracker is enlightening: if a firecracker explodes in your open palm, you end up with singed skin, but if it explodes in your closed fist, you lose fingers.

In any case we should immediately stop daydreaming about building breeder, fusion, or hybrid reactors—including Rapid-L type reactors—using lithium-6 as a fuel or coolant. These types of reactors would not be safe even if they were built hundreds of feet underground in bedrock, because lithium-6 can be used to construct crude but extremely powerful, two- or three-staged nuclear weapons. Other kinds of breeder reactors or so-called Generation IV reactors also would be highly problematic, not least of all because of the extremely high enrichment levels of the plutonium, uranium-233, or uranium-235 involved in most designs.

The fuel for our current nuclear reactors contains 0.7–3.6 percent uranium-235. This kind of fuel cannot be used in the first stage of a nuclear weapon without further enrichment. According to Oak Ridge, Los Alamos, and Lawrence Livermore national laboratories, the uranium-233 content in uranium has to be enriched to at least 10 percent and the uranium-235 content to at least 20 percent in order to create a single-stage nuclear weapon or the first stage of a more complex device.

All the proposed breeder reactor designs I have seen would use fuel containing at least 15–20 percent plutonium, uranium-233, or uranium-235 in at least one part of the reactor. The fuel of Rapid-L reactors contained 60 percent uranium-235, and the proposed thorium reactors (converting natural thorium to uranium-233) would contain almost pure uranium-233 in their cores.

In other words: if we move to a breeder reactor economy, every movement of fuel to any of these reactors would give terrorist organizations a new chance for acquiring the key component of a nuclear weapon.

Rapid-L would be an especially dangerous design, because it would contain both lithium-6 and uranium fuel with 60 percent of isotope 235. In *Lithium-6*, the terrorists can't use the uranium-235 because the reactor has already been operating for a while. This means that the fuel would already be so radioactive that its gamma radiation would kill the whole team in a couple of minutes, even if the terrorists somehow managed to remove the fuel rods from the reactor. However, if the terrorists could have struck just before the reactor started, they would have gotten almost everything they needed at once.

Luckily, the economics of breeder reactors do not look very promising. The Americans, Soviets, Germans, Japanese, French, and Chinese all tried to develop large breeder reactors for power-generation purposes in the 1970s and 1980s. All these programs were abandoned because of numerous sodium leaks, near accidents, and other difficulties.

The only large breeder reactor that has ever produced significant amounts of electricity was the Superphénix in France. The Superphénix operated for eleven years but only provided 7.9 billion kilowatt-hours of electricity before it was finally shut down, after the mass of steadily accumulating problems became too much to deal with. The "load factor" (the ratio between nominal power and average power) of the Superphénix was 6.6 percent, meaning that the power it produced was at least one hundred times more expensive than electricity now produced by ordinary nuclear power plants.

Nuclear reactions occur very quickly. One hundred million links in a reaction chain can happen in a single second. For this reason even very small deviations from equilibrium can move a reactor from critical to supercritical. According to Ted Taylor and Freeman Dyson, a runaway reactor is, in a way, almost like a partially misfiring nuclear bomb. The nuclear power plant destroyed at Chernobyl used only 1.8 percent uranium-235 as its fuel, but the first explosion was still a tiny nuclear explosion.

Lithium-6

One day it may be possible to build a fusion reactor that produces clean nuclear energy. But that would mean the reactor would have to use helium-3 fuel. The atomic fusion of helium-3 produces protons instead of neutrons. Because protons have an electric charge, they can be directed with magnetic fields. Unfortunately, the nearest sources of helium-3 are the Moon, the solar wind, and the atmospheres of Jupiter and Saturn. This is why the joint US-Japanese-European Union International Thermonuclear Experimental Reactor would use deuterium and tritium (lithium-6) for its fuel. The fusion of deuterium and tritium produces neutrons, which have no electric charge and which therefore cannot be controlled with even the most powerful magnetic fields.

The neutrons produced by deuterium-tritium fusion impact the shielding of ITER-type reactors at high velocity. Because of this the entire shield becomes just as radioactive as the spent fuel produced by a normal nuclear power plant. A good explanation of the differences between various kinds of fusion power plants can be found in *Return to the Moon* by US senator and lunar astronaut Harrison Schmitt. Schmitt openly states that the shielding of a deuterium-tritium reactor would have to be replaced at least every few years. The result of this is a few hundred or even thousand tons of highly radioactive waste, depending on the size of the power plant. A normal nuclear power plant produces a few dozen tons of spent fuel rods every year, but the power plant itself does not become terribly radioactive.

Contrary to popular opinion, small amounts of plutonium do occur in nature. There seem to be some kind of natural nuclear reactors inside the earth, because many fumaroles—a type of thermal gas vent—emit material containing uranium that has as much as seventeen grams of plutonium per ton. Even so, natural plutonium is rare, and it is only found in some of the most difficult places in the world to reach. Spent fuel from nuclear power plants contains about a thousand times more plutonium, up to twenty kilograms per ton. In other words, each year a big nuclear power plant produces enough plutonium to build dozens of nuclear bombs, even if the plutonium was used to make the entire bomb and not solely the igniters for hydrogen or hydrogen-uranium bombs.

Plutonium is a fast, cheap road to a nuclear weapon. Without plutonium, building nuclear weapons requires an industrial effort on the scale of the Manhattan Project. Separating the various isotopes of uranium from each other is a complicated, arduous process. Producing the raw material for one nuclear bomb this way requires running several thousand gas centrifuges for years. For example, the current conflict between Iran and the West relates to the fact that Iran has upward of twenty thousand gas centrifuges it is using to produce fuel for a nuclear power plant that is under construction.

Once a nation has a working nuclear reactor, it can build nuclear bombs simply by dissolving spent fuel in nitric acid. Because uranium and plutonium are different elements, they can be separated from each other chemically without any gas centrifuges. It is not absolutely necessary to separate the different isotopes of plutonium to make nuclear weapons. The plutonium produced in nuclear reactors starts out as the isotope best suited for bomb building, plutonium-239. As the reactor runs, other isotopes of plutonium also begin to build up, especially plutonium-240. The growth in their proportion complicates the construction of a nuclear bomb a little but not significantly.

For example, North Korea, which is not generally considered a high-tech wonderland, was able to follow the plutonium route to its first nuclear bomb within a year of George W. Bush's astonishingly irresponsible "Axis of Evil" speech.

Spent nuclear fuel can also be used, without further processing, as an effective weapon of mass destruction. You don't have to go all the way to a nuclear bomb. During the Second World War, Manhattan Project scientists, including Robert Oppenheimer, drew up plans for contaminating the fields of Germany with radioactive substances so the resulting lack of food would force Germany to surrender. The Allies also feared that Hitler would stop the Normandy invasion by creating an impenetrable zone poisoned with radioactivity.

I wrote *Lithium-6* between 2005 and 2007. Many things have changed since then. Before the Fukushima disaster in 2011, the serial production of Rapid-L reactors was a serious venture, actively promoted by Japan's national nuclear research center. But since Fukushima the idea of installing small nuclear reactors in every basement has become psychologically impossible, at least for the time being.

Today, the possibility that many, if not most, tobacco-induced cancers might be caused by radioactive substances present in tobacco smoke is taken much more seriously than in 2007. This change is mostly because Brianna Rego, a Guatemalan-born scientist living in the United States, reminded the world—in a now-famous article entitled "The Polonium Brief: A Hidden History of Cancer, Radiation, and the Tobacco Industry"—of old research conducted in the United States in the 1960s and 1970s that linked polonium-210 and tobacco-induced cancers.

The original insight was provided by an almost forgotten researcher named Vilma R. Hunt. In 1964 she proved that the polonium-210 in tobacco leaves is not present in tobacco ash but is inhaled into the lungs with the smoke. Later research showed that the polonium in tobacco tends to concentrate in the bifurcation points of the tiny air tubes (bronchioles) inside the lungs, where it forms radioactive hot spots in these extremely vulnerable parts of our anatomy.

According to scientific experiments, some of which were conducted half a century ago, it is very difficult to cause lung cancer in laboratory animals with tobacco smoke that does not contain any radioactive polonium-210. On the other hand, it is very easy to cause lung cancer in 94 percent of laboratory animals by forcing them to inhale tobacco smoke rich in polonium-210.

When filters were added to cigarettes, they reduced the amount of chemical carcinogens in tobacco smoke by four-fifths. At the same time the average amount of polonium in tobacco increased at least threefold and possibly sixfold, and tobacco's ability to cause cancer doubled or tripled. All this points toward the conclusion that a substantial part of tobacco-induced cancer might actually be caused by radioactive substances.

I was not aware of this old body of research until Brianna Rego's articles drew my attention to it. However, my own observations about wood fuel smoke causing relatively few cancers in India—compared to tobacco smoke—pointed toward a similar conclusion.

Upon discovering them, I sent Brianna Rego's papers to several members of the European Parliament, which led to some serious discussions in Brussels and Strasbourg during 2013. The Committee for Environment, Public Health and Food Safety of the European Parliament proposed an act calling for a low threshold for polonium-210 in cigarettes, as well as the development of a standard measuring technique (an ISO standard) for its levels in tobacco.

The same members of the European Greens parliamentary group who had raised the issue in the Committee for Environment, Public Health and Food Safety also presented a proposal to revise the Tobacco Products Directive to restrict the amount of polonium in tobacco to roughly 5 percent of the present average (to 0.002 picocuries per cigarette). This proposal was defeated by a strong combined lobby of nuclear and tobacco interests by an even vote, 35–35. In a draw, the original proposal of the European Commission won.

There is no certainty about what will happen next, but it seems that the story about Ted Taylor lighting a cigarette with a small parabolic mirror and a nuclear bomb—which I have mentioned several times in *Lithium-6*—may have even greater symbolic value than I imagined when I was writing this novel.

I have provided a more detailed analysis of these issues in a nonfiction book, *Rethinking Nuclear Power: Nuclear Electricity and Nuclear Weapons Proliferation*, published in New Delhi by the Coalition for Nuclear Disarmament and Peace (CNDP) of India and as an e-book by Into Publishing in Helsinki.

—RISTO ISOMÄKI, JYRKÄNKARKI-MALMI,
MAY, 2015

About the Author

Photo © 2011 Pertti Nisonen

Risto Isomäki is an author, science editor, and environmental activist. He has worked on several international projects in Africa and India, and he has published numerous nonfiction books on environmental affairs, development cooperation, and the third world. Isomäki's fiction titles use solid scientific expertise and research-based facts to create fantastical visions of the future. His novel *The Sands of Sarasvati* was nominated for the Finlandia Prize in 2005 and also received the Thank You for the Book medal in 2006.

About the Translator

Photo by Pekka Piri

Owen F. Witesman is a professional literary translator with a master's in Finnish and Estonian area studies from Indiana University. He has translated more than thirty Finnish books into English, including novels, children's books, poetry, plays, graphic novels, and nonfiction. His recent translations include the novels *My First Murder*, *Her Enemy*, *Copper Heart*, and *Snow Woman* from the Maria Kallio series by Leena Lehtolainen (AmazonCrossing), the novels in *The Snow White Trilogy* by Salla Simukka (Skyscape), the satire *The Human Part* by Kari Hotakainen (MacLehose Press), the thrillers *Cold Courage* and *Black Noise* by Pekka Hiltunen (Hesperus), and the 1884 classic *The Railroad* by Juhani Aho (Norvik Press). He currently resides in Springville, Utah, with his wife and three daughters, two dogs, a cat, and twenty-nine fruit trees.